Also by Anna Bell

We Just Clicked
If We're Not Married By Thirty
It Started with a Tweet
The Good Girlfriend's Guide to Getting Even
The Bucket List to Mend a Broken Heart
Don't Tell the Brides-to-be
Don't Tell the Boss
Don't Tell the Groom

PRAISE FOR ANNA BELL

'Warm-hearted and hilarious. It will make you giggle and
want to hug the book when you finish it. I flippin' loved it!'
Miranda Dickinson, *Sunday Times* bestselling
author of *Take a Look at Me Now*

'A brilliantly funny, uplifting yet emotional
rom-com that I just lost myself in'
Elle Spellman, author of *Running Into Trouble*

'Romantic and refreshing'
Mhairi McFarlane, *Sunday Times* bestselling author

'The perfect laugh-out-loud love story'
Louise Pentland, *Sunday Times* bestselling
author of *Wilde Like Me*

'Smart, witty and completely fresh'
Cathy Bramley, *Sunday Times* bestselling author

'Funny, romantic and uplifting'
Cressida McLaughlin, author of *The Cornish Cream Tea Bus*

'This is the fun breath of fresh air we need right now!'
Fabulous

'Funny and touching'
My Weekly

'Perfect for fans of Sophie Kinsella'
Take a Break

'A funny, feel-good read'
Closer

'Romance, comedy and drama sparkle in this fun, fresh
and frothy concoction'
Lancashire Evening Post

'A fun, bouncy, brilliant tale'
Heat

'Funny, relatable and fabulously written'
Daily Express

Anna lives in the South of France with her young family and energetic Labrador. When not chained to her laptop, Anna can be found basking in the summer sun, heading to the ski slopes in the winter (to drink hot chocolate and watch – she can't ski) or having a sneaky treat from the patisserie – all year round!

You can find out more about Anna on her website – www.annabellwrites.com or follow her on Twitter @annabell_writes.

THE
MAN I
DIDN'T
MARRY

ANNA BELL

ONE PLACE. MANY STORIES

HQ
An imprint of HarperCollins*Publishers* Ltd
1 London Bridge Street
London SE1 9GF

www.harpercollins.co.uk

HarperCollins*Publishers*
1st Floor, Watermarque Building, Ringsend Road
Dublin 4, Ireland

This edition 2021

3
First published in Great Britain by
HQ, an imprint of HarperCollins*Publishers* Ltd 2021

Anna Bell asserts the moral right to be
identified as the author of this work.
A catalogue record for this book is
available from the British Library.

ISBN: 978-0-00-834080-3

MIX
Paper from
responsible sources
FSC™ C007454

This book is produced from independently certified FSC™ paper
to ensure responsible forest management.

For more information visit: www.harpercollins.co.uk/green

This book is set in 10.7/15.5 pt. Sabon by Type-it AS, Norway

Printed and bound in Great Britain by
CPI Group (UK) Ltd, Croydon, CR0 4YY

For Jessica,
For inspiring me to always be braver.

Prologue

When deciding to go to Comic Con this year dressed as Wonder Woman, with a very short skirt and tiny corseted top, I had not factored in the possibility that we would end up in a meat market of a club afterwards. I tug down at my skirt, which seems to have become even shorter in the few minutes since I last pulled it down, before I squeeze through the dance floor, fending off bum pinches and guys trying to grind in my direction. Ugh. To think I've been wearing this outfit all day and I didn't have one unwelcome advance. And yet, I've been in this club less than an hour and I've been slapping hands away left, right and centre.

I didn't really want to come, but my friends dragged me here and I've only gone and lost them. Neither of them are answering their phones, so I've spent the last twenty minutes searching the different floors, which are so dark and full of sweaty bodies, trying to find them. You'd think that dressed as the Incredible Hulk and HawkGirl they'd be easy to spot. It's late and it's been a long day, and if I can't see them on my final scan of the upstairs dance floor, I'm going to call it a night.

I look over at the people standing around the tables at the edge of the dance floor and my heart almost stops. Standing at one of those tables is Max Voss – my best friend Rachel's brother, aka my teenage crush. I haven't seen him in years, but he is every bit as gorgeous as he was when we were younger, perhaps even more so. I can't stop staring. I feel like I'm 15 again, trapped in his power.

It's one thing to be a gormless 15-year-old with an embarrassing crush; it's quite another to be behaving the same way at the ripe old age of 28. Yet, I can't help it. This is exactly why I don't meet up with Rach at her parents' house if I know he's going to be there.

He must sense me staring at him as he looks up and our eyes meet. I expect him to quickly turn away – I doubt he'd recognise me with my hair this long and without the trademark thick glasses that I wore until I was in my early twenties – but to my utter surprise he starts furiously waving at me. I look behind, expecting to see some leggy blonde, but no one behind me is paying him any attention. He points at me again and, thanks to the rum and Cokes I've been drinking, I've got the confidence to go over.

'Hey,' he says, beckoning me closer and shouting in my ear. 'You're here.'

He's so close that I can feel his breath on my cheek when he talks. It's the closest I've ever been to him; he's certainly never been this friendly with me before.

He puts his hand on the small of my back, causing me to melt at his touch. I reach out to hold onto the table beside me to stop my legs from buckling. I hate that my teenage crush still has such a hold on me.

'I thought you weren't coming,' he says.

'I'm sorry?' I say.

'Come and meet Dodge,' he says, ignoring my confusion.

He takes me by the hand, leading me to his group of friends, and places me in front of one who is dressed in a lime-green Borat mankini. Out of all the costumes that I've seen today, this is by the far the worst assault on my eyes. I try to ignore the hair and bits of flesh popping out from where they're not supposed to.

Max whispers something into his friend's ear and his friend looks me up and down; a huge grin appears on his face.

He comes towards me, holding out his hand, and I don't know what to do other than to shake it.

The rest of Max's friends seem to have taken great interest in what's going on and they've formed a circle around me. A couple of them start to shout and sing the *Wonder Woman* theme tune; they're smiling and clapping and, because it seems like a good idea after my rum and Cokes, I start to join in with them, putting my hands above my head and moving my hips to the music.

The chanting starts to change and it's hard to make out what they are saying at first, but then I hear the word 'kit' and then 'tits'. Why would they want me to strip? Unless? I suddenly stop, looking down at my outfit and thinking of Max's reference to him thinking I wasn't coming. The fact that they're all men in their group. The fact that he didn't make any reference to my name or knowing who I was. Oh God. I think he thinks I'm a stripper.

The man in the Borat mankini is nodding encouragingly at me, presumably waiting for the show to start, and I look over at Max in horror.

I watch his facial expression change from one of amusement to one of confusion.

'Wait, I know you,' he says, taking a step forward, his eyebrows furrowed. 'Oh my God!' he shouts. 'Spider, it's you!'

I cringe at the use of the nickname he used to call me. I haven't heard it in years. When I was younger my glasses were really thick and, if you looked through the side of them, it often looked like I had multiple eyes. Add to that my tall, gangly limbs and my flat chest, and Max had once said that I looked like a spider, and the name stuck. Heartache and pain coming flooding back, of having the kind of teenage crush that consumed every fibre of my being, only for the object of my affection to see me as a spider.

Tears start to form as the memories come in thick and fast, Max's friends all still calling for me to strip. It's too much. I turn and push my way through the crowds on the dance floor and down the stairs towards the exit.

'Spider, wait!' I hear as Max thunders down the stairs after me.

I ignore him and find myself out on the pavement, wrapping my cape around me to counter the chill in the air.

'Spider, please. I'm sorry,' he says, turning me round gently from my elbow.

'You thought I was a stripper?' I say, putting my hands on my hips. My cape billows out behind me in the wind.

'I'm sorry,' he says again, taking me by the hand and walking me away from the bouncers who are trying not to laugh at us. 'It was the outfit. My mate Jez said he'd booked one and then you were standing right in front of us and you were looking over and I just thought... Shit, I'm so sorry. But look at you, Spider, all grown up.'

I'm aware that he's looking at my boobs, which are squeezing over the top of my corset, and my cape is no help; no matter how many times I try and wrap myself in it, it keeps flying back in the wind.

'Um, Max,' I say, waving and pointing at my face. His eyes flick up.

'Oh yeah, sorry, it's just. That outfit. Do you always dress…'

'I went to Comic Con today.'

'Comic what?'

'Never mind.'

'Are you here with friends?'

'I was, but I lost them. I was looking for them when I bumped into you. But I think I'm just going to go home,' I say, scanning the street for a cab.

Two bouncers struggle out of the club; they're manhandling Max's friend in the Borat mankini. They practically throw him into the arms of his waiting friends, who have scrambled out after him.

'What the hell happened?' asks Max.

'Rodge's just been sick on the dance floor.'

Max winces.

'We're going to take him home,' says his friend.

'I'll help.'

'Nah, mate, we've got him,' the friend says, tapping Max's chest. 'You stay here.'

He gives me a big grin and then he helps prop Rodge up and they lead him down the street. It's then that I see Rodge's bare bottom.

'Oh, that costume,' I say, wishing I could unsee it. 'Is it his birthday or something?'

'His stag do.'

'He came here on his stag do?' I say, raising an eyebrow at the exterior of the cheesy club.

'If you knew Dodge, you'd know it was pretty fitting. So, Spider—'

'The name's Ellie.'

He screws up his face. 'Of course, Ellie. Shit, I'm supposed to be apologising and I'm digging myself a deeper hole. Look, I can't remember the last time I ate, can I make it up to you by buying you some food?'

Max Voss has just asked me if he can buy me food? Didn't I always fantasise about this moment? Play it cool, Ellie. 'Why not,' I say with a simple shrug.

'Great,' he says, turning and walking into the fried chicken shop next door. Not quite what I had in mind.

We order some chicken and chips and when it arrives Max carries the tray over to the red plastic chairs by the window. My skirt is so short that I'm concerned that my skin's going to get so stuck to the plastic that it'll peel off when I stand up.

'Of all the people to bump into here, I never expected to see you in a club. Didn't think it would be your kind of thing,' he says, taking the cardboard boxes off the tray and handing one across to me.

'Oh yeah, and what did you think would be my kind of thing?'

'Oh, I don't know, sci-fi conventions. You always were a geek,' he says with a cheeky grin. I throw a chip at him and he laughs. 'Ow, bloody hell, they're hot.'

'I know, I just burnt my fingers,' I say, laughing.

'I didn't mean to offend you. I just meant that, you and Rach, well, you weren't exactly known for going out. The only time I can remember is when I had to escort you both into a party because you were too scared to get out of the car.'

'Well, I've got slightly more confident in the last twelve years,' I say, cringing at the thought. Him walking us into the party wasn't the embarrassing part...

He gestures briefly at my chest. 'And I see you have no need for tissue paper any more.'

That was the embarrassing part.

I close my eyes and I'm instantly transported back there. Max had driven us to the cricket club and – when Rach and I had been too nervous to walk past a group of cool boys hanging around outside – Max had walked us over. Rach and I were just saying goodbye to Max when he pulled at what he thought was a rogue bit of tissue stuck to my top, only to pull out a long strip of toilet roll that had been stuffed inside my bra.

'I never did thank you for that night, for not laughing at me.'

When Max had pulled the first bit of loo roll from my top, it had torn and left a part of it hanging out. Instead of laughing at me, like most teenage boys would do, he'd stepped forward and hugged me to discreetly pull the rest of it out. I might have been left with wonky boobs, but at least the whole school didn't find out I'd stuffed my bra in the first place.

'I did what anyone would have done.'

'No, you didn't. It was really kind.'

'Well, you were always at our house and you became like a sister to me.'

'Huh, and do you still see me as that now?'

His eyes keep flitting between my outfit and my face and I can see he's still quite drunk by the way he's swaying.

'That outfit's playing tricks with my mind and I don't know what I'm thinking any more.'

My cheeks go red. Is he flirting with me?

'I don't think your girlfriend would like you saying things like that to me.'

'Girlfriend?'

'Sorry, I thought Rach said a few months ago that you were seeing someone and I just assumed.'

'Oh yeah, didn't work out. She moved abroad,' he says, shrugging his shoulders. 'We weren't serious or anything.'

'Oh right,' I say, feeling a little awkward bringing it up. 'So, what did you do for the stag do?'

'Now, I can't tell you that, but it's been a long day, that's for sure. We started drinking at eight in the morning.'

'Bloody hell, how are you still going?'

'Tactical nap at… an undisclosed location that had some comfy chairs. Plus, I switched to vodka Redbulls, so I might not sleep until next Tuesday, but I outlasted Dodgy Rodge, which is sort of an unwritten rule of a stag do.'

'What are the other unwritten rules?'

'I don't think I can tell you them either.'

'Right, I like the fact you're creating an air of mystery for something that, to be honest, is pretty much about you guys getting as wasted as possible and going to strip clubs.'

Max laughs.

'Were you always this funny, Spid— Ellie?' he says quickly as I go to scowl.

'Yeah, you were just too cool to talk to me.' I pick up a chicken wing, planning to eat a small delicate bite, but I've well and truly got the booze munchies and I ravage it like a caveman.

'That's not true,' he says, but we both know it is. Max was one of those kids at school – the ones that everyone worshipped, whereas Rach, his sister, and I... well, we'd struggle to find anyone that knew our names.

'So, aren't you like some kind of rocket scientist?' he asks.

'A data analyst, so not quite.'

'Still impressive,' he says with a head bob. He eats a chicken wing quicker than I did. 'And do you live around here? I know Rach comes up to stay with you, but I thought you lived in Ealing or somewhere out that way.'

I'm slightly flattered that he knows where I used to live.

'Yeah, I used to, but I got a new job and was finding the commute too long. I live in Clapham North now.'

'Oh, not far from me. I'm in Brixton.'

Of course I know this fact.

'Cool,' I say.

We both look down at our food that we've decimated.

'I guess we were hungry,' I say.

'Yeah. I needed that. So, um, did you want me to make sure you get home safely?'

'Sure,' I say, and as we leave to find a taxi I try and stop myself from having a mild panic attack. He's just being polite and he'll drop me off on his way past in a cab.

It turns out that Max wasn't just being polite because he is now standing in my living room drinking a quick nightcap of limoncello, which was the only spirit I had in.

'You know, it's a really long way back to Brixton,' says Max, stretching out his arms and faking a yawn.

'Yeah,' I say, agreeing, even though I know it's a very short bus ride away. 'You know, you can always stay here.'

'Thanks, that would be great. Of course, I'll sleep on the sofa.'

'How perfectly gentlemanly of you,' I say.

'Naturally,' he says, and he takes a step closer to me. My heart is pounding. He's looking at me in the same way he was looking at his chicken before he devoured it.

'But, you know, I think I'm going to have a little trouble getting this costume off.'

'I could help you out of it.'

'Well, that would be the gentlemanly thing to do.'

He nods.

'It might be easier to do it in my bedroom.'

'Of course,' he says, holding his arm out as if to say lead the way. He follows me into my room and, as soon as the door slams shut, he launches himself at me, kissing me furiously.

We fall on to the bed and there are drunken hands everywhere running all over each other's body. It's not the most co-ordinated of efforts but there's a kind of hot and heavy panting that comes from a lot of lust.

'The costume,' I pant.

'Gotcha,' says Max and he starts to wrestle the top, but it won't budge. We sit upright and he gives the zip at the back another tug, but it's stuck.

'Hang on, let me have a go,' I say and I put my arms round at the back, just as Max bends down to have a better look, and I whack him in the face with my elbow.

'Ow, fuck,' he says, cradling his eye.

'Shit. Let me see, hold still,' I say, leaping up.

He's clutching at his face so tightly that I have to prise his fingers away to make sure there's no blood spurting out of anywhere.

'It doesn't look like it's bleeding,' I say.

'It fucking hurts, though.'

'And your eye's still there; that's a good sign, right?'

I curse my Wonder Woman costume. I have dreamt about this moment for years and years and the one time I get Max in my bedroom I accidentally assault him.

'I'll go and get you some peas, OK? Stop the swelling.'

I hurry into the kitchen, find half a bag of peas and wrap them in a tea towel.

I make it back into my bedroom in record time but Max is passed out on the bed. Oh shit. I can feel my heart racing in a completely different way; now it's in a sheer terror – what if he's got a concussion?

I bend over to him to check his breathing and he's lightly snoring. Do people snore if they've got a concussion? The clock on my desk reads 3.32 a.m.; it's the kind of ridiculous situation where I'd usually phone Rach for advice, but I don't think it's quite the time to broach the subject of what I was doing in bed with her brother.

In a panic I go back into the kitchen and fill up a glass of water and I rush back to Max. I check his vital signs once more before I tip the water over his head, wincing as I do it.

'What the...' he shouts, sitting bolt upright and shaking the water off his face and out of his hair.

'Oh, thank goodness,' I say. 'I thought you had concussion.'

'No, I'm just drunk,' he says, and he reaches out his hands and pulls me in, wrapping his soggy arms around me. He nuzzles into the back of my neck and goes back to sleep.

And I just lie there, in my Wonder Woman costume, trying to ignore the worry of the inevitable awkward morning after the night before, because I've got Max Voss in my bed and, even if it's just for this moment, I feel like all my wildest dreams have come true.

Chapter 1

'Here we go,' says Max, rummaging through my wardrobe. 'Why don't you wear this?'

I take off the dress I'm wearing, my bump feeling relieved to be free. It was definitely wishful thinking that, at this late stage in my pregnancy, I'd be able to slip into that dress.

I turn around to see what Max has found lurking in my wardrobe, to find him holding up a green catsuit with a big grin plastered on his face. 'I'm pretty sure this is stretchy.'

'Max Voss,' I say in my best scolding voice, 'that catsuit is what got us into this predicament in the first place, plus there's absolutely no way this bump or these boobs are getting into that.'

There's a flicker in his eyes and I know exactly what he's thinking. I wouldn't say that we're a married couple with telepathy but I can tell in an instant when my husband's horny.

'Put it back in the wardrobe,' I say firmly.

The catsuit belonged to the costume I'd made for our daughter Sasha's first birthday. The theme was children's books and I'd dressed as the Hungry Caterpillar, but the catsuit was more skin tight than I'd expected and I'd spent most of the party running away from The Gruffalo, aka my husband, until Sasha had gone to sleep and all the guests had left, and then the Gruffalo'd had his wicked way with me. Seven months later, we're now expecting the Gruffalo's child.

I'm actually a little flattered, though. When I was pregnant with Sasha we were at it like rabbits, but between moving house a few months ago, having a toddler and working demanding jobs, we haven't been having a lot of sexy time lately.

'I'm going to have to go in my underwear at this rate,' I say, planting my hands on my hips.

'Well, I for one would be very in favour of that,' says Max, taking a step closer to me. 'Are you sure we even have to go? Mum and Graham are looking after Sasha and we've got the whole house to ourselves. When does that happen?'

'Never,' I say, and he steps into touching distance. 'But we're going to these birthing classes.'

'Why? We've done this before; we know what to do. I have to give you my hand to hold which you'll crush, and I'll tell you to breathe and you'll tell me to fuck off.'

I pull a face.

'That's why we're going this time, so that it'll be different.'

'Good, I'm looking forward to not having to have my hand X-rayed for fractures after.'

He leans over and gives me a kiss. My arms instinctively wrap around him and I kiss him back.

'No, no, no,' I say, pushing him gently away even though my heart's racing furiously. 'We don't have time.'

'Come on, that was at least a seven kiss.'

Max and I have this game that we play where we rate kisses out of ten, usually when we're watching a film or TV programme. I don't remember how it started, but pretty much only Ryan Gosling and Rachel McAdams in *The Notebook* have been awarded a perfect ten by both of us. Not that Max has sat through the whole film, but I did make him watch *that* kiss in the rain.

'I dunno, I reckon that was only a five,' I say, lying. Usually seven and above kisses end in sex and we really don't have time for that.

'Gee, thanks, and there was me trying to spice up our marriage a little,' he says, taking the piss out of an article I was reading on my phone this morning.

'I promise, there'll be plenty of time for that before the baby arrives and I'm on maternity leave. We can do all the spicing, and role play, and whatever else they suggested then. Anything to make this baby come along quicker.'

I put on the very first dress I tried on and check myself out in the mirror, still not satisfied. 'Maybe I should try and find some leggings and a tunic?'

'If we don't have time to have sex, you don't have time to change again. Plus, it's boiling outside and you'll roast.'

I laugh. He's right.

'OK, OK.'

'I don't know why you're so worked up about this, anyway,' he says, shoving a black v-neck T-shirt on. Men have it so easy with clothes. 'You do realise that you've already given birth *and* done these classes before.'

I only have to raise my eyebrows and tut. My raging pregnancy hormones are not to be messed with at the moment.

'Yes, but we all know it's not actually about the course. I want to find mums I can hang out with here and I don't think it'll be a bad thing for you to have some local dad friends.'

'I don't think I want to be friends with other "dads",' he says, pulling a face and doing air quotes.

'You know they're just men who happen to have a child, like you,' I say, laughing. Why is it men never feel the pressure to make friends the same way women do? 'Plus, you need more friends; you hardly see anything of Owen any more.'

'That's because he's sowing his wild oats now that he and Sarah have split up.'

We walk out of the bedroom and I try not to notice the worn floral carpet underfoot as I plod down the stairs. I equally try and ignore the textured pink stripy wallpaper covering the walls, or the glossy pink banister, and the seascape mural that covers an entire wall of the hallway downstairs. In fact, I've got quite good at blocking out the decorative features that the previous owners, who seemed to be allergic to taste, had installed.

When we outgrew our tiny flat in London, Max and I decided to move to our hometown of Fleet, which was still commutable to London but conveniently close to our parents. To get the type of house we wanted within our budget – where we wouldn't be mortgaged to the hilt and have to sell both our kidneys and probably any future children – we'd bought one that was a bit of a 'project'. What we'd really love to have done was gut the whole house and have a fancy renovation with a big open-plan living space, big windows and bi-fold doors, but there's no way that we can afford that. Instead we drew up a list of all the cosmetic bits that could make the house look less like an experimental art exhibit. Only we moved in three months ago and I'm still waiting for the enthusiastic DIY-er that Max turned into when we viewed the house to make another appearance.

I sigh, looking up at the seascape that I hate so much.

'I'll get to it soon,' says Max, grimacing. 'You know, when work calms down a bit.'

He's been working ridiculously long hours for the last month, often catching the train into London at the crack of dawn and arriving home late at night.

'I'd forgotten what it's like to leave the house without Sasha – look at us, just breezing out the door,' says Max.

'I know, no scrambling round to find shoes and coats and look! I'm using a tiny handbag for the first time in for ever,' I say, slipping it over my shoulder.

Max chuckles as he opens the door and we head outside. 'You know, this has definitely been the best bit of moving back home, having the grandmas around to babysit.'

'We didn't move back to Fleet just for that.'

'I know, but isn't it a bloody brilliant upside? Two sets of babysitters nearby.'

'Well, one set. You know my parents are never here with all their cruises,' I say, climbing into the car. My parents downsized into a tiny flat above a fish and chip shop a couple of years ago, and since then have been spending all the money they made from selling their first and only house – bought in the 1980s – on cruises around the world.

'When do they get back from this one?'

'In about five weeks. Don't worry, I've made sure they're going to be back in plenty of time for this one,' I say, patting my bump.

'I think we're going to need all the help we can get,' says Max, starting the car engine.

'So, today, with the people,' I say, choosing my words carefully, 'can you, um, just tone things down a little – you know, with the jokes?'

Max stops reversing the car and snaps his head back at me. Usually Max makes an excellent first impression, but when it comes to talking about female anatomy, he seems to turn into a teenage boy making inappropriate jokes.

'Tone it down?' he says, narrowing his eyes.

'Yeah, you know... perhaps not make the jokes you did last time. The one about the stitches.'

'What? The guys totally laughed their arses off.'

'The guys might have done, but the girls didn't. We didn't even meet for a pre-baby coffee in the end. I'm sure it wasn't all about that joke, but I just think we should do everything we can to make friends. Just try to fight the instinct to be funny.'

'OK, one boring bastard coming up,' he says.

'Oh no, you've got to be interesting,' I say, as he pulls off the drive. 'They've got to like you. Women judge their friends on what men they pick to be their husbands.'

'Then you will have absolutely nothing to worry about,' he says. 'I can charm anyone.'

I rub my sweaty hands on my thighs hoping that he's right. Our move to Fleet hasn't exactly been as I pictured it, and it would be nice for something to finally go our way, and a ready-made friendship group could be just it.

'Right then, everyone,' says Mary, the course leader, standing in front of the class. 'I'm glad that you're all settled in nicely. It's my job to hopefully ease any of those fears and apprehensions that you might have about the next few months of your life as you transition into your new role as parents.'

It's a good job that the plastic chairs we're sat on are so ridiculously uncomfortable or else her soft, soothing tones would send me right off to sleep. Although at seven months pregnant, pretty much any sitting down for more than ten minutes has me nodding off. Perhaps that's why they've kept the chairs of torture.

Mary starts to talk about the importance of positive thoughts and I start to look around at my potential new BFFs. Discounting the husbands, there are four other women. There's a woman who looks like she's impersonating a royal with her perfectly styled hair, smart tailored dress and sensible court shoes; she is sat on a plump cushion, which I'm very jealous of. Another with cascading blonde curls who's got her notepad out and is studiously making notes. One with long brown hair and a gorgeous maternity dress, who looks absolutely terrified. And finally the woman sat beside me, with a short blonde bob, who catches me looking and gives me a smile in return.

'Now,' says Mary, 'you're not far off the end of your pregnancy journey, and you've got so much to look forward to.'

'Yes, like delivering a watermelon out of your vagina,' says the woman with the blonde bob.

Her husband groans.

'What? We're all thinking it and it's terrifying,' she says, and I give her a nod in solidarity before we turn our attention back to Mary.

'Yes, it's true that birth can seem very daunting, but we will come to that. By the end of these sessions, you'll realise that no matter how big the watermelon is – and sometimes the watermelon can be very big – your body will be able to cope. In fact, last month one of our course members gave birth to a ten-pound baby,' she says, and the woman next to me almost shrieks in horror.

'Who was that, Mary?' asks the smartly dressed woman.

'Ah, Anneka, I forgot that you took last month's class too.' That at least explains how she knew to bring a cushion. 'It was Aimee with the long blonde hair.'

'Oh,' Anneka says, nodding her head.

'Now, before we get into all the serious stuff, I thought that it might be quite fun to do an ice-breaker,' says Mary, getting us back on track.

The woman with the blonde bob next to me mutters what sounds like 'FML' under her breath.

'I'm going to give you all a pack of ten different coloured bits of wool, which are all different lengths. You'll also see that around the walls there are cards with writing on them, like *length of cervix when fully dilated*, *length of bump at full term*, and what you've got to do is match the different lengths of wool with the cards. Don't forget the idea is to talk as you go round and discuss it with your fellow classmates,' says Mary, handing out our packets of cut string.

I'm sorting through the strands of wool when Max holds one up and looks at it.

'Length of my penis,' he says with a grin.

'Firstly, what did we say about anatomy jokes, and secondly,' I say, taking hold of his piece of string and dangling it in front of his eyes, 'only in your dreams.'

'Ouch,' he says, laughing and snatching it back.

There's an uneasy scraping of chairs as people get up and walk about.

I separate from Max and start looking at the card closest to me. *Circumference of average baby's head during birth.* I wince. Despite the fact I've already gone through this once, I tried my best to block out the memories of it.

'Do you reckon any of this wool is big enough to wrap around our necks?' says the woman, who was sitting next to me, attempting to do it. 'Sorry if that was really bad taste; I pathologically hate ice-breakers.'

'Me too,' I say. 'I'm Ellie.'

'Helen.' She turns to read the card and pulls a face. 'You know there have got to be better ways to make friends with other mums-to-be. You know, some kind of Tinder for pregnant people. That way we could swipe left and right and select our friends without having to be traumatised for the rest of our pregnancy.'

'Probably pretty niche, isn't it, in Fleet?' I say, laughing. 'Plus, what if people lied on their profiles? At least this way you get to vet them.'

'True,' says Helen, nodding. 'And I bet you'd get pervy men catfishing. You know, ones who have a thing for pregnant women.'

'Do men have a thing for pregnant women?'

Helen nods again. 'I bet they do.'

The woman in the royal blue dress walks up to us and has a quick read of the card on the wall before she looks us up and down and then breaks into a polite smile. 'So, November babies, huh?' she says, pointing at the bumps. 'When are you due?'

I look at her incredibly neat bump that almost looks like she's just shoved a beach ball up her dress.

'Fourth,' says Helen.

'Third for me,' I say.

'Oh, that woman over there is due on the fifth. Isn't it an amazing coincidence that you're all due around the same time?'

'I know,' says Helen. 'It's like there's some kind of romantic day that happens in February that results in all these early November babies.'

We all giggle, even though I know mine was more to do with Sasha's birthday party on 12 February rather than Valentine's Day.

'I'm Anneka,' says the woman, and Helen and I introduce ourselves.

'When are you due, Anneka,' I ask.

'Twenty-fifth of October, although I'm having a C-section the week before.'

'How are you smaller not bigger than us?' asks Helen.

'My gynaecologist says that I haven't put on one pound of non-baby weight.'

'Sod that. If I'm not allowed gin for nine months I'm damn well eating cake,' says Helen.

'Me too,' I say.

'Gestational diabetes is a real thing you know,' Anneka says horrified.

'Oh, so you'll be the first one out of us to have the baby then,' I say, trying not to spoil the group harmony I'm so desperate to create.

'I guess you've saved us from any awful ice-breaking games of guessing who's going to be the first to have their baby,' says Helen.

'Well, you never know. I did one of these classes last month and one woman went into labour just after the class, at thirty-two weeks,' says Anneka.

'Was the baby OK?' I shudder at the thought.

'Oh yes. It turns out that there had been a bit of a miscalculation of the dates. But mother and baby are doing fine – or at least as fine as you can be after your boyfriend walks out when he realises that he can't be the father of the baby.'

'Crikey. Sounds a bit dramatic.'

'I know, if only Jeremy Kyle was still on air, they would have been a shoo-in for the show.'

'So how come you're doing this group twice?' I ask.

'Because my baby is due late October, it straddled the two groups, so I thought I'd do both and pick which group I preferred.'

'And how are we doing compared to the last group?' asks Helen.

'Gosh, they weren't my type of people at all. Didn't have a single thing in common, and did I mention the whole Baby Daddy scandal?' she says, coming across as a bit of a snob. 'Despite that, I'm sure I would have picked your group as you all seem lovely.'

'Hmm,' I say, not knowing quite what to make of her.

'I'm going to go and talk to the other ladies over there.'

She points at the other two members of the group who are chatting away.

'FYI,' says Anneka, 'the string you were going to use here for the baby's head is actually the length of your birth canal. Try this one instead,' she says, selecting one of the larger lengths of wool in her pack.

I gasp in horror at the length of it as she pins it up.

'I think I preferred it when I only thought it was a watermelon coming out,' says Helen. 'Isn't this class supposed to ease our tensions, not scare us silly?'

'I know. I've actually been through this all before with my little girl, but I think there are some things I'd rather not know.'

'Come on, ladies, rotate, rotate,' says Mary, clapping her hands.

'How much more have we got of this?' says Helen, raising her eyebrows as she goes off and talks to one of the husbands who's looking cluelessly at another card.

I start to relax, feeling like this whole making friends malarkey might not be so hard after all.

By the time the intensive course draws to a close I've met all the other couples. I've particularly warmed to Helen with her sharp wit, and Polly reminded me of myself in my first pregnancy – like a rabbit caught in headlights. Anneka took a shine to Max and his charming personality, and despite his risqué jokes she still prefers us to her previous group. Then there's Nina with the cascading curls who's funny and friendly.

'You see,' says Max, as we climb back in the car, twenty minutes later. 'That went pretty well. And I wasn't embarrassing and at least I showed up, unlike Anneka's husband, what's his name?'

'George… I think he went last month with her and what do you mean you weren't embarrassing? At one point you licked the poo from the nappy.'

'I didn't lick it; I licked my finger, which it had leaked on, and it was Nutella. But despite that, I think everyone liked me and you, so that's the main thing, right?'

'Yep, I guess so.'

We all swapped numbers after the session and Anneka had put us all in a WhatsApp group, and set up one for the men, before we'd even made it to the car.

'See, I told you there was nothing to worry about, and, as Mary says, you've got a couple of months to sit back and chill out before the little one arrives.'

'Ha, ha, ha,' I say, laughing. 'I'm going to still be working, even if it is from home.'

'Yeah, yeah, you're going to be working in your PJs on the sofa with *This Morning* on in the background,' he says, taking the mickey. 'Plus, you've only got another month of it, then you get a whole year off,' he says.

'You know maternity leave isn't actually a holiday, right?'

'Come on, this new little baby will be as easy-going as Sasha.'

I splutter a laugh. 'Sasha, easy-going?'

'Yeah, she is when I have her.'

'And how often do you look after her alone?' I say, meaning it as a joke, but it comes out a bit sarcastic.

'I'd take her more, but you always want to do things as a family at the weekend.'

'Yeah, because I want to see you too,' I say, trying to soften the mood. 'It's all going to be fine, isn't it?'

'Relax, Ellie,' says Max, starting to mimic Mary's dulcet tones. 'Your last two and a half months of pregnancy are going to be completely calm and stress-free, I'll make sure of it.'

I laugh and hope that he's right.

Chapter 2

I absolutely love waking up to the feeling of not needing to rush around, which is why Saturdays are always my favourite day of the week. Today it's even sweeter because I had my last day in the office yesterday, and whilst I've got a month left before my proper maternity leave kicks in, the fact that I am going to be homeworking and no longer have to commute is reason enough to celebrate.

'What do you fancy doing today?' I say, strolling into the kitchen. Max is sat at the table with a coffee in his hand, scrolling on his phone. Sasha's sat in her high chair eating some toast that I'm guessing was off his plate. I sigh; now she's not going to touch the porridge I was just about to make her. I try and let it go, not letting it ruin my good mood. 'The weather's going to be nice, we could go for a picnic?'

Max follows my gaze out of the kitchen window and we both wince at the sight of the waist-high weeds and grass growing in our tiny garden.

'Actually, I've got to head into work.'

'Into work? On a Saturday?' I say, leaning my back on the horrible kitchen cabinets, which are different varieties of wood. Max is a project manager at a large asset management company and, whilst Saturday work isn't unusual when they're coming to the end of a project, it's very rare for him to go into the office at a weekend when so much can be done remotely.

'I know, I'm sorry. It's just something cropped up late last night, and I went to tell you but you were already asleep.'

He gives Sasha another bit of toast and she takes it greedily.

'Oh right,' I say, popping the kettle on. 'And it couldn't wait until Monday?'

'No,' he says. 'But I won't be in all day. We could do something late afternoon.'

'It's your mum's birthday dinner tonight.'

'Oh, that's right. First special family dinner with Graham, how did I forget that?' he says, pulling a face at the reference to his mum's new boyfriend, his dad's former best friend.

'It'll be good; she's really happy with him.'

'I know, I know, and it's not like he's not been there for other birthdays when Dad was there, but—' he shrugs his shoulders '—I guess I should be glad she's with him – at least he's a nice guy.'

'Yeah, he is,' I say, popping Sasha's sippy cup on her high chair. 'Juice,' I say to her, as she starts to babble away to me. 'Yummy juice.'

'Do you think Dad knows about Graham?'

'Oh,' I say, distracted from my little conversation with Sasha. 'I don't know. You see, if you were talking to him, you could ask him.'

'Or you could when you skype him. So, is Rach coming tonight?' he asks, deliberately changing the subject. I know not to push about his dad. Max has barely spoken to him since he went on a golfing holiday to Portugal a few years ago, met a young Pilates instructor named Ruby and never came home.

'Yeah, she's coming but Gaby can't make it because she's on call.'

'The downside of being a doctor. Or maybe it's an upside; she gets a get-out-of-jail-free card for any family social gathering.'

I laugh.

'Why don't you give Rach a call, see if she'll come up before?' he says.

'That's a nice idea,' I say, wondering why I didn't think of that.

When I got together with Max I didn't really factor in how much it would change my friendship with Rach. I still see her a lot, maybe even more than I did, but it's usually in a family setting. It's rare for us to spend time just the two of us, and when we do it's not the same as it was. She was worried that he was going to hurt me in the early days and I guess that's made me more guarded when I talk to her, not wanting to present anything but a perfect view of our marriage. Plus, it's not like she really wants to hear about her brother's sex life.

'It'll be good for you to spend some time together and hopefully she'll give me less crap about stealing you away from her,' he says, draining his coffee and standing up. He gives Sasha a kiss on the head and ruffles her hair as he leaves the table.

'Oh, I meant to say Rach and Gaby are going to a festival down in Dorset in a couple of weeks. It's supposed to be family-friendly and they wondered if we wanted to come along with Sasha.'

Max laughs out loud and then stops when he realises I haven't joined in.

'Sasha in a tent? And you? Ellie, sleeping with you at the moment is like going nine rounds with Tyson Fury. You can't get comfortable at the best of times; how the hell are you going to get comfortable in a tent?'

'I think I'd manage.'

He raises an eyebrow.

'Think of all the kit we'd have to lug from the car. I'm weighed down like a pack horse going out with Sasha as it is without having all our camping gear too.'

'I'm sure Rach and Gaby will give us a hand. Plus, Pilot Dawn are headlining.'

Mentioning one of his favourite bands has piqued his interest but he's still pulling a face that looks like it's going to be a no.

'I'll think about it,' he says, which is his way of shutting something down.

'OK,' I say, feeling deflated.

He clearly picks up on my disappointment as he sighs theatrically.

'Why don't we talk to Rach about it tonight, see how it might work?' he says, and I do a little fist pump. 'I'm not promising anything. I mean, wouldn't you rather go away somewhere with four walls, an en suite and a babysitting service?'

'Where's the fun in that?' I say, laughing.

'I'll try and get home as quick as I can,' he says.

'You better do, as now I'm not going to be commuting I'm going to have all that extra energy – and weren't we talking about having more sexy time?' I say the last bit in a bit of a whisper, not wanting sexy to be the next word that Sasha starts trying to mimic.

He laughs from the pit of his belly and it's nice to see him less stressed about work.

'The role playing, gotcha. You never know, I might bring you back something from London. Do you think you can get kinky maternity outfits?'

I flick him with a tea towel.

'Don't you dare.'

He winks at me and kisses me on the top of the head, much like he did Sasha, but I'm glad that he doesn't ruffle my hair like he did hers as it looks messy enough already.

Sasha's getting bored in her high chair so I scoop her out and sit her on the tiled floor. She starts tipping out the Tupperware from the bottom drawer – which is one of her favourite pastimes – and I pick up my phone to text Rach.

'Let's see if your auntie Rach fancies coming for a walk.'

'Walk, walk,' Sasha repeats the best she can, and I grin. Perhaps today's not going to be a write-off after all.

Luckily for Sasha and I, Rach is free this afternoon and she jumped at the chance of coming with us to Fleet Pond, a large nature reserve with a rabbit warren of paths on the outskirts of town.

'I'd forgotten how nice this place is,' says Rach. She steps round a big puddle on the path and I wheel Sasha's stroller through it, trying not to splash mud up my legs. 'I haven't been out here in years.'

'I love it here too. It's one of the reasons we moved back

here, having this kind of nature on our doorstep. I've got so many happy memories of coming here as a kid.'

'Me too,' she says. 'Do you remember when we ran away here when our parents wouldn't buy us Robbie Williams tickets?'

'I do,' I say, laughing at the memory of the little den we built of an old sheet under a tree. 'It was fine for the first hour or two, but then, didn't we run out of food?'

'Yes, although it probably wasn't surprising when we'd only packed a big bag of crisps and a Mars Bar.'

'And then it started to rain.'

'We hadn't really thought through the sheet not being waterproof.'

'No, it was lucky Max came to find us,' I say, laughing.

'Yeah, but only because I'd stolen his Discman, not because he was genuinely worried.'

I haven't thought about that in so long.

'How old were we? Ten? Eleven?' she asks.

'Yeah, maybe eleven or twelve. I think we were in Year 7.'

'Who would have thought then that you'd marry my brother, and you'd give me a niece? My beautiful, sleeping niece.'

'Ssh, don't jinx it; she never usually naps for this long,' I say, and she smiles.

'You know, Mum kept trying to cajole me into coming over to help her bake her birthday cake. But we all know how twitchy she gets when she's baking. She won't even let me lick the bowl out.'

'I did offer to buy her one, but she insisted on making it,' I say, laughing.

'She sounded so excited, though. She's really happy with Graham, isn't she?'

'Yeah, she really is. We've seen them quite a bit since we moved and they get on so well.'

'Still, I'd never in a million years have put those two together.'

'I know, me neither. But I'm so pleased; I think she deserves to be happy after everything she went through with your dad.'

Rach nods, looking sad at the mention of her dad. His sudden departure to Portugal hit the whole of the Voss family badly.

We move out of the way for a woman who's being tangled up in the leads of her Yorkshire terriers.

'So, what's Max up to today? Tackling that attractive hallway of yours?' asks Rach.

'No, funnily enough,' I say, ducking under a low hanging tree, 'he's working today.'

'Jeez, on a Saturday?'

'Yep. He's been working really long hours lately, finishing his projects so that he's ready to take paternity leave.'

'Is he just taking the standard couple of weeks?'

'Yeah – could you imagine him looking after the two of them on his own if I went back to work?' I say, chuckling. 'I'd feel like I was working two jobs, having to prepare everything for them before I left.'

'Ha, that's true, but at least it makes it easy for you to decide what to do. I think Gaby and I will be fighting over who would have the leave,' she says with a half laugh.

'Ooh, I know you said you both wanted kids, but that sounds like you're talking about it…'

Rach looks uneasy.

'Sorry, I shouldn't have pried,' I say quickly.

'No, it's fine,' she says, letting out a deep breath. 'It's just… actually it might help if I talked to you about it, if you wouldn't mind?'

'Of course not. Why don't we stop for a drink? We're nearly at the little coffee van and it's got tables and chairs for us to sit at.'

'Wouldn't that wake up Sasha?'

I peer through the plastic flap on the stroller hood.

'She looks pretty far gone. I'll just rock her,' I say as the coffee van and its excellent flapjacks come into view.

'Great, I'll order then, so you can stay with her. What do you fancy?'

'Decaf skinny latte and maybe a flapjack. For Sasha, for when she wakes up, of course.'

'Of course,' says Rach, with a conspiratorial smile. 'I might go for one too, for that very same reason.'

She walks off to queue and I wander over to an empty table, making sure that I've got room to push Sasha's stroller with my foot. The queue seems quite long and I hope it moves quickly as I'm intrigued to hear what Rach's got to say.

I slip my phone out of my pocket in a bid to distract myself and I see there are some messages in the group chat that Anneka set up, about the meet-up we've got arranged for Monday.

Since our antenatal class a week ago, we've been messaging each other quite a lot, bemoaning everything from swollen ankles to listing everything we will eat/drink/do after the babies are born. The evening at Anneka's on Monday will be our first proper meet-up and I'm really looking forward to seeing them.

Anneka:

Morning, ladies! Just need to confirm that you're all on for Monday evening? It's at seven o'clock sharp. Do let me know if anyone's got any dietary requirements, other than the pregnancy ones, of course, as I'll be doing the Ocado order in a bit. Looking forward to seeing you all for some moderated fun!

Helen:

I am confirming my place and availability for Monday, only I don't do fun in moderation. My dietary requirements are lots of cake and carbs to make up for the lack of alcohol. See you on Monday at 7.30 x x

Anneka:

It's 7 sharp and I've ordered healthy snacks now.

Helen:

It's OK I am happy to visit an actual shop and will bring unhealthy snacks too – to give us a balanced diet, and FYI I'm always late, will aim for 7 aka see you 7.30.

Polly:

I'm there. Really looking forward to it, you have no idea what a relief it is to have found such a lovely group.

Nina:
Thanks for the invite, Anneka, but I don't think I'll be coming along to the meet-up. I have a really large social group and it's always so hard fitting everyone in as it is. You seemed really nice though :) Best wishes with the bumps, births and babies x x

Nina HAS LEFT THE GROUP

I stare at my phone in shock. I quickly scroll down to see my friends' reactions. My phone's making little noises every couple of seconds letting me know more messages are being added.

Anneka:
WTF???? How dare she leave us?????

Helen:
Perhaps this is how the other group felt when you left. ;)

Polly:
Do you think it was something I said to make her leave?? Did I come on too strong?

Helen:
Maybe a little. Maybe you should have waited until after Monday to confess true feelings… Kidding, obviously she's a weirdo.

Anneka:
What am I going to do with all the carrot sticks???

Helen:
Do you want the 31-week pregnant bitch reply to that or the polite one?

Polly:
I'll bring some hummus… x

I quickly type a response when I get to the bottom of the conversation.

Ellie:
OMG, what a shocker! Looking forward to seeing you on Monday and discussing it x x

Definitely Nina's loss, IMHO. The conversation finishes and I put my phone on the table. I look over to the coffee van to see that Rach is nearly at the front of the queue.

'Eleanor, Eleanor Smith?' says a voice and I turn to see a woman squinting at me. It's her cheekbones that makes me instantly recognise her as the extremely stunning Cara Worthington, someone I went to school with.

'Um, yeah, although it's Voss now. How are you, Cara?'

I watch her eyes widen at my surname. Everyone at school knew who Max was, and I'm sure she wouldn't be the only person to be surprised I married him. But she quickly composes herself, fluttering her eyelashes and breaking out into a big smile like we're long-lost friends, when, in truth, I'm surprised she even knew my name. Or at least she knew the name teachers called me at school – anyone who was truly my friend would have called me Ellie.

Cara Worthington was one of the popular girls in my school year and we didn't exactly mix in the same circles. She used to swan around with her perfect make-up and an inordinate number of little butterfly clips in her hair, a trail of hot boys in her wake. Whereas I used to shuffle around school with the odd spot covered with bright orange cover-up, my hair in a tight bun with two escaped tendrils hanging down at the front and the only boys following me were from the Dungeons and Dragons role-playing club we'd formed.

'I'm fine. I'm so pleased you recognised me. Especially when I'm looking like this,' she says, as if fresh glossy hair was some kind of disguise. She's dressed head to toe in Lycra, but, being Cara Worthington, it's not any old Lycra, it's Lululemon, which makes the out-of-shape yoga bottoms that I'm wearing seem even more frumpy. 'It must almost be twenty years now. We missed you at the ten-year reunion.'

'Oh yes, shame I couldn't go,' I lie. When the invite came through on Facebook I promptly deleted it, not wanting to relive my school days. 'I was living up in London at the time and busy and um...' I say tailing off. 'So, do you live around here?'

Since we moved back a few months ago I keep seeing people I went to school with. After years of living an anonymous life in London, where even my next-door neighbours pretended not to know me, I can't get used to it. It seems that a lot of people escaped Fleet, but the lure of familiarity and free babysitting from family members has pulled many back.

'No,' she says with a tone of horror. 'I'm just back visiting my mum. I live in Manchester now.'

'Oh, I like Manchester,' I say, nodding.

'Yeah, it's great. I work for the BBC up there.'

'Wow, impressive.'

'Yeah,' she says, beaming again and giving her hair a flick.

It's scary how alike she is to her teenage self and I hope that she's not thinking the same about me.

'So, it's Voss, then?' she says, her eyes starting to twinkle. 'You don't mean you married—'

'Uh-huh,' I say, a little bit proud of the fact.

'Wow,' she says, looking impressed. 'Do you mind if I pull up a chair?'

'Oh, um, of course,' I almost gasp in shock. The only time Cara spoke to me at school was if she needed to borrow my maths homework, and I'm pretty rusty on trigonometry now. 'Rachel's just getting us drinks, did you want me to shout over to get you one?'

'No, no,' says Cara, looking over at Rachel and smiling. 'No, I'm on a juice diet at the moment.'

She sits down at the empty chair opposite me, placing her elbows on the table and cupping her chin in her hands.

'So, Eleanor *Voss*,' she says, weirdly emphasising my surname, 'I want to hear about what you've been up to. I see you've… had a baby.'

'Uh-huh,' I say again, 'and I'm expecting another one.'

I pat my belly and her face lights up.

'That's so *amazing* for you both.'

My phone starts to buzz across the table and I see that it's Max's mum Judy.

'Do you need to get that?' says Cara.

'No,' I say, sending it to voicemail.

I feel guilty not answering it, but Judy's one of those people where if you answer and ask her if you can phone back, she'll just tell you that it'll only take a second and rattle off what she wanted to say regardless of how long it'll take. I'll give her a ring when Cara's gone.

'So, which one of you is going to stay home for the baby?' she says, tilting her head.

I'm thrown by the question, which seems awfully progressive. It's the second time today I've been asked this, and it's starting to make me feel guilty for womankind that Max and I didn't even discuss it.

'Well, predominantly me. It's easier with the breastfeeding,' I say, feeling like I have to justify it.

'So, you're taking the whole year,' she says, almost shocked.

I nod, feeling even more guilty.

'I don't know if I could leave my job for as long as that,' she says. 'I love it so much. It's like a calling. Plus, I've worked so hard to get to my position, I'd hate to take a step back,' Cara says.

I want to scream out that I have too. I think of how hard

I've worked climbing the rungs, all those years of study, all those hours of overtime that I had to effectively push aside when I had Sasha. So far, I've just about managed to keep my position – they've let me work a three-day week, but with another baby in tow, and the mum guilt creeping in of wanting to spend more time with the kids when they're young, I'm not sure how long that's going to be the case. Especially when I have so many male colleagues who don't seem to suffer the same fate when they have kids. But I don't say any of that; I just nod along.

'So, Eleanor *Voss*, are you due soon?'

'I've got another nine weeks or so to go, Cara Worthington.' Why does she keeps using my full name?

'Bloody hell, nine weeks, so you're going to get even bigger than that?' she says. 'No offence, it's just that usually tall people have those small bumps...'

I suddenly hope that they've run out of flapjacks.

'Here we go,' says Rach, balancing the tray on the table, when she looks up and sees who's sitting opposite her. 'Oh, um, hi.'

'Hi, Rachel, you remember me, right? Cara Worthington from school.'

'I remember,' she says with a nervous laugh.

'So, another little baby?' Cara says, staring directly at Rach.

'Um, yeah, we're all very excited,' she replies and turns to me, her eyes begging for me to take over the conversation. Rach seems to have regressed to her school self, where she couldn't even look, much less talk, to anyone popular.

'I couldn't imagine having two kids. Not that I need to. I don't even have time to go on a date with my job, let alone have a baby,' she says with a tinkle of laughter.

40

'So, do you work on TV?' I say, taking the pressure off Rach.

'Behind the scenes. I think it's more rewarding than being on-air talent,' she says, nodding as if she's agreeing with herself.

'I imagine it is,' I say.

'And what do you two do? Rachel?' she says, raising an eyebrow.

'Um... I...' says Rach with a bit of a stutter.

'She's a researcher at the University of Surrey.'

'Impressive,' she says and Rach blushes. 'And what do you do?'

'I'm a data analyst.'

'What's that?' she says, screwing up her face.

'In basic terms I look at a company's data and try and make patterns to see if there are elements of their businesses that can be streamlined.'

'Oh right. Sounds... heavy. Probably why you're desperate for a break. Although I would have thought that, in your situation, you would want it do it a bit more fifty-fifty, rather than you giving up your job, Ellie,' she says, looking between me and Rach.

'In my situation?' I repeat.

She nods. 'Yes, you know. I mean you're carrying the baby and then you're getting all the time off with the baby too.'

'Well, that's usually how it goes,' I say.

I pick up my coffee, in a bid to drink it as quickly as possible to get away from Cara and her weirdness, only to find out that I don't have an asbestos mouth and it burns my tongue.

'I've always wondered about these things. You know, how it works? How you decide how you're going to get pregnant.' She's still looking between the two of us.

41

Cara was always goofing around in our human biology lessons – probably because she was one of the only teens in our class that had already conducted her own experiments – but perhaps she should have been paying more attention.

'Well, there's a man and a woman...' I say with laugh and a bit of a snort.

'And you didn't mind?' she says, looking directly at Rachel.

'To be honest, I try not to think about her having sex with my brother,' she says.

Cara's jaw drops and it only highlights her perfect cheekbones more. She's clearly as shocked as I am that Rach has managed to reply in a full sentence to her. She peers closely into the stroller that I'm rocking. Sasha's eyes fly open, as if she senses that she's being watched, and for a moment she's too startled to cry.

'Oh my God, she looks so much like him,' Cara says.

I scramble underneath the stroller, rooting in the bag to her milk.

'Don't worry, honey, you've been sleeping, but I've got some milk for you.'

'Doesn't it feel weird for you to look at her and see him?' Cara asks Rach.

'Not really, he's her dad.'

'Mmmhmm, absolutely,' says Cara, nodding away. 'But it must be hard looking at her and seeing his resemblance every day.'

'I don't see Sasha every day, I live in Guildford,' says Rach, frowning.

I finally find the milk at the bottom of the stroller.

'Here you go, sweetie,' I say, placing it in her hands and stroking the side of her face.

'Surely Guildford's commutable from Fleet,' says Cara. 'Why wouldn't the two of you live together?' She gestures to me and Rach.

'Why *would* we live together?' I say, confused, sitting back up from the stroller now that Sasha is preoccupied with drinking from her sippy cup. I pick up my coffee cup and take a much-needed sip.

'Because you're married,' she says, looking between us both. 'You're Mrs Rachel Voss.'

'You think Rachel is my wife?' I say, spluttering out my coffee.

'That's what you said. I asked if you married her and you said yes.'

'Er, no you didn't. I'm pretty sure I would have remembered that.'

'Oh, right. So, you two aren't…?' she says, raising an eyebrow. 'God, I'm so sorry, but you know there were all those rumours at school about you two being lesbians; I just assumed.'

'All those rumours at school?' I say in a slightly high-pitched voice whilst this all sinks in.

'Yeah, you two were always together and didn't you have your own language?'

'It wasn't really our own language, it was a variant of gibberish,' says Rach, who is more amused than stunned. 'Did everyone think we were together?'

'I think so,' she says, shrugging her shoulders. 'It could have been worse; we could have thought you were dating one of those boys you used to hang out with from that sci-fi club you used to have.'

I curl my hands tighter around my coffee cup, despite it

practically scalding me, as I try and digest this revelation. Rach has started to laugh. Sasha starts to laugh too and somehow it makes the whole situation seem all the more funny.

'I can't believe everyone else knew I was a lesbian when I didn't.'

I crack a smile. Rach came out to me when we were in our mid-twenties, although she didn't tell anyone in her family until just after her parents split up.

'So, wait, hang on. If you're not married to each other, and she's your brother's baby,' she says, nodding her head towards Sasha, 'does that mean you married Rachel's brother?'

'That's right.'

'Oh, it's just that I thought Max was your only brother.'

'He is,' says Rach.

'*You* married Max?' she says, turning to me, her voice tinged with disbelief. 'You married Max Voss? Max Voss who we voted Most Fuckable of 1997?'

I know that I looked different in school and I wasn't the most comfortable in my skin back then, but surely it's not that shocking that I could have married him, is it? I mean, he might have been *the* Max Voss back in school, but now he's just Max.

'Yes, Ellie did, I don't know why it's a surprise,' says Rach. 'She's fucking awesome – in fact, Max is bloody lucky that she married him; she's more of a catch than he is.'

I'm grateful to Rach, and I try and smile in appreciation but I've started to shake. Cara still can't see past the gangly girl in the glasses. The funny thing is, that whilst my glasses might be thinner, I'm still that girl, studious and a bit geeky at heart, but I'm also warm and funny and generous and she would have seen that both then and now if she'd actually looked, but she won't.

'Of course, I guess it was just a shock at first, but of course there's no reason that she couldn't have married him...' says Cara, still seeming shocked. 'Just out of... curiosity... does he still look like...'

'A Hemsworth brother, uh-huh,' I say, feeling uncomfortable that my life is now being validated by how hot my husband is. Sasha's starting to wriggle in her stroller and I take her milk away, before unclipping the stroller straps and pulling her on to my lap.

'You are one lucky woman,' she says.

'So are you, you've got your work,' I say, trying not to sound too sarcastic as I bounce Sasha on my knee and clap her hands together. 'And it's your calling.'

'Hmm. Yes, I guess so.' She slips her jacket back on and slides her chair back. 'God, it's such a shame you weren't lesbians. We were planning this feature for next month on the show and it's about same-sex couples who adopt and we've got a few men but we're short on women.'

And finally, the penny drops as to why she was so keen to sit down and chat.

'Sorry we couldn't help,' I say, flatly.

'No worries,' she says, standing up. 'I probably should get going. Perhaps I'll see you at the next reunion.'

She slips her tiny bag over her shoulder.

'Hey, yeah, perhaps we can come together,' says Rach, patting my hand. 'Cause a real stir.'

Cara half smiles before hurrying away.

Rach and I exchange looks, trying desperately not to laugh until she's out of earshot.

'Bloody hell, she hasn't changed a bit from school. She's

still a massive bitch,' says Rach, when she finally disappears out of view.

'That's a bit harsh,' I say.

'Oh, come on, did you see her face when she realised you were with Max?'

'She's not the only one that does that,' I say. Sasha starts wants to wriggle off my lap so I let her and she toddles between me and Rach, excited for her new-found freedom.

'No, but she's probably the only one that would say it to your face. I can't believe we used to want her to notice us.'

'I know.'

'So, now that she's gone, shall we get back to what you wanted to talk about?'

'Oh yeah,' says Rach, exhaling a deep breath.

My phone vibrates across the table again. I pick it up.

'It's a voicemail, your mum phoned earlier.'

'Answer it,' says Rach. 'She's probably just got an icing sugar emergency.' Sasha reaches out to her and Rach tickles her, much to her delight.

I laugh at the two of them. Sasha keeps toddling away but going back for more each time, but as the message starts to play the smile slides off my face.

'Ellie, it's Judy um... Max is here and he's... well, he looks fine, but I think there's definitely something wrong with him. I think you need to get over here as soon as you can.'

My heart starts to beat rapidly.

'What's wrong, Ellie?' says Rach, sitting forward.

'It's Max,' I say, dialling Judy's number but it's engaged and I leave her a quick message asking her to call me, but then I see that my battery is almost dead. 'Your mum says that there's something wrong with him. Shit, why didn't I charge my sodding phone?'

I try Max's number but it goes straight through to voicemail.

'I left mine charging at Mum's,' says Rach. 'Come on, let's go straight there.'

'But it'll take us half an hour to walk there.'

'Or twenty if we hurry. Come on.'

I can't seem to make my feet work.

'But we were going to talk about you and Gaby.'

Rach pops Sasha back into the stroller. 'Don't worry about that now; we need to make sure Max is OK.'

'OK, OK,' I say, my voice unsteady.

'Come on.' Rach takes hold of the stroller and starts marching down the path and I follow after. 'I'm sure there's nothing to worry about. You know what Mum's like; she loves her amateur dramatics.'

I hope that Rach is right, but my stomach is churning at the thought of how scared Judy sounded and I get the feeling that something is very wrong.

Chapter 3

By the time I get to my mother-in-law's house, Sasha is asleep again, and Rach and I are red-faced and sweaty.

'I'm going to put the stroller under the tree in the back,' I say, as Rach heads straight to the front door.

'OK, see you in a sec,' she says, putting her key in the lock. I unlock the side gate and wheel Sasha into the shade of the big oak tree and head towards the back door. I glance through the kitchen window and sigh with relief as I see Max poking his head in the fridge – he's all in one piece.

'You,' I say, opening the door and pointing a finger at him. 'You are in big trouble.'

He jumps back in surprise and holds his hands up.

I give him a once-over. There's not a scratch on him. Bloody Judy. She should know better than to leave a message like that on the answerphone of a heavily pregnant woman. I'm not sure why Max came here instead of heading back home, but knowing him, he probably lost his keys and his phone battery had died like mine.

'Come here,' I say with relief as I walk towards him and throw my arms around his neck. 'What are you doing here?'

He steps backwards, hitting the kitchen wall with a thump, his face panic-stricken.

'This is my mum's house.' He narrows his eyes before a small smile spreads over his face. 'Spider, blimey, I almost didn't recognise you.'

I stop still. He knows I hate that nickname. He hasn't called me that since the night in the club when we got together. I push my much thinner-lensed glasses up my nose.

'Very funny, Max,' I say, taking a step back.

'Bloody hell. You sure grew up, didn't you? It doesn't look like there's much tissue paper in there today,' he says, dropping his voice and giving me a wink.

In fact, he said that that night in the club too.

'Is this some kind of role play we're doing?' I say, confused. He's looking at me with the same sort of look that usually leads to us abandoning clothes and ending up in the bedroom.

I'd only been kidding about it this morning, but he's obviously spent time concocting this.

'Role play? Yes, you were always into that, weren't you? You and Rach used to be in that club at school, what was it – *Dungeons and Dragons*?' says Max with a laugh.

Pretending like we haven't seen each other from school is not the role play I'd had in mind, but, fresh from the encounter with Cara Worthington, perhaps re-enacting a fantasy where the geek that got the guy would be fitting.

'Oh right, gotcha. So, Max, do you come here often?' I try and purr but it sounds more like I've got a fur ball stuck in my throat.

'Well, it is my mum's house...'

'Oh yeah.' I'm so rubbish at this acting malarkey, unlike

49

Max who's taking it very seriously, playing hard to get. 'But your mum's not here now, is she?'

'Er, no, she's in the lounge, on the phone.'

I edge forwards and he presses himself almost flat against the wall. My bump is pinning him in place – he's not going anywhere.

'That's handy,' I say, running my finger down the buttons of his shirt.

'What are you doing, Spider? I know that you used to have a bit of a crush on me but I never thought you'd do anything about it… I had no idea what you were really like.'

'Oh, really?' I say, finally nailing the purr. 'Those abs…' I reach out and stroke them. 'And that bum of yours.'

'Spider,' he says again in shock as I cup his bum and it only makes me giggle more. I'm actually quite enjoying this. Who knew this could be so fun?

'You know,' I say, 'when we were teenagers eating at that very table, I used to imagine what it would be like to have sex with you on top of it.'

'Bloody hell, my mum is only in the next room,' he says, looking horrified and wriggling away from me and the kitchen wall. 'This is wrong on so many levels, not least because you're pregnant and,' he says, grabbing my hand, 'you're also married.'

I mock-roll my eyes.

'Oh, don't worry, my husband doesn't need to find out. Plus, you're much better-looking than him.'

Max momentarily puffs out his chest at the compliment; he is so in character it's almost funny. He starts to back away from me, walking behind the table, and I follow him, finding myself chasing him slowly round it.

'This is wrong,' he says.

'But isn't that what makes it so right?' I say in an over-the-top voice, finally grabbing hold of him and pinning him with my arms more forcefully against the wall and leaning up to kiss him.

'Right, Mum's filled me in. She's phoned Gaby—' says Rach, bursting into the kitchen and causing us to leap apart. I try and compose myself, whilst Max just stares at me like he's been hit by bus. 'Oh, sorry, I didn't mean to interrupt.'

'You didn't,' I say, pretending I'm not mortified.

'I guess everything is fine, then?' says Rach, folding her arms across her chest and staring between us.

'Everything is fine,' I say, straightening my top. 'I was just about to fill Max in on the fact that we bumped into Cara Worthington from school.'

'I remember her, the one with the blonde hair and the big boobs.'

Rach and I snap our heads round and stare at him.

'What?' He shrugs, digging into the fridge. 'That's what she was known for at school. That, and she'd swallow.'

My mouth drops open.

'Come on, Spider, you shouldn't look so shocked. You didn't seem that shy a few minutes ago.'

'Spider?' says Rach in a low voice, studying my face for a reaction.

'Oh God. We were pretending not to be together. You know how couples do to, um—' my cheeks flush even more '—um… well, never mind.'

'I'm just going to pretend that I don't know that you two do stuff like that, but Ellie, Mum said that there's something wrong with Max.'

Max sighs loudly.

'There's nothing wrong with me. It's all of you that are acting weird. You, Mum, Spider. Do you know she came on to me? I mean, if anyone was acting weird it's her. She kissed me, and she's married and up the duff,' he says in an almost whisper towards Rach.

'No shit, Sherlock,' she whispers back.

'Well, it was her fault, she came on to me, so don't you be having a go that I came on to her. She's the one with the husband.'

'Max, stop this, it's one thing for us to pretend amongst ourselves, but don't drag Rach into it,' I say, mortified.

'What do you mean, stop pretending – pretending what?' he says.

I can sense Rach's eyes burning into me.

'Ellie—' she starts, but I don't let her finish.

'You. You are my husband. This is your baby.'

Max narrows his eyes and looks at me before he starts to laugh.

'Good one, Spider. Look, can everyone stop joking?'

'I've found my keys,' says Judy, bursting into the room. 'Have you brought Ellie up to speed? Ah, darling, there you are.'

She comes over and takes hold of both of my hands.

'Did Rach tell you that I phoned Gaby? She says that we should go straight to A&E to get Max looked at.'

He groans.

'I've told you, Mum, I'm fine.'

'Max? What is going on? Why would you need to go to A&E?' I feel panicked. None of this is making any sense.

'There's absolutely nothing wrong. My mum, as per usual, is overreacting about everything. What time's Dad going to be home, he'll calm you down.'

'Your dad? But—'

'He's not back anytime soon, love,' says Judy cutting me off and shooting me a look.

'Shame, as he'd sort this right out,' Max says with an exasperated sigh.

'Would someone please tell me what's going on?' For someone whose profession it is to connect the dots between pieces of information, I'm doing a pretty bad job of it here.

'Everyone's gone flipping crazy, that's what,' says Max. 'From Mum and Rach trying to pack me off to the hospital and you sticking your tongue down my throat. All I want to do is have a beer and watch the football.'

My heart is starting to pound loud enough for me to hear.

'But Gaby says we should go to A&E right away,' says Judy.

'Well, whoever Gaby is, she's wrong,' he says, leaning into the fridge and taking out a beer.

'What do you mean, whoever Gaby is?' I say.

I'm starting to feel light-headed and sick now that this is moving beyond a joke and I sit on a chair before I fall down.

'I don't know, but whatever trick you're playing it's not funny. I'm going to watch the football,' he says, storming out.

As I look between Judy and Rach, the faint sound of the TV in the lounge drifts in.

Rach sits me down on a chair and pulls up one for herself.

'Max turned up here about an hour ago and he's a bit confused,' she says quietly.

'Confused?'

'He said he was in Chiswick and he didn't know what he was doing there, so he went to his flat in Brixton but there was someone else living there. Then he saw his train pass for Fleet in his wallet and he came here.'

It takes a moment for what she's saying to all sink in.

'Brixton? Why would he think he lived in Brixton? He's moved twice since then. And what was he doing in Chiswick? That's nowhere near his office.'

My wrists begin to tingle and it travels up my arms to my neck, before my whole body starts to burn.

'We really don't know what's going on, but it seems like he's lost his memory,' says Judy.

'His memory?' I say scrunching up my face. 'People don't just lose their memory. Surely that only happens in the movies.'

'It's the only thing we can think of. He still thinks he's thirty-two and that he lives in Brixton. He doesn't remember you two getting together or that you've moved to Fleet.'

I shake my head. He can't have forgotten the last five years of his life. I stand up quickly and have to clutch the table as my head is spinning wildly.

'This isn't happening,' I say, marching towards the lounge and throwing open the door.

Max is sitting on the couch flicking through the channels with the remote.

'I keep trying to find the sports channels, but they're blocked. Dad'll be furious that they're not working.'

I grip the back of the sofa, my legs still unsteady.

That's the second time he's mentioned his dad; he's barely spoken about him in four and a half years.

'Ellie, love,' says Judy, walking in, her face as white as

a sheet, 'we need to get him to the hospital. I'm worried that he's had some sort of fall and hit his head.'

Max runs his hands through his hair and familiar butterflies stir in my stomach – only today it's with nerves, not lust.

'I can hear you, you know. And I'm fine,' he says, shrugging. 'Mum, what's happened to Sky Sports?'

'We got rid of it,' she says.

'Why would Dad do that?' he says, screwing his face up, but before Judy can answer there's a whimper from the hallway and Rach walks in with Sasha in her arms.

'Look who's just woken up,' she says, and Sasha pulls towards me.

'Is that your baby?' says Max, standing up from the sofa. 'Do I know the father?'

I'm too stunned to reply. I don't want to believe that Rach and Judy are right but if he's not trying to spice up our sex life, then I'm running out of logical reasons as to why he's doing this.

Sasha sees Max and lunges towards him. I instinctively pass her over but I don't miss the look of horror on his face.

'What am I supposed to do?' he says, taking her a little awkwardly. But as soon as she's in his arms, he balances her on his hips and starts to smile at her.

For a minute I think everything's going to be OK. I look over at Judy with relief. Whatever little episode that was, it's over now, and he's back to normal.

'I think she's done something in her nappy,' he says, quickly holding her out to me. 'I'm going to get another beer before I try and work out what's happened to the sports channels. She's cute, though, despite the smell.'

He leaves the room and I turn to Judy and Rach.

'What the bloody hell is going on?' I say, holding on to Sasha just a little too tight.

'You have to be careful, love, you don't want to upset the baby.'

'Upset the baby? Judy, my husband doesn't have a clue that we're married or that he's a dad. How could I not get worked up?'

'I know it's hard,' Judy says, trying to sound calm when she's anything but. 'It's just that now is not the time for this baby to arrive, OK?'

'I know, I know,' I say, breathing out heavily. 'I just don't understand what's happening.'

'Gaby said it could be any number of things and that he probably needs to see a neurologist. She said not to worry as in most cases amnesia is very short-lived,' says Judy.

Rach takes Sasha from me before helping me sit down on the sofa.

'Amnesia,' I say, confused. 'How can it be amnesia? He remembers who we all are.'

Judy rubs her forehead and exhales deeply.

'But he doesn't seem to remember the last five or six years.'

'The last five or six years,' I say, choking up. So much has happened since then. His dad leaving. Us getting together. Us getting married. Sasha being born. Me getting pregnant again. 'He's got to be putting it on. He isn't acting like someone who's lost their mind. He doesn't seem upset or traumatised like you'd imagine he would be – in fact he's the most relaxed I've seen him look in ages. Gaby must be wrong.'

Judy winces. 'Let's not second-guess everything. Gaby said to go to the hospital and get it all checked out.'

'He's under so much pressure from work at the moment, what if it's tipped him over the edge?' I try to take deep breaths as adrenaline starts to kick in.

'I'm sure that's all it is,' says Judy in a calming voice. 'But let's get him checked out sooner rather than later. OK?'

'How about I stay here?' says Rach. 'I can look after Sasha.'

'Would you mind?' I say, relieved, as right now I don't think I can manage to look after her and worry about Max.

'Of course. Get him sorted and then come home and we can gossip properly about what the hell happened with Cara Worthington.'

'Oh yes, Cara with the big boobs,' I say sarcastically.

'He's going to be fine, Ellie,' she says, leaning forward and putting an arm around me. 'He'll be just fine.'

I nod and give Sasha a big kiss. It has to be OK. Both Sasha and this baby need their daddy just as much as I need my husband back.

Chapter 4

I always think I'm good in a crisis. I'm generally level-headed and not known to panic, but it's not every day that your husband is treating you like you're a deranged stalker.

The longer we've been in hospital, the more worried I've become. I think I expected the A&E staff to tell us we were overreacting but the fact that they gave him a full examination and immediately called for a neurological consultant hasn't done anything to settle my nerves.

Max, meanwhile, is taking everything in his stride. He's had a nap, eaten a share bag of M&Ms and flirted with the very pretty doctor that first saw him. I did try and remind him numerous times that I was his wife, but he keeps laughing me away. And when he's not laughing, he's pointing to the lack of wedding ring on his finger. I've given up telling him that he takes it off when he showers, and nine mornings out of ten he forgets to put it back on, because he's having none of it.

Judy, on the other hand, is taking the altogether different approach of sitting calmly next to him and not saying a word.

'Do you think this is going to take much longer?' asks Max. 'Only I'm sure I'm missing the football.'

'Forget about the sodding football,' I say, pulling out my

phone and swiping to find the results. 'Brighton got beat by Man City 4-0. There, you happy?'

He narrows his eyes.

'For fuck's sake, now I know you're winding me up. How could Brighton be playing Man City?'

'Because they're in the premiership now,' I say, wondering if he'll at least believe that.

'Ellie, I think it's better not to tell him anything about what he's missed until the doctor comes along.'

'What? So the bump and I are supposed to sit here and pretend we don't exist?'

Judy bites her lip and I feel bad. This can't be easy for her either. Her life has changed drastically in the last few years and it won't be easy explaining all that to Max again. But it's infuriating, Max is acting like a bloody teenager. It's as if he's forgotten fifteen years rather than five.

There's a screech of metal as the cubicle curtain is pulled back and another blond doctor walks in. I almost sigh with relief that this time it's a man and at least I'll be spared from watching Max flirt outrageously.

'Now then, Max, what's been going on?'

'We're wasting your time, that's what's going on,' says Max, folding his arms over his chest.

'It's OK, Max, I'm Sam, and I'm going to just ask you a few questions about everything. First off, do you know where you are?'

'County Hospital,' he says, sighing as if he's a moron.

'OK, and what's the year?'

'2014,' he says without blinking.

'OK, and the prime minister is?'

'David Cameron.'

'And Brexit is?'

Max scrunches up his face.

'I'm sorry, I don't understand.'

'Oh good God,' says Judy. 'I want whatever he's got.'

I suppose I was really naïve when it came to thinking about his memory loss. I hadn't really considered that it wasn't just us he'd forgotten about, but everything that's happened in the world.

'2014,' I say slowly. 'Obama is president?'

'Uh-huh, who else?' he says. 'Aren't you supposed to be some sort of genius, Spider?'

I flinch at the name and the consultant turns around and looks at me.

'Are you his wife?'

'Yes, I'm Ellie and this is his mum, Judy.'

'She's not my wife,' interrupts Max. 'She's my sister's best friend, who I haven't seen for years. They're playing some sort of joke on me.'

Sam, the consultant, looks at me before looking back at him.

'So, you don't think you're married?'

'Of course I don't, because I'm not. I think I'd remember that,' he says, spluttering a laugh. 'Look, no ring.'

I scrunch my hands into a ball, digging my nails into my palms to ground myself with the pain.

The consultant makes a couple of notes on his iPad and then turns to me.

'Perhaps it's better if I speak to Max on his own,' says Sam.

'But—'

'It's often easier that way. There are chairs opposite the cubicle. I'll come and chat to you when we're done.'

'But I really think that—'

'Please, just a few minutes,' he says in a tone that makes me pick up my bag and shuffle out.

'Come on, Ellie, it's for the best. Give Max a bit of space.'

'But he's confused, he's—'

'That's why we need to give him space,' she says, sitting down.

Judy and I sit in silence at first. I don't think either of us wants to vocalise the magnitude of the situation. I pull out my phone and ring Max's best friend Owen, only for it to go straight to answerphone. I leave a message explaining what's happened and asking him to call me when he gets a chance.

'Was that your mum?' asks Judy.

'No, Mum is definitely not one for a crisis. Besides, she's somewhere in the Caribbean at the moment. I was phoning Owen.'

'Oh, good idea. Maybe he might have known what Max was doing in Chiswick.'

I nod and slip my phone back in my pocket and we sit in silence once more.

'Imagine not knowing about Brexit,' says Judy eventually.

I close my eyes and wonder what that would be like. Going back to a much less confusing time.

'Or about Donald Trump,' I say, thinking about the order of events.

'Or that David Bowie died,' says Judy.

I turn and look at her.

'Bloody hell, 2016 – the year all the good ones died. Max loved Alan Rickman. He insists that *Die Hard* is the best Christmas film ever and that it's all because of Alan.'

Judy takes my hand and squeezes it. It's hard to process how much he doesn't know.

'Prince died.'

'Noel Edmonds,' says Judy, shaking her head.

'Noel Edmonds? No, I'm pretty sure he's still going.'

'Really?'

'No,' she says, quite forcefully. 'I'm sure he died a couple of years ago. Isn't that why *Deal or No Deal* finished?'

'I think it had just run its course.'

'Hmm,' says Judy, unconvinced. She pulls out her phone and taps away. 'Ah, it was Keith Chegwin. Got the wrong one.'

'They're nothing like each other,' I say, stifling a laugh.

'They were both on *Swap Shop*, probably before your time. Gosh, think of all the TV he'll have missed.'

'Yes,' I say, thinking of all the boxsets we've watched since we've been together and how binge-watching them has become such a big part of our relationship. 'He won't remember that he saw *Dark Energy* and it took me years to convince him to watch it, *years*.'

Max doesn't do sci-fi and I had to beg him to watch my favourite cult classics.

'He'll be mad about them removing the toffee from the Quality Street box, though, do you remember that?' she says.

'How could I forget toffeegate?' My lips start to curl and a small laugh escapes me, and Judy laughs too. Only when we stop, sadness hits me. 'How could he forget all that?'

'This all could be a blip, you know; he could wake up tomorrow and it will all seem like a bad dream.'

Judy's ever the optimist. I only hope she's right.

After what feels like an eternity, the consultant comes out into the corridor. We go to stand but he motions for us to stay put and he pulls up a chair and sits down next to us.

'So, I've had a quick check over Max and the good news is that his test results so far seem good and there's no obvious outward signs of a head injury. The next step is to do an MRI scan and an EEG to make sure that he hasn't had a stroke or a seizure of some kind, but I think from the way he's acting and his blood tests not showing anything unusual, I'm leaning towards a diagnosis of dissociative amnesia.'

'That sounds serious,' says Judy; her grip around my hands tighten.

'It is and isn't.' Sam takes a big deep breath before he explains. 'It's obviously serious in that he's missing years of his life, but if the MRI scan comes back showing no signs of physical damage to his brain, it would mean that those memories are still there.'

'But I don't understand; if they're still there, why can't he access them?' I say.

Sam takes another breath and puts a reassuring smile on his face.

'Now, this isn't my area of expertise, and the psychiatrist will explain better, but we don't always know why this happens. Usually, people do this when they've witnessed or experienced a traumatic event. We think it's caused by extreme stress in a trauma. What was Max doing earlier today?'

'He went to work,' I say, feeling like something isn't quite adding up.

'Going to work can be pretty traumatic,' says Sam, trying to lighten the mood, but it doesn't. 'You don't know if he got in an accident or anything?'

'No, we don't know,' I say.

'OK. Well, in most cases where this happens, patients recover quickly,' says Sam.

'When you say quickly, are we talking days or weeks?' says Judy.

'I think generally it's hours, sometimes days or weeks, possibly even months or years but only in very, very rare cases,' he says quickly, after Judy and I gasp. 'I'm going to order for a psychiatrist to consult whilst we wait for the MRI scan.'

'A psychiatrist,' I say, shutting my eyes. 'Doesn't he need a neurologist like you to fix him?'

'If this is dissociative amnesia then unfortunately there's nothing that I can do to unlock those memories. When Max's memory comes back it will hopefully be in one big bang. Quite often something triggers that bang, like finding out the root of the trauma. But you have to remember that whatever caused him to shut down part of his brain is something that he doesn't want to relive – so the psychiatrist will probably recommend that he sees a psychotherapist, who would help him through it with counselling in a supportive environment.'

I'm quiet for a minute whilst I try and take it all in.

'I'm sorry,' says Judy, speaking her mind as usual. 'But this sounds like bullshit to me. You're essentially telling me that my son has hidden his memories.'

Sam taps a couple of times on his screen.

'Yes, I am. Our brains can work in very complicated ways to protect us.'

'There has to be more to it,' says Judy. 'I mean, if he's properly lost his memory, why isn't he bothered? You've seen him; he's not even distressed.'

'That's one of the symptoms of this type of amnesia. Generally, if you've lost your memory as a result from a problem in your brain, you get upset and anxious as you know something is not right. But in Max's case, because his brain is hiding something from him, it's pretending that everything is normal. It might not be the normal as you know it, and he might be acting out of character, but he doesn't realise that.'

Now it's my turn to squeeze Judy's hand.

'What can we do to help him to find those memories?' I focus on the cure rather than the diagnosis.

Sam gives me one of his sympathetic looks. 'Support him with the psychotherapy, perhaps remind him of memories to try and see if anything jogs it. Going about your daily routine might trigger something. But you have to be careful, you want to create as safe and supportive an environment as possible for him to regain his memories. You don't want to shock him any further, so don't feel like you need to tell him everything at once. He's going to regain these memories pretty soon, so I think the best thing you can do is to carry on as normal until he does.'

'But what about his job?' I say in a panic. 'He won't remember what he's working on.'

'I'm sure the psychiatrist will sign him off temporarily. I've ordered that consult and the MRI – both are a bit of a waiting game, I'm afraid. Saturday isn't the best day to be in A&E,

especially with sports starting up again after the summer. I'll leave you to let this all sink in and then I'll be back to do an EEG a bit later on.'

'And in the meantime?' I say, not even questioning what an EEG is.

'Go and talk to him,' he says, shrugging and looking at his watch.

'Thank you,' I say. He gets up, assuring us he'll see us after his tests.

I head towards the curtain but Judy pulls me back.

'Do you think we should decide what to tell him?' she asks.

'How do you mean? The doctor said—'

'I know, but I was thinking about his dad.'

'Oh,' I say. 'It's going to be awful for him have to go through that all again.'

'Which is why I don't think we should tell him. He's probably going to get his memory back in a few hours; there's no point in distressing him.'

I feel uneasy. It's a pretty big part of his life to miss out.

'What if this goes on for months?'

'Then we find a way to tell him, gently. Ease him into the idea.'

'And in the meantime how are we going to explain that he's not at your house?'

'We'll tell him he's on a golfing trip with Graham. I really think this is best for Max.'

'OK,' I say, staring back at the curtain. 'And what about Mick? Are we going to tell him that Max has lost his memory?'

She fiddles with the strap on her handbag.

'Judy, he's his son; he'd want to know.'

'I know, I know, but can we wait and phone him in a few days? Let's just see if he gets his memory back first. The last thing we want is him flying over and upsetting Max.'

I bite my lip. I'm torn over telling Max the truth and causing more upset in the family. The last time I got involved I suggested that Mick be allowed to video call to see Sasha, and whilst Max reluctantly agreed – he doesn't want to stand in Sasha's way of having a relationship with her granddad – he always leaves the house when we do it.

'OK,' I say, nodding.

'I'll text Graham and Rach and let them know what's happening.'

I step forward and open the curtain to find Max grinning back at me. I hold my breath, hoping his memory is back.

'You look pleased with yourself,' I say, hiding the expectation in my voice. 'Have you remembered?'

'No,' he says, 'but Sam told me that Brighton did play Man City this afternoon. You were right, Spider. Brighton are back in the premiership!'

Judy looks at me and shakes her head. Trust Max to focus on this and not the fact that the doctor has just told him he's lost five years of his life.

I look at him, and in one way he's the Max I know and love, but in another he's not the man I married at all.

Chapter 5

I wake up to the sounds of Sasha muttering and it takes me a few seconds to work out where I am. I roll over and spot her standing up in the travel cot and yesterday comes flooding back to me.

I dread to think how little sleep I got last night. It was late by the time Max was discharged from hospital and we got in and went straight to bed, staying at Judy's house, given that Sasha was fast asleep there.

I scoop her up and she starts babbling away. I'm trying to listen to her, but I can hear Max laughing downstairs and I'm filled with hope. I hurry down the stairs and burst into the room to find him opening and closing the cupboard doors.

'Hey,' I say, a little breathless.

Sasha wriggles out of my arms and I pop her on the ground and she toddles away.

'Hey, Spider,' he says, pulling out a frying pan and placing it on a hob.

My heart almost breaks. Sam did warn that it might take days, weeks or months to come back, but I hadn't realised how much I'd been pinning all my hopes on him waking up today with his memory back.

Whilst I find it incredibly disconcerting that he's acting as if this a typical Sunday, the consultant did tell us that that's how he'd react. I guess I should be grateful that he's accepted that I'm in his life even if he is ignoring the fact that we're actually married and avoiding talking about the life we live.

'I'm making breakfast for Rach if you want some? I make a mean omelette,' he says.

'Sure, and Sasha would too,' I say, sinking down into a chair. In my desperation to check on Max I hadn't noticed Rach sitting at the table, and she gives my arm a rub, before she holds her hands out to Sasha who's launched herself at her.

'OK,' he says, and I watch him chopping up the ingredients.

'You'll have to chop the peppers up small for Sasha, though.'

It seems strange having to spell things out that only yesterday would have been second nature to him.

'Oh right, OK,' he says, nodding but not acknowledging her. He's usually magnetically drawn to her when she enters a room.

'I just need to find where the herbs and spices are,' he says, opening and shutting another cupboard.

Rach stands up, still clutching Sasha, and opens a cupboard next to the stove. 'Here. You know they've been in exactly the same place for the last twenty-eight years.'

'I don't think I've ever cooked here before,' he says. 'Why would I when Mum does it so well?'

'You don't have to brown nose when Mum's not even here.'

'Did I hear my name?' says Judy, walking into the room.

'They're just laughing about Max not knowing his way around your kitchen,' I say, filling her in.

'I didn't even know he could cook,' says Judy.

She goes to take over but he bats her away.

'It's fine, I'm making an omelette. Do you want one?'

'OK,' she says, giving Sasha a hug before she sits down at the table with Rach.

Max pulls out Herbes de Provence and puts them on the counter next to the carton of eggs.

'Where do I find a whisk?' he says, digging around in the pot of utensils until he finds one.

'This feels almost like when you used to sleep over when we were kids, Ellie,' says Rach. 'Well, except for Max's cooking – we wouldn't have been eating anything he cooked.'

'You were missing out. Do you not remember that macaroni cheese I cooked in home ec? I got an A in it.'

'I'm pretty sure you just used to get Carly Simmons to cook for you,' says Rach, rolling her eyes.

'Hey, I think most of it was my own work, thank you very much,' he says, flashing a winning smile. 'Or at least I did provide all the ingredients.'

'Mum used to weigh it all out and put it in little Tupperware pots for you.'

'Did I?' says Judy, a small smile on her lips.

It stings that Max is acting exactly the same with Rach and his mum as he normally would, yet almost like a stranger with Sasha and me. This new normal is going to take some getting used to.

'That was delicious, even if I do say so myself.' Max pushes his plate away and picks up his phone after he's finished his omelette. 'I'm pleased I use the same password for every phone or else I'd have been screwed,' he says, cracking a joke, like only Max could at a time like this.

'Actually, you've got fingerprint recognition on this phone. There, on the back, it scans your fingerprint,' I say, turning it to show him.

'Holy shit, we do live in the future,' he says, his eyes lighting up. 'What else has happened tech wise? I see we haven't got a robot washing the dishes yet.'

For the first time since leaving the hospital, he's actually excited about discovering something about his new life, and it's not even related to football.

'Um, pretty sure they had dishwashers in 2014,' says Rach. 'But, knowing you, you probably wouldn't have known what one was.'

'Very funny. You know what I meant.'

'Unfortunately, we don't have any real-life robots,' Judy says. 'Alexa, what are the biggest technological advances from the last five years?'

The mechanical voice of Alexa fills the room. '*The top ten technological advances in the last five years are practical augmented reality, AI in apps...*'

Max spins round and stares in wonderment at the little speaker on the counter and listens with great interest to the list.

'I can't believe you have this. Mum, when did you get all tech savvy?'

'You bought it for me for Christmas, but I quite like her. She keeps me company.'

'I bet this is all your doing, isn't it? It's a bit *Star Trek*,' he says to me.

'Sometimes I think there are two women in our marriage and Alexa's one of them. You're very fond of her,' I tell him.

'Am I? What do I use it for?'

'Everything. Football results, music, the weather.'

'Huh. How do I do it?'

'You say, "Alexa," and then you ask your question.'

'OK. Alexa, what division are Brighton in?' he says slowly and loudly, like a British person abroad that doesn't speak the language.

'Brighton and Hove Albion FC are in the Premiership.'

'Yeah, they are,' he says, doing a fist pump.

He picks up his phone again and starts swiping.

'Are you looking for things to jog your memory? Maybe looking through your messages will help,' says Rach.

'No, I was going to text Dad to see what time he was going to be home.'

Judy and I exchange looks.

'Have you not told him about Dad?' says Rach, looking at us in horror.

'What do you mean, tell me about Dad?' says Max; he's only half listening as he's scrolling through his phone.

'Just that he's away, on a golfing holiday, with Graham, and he won't be back for a few weeks,' Judy says, parroting it out in a way that makes me think she rehearsed it.

Rachel opens her mouth to protest. 'Ouch,' she says, looking under the table where I imagine she just received a kick.

'But when I spoke to him yesterday, he said that he'd be back tomorrow, which is today,' says Max, looking up over his phone.

'You can't have spoken to your father yesterday,' says Judy;

72

she starts fiddling with the collar of her high-necked blouse. 'He's got bad signal on his holiday.'

Rachel's eyes are practically bulging out of her head, but she doesn't say anything.

'It seemed all right. I called him when I found someone living at my old flat in Brixton and he told me to come back here and that you'd help me. That's when I found my season ticket.'

Judy's neck starting to turn red where her blouse is scratching against it. I open my mouth to tell them that I think it would be best to tell him the truth when the doorbell rings. We all look at up at the kitchen door that leads to the hallway.

'Maybe that's him now,' says Max, scraping his chair along the floor as he gets up. 'Forgotten his key or something.'

Judy looks at me in horror and we're both thinking the same thing: that it can't possibly be him.

Max walks out of the room and Rachel gets up and closes the kitchen door before turning her attention to us.

'Bloody hell, you were at that hospital for hours and when you said you were filling him on what's been going on I thought you'd told him the big stuff,' she says.

'We had, there's been a lot he didn't know about Brexit, Trump, Boris becoming PM, the climate change emergency, *Supermarket Sweep* making a comeback,' says Judy, not looking her in the eye.

'For God's sake,' says Rachel.

'It's just not the kind of thing you can blurt out sitting on a hospital bed,' Judy says. 'Those curtains are so thin.'

Rachel rolls her eyes again. She's always been the rip-off-the-band-aid kind of person who will always tell you exactly how it is. It's actually a great quality in a friend once you get used to someone being brutally honest at every moment. It's saved me from a lot of things over the years; getting my hair permed in Year 8; dodgy midnight snogs with undesirable men when I was wearing beer goggles; a fishtail wedding dress that would have seriously hampered my ability to dance.

'You should have told him yesterday,' says Rach.

'Look, the doctor thinks that Max's memory loss is only going to be transient. He should remember everything in the next few days and then we'd have put him through all that for nothing,' says Judy, crossing her arms over her chest.

'What if he really has spoken to Dad and that's him at the door?'

'It's more likely to be Elvis,' mutters Judy. 'He won't have got on a plane, he just won't have.'

We hear a woman's laugh.

'I knew Mick wouldn't have come,' says Judy, sighing with relief.

'I'll go and see who it is,' I say, not wanting a repeat of last night where Max was hitting on any woman that he saw.

'Oh, Gaby,' I say, relieved to see Rach's girlfriend at the door.

'Sorry, I don't want to intrude but I finished my shift on call and I thought I'd come.'

'Of course, come in.'

'Yeah, come on in,' says Max and I notice his demeanour has changed. He's standing a little bit taller; he's smiling a little bit more. Oh no. This is just what Max was doing with the female doctor last night.

Max ushers her in and leads her to the kitchen.

'I'll shut the front door then,' I mutter, slamming it shut and following them down the hallway.

'Hey, you came,' says Rach, sounding surprised as we walk back into the kitchen.

'So, you're Rach's doctor friend. Have you come to check me out too?' he says with a wink.

'Oh,' says Gaby, throwing me a quizzical look, 'it sounds to me like your doctor yesterday gave you all the right advice. Be gentle, don't force things, and hopefully with the help of the psychotherapist your memories will come back soon. And in the meantime, I'm here to support you all.'

'That's a very nice, friendly thing to do. Rach is lucky with all her friends; she has so many pretty friends now.'

'Yes, including the one that's your wife,' I say, putting my hand up.

'Oh yeah,' he says with a hint of a laugh, almost like I've told a joke. It's as if he can't take us being together seriously at all. 'It's hard for me to go from being single to suddenly being "taken",' he says, turning back to Gaby and doing air quotes.

Gaby's eyes widen slightly and she looks at me. I shrug back. I'm trying to keep telling myself that this is not my husband, that he doesn't know any better.

'That's OK, Max,' she says, giving him a pat on the arm that's almost like a slap. She walks over and puts her hand on Rach's shoulder. 'I'm taken too.'

Rach rubs Gaby's hand.

'Max, this is my girlfriend, Gaby.'

'Yeah, she said she was your friend,' says Max, and it dawns on me that Max doesn't know that Rach is a lesbian.

'No, I mean, she's my partner.'

'Your partner,' he says slowly as if it's sinking in. 'You're...'

'Uh-huh,' says Rach and Gaby sits down next to her and they hold hands.

'Oh right, wow. OK, that's a lot to take in. So, Robbie was...?'

'Yeah, I guess I knew that something wasn't quite right,' says Rach, shuddering at the mention of her ex-boyfriend.

'Right, OK,' says Max. 'Let's get this straight then. I'm married to Ellie, Rach is a lesbian and is dating Gaby here, and I have a daughter who is almost two.'

'Plus, you have another child on the way,' chips in Rach.

'Right,' he says, screwing up his eyes like it's too much to take in. 'At least nothing's changed with you, huh, Mum?'

He laughs and Judy's face turns pale. She goes to open her mouth but the sound of a key turning in the front door lock stops her. We all look around the kitchen, looking to see who's not here, before Judy shrieks with alarm.

'That'll be Dad,' says Max.

The door slams shut and footsteps come down the hallway, and then, sure enough, Mick walks through the door with his dark tanned skin.

'What the actual—' says Rachel.

'I got here as soon as I could. I was so worried after your phone call yesterday. What's going on?'

For a second no one says anything but then Max walks forward and wraps his arms around him.

'Dad, you came back early.'

'You asked me to come, so I did.'

Tears are welling up in Mick's eyes; I know that Max's refusal to speak to him over the last few years has hit him hard. I glance at Judy; her eyes are wild with panic. But then I look back at Max and see how happy he is to see his dad and I feel awful that any second now we're going to have to burst that bubble.

Chapter 6

Max wastes no time filling in the details of his memory loss with his dad. At any moment I'm expecting Judy to wade in and tell him the truth about their marital status, but she doesn't. She's standing there, her shaking hands, fiddling with the collar of her blouse.

Judy starts walking across to Max; I think that she's realised that now is the time to come clean, but it's not Max she's making a beeline for, it's Mick.

My whole body tenses. The last time they were in the same room was at our wedding, and they almost came to blows. After that, things still hadn't improved, particularly since they'd started discussing selling the house, but now a smile spreads across her face leaving me even more stunned.

'Darling, you're home,' she says in an overly theatrical shrill. My mouth drops a little as I watch her slip her arms around him. I see that Rach's does, too. 'I'm so pleased you could cut your trip short.'

Mick flinches as she wraps him up in a big hug. Max, unaware of the awkward tension, sits down at the table and Judy seizes the opportunity to whisper something in Mick's ear. Mick's brow wrinkles and he nods before Judy pulls out of the hug and takes hold of his hand. It reminds me of the type of handhold I do with Sasha when I'm trying to drag her along the pavement in a direction she doesn't want to go.

'We're just trying to bring Max up to speed with what's been happening, seeing as though he has lost his memory of the last *five* years,' Judy says, leading Mick over to the table. 'Although we're trying our best not to overwhelm him. So much has happened in the world in that time. Can you even remember what *we* were doing five years ago?' she says, tinkling with laughter and squeezing his hand tighter. 'He's just found out about Rach and Gaby.'

'All right, Rach?' he asks, giving her a tentative smile.

Rach nods back. 'Yeah, thanks, Dad.' Her voice is strained. They still at least talk to one another, but they're nowhere near as close as they used to be.

Rach and Gaby went and stayed at his new house for a night when they were in Portugal last year – she didn't really want to go into details but reading between the lines I don't think she gelled with her potential new step-mum Ruby.

'Nice to see you, Gaby,' says Mick.

'You too,' she says.

'Isn't this a nice belated birthday present?' says Max, smiling at his mum, ignoring all the subtext of the glances and hostile body language around the table. 'Having Dad back early.'

'Oh, absolutely. Happy birthday to me,' she says, smiling through the sarcasm.

'Oh yes. Happy birthday,' says Mick, looking a bit flustered before he leans forward and gives his ex-wife an awkward peck on the cheek. 'Sixty-five?'

'Ha ha ha. Always the joker,' she says through gritted teeth. 'Sixty-two.'

Sasha drops her bowl off the high chair and Mick spins round and looks at her in wonderment. I've sent him photos of Sasha, and we skype so that he can see her, but this is the first time he's ever met her in person.

'Sasha,' he says warmly.

Thank God she can't talk properly. I'm grateful that he doesn't try and reach out to take her. She's not good with strangers. But she looks up and smiles at him at least.

'You must be tired after your trip,' says Judy, swooping in. 'Do you want to rest a little upstairs?'

'Um,' he says, faltering. 'I'll just have a coffee instead.'

'I'll make one,' I say, jumping at the chance to leave the awkwardness at the table.

'And I'll help,' says Gaby, clearly thinking the same.

Mick starts quizzing Max and Judy about what was said in the hospital while Gaby picks up the kettle and the two of us go over to the sink at the end of the kitchen.

'Surely we should tell Max about his mum and dad splitting up?' Gaby says to me, with a frown.

'Of course we should, but it's not our place,' I say. 'This has got to be their decision. The doctor last night said not to shock him.'

'I don't think this is what he meant,' she says, sighing. 'As a doctor, I'd advise you all to tell him.'

'And as the girlfriend of his sister what do you advise?'

'Not to get on the wrong side of the mother-in-law,' she says with another sigh. 'I guess that's why you can't treat family members.'

We both look over at the table where Judy and Mick are sitting, holding hands.

Gaby turns off the tap and goes to plugs the kettle back in, whilst I start spooning ground coffee into the cafétière.

'How's Graham, Dad?' asks Max. I spray coffee all over the counter and spin around.

'Oh, I'm sure he's good, wouldn't you say, Judy?' says Mick, raising an eyebrow. I hadn't even considered how Graham would fit in to all this. If Judy and Mick are pretending to be together, Judy can't exactly have him as her boyfriend.

'Of course, but obviously you'd know better having spent the last couple of weeks playing golf with him,' she says, with a smile that contradicts the forceful look in her eyes.

'Two weeks playing golf?' says Max, slapping a confused-looking Mick on the back. 'Retirement's suiting you well, then? And there was us worrying that you weren't going to know what to do with yourself when you stopped working.'

'Oh, Mick's had no trouble filling his time since he stopped work. Golf, Pilates,' says Judy, pleased with her subtle dig.

Mick laughs back and he gives Judy a squeeze that induces more fake laughter.

It's the first time in years that I've seen the two of them act civilly with each other; I didn't realise they were still capable of doing so – even if they are putting it on for Max's benefit.

To think I'd considered Judy a terrible actress for all these years. We were once reluctantly dragged to watch her in an amateur dramatics play, but if she acted this well, I'm sure the show would have been a sell-out.

Sasha starts to get bored in the high chair, so I wipe her mouth with some kitchen roll and pick her up.

She pulls towards Max, muttering her favourite 'Da-da-da' noises.

'Is she saying "Dad"?' he says, still looking at her with a degree of caution.

'Her version of it; it was her first word. Do you want to hold her?' I say, hoping he will, because right now she's so wriggly it's uncomfortable holding her.

He pushes his chair back and takes a deep breath.

'OK, OK,' he says, wincing. 'How do I do this?'

'Just take her and she'll do the rest,' I say, handing her over.

She soon settles herself on his lap and starts tugging at his ears, causing him to laugh and my heart to swell. I turn back to finish making the coffee but Gaby's already done it. She places the cafétière on the table and I start putting out the mugs so that everyone can help themselves.

'What's your golf handicap after your holiday?' asks Max.

Mick freezes in panic and I interrupt.

'You know, I'm a bit hungry,' I say.

'Do you want me to make you another omelette?' asks Max, looking up.

'No, it's not that kind of hunger. It's a pregnancy craving. What I really fancy is pickles. Do you think you could run out to the little Sainsbury's and pick me up some?'

I do my best sweet smile.

'Pregnancy cravings? Do you have them a lot?'

'Uh-huh,' I say, lying. Aside from my diet of ginger nuts in the first three months, the only cravings I've been having are for the things I'm not allowed to have, like gin.

'OK, then,' says Max.

'Hang on, I've got some cornichons,' says Judy, jumping

up, ignoring the daggers I'm shooting her way. 'I think I got some in for Christmas.'

'Mum, it's August,' says Rach.

'I know that,' she says, getting up and digging through one of her cupboards. 'But you have to get these things whilst you see them or else you'll forget and they'll sell out nearer the time.'

'I'm pretty sure they sell them all year round,' says Rach, shaking her head.

'Aha! Here they are,' she says, sliding the jar along to me, followed by a fork and a plate.

I stare at it in horror. I hadn't really thought this through at all. My stomach lurches at the thought. Cornichons are probably the last thing I want to be eating at nine o'clock in the morning.

'Stroke of luck,' says Mick, 'now Max can stay right here.'

'Yes, how lucky.' I twist the lid off and try not to gag at the smell of vinegar. I stab one wrinkly little pickle with my fork; it looks so unappetising but I pop it in my mouth anyway. I'm chewing, chewing as quickly as I can, and I wash it down with some orange juice.

'Did that hit the spot?' asks Judy.

'Almost, but now that you've mentioned Christmas, I fancy a cherry bakewell. Max, do you think that you could get me some?'

'Yes, nothing screams Christmas like a cherry bakewell,' says Rach.

'What, they're almondy; that's festive!' I say, throwing her a look and hoping she gets what I'm trying to do.

'I might have some of those too,' says Judy, about to get up.

'No, Judy. I don't think you do,' I say. 'I ate them on Wednesday afternoon when I came over.'

'You were only here for a couple of hours,' she says in shock. 'I had two packets.'

Judy had asked me to wait in for a parcel she was expecting, as she and Graham were off to their gardening club's AGM and she knew I had Wednesdays off work. I'd been delighted to escape my tasteless house and hang out in a neutrally painted space for a few hours.

'Sasha and I were hungry.'

'You and a toddler ate twelve of them?' she says, disbelieving.

'Uh-huh and now I really want some more. Max, can you run up to Sainsbury's. It's still on the main road,' I say, getting up and passing his wallet that is on the side. 'I'd go myself, but I'm feeling a bit sluggish.'

'Probably the twelve cakes you ate last week,' says Judy, causing Rach and Gaby to giggle at my scolding.

'I guess I can go,' say Max standing up, looking unsure. 'Do you need anything else, Mum?'

'No, I don't think so,' says Judy. 'Unless Ellie's raided anything else.'

'No, that's all.'

'I'll come with you,' says Mick. 'Might do me good to stretch my legs.'

'No,' I say quickly. 'I think Gaby should go.'

Both she and Rach look at me in confusion, before Gaby nods.

'Come on, Max,' she says firmly as she stands up, and Max has no choice but to follow her out of the kitchen. He hands Sasha over to me as he goes.

'You know, you've got to watch your sugar intake,' Judy says to me. 'I'm surprised Gaby didn't tell you off.'

'I haven't eaten all the bakewells; they're still in the cupboard. I just needed to get him out of the house.'

'Why?'

'To discuss what we should do for his birthday... Why the bloody hell do you think?' I say, letting Sasha wriggle off my lap. She heads straight for the corner where Judy has a box of toys she's picked up from charity shops.

'Too right,' says Rach. 'Someone's got to talk some sense into the two of you. I mean, what are you playing at, pretending you're together?'

'It wasn't my idea,' says Mick. 'Your mother just bamboozled me into it.'

'I didn't bamboozle you into it. Ellie and I decided last night that it would upset Max to tell him about the break-up.'

'Whoa, hang on, that was before Mick turned up,' I protest. 'You can't just pretend you're still a couple.'

'Why not?' says Judy.

'Because Max thinks that Mick lives here and, if you don't tell him, Mick is going to have to live with you until Max gets his memory back,' I say.

'Well, we can pretend when you come over, can't we?' says Mick. 'I can stay in the spare room the rest of the time.'

'That's if Max wants to come home to our house,' I say. 'He hasn't been that keen to leave here and I don't think you can keep up the charade with us all living under one roof. And what if he doesn't get his memory back for months? You can't stay here indefinitely.'

Judy flinches.

'I'm sure it won't be that long,' says Mick. 'We'll cope. Won't we, Judy?'

I rub at my temples.

'What about Ruby?' Rach asks. 'Surely she won't be that understanding about you staying with your ex-wife.'

'I'll just have to tell her that I'm staying with Max and Ellie,' he says.

'Pah,' says Judy. 'What a surprise. You're lying to her too.'

'See, you're bickering already,' says Rach. 'This is going to get out of hand. The sooner you tell Max, the easier it'll be.'

'But then he won't speak to me all over again,' says Mick. 'Did you see how he hugged me?'

'And it crushed him the first time, really crushed him,' says Judy. 'Rach, surely you remember. He went all out of control with his drinking and I can't watch him go through that again. Not with Ellie pregnant, and having Sasha to look after; we want Max to be stable. Look, the doctor says that his memory is going to come back any day now. And we don't want to give him any nasty shocks; we don't want to make his memory loss any worse.'

'Yes, but—' I start.

'It's in his best interests,' says Mick.

For once they're presenting a united front.

'You know that when Max finds out – and let's face it, he's going to – he's going to be even more hurt that you lied to him,' I say.

'No one wants to hurt him,' says Mick, sighing. 'I've hurt him enough for a lifetime.'

'We haven't got any other choice,' says Judy.

The front door goes again, Gaby and Max come walking back in, clutching boxes of cakes. Judy and Mick give Rach and me pleading looks.

'Here you go,' says Max, sliding the packet across to me.

'Coffee?' says Judy, touching the cafétière to make sure it's still warm. 'And then we can all have one of those cakes.'

Sasha hears the sound of food packaging and cruises round the back of chairs to get to me – she truly is my daughter. I break her off a bit of pastry and hand them out to everyone, before digging into one myself. They're so good that had I found them on Friday I probably would have eaten all twelve.

'So,' says Gaby, 'are you any closer to working out what Max was doing in Chiswick in the first place?'

We all look at Max and his blank face.

'What, you haven't worked that out?' says Mick.

'Of course not, or he'd probably have his memory back already,' says Judy.

'What have you got so far?' says Gaby, cutting through the tension.

'Um, well, we haven't exactly. We've been so busy catching Max up,' I say.

Mick sighs and rolls up his sleeves, revealing a deep dark tan that couldn't possibly be the result of a two-week holiday. He stands up and walks over to the blackboard that Judy writes her shopping list on and wipes off her list, before taking it off the wall and propping it up on the work surface so that we can all see it.

'Oi!' says Judy.

'I'll remind you that you need washing powder,' he says. 'Let's write down what you know so far.'

Judy folds her arms.

'Five minutes through the door and already taking charge of the situation,' she says.

'Well, darling,' he says, giving her a big smile, 'it's what I always do, isn't it?'

Judy looks like a pressure cooker about to explode, and, for a minute, I think the truth is all going to come tumbling out.

'Hmm, what would we do without you?' she mutters, digging deep in her acting skills and smiling back.

Mick starts writing and I squint to see that he's written the word 'Chisick'.

'There's a silent "w" in it, after the "s",' says Judy.

'Thank you, darling,' says Mick, correcting it with such force that I'm worried the chalk's going to snap.

'Ooh, this is just like *Line of Duty*,' I say, my eyes lighting up.

'What's *Line of Duty*?' says Max.

The hours that we've spent at this very kitchen table discussing plot twists and joking in acronyms as a piss-take of the show's verbal diarrhoea of OCGs, UCOs and AFOs.

'It's a TV programme, and it's brilliant,' says Rach, and Max gives an apologetic shrug.

'Max found himself wandering in *Chiswick* with a "w",' Mick carries on. 'And then he travelled to *Brixton*. I take it that I've spelt that right?'

'Yes, dear,' says Judy.

'Then he phoned me before travelling to *Fleet*. He's lost five years of his life.'

He underlines the year three times and then turns to look at us.

'What else have we got?' he says, raising an eyebrow in hope.

Judy, Rach and I exchange glances.

'We haven't got anything else,' I say.

'Nothing else? What about his phone? Have you been through the records, text messages, WhatsApp, Facebook?'

Max shakes his head.

'I've had a quick look and couldn't see anything,' he says. 'There's only really messages from Ellie, which don't make a whole lot of sense. Stuff about caterpillars.'

He picks his phone up from the table and I'm worried he's going to read them out loud, and I put my hand over to cover his screen. Since the night of the Hungry Caterpillar costume it's become our codeword if either of us is feeling a bit horny.

'We don't need to go into those,' I say dismissively. 'What about a work calendar? Or work emails? That's where you were headed yesterday morning when this all happened.'

'I like your thinking, Ellie,' says Mick, pointing at me with the chalk.

Judy purses her lips.

'I've been trying to find my work emails,' Max says.

'Here, I can do it,' I say, reaching out for his phone.

He pulls it closer to him.

'Or Rach could look; she's good with tech,' I say, hurt that he doesn't trust me enough to be let loose on it.

Max unlocks the phone with his thumbprint – still in awe of the technology – before he hands it to her.

Mick is poised with the chalk waiting for any new information.

'Nope,' says Rach, wrinkling her nose up. 'Nothing on here about a meeting or anything about heading into work on Saturday.'

'There has to be,' I say. 'Max told me that he'd found out late Friday night that he had to sort something out in the office.'

'I can't see it in the inbox,' says Rachel. 'What about your personal email?'

'I don't usually mix the two,' says Max, 'although who knows about future me. Maybe he does.'

I shake my head. 'You barely use your personal email; usually you chat to everyone via WhatsApp.'

'Does your office use Slack or anything?' asks Rachel, swiping around the phone.

'I don't know,' he says, shrugging. 'We didn't, but I guess things can change.'

'You don't have any apps on your phone,' she says, shaking her head.

'What about Owen? Did you call him?' I say, realising that he hasn't returned my call.

Rach taps around.

'Looks like you haven't spoken to him for a few weeks.'

'That's weird,' I say. 'You always speak to Owen.'

'Did he call you back last night, Ellie?' asks Judy.

'No, but it went straight to voicemail so maybe his battery was flat and he hasn't charged it yet.'

'Have you tried ringing Sarah?' asks Max.

'Oh,' I say, closing my eyes again at yet another thing he doesn't know. 'Sarah and Owen split up last year.'

'What? As in they're taking a break?'

'No, they're getting a divorce. It was all pretty amicable,' I add quickly.

'What? No, not Owen and Sarah, they're like... they're like,' says Max, clearly struggling, 'one of those couples that are inseparable.'

'He told us they'd married too young, that they decided they wanted different things,' I say, feeling awful that I'm the one to tell him.

'Wow,' says Max, shaking his head.

Mick writes *Owen* on the board. 'OK, so we will need to follow up with him just to double-check that he doesn't know anything.'

'Is he still in Dalston?' Max asks.

'He lives in Surbiton now.'

'Surbiton? Bloody hell. Why have we all moved out to the sticks?'

'Um, it's hardly the sticks. It's Zone 6,' I say, laughing.

Sasha starts to get a bit restless and Gaby goes down onto the floor to play with her. I shoot her a grateful smile.

'What if I was meeting Rodge or Jez?' he asks.

'You don't really see them that often these days.'

'I don't?'

'No, we only tend to meet up with them if it's someone's birthday.'

'Right,' he says. 'So, who do I hang out with now?'

'You still do your five-a-side footie thing when you're not too busy at work. We were really good friends with a couple we knew from my work, Howard and Keely, but they moved to Edinburgh a few months ago. To be honest, you mainly just spend your time with me and Sasha.'

He gives me a long lingering look as if it's dawning on him how much of his life has changed and how much I'm a pivotal part of it.

'It's just so hard to get my head around,' he says, for the first time addressing the elephant in the room.

'I know, for me too,' I say, and he smiles at me. There's a flash of solidarity between us that gives me a little bit of hope that my Max is still in there somewhere.

'Shit,' he says, exhaling loudly. 'OK, so if I wasn't meeting any of my non-existent friends, and I was supposed to be doing work, then maybe I was meeting a client?'

'On a Saturday?' I say.

'Yeah, that does seem odd,' he says.

I stare hard at the board, trying to see a connection. I'm usually good at spotting patterns for work, but there's not enough to go on.

'So,' says Mick.

'Looks like we're no further forward,' I say, thinking what a mess everything is.

'Don't look so disheartened,' says Gaby. 'Your type of amnesia doesn't last long, and I bet you'll go home and something will trigger your memory and suddenly it'll all come flooding back.'

'Back home?' says Max, looking at his parents. 'I thought I'd just stay here.'

'You can't do that,' says Judy, jumping up. I'm guessing she and Mick will need respite from their acting. 'I mean, Gaby is right, being with your family, it will jog your memory quicker, I'm sure. Plus, you and Ellie need to be on your own to work things out, spend time together.'

'But what about... sleeping arrangements,' says Max, looking flustered.

'We've got a spare room,' I say. 'It's filled with boxes, but underneath them somewhere is a mattress.'

He looks relieved and it stabs at my heart. I'm dreading us being alone without his family to hide behind. With other people around I'm just about holding it together, but Max treating me like a stranger in our own home is going to be a whole other level of heartbreak.

Chapter 7

The rest of the morning and the afternoon pass in a bit of a blur. As my brain finally started to process everything, I took a step back and let Max's family rally around him, filling him in with heavily edited versions of the last five years.

They showed him photos of our wedding and of when Sasha was born. They pulled up news clips online of Donald Trump that Max thought were parodies. They explained to him in basic terms what Brexit was and the shambles it had become. They told him of the war on plastics and how we've moved to reusable items where possible. It was hard to tell what he was thinking; he sat there nodding, taking it all in, but not saying much.

You don't see the world changing when you're living it every day; it's only when we stop and reflect that you realise how much can change in five years.

'Here we are,' says Judy, pulling up on the street outside our house, in the early evening. Neither Max nor I are relishing the idea of playing happy families, but we know Gaby is only echoing what the doctor had said last night about living our normal life.

Max, Sasha and I are wedged into the backseat of the car

and I struggle to bend down to retrieve my handbag and the keys.

'Home sweet home,' I mutter, unclicking my seatbelt and opening the door.

Max looks at the house with trepidation. I don't know whether it's the thought of seeing where he now lives or being alone with me.

He's going to hate the house. His old flat in Brixton, where he remembers living, was in a converted school house that had huge floor-to-ceiling arched windows, dark wood parquet floor, minimalist furniture and tech everywhere. It was jaw-dropping – whereas, while this house might look normal from the outside, inside it's jaw-dropping for all the wrong reasons.

'Are you sure that we can't just stay at yours?' says Max.

'No,' says Judy, with a stern voice. 'You've got to go about your normal routine.'

'But I'm not going to be, am I? Simon won't let me go into bloody work.'

Max hasn't taken the prospect well of being signed off work for a month. He thinks that because he still works at the same company – doing more or less does the same job that he was doing five years ago – that he'll be able to pick up his new projects.

'You know you're not legally allowed to once a doctor has signed you off,' says Judy.

'Are you sure there was no wriggle room?' he says, raising a pleading eyebrow at me.

I was the one that had to phone his boss this morning to fill him in on the situation and, whilst the main reason he isn't allowed back is the sick note, it's also because they deal with multi-million-pound projects and no client would want him anywhere near them when he can't even remember his own wife and child.

'No, but Simon did say that he'd email over some old project briefs and evaluations so that you can see what you've been doing over the last few years.'

Max sighs like a sulky teenager.

'Look, Max,' says Judy. 'You need to spend time with Ellie and Sasha *alone*. Hopefully that way your memory will come back and, the sooner it does, the sooner you can go back to work.

'Plus, now that Ellie's on maternity leave you'll get to spend lots of time together.'

'She gets to babysit me and Sasha; aren't I the lucky one?'

I grit my teeth. This wasn't how I envisaged the last eight weeks of pregnancy. I'd been looking forward to my home-working, but when I phoned up my boss and explained the situation, she suggested that I start my maternity leave early. I've just got to tie up my loose ends and reallocate the reports I had to write. It means that I'll now have a month less with the baby at the end of my leave, but I just can't imagine working at the moment with all this going on.

'So, are we going to go and see this house?' asks Max.

We all get out of the car and I pull Sasha out of her car seat. Judy reaches out and takes her and I unlock our door.

'So, um, this is it,' I say, watching Max's mouth fall open at the sight of the mural.

'Whoa,' says Mick, wrinkling up his face. I'd forgotten that he hasn't seen the house either. 'Surely you remember that, Max? No one could see that and forget it.'

He runs his hand over the textured paint and shudders.

'Did we put this in?' says Max, squinting at it.

'Ah-ha, I did it myself,' I deadpan before I remember he doesn't know my sense of humour. 'No, it was here when we bought it. We've not had the time since we moved in to get rid of it.'

Mick keeps pulling faces; he's clearly as horrified by the property as his son.

'It doesn't look like it would take you long to change it,' says Mick, giving away that he's not seen it before. Judy elbows him in the ribs, but Max hasn't really heard what he's said. He's still looking on with horror.

'Uh-huh, it's all cosmetic. Max, you'd planned to do most of the work, as we stretched our budget to buy it. You've just been so busy at the office lately; you haven't had a chance.'

'Well, I'm not going to be busy over the next month, am I?'

'Your dad could give you a hand,' volunteers Judy, and Mick gives her a hard stare. 'It would be nice to get you out of the house and out of my way,' she says with the fake laughter that's fast replacing her normal laugh.

'OK, I guess it would be nice to spend proper time with you,' says Mick.

'Steady on, Dad, you sound like you're going soppy in your old age.'

'I just mean that you've been so busy working, I haven't spent a lot of time with you lately.'

'Let's hope I haven't forgotten how to use a paintbrush.'

Max steps into the lounge straight ahead and quickly retreats.

'It's bright orange and pink? Who the hell lived here before? Laurence Llewelyn-Bowen?'

I laugh and snort, and Max looks at me in alarm. Usually he takes the piss out of me whenever I accidentally snort, and then I pretend to get offended by it, and then he'll wrap me in his arms and tell me he finds it endearing. It's all these nuances that make up our relationship and their absence is going to take a lot of getting used to.

'So, I think we should be going,' says Judy, looking over at Mick.

'Er, right,' he says, reluctantly.

'Do you have to?' says Max, 'You could stay for dinner. We could get a takeaway or—?'

Judy pats him on the arm.

'I think you need some time as a family,' she says. 'But we're only round the corner. You can come over anytime. That goes for Sasha too. We're more than happy to help out and have her whenever we can, during this... uncertain time.'

'Absolutely,' says Mick, leaning into Sasha to pinch her cheek, only she turns and buries her head in Judy's chest.

Judy holds her out to me and she nestles into me straightaway.

'I'll give you a ring in the morning, love,' says Judy. 'And don't forget, Gaby said you can always call her too, if you need a doctor's point of view.'

Max nods slowly and Judy and Mick hug us all before heading out the door.

We wave at them as they drive off and we step back into the house and close the door.

Max looks at me and my heart starts to beat faster. This feeling reminds me of the time when we were teenagers and I'd bump into him at Rach's house, when I'd get nervous at seeing him.

'So, um...'

'So,' I say, unsure what we're supposed to do or say now. I've been so reliant on his family to talk him through our life; now that it's suddenly just us, it hits me how much of a stranger I've become to my husband. 'Sasha probably needs to go to bed. I guess I'll bath her and put her down and then we can talk.'

'Sure, OK,' he says, smiling uneasily. 'I'll, um, wait in the kitchen.'

I point him in the right direction and take Sasha upstairs.

'Come on then, poppet,' I say, thinking how nice it must be to be oblivious like her.

An hour later, I walk into the kitchen and find Max sitting at the table, his head in his hands. I don't want to disturb him at first, he looks like he's deep in thought. My mind is being completely blown by what's going on, I can only imagine what's going on in his and how confusing everything must be for him.

He senses me and lifts his head, giving me a little smile.

'Hey,' I say, walking over and leaning against the worktop.

'Hey. Is she asleep?'

'For now. Sometimes she wakes in the night, but it's been a busy day so hopefully not.'

'Right,' he says.

There's an awkwardness in the air as neither of us know what to say.

'Do you want a drink?' I ask.

'Desperately,' says Max, and it makes me laugh.

'Gin?' I say, reaching up to the cupboard and pulling out his favourite rhubarb and ginger gin.

'Can't stand the stuff,' he says. 'Have we got any Jack Daniels?'

I shudder as I've never been able to stand the smell of JD.

'Trust me, you drink this all the time,' I say, opening a can of ginger beer from the fridge and pouring it over his gin. I put the rest of the can of ginger beer in a glass for myself.

I sit down opposite him and slide his drink across.

'Mmm,' he says, taking a sip. 'That's actually pretty good. You really do know me better than I know myself.'

'Just temporarily,' I say. There's another pause.

'So, this is a bit of a head fuck, huh?' he says eventually.

'Such a head fuck.'

'You and me, this house. I mean, what's this place all about? I know that you said it was structurally sound and I'm glad that we've managed to be in the position of owning a house, but still...' He looks at the mismatched kitchen units. 'And it's in Fleet; I never imagined I'd end up living here again.'

'Me neither, but things changed when we had Sasha. I guess we saw things differently. And Fleet's got a lot going for it, and it's only fifty minutes from London.'

'It feels like a world away, though, doesn't it?' he says.

'It was voted one of the best places to live in the UK.'

He scrunches his face up. 'But I love living in Brixton. I love everything being on my doorstep. I just feel like I'm missing something.'

'You are. Five years' worth of somethings.'

Out of all the years he could have forgotten, he can't remember the most eventful years of his life: his parents splitting up; Rach coming out; him growing tired of serial dating; us meeting and marrying; having Sasha.

99

'Before we got married, we moved to a slightly bigger flat in Herne Hill. It was close to Brockwell Park and the whole area has a bit more of a family feel to it. But when Sasha came along...' I shrug. 'I don't know, we loved it less and less. We started to get tired of the neighbours that rolled in at two a.m. and threw parties when we'd just gone off to sleep, or when we wanted to get anywhere and it was such a nightmare taking a pram on public transport. We'd come down and visit the parents here and we'd walk around the pond, or stroll up to the high street with the pram, and it just seemed so much easier.

'I guess we just remembered how nice it was growing up in a relatively small town and we wanted Sasha to have a similar childhood to us.'

'But surely we could have found a house up there, or somewhere that was near the end of a tube line?'

'I guess we could have done, but we didn't really look. When we thought of suburbs we both thought of here.'

He blows through his teeth. 'I never thought I'd be one of those people that moved back.'

'Me neither,' I say with a shrug.

We sit there in silence whilst he seems to contemplate it.

'So, you, Spider, how did we...?'

'*Ellie*, you've got to call me *Ellie*. I haven't been Spider for a very long time.'

'Sorry, old habits. Of course, I guess that wasn't the nicest of nicknames.'

'Not really.'

'It's just whenever I see you, I think of you and Rach and how you used to be. You were round our house so much when we were kids that I almost felt like you were my sister. I don't understand how we went from that to this. I mean, we have a daughter who's sleeping upstairs, so I presume we... you know, and the fact that we've got another one on the way means...'

'We did it twice,' I say. If this wasn't so tragic it would be funny. 'You know, I'll let you in on a little secret: we do it quite a lot.'

His cheeks pink and then he coughs.

'But presumably when we met up again a few years ago I did still see you as my kid sister's friend at first?'

'Oh yeah. When we met we were very drunk and had a quick kiss and fumble before we passed out, then the next morning you told me quite clearly that you thought of me like a sister and that we should just be friends.'

Max is nodding as if he's thinking the exact same thing now.

'Only the second time we met up, let's just say you saw my boobs and pretty much gave up on thinking that I was like a sister to you.'

He looks shocked but there's a small smile creeping over his face.

'Well, maybe they're the key to this whole thing,' he says. 'Perhaps you should give me a quick flash now and it all might snap back into place.'

It's exactly the type of cheeky thing my Max would say and it's so hard to reconcile that this isn't him – or at least, not the him that I know.

He's raising an expectant eyebrow and has a little wicked grin on his face. He's seen me naked hundreds, if not thousands, of times before, but it feels different now.

'It's hard because you're still the same Max, yet you're completely different.'

'I'm guessing you feel like you've lost a husband.'

'I hope I haven't,' I say, a lump catching in my throat. 'Perhaps more temporarily mislaid him.'

He smiles at me with pity and my heart breaks a little more.

'I've just never been the long-term-relationship kind of guy. I've never really felt the need to settle down and move in with someone. I'm happy in my flat, hanging out with my mates and going out and...' He shakes his head. 'I'm sorry if this isn't what you wanted to hear. I'm just trying to be honest.'

I blink back a tear. It's not like I expected him to come home and for us to magically get back to how we were, but I guess I hadn't really considered that he wouldn't want to try to reconnect with me.

'Ellie,' he starts, but there's a soft knock on the front door.

'I'll get that.' I'm relieved to be able to leave.

Max reaches out and touches my arm, causing me to stop as my whole body tingles from his touch. I wonder if he feels it too.

There's another knock at the door and I pull myself away. I walk down the hallway wiping my glistening eyes with my sleeve.

I open the door and I'm so relieved to see Max's best friend Owen standing there that I throw myself into a hug.

'I'm so glad to see you,' I say.

'Sorry, we were in the New Forest for the weekend and the signal was crap. I only got your message about an hour ago, and when I called back you didn't answer, so I thought we'd stop off en route home as we passed on the motorway.'

The word *we* startles me; it's then that I notice the redheaded woman behind him.

'Oh,' I say, pulling away from him and trying to compose myself. 'Hi, I'm Ellie.'

'Claire,' she says, rocking on her heels like she's nervous.

'So, is it true? Your message, about Max... he's really lost his memory?'

'Yep, last five years,' I say, causing Owen to blink rapidly. 'Come on in, see for yourself.'

'I don't understand,' says Owen, and, as I usher them inside, I fill them in on the past twenty-four hours.

'Mate,' says Max, with a sigh of immense relief when we walk into the kitchen.

He walks up to him and gives him a hug and Owen's a bit taken a back.

'Thanks for coming.'

Owen doesn't say anything at first; he's too busy looking between me and Max.

'This is real?' he says. 'I can't get my head around it.'

'None of us can,' I say.

'I'm sorry,' says Max, walking up to Claire. 'I'm sure I probably know you, but seeing as I've lost the last five years, I can't remember meeting you.'

'Actually, we've never met,' she says with an awkward smile. 'I'm Claire.'

'Claire, nice to meet you,' he says. 'That's actually good. You're the first person I've met since this has all happened who I'm not supposed to know. Are you two an item or...?'

'Yeah,' says Owen, not elaborating.

I didn't realise he was seeing anyone, certainly not anyone

he'd go on weekends away with. I wonder why Max hasn't mentioned it.

'I'm having trouble with all of this. If you don't remember the last five years, does that mean you don't remember getting together with Ellie?'

'Nope.'

'Wow, you don't remember your own wife?' says Claire, tucking her hair behind her ears.

I feel a bit sorry for her being thrust into this situation when it's the first time she's meeting us.

'I know, it's been quite the weekend. Hey, why don't we all go and grab a pint? Where's our local, would it be The Station? We can get to know Claire properly. It'll make a change to learn all about you rather than my missing years.'

'We can't go out, Max. Sasha's in bed upstairs,' I say.

'Oh right, yeah,' he says. 'I keep forgetting you have a daughter.'

'*We* have a daughter,' I say, frustrated that the new reality isn't sinking in. 'But look, why don't you go for a drink?'

'We're not just going to leave you on your own, Ellie,' says Owen. 'Why don't I put the kettle on?'

'The kettle?' says Max.

'I'm driving, mate,' says Owen.

It's odd because there's an edge to his voice that's not usually there.

'OK, well, Claire – you'll have a beer with me, or one of these gins that I'm drinking, won't you? I have to drink with someone and Ellie can't because of the baby.'

Claire looks a little torn and glances at Owen, who gives her a shrug, before she smiles back at Max.

'Sure, I'll have a beer, thanks.'

He goes into the fridge, takes one out and pops the lid and hands it to her.

'Right, shall we sit down in the lounge and get to know each other properly? I warn you that you might want to put your sunglasses on to sit in there,' he says, pointing at the ones on top of her head. 'Come on.'

Claire looks nervously over her shoulder at Owen.

'Go, we'll be there in just a second.' He gives her a quick kiss on the top of her head and she smiles back at him. The show of intimacy makes my heart pang as Max would usually do something similar when he left a room.

Owen shuts the door gently behind them as they leave.

'What the hell is going on, Ellie? He's acting like there's nothing wrong?'

'I know, it's a symptom of this type of memory loss.'

'And it's genuine? He's not putting it on?'

'Why would he?'

'I don't know,' he says, letting out a deep breath.

'He's definitely not putting it on. His dad flew in today and they're acting like they're the best of friends.'

'Shit,' he says. 'How did he take hearing about the divorce?'

'They haven't told him. They're pretending they're still together.'

Owen's eyes nearly pop out of his head.

'They're *what*?'

'It's all so fucked up, Owen.'

'And nothing came up in the tests?'

'Nope, they were all clear,' I say, almost wishing something had come up because at least it would explain things. I know this is a better outcome, that there isn't anything physically wrong with Max, but it's awful to think that he's hidden his own memories from himself.

'Shit, Ellie.'

'I know, and he doesn't remember Sasha, and we've only got nine weeks until this one comes along,' I say, patting my bump.

Tears that I've fought very hard not to fall start cascading down my cheeks.

'Ssh,' says Owen, putting an arm around me. 'It's going to be OK. You said it was only going to be temporary, I'm sure he'll get his memory back soon.'

'Yeah, we're hoping we can work out what he was doing on Saturday and find out what happened. Do you have any idea why he might have been in Chiswick?'

He hesitates and I almost get the impression that he's going to say yes, but then he shakes his head. 'No,' he says, 'I haven't spoken to him in a while.'

'That's not like you guys. I know he's missed a few of your five-a-side games because of work, but don't you meet up sometimes for lunch?'

'Yeah, but I've been busy lately. We've been doing the whole telephone tag thing. And plus, I've been seeing a lot of Claire. Speaking of whom, we should probably go and rescue her,' he says, edging closer to the door.

'Yes, yes of course,' I say. 'I'll make your tea and bring it in. Milk no sugar, right?'

'Yep, thanks, Ellie.' He's started walking away when he turns back. 'He's going to be fine, it'll all work out.'

'Of course,' I say, putting a brave smile on my face, which slips off the minute he walks out of the kitchen.

I flick the kettle on, and I hear my phone beeping in my bag. I root around and pull it out to see a message on our Yummy Mummies group chat.

Anneka:
Don't forget, Polly and Ellie: 7 p.m. sharp! Don't forget, Helen: 6.30 p.m. sharp!

Helen:
Nice try. See you at 7.30 x

With everything that had happened over the weekend, I'd forgotten all about tomorrow night's girls' night. I start writing out a message to tell them I won't be able to make it after all when I see it says Anneka's typing.

Anneka:
FYI Only valid excuse for not turning up is actual labour.

I laugh out loud, my fingers hovering over the keys. I can't leave Max alone with Sasha. What if he forgets about Sasha again and goes to the pub? Perhaps I could ask Judy or Mick to pop over and keep him company. Going out for a couple of hours will probably do me some good. Sasha will be in bed, and I'm only going to be ten minutes down the road, so I can always come back if there's an emergency.

Ellie:
See you tomorrow x x

Whilst the kettle boils, I start taking deep breaths and repeating Owen's words in my head: *It'll all work out.* It has to, we've got no other option. I brush the tears away and splash cold water on my face, before I make Owen his tea and take it down to the lounge.

Chapter 8

Our getting-to-know-each-other time so far hasn't gone the way Judy had hoped. We've been home for twenty-four hours, and yet we've barely spent a moment alone together. Owen and Claire left late last night and we were so exhausted that we went straight to bed – in our separate rooms. Then this morning, Mick turned up at 9 a.m. dressed in overalls – and carrying enough supplies to paint the whole street. Whilst Max and Mick made a start on the lounge, I spent the day reassigning projects and tying up as many loose ends as possible during my first and last day of homeworking. And now, I'm heading out for the evening at Anneka's.

'Are you sure you're going to be OK?' I say to Max and Mick, now sitting on the plastic-covered sofa having a beer, reflecting on their hard day's graft. 'I don't have to go tonight.'

'Go,' says Max. 'Dad's here to help me. I'm sure that he babysits Sasha all the time.'

Mick grimaces slightly before giving me a wink.

I'm not entirely reassured by the fact that Mick is helping Max when he also has zero experience of looking after Sasha, but I need to escape.

'We'll be fine. We've got your number and she's fast asleep,' says Mick.

'OK, I won't be late,' I say, practically running out the door before I lose my nerve.

I drive away and I barely get along the next road before my phone rings and my heart sinks as I assume it's Max and Mick. I pull over and I almost sob with relief, happy to see it's a Skype call from my mum.

Why is it that whenever there's something wrong it's always your mum that you want to talk to?

'Hi, Mum,' I say as I answer, but there's a delay and I can just about see a grainy image of her.

'Hello, darling, how are things with you?' Or at least that's what I think she says as the sound is a bit muffled.

'Something's happened to Max and he doesn't remember us at all,' I say.

'Oh, darling,' she says; the screen pixelates, but when it clears, she has a big smile on her face. 'You're having a December ball. Lovely.'

I look at her in disbelief.

'No, Mum,' I say. 'He can't remember.'

'Oh… November,' she says, nodding before saying something else that I can't catch.

I scrunch up my eyes. The pixelating screen and the misheard conversation reminds me that she's half a world away. As much as I want to tell her to make myself feel better, all she's going to do in any likelihood is worry and it'll ruin her holiday.

The picture disappears and when it returns my dad is sitting next to Mum.

'Hi love, how's Sasha and the dump?' I presume I misheard and that should have been bump.

'They're both fine. This is a really bad line,' I say as the picture cuts out and comes back frozen. 'Can we try again soon?'

'Yes, of course. We'll... you... Antigua...' she says before the picture cuts out.

I fill in my own dots; she's either been or is going to Antigua and she'll try me again soon. I usually follow her cruises on an app to make myself jealous of the exotic places she's visiting, but I haven't looked over the last few days.

I sigh and hang up, and carry on to Anneka's.

When I arrive, I'm not surprised to find that she lives in a massive house. It's in one of the nearby villages and has sweeping views over the countryside. It's the kind of house that I'd lust over on *Escape to the Country*. A barn conversion with centuries-old big wooden beams mixed with fresh brickwork and lots of glass. I can only imagine how good the inside is going to be. Anneka's husband is a solicitor specialising in divorce, and judging from the size of the house business must be booming.

I knock the chunky door handle, envying that too.

'Ah, Ellie, look at you, bang on time. I like that,' says Anneka, opening the door.

I don't tell her that I was too scared to be otherwise. A beat-up-looking car pulls up on the drive and I notice Polly behind the wheel, mouthing something along the lines of *holy shit*.

I give her a quick wave and she waves back before waddling over to join us.

'This place is amazing, Anneka,' she says, as she draws close. 'Remind me never to invite you to our house.'

'I know. I thought our little house was going to be something special when we finished painting it, but this,' I say, as we walk into the entrance hall, 'this is incredible. Did you have it built?'

'The house, no,' she says, shaking her head. 'We bought it last year when we thought we'd start a family. The place we had before only had four bedrooms.'

'Only four,' I say with a laugh, and Polly raises her eyebrows.

'George has children from a previous marriage and we didn't want them to feel left out with the new baby. Plus, we thought it would be handy to have a guest annexe for when we need staff. I've already registered at an agency to find us a Chinese au pair. So important for them to start learning languages early and Cantonese is going to be the language of the future.'

'Oh, absolutely,' I say, trying to nod along as if I'd considered something similar.

I hand Anneka the bottles of non-alcoholic fizz that I brought with me and she takes them and walks us down a light and airy hallway.

I walk along open-mouthed, glancing into the different reception rooms along the way.

She leads us into the kitchen of dreams, which has a large open-plan living area attached to it, housing a big dining table and multiple sofas, complete with bi-fold doors spanning the whole back of the house that lead on to a large garden that overlooks fields.

'So, what are we all drinking? Do we want some of this fizz that Ellie's brought?'

'Fizz is good with me,' says Polly.

I nod and try to perch on one of the breakfast-bar stools, keeping one foot on the floor so that I don't topple over.

'Oh, don't sit there, they're buggers to sit on. Go and sit on the sofas.' Anneka points at the very brilliant white ones in the corner.

'But they're so white,' I say, walking over. 'They don't look like they've ever been sat on.'

'Don't worry, they're Scotchgarded and our cleaner does wonders with them.'

Polly gives me a terrified look but we do as we're told.

'So, how are you getting on?' I ask her.

'I'm OK, I think,' she says, answering my earlier question. 'I'm just so tired all the time. I think it'll be better when I stop working. I've got another month and a half to go and I can't wait.'

Anneka comes along and deposits our drinks in front of us, followed by a platter of crudités.

'Help yourselves and there's dip, too, low-sugar salsa and fat-free tzatziki.'

I glance at the sofa again, but Anneka's looking at me expectantly and that's terrifying me too, so in the end I plump for the tzatziki, which is the least stain-y option.

'So, how about you – are you now homeworking?' Polly asks me.

I'm about to respond, but the doorbell rings.

'Five minutes late,' declares Anneka from the kitchen island where she's sorting out the drinks, before she click-clacks off towards the front door.

'I don't think I've ever been on time anywhere in my adult life,' says Polly. 'This was an absolute first because she scares the bejesus out of me.'

'I know. Me too.'

'Thank goodness it's not just me. I'm terrified of what it's going to be like when I've got the baby in tow. When my sister's kids were little it took her an hour or two to leave the house.'

'I know, most of the time, when I'm going out with Sasha, I have to try and leave the house an hour earlier than I'm supposed to,' I say.

'Maybe that's why Nina left the group. Couldn't handle the pressure.'

'Ha, perhaps we'll all be joining her,' I say, laughing.

Helen walks into the room behind Anneka, clutching a big box from a local bakery.

'Hello, hello,' she calls, waltzing straight over and nudging the healthy snacks aside a bit before setting down the box, which is full of little fruit tarts. 'I listened to the memo,' she turns to Anneka, 'they've got fruit in them, at least.'

Anneka wrinkles up her nose. 'And jelly, sugar and custard.'

'Yeah, but the fruit counts as one of our five a day. So...' She shrugs and sits down. 'And I also bought us this, you know, in case we needed a bit of an ice-breaker.'

I stare hard at the DVD.

'Nothing says "ice-breaker" like *Magic Mike XXL*,' I say, pulling a face.

'Thought it might help us bond, you know, through the cringing – and to be honest, it's the closest thing I can get to a man these days. Since the bump has become bigger, Toby won't let me near him. He once saw the baby kicking when we were getting down to it and it freaked him out.

'I know, sorry, probably a bit of an overshare. But none of my other friends get this kind of stuff. I'm the last of them to have kids, they've all been there done that, and they don't have sex any more anyway now that their kids are bigger and go to bed late.'

'Oh my God, is that a thing?' I say. Max and I haven't had much of a problem with that as Sasha goes to bed around 7 p.m.

'Apparently, when they're teenagers, it makes it harder as they go to bed so late and they get all freaked out if they hear any sort of creaking.'

My jaw drops in horror; I hadn't thought of my babies ever becoming teenagers.

'Oh, it's not so bad. You just buy them an expensive pair of AirPods and extend their WiFi privileges by an hour or two,' says Anneka, batting away her hand and handing Helen a glass of fizz. 'George has two teenage children from a previous marriage and we were on quite a rigid sex schedule to try and conceive this little one. We didn't have time to be precious about when other people were in the house. If it was the right time, it was the right time.'

'Blimey,' I say, drinking my fizz and wishing it was alcoholic.

'Besides, we won't need to worry about that with these ones. By the time they're grown up they'll be hooked into all sorts of gadgets that they'll have no clue what we're up to,' says Anneka.

'Something to look forward to either way, huh?' says Helen, pulling a face and Polly and I laugh.

'So, this is exciting, isn't it?' says Anneka. 'We don't even need the woman that shall not be named.'

'Nina?' volunteers Helen.

'Thank you, I didn't want to waste my breath on her name, but yes, her. Look at us all bonding away. I'm sure over the next year we're going to share everything,' says Anneka. 'I just wanted to say that I am so pleased to have you all here and that I have found you. I just knew when I met you that you were going to be my group.'

'And that you were running out of time to do the class again,' says Helen.

Anneka chooses to ignore her.

'And on that note, I'd like to propose a toast. I hope that we'll be a happy, nurturing and supportive group and that we'll be there for each other. It's going to be a tough time going into motherhood and we're going to need people that we can rely on and I hope that we have found just that. Cheers.' Anneka raises her glass.

My eyes start welling up – that's just what I needed to hear – and we all drink.

'That was lovely,' says Polly.

'I've been planning it all day. My hairdresser Cassandra has been coaching me to be a better person. Did it work? Did I sound nice and normal?' she says, raising an eyebrow.

'You did until you asked us afterwards,' says Helen. 'Are you all right, Ellie?'

I sniffle back the tears that have involuntarily started to fall.

'I'm sorry,' I say, dabbing them away. 'It's just I've moved down here and I don't really know anyone any more and I haven't really got any friends in town yet and that just meant so much, especially as this weekend...' I can't quite get the words out.

'I'm an emotional wreck at the moment too,' says Polly. 'Last night I cried at *Dragon's Den* every time someone got offered a deal.'

'Those look more than just hormonal tears,' says Helen, nudging the box of fruit tarts towards me.

'They are, but I feel a bit bad unloading about it to you all as we don't know each other that well.'

'Don't worry about that,' says Anneka. 'We're all friends here. I can give you a card, if you need George's services.' She looks at the horror on Helen and Polly's faces. 'What? You would not believe what went on with the last group.'

'It's nothing like that, Anneka. Or at least I hope it won't be,' I say, taking a deep breath. 'Max lost his memory.'

The three of them stare at me blankly.

'You know, I was waiting for something a bit more scandalous,' says Anneka. 'George is terribly forgetful. But that's because he's in his sixties.'

The picture she's painting of George becomes even clearer. But now isn't the time to find out more about him.

'He's not forgetful; he's forgotten *everything* about the last five years.'

'What the actual—' says Helen

'Don't say the f-word,' says Anneka. 'We're not swearing in front of the babies.'

'They're not even born yet; what the fuck are they going to do about it?' says Helen. 'Oh shit, sorry.'

She clasps her hand to her mouth, pretending it was accidental, and Anneka's nostrils flare.

'Do you know how much foetuses can hear? Anyway, we're getting off the topic. Ellie—' she waves her hand for me to continue '—what on earth happened?'

'I guess I better start at the beginning,' I say.

'This sounds just like that movie,' says Polly, helping herself to another mini tart. 'I think it has Channing Tatum in it, or someone similar anyway. And it's the wife that loses the memory, not him. But it's like totally the same thing – she has to fall in love with her husband all over again.

'Of course there's her family, who are trying to manipulate her and steal her away. But apart from that…'

'Apart from that,' I say, wishing my situation *was* a movie and not real life.

'Oh, I've seen that one,' says Helen, and we all look at her. 'Come on, *Magic Mike* is not the only Channing Tatum film I've seen.'

'Perhaps if I'd watched it I'd know what to do.'

'Oh yes, it might give you some tips,' says Helen. 'You could be like the family and manipulate Max into doing things that he normally wouldn't do. You know, telling him he always puts the bins out or always sorts through the laundry. Or maybe he cooks for you every night. Or he rubs your feet without you having to ask when you get home from work. And he has sex with you all the time when you're pregnant,' she says wistfully, getting caught up in the fantasy.

'I'm sensing a theme here,' I say. 'Do we need to talk about your marriage?'

'Oh no, I mean we probably *do*, but now is all about you. What can we do to help?'

'There's nothing I think any of you can do, really, unless you either know why Max was in Chiswick or you've got any idea how I can get his memory back.'

'Imagine not knowing how you fell in love with one another,' says Polly, a tear rolling down her cheek. 'Not that I know how you two fell in love, but I know that if my husband forgot I'd be really upset.'

'It's hard. You don't realise how much of your shared history is part of your everyday life and vocabulary. And it's lonely too. I mean, it's only been three days, but going through even basic everyday things – like when the baby's kicking or when I've got awful heartburn – I don't feel like I can turn to him. Even though he shouldn't feel like a stranger to me, he's become one because I'm a stranger to him.'

Polly reaches over and rubs my back and I blink back the tears.

'You know you can message us,' she says. 'That's what the WhatsApp group is there for.'

'Absolutely,' says Helen.

'But hopefully if the doctors are right, then he'll be getting his memory back any day now,' says Polly.

I nod. 'That's what's keeping me going at the moment.'

'But aren't you worried about what happens if he doesn't get his memory back?' says Anneka, helping herself to some of her carrot sticks dipped in salsa.

Helen shoots her a look.

'What?' she says, chewing on her carrot. 'I'm sure we were all thinking it. I'm just thinking out loud.'

'I'm sure it's not going to come to that,' says Polly, patting my arm again.

'I'm just trying to be realistic,' says Anneka. 'Surely you should be using this time to get him to fall back in love with you because if he doesn't get his memory back, he's still going to be a stranger. And this isn't about me being tactless or blunt. You went to antenatal classes to prepare to give birth and have a newborn, so why wouldn't you prepare in case he never remembers?'

'I hate to agree with her,' says Helen, 'but there's a certain amount of truth to what she's just said. I'm sure that Max is going to get his memory back, but maybe it wouldn't hurt for him to try and get to know you all over again.'

I take a sip of my drink and consider what they're saying.

'Look, what Anneka and Helen are suggesting is the worst-case scenario,' says Polly. 'What happened to thinking positive?'

'I can do positive too,' says Anneka. Helen raises an eyebrow with suspicion. 'It's just that I like to be practical. We're all rooting for him to get his memory back as soon as possible but, in the meantime, I think your best bet is to make him fall in love with you again.'

'Oh yes, I'll just wave my magic wand,' I say, running my hands through my hair. 'It's not that easy, is it? Falling in love, I mean. There are so many variables to consider and everything has to be just right. There are tons and tons of stories of people meeting their soulmate but it not being the right time for one of them, or something's prevented them from getting together. If I'd have re-met Max a few years earlier I'd doubt we'd be together now. He was out with the lads most nights and having flings with drop-dead-gorgeous model types.'

The words tumble out of my mouth before my brain catches up with me. Max still thinks he's living that life. And he said it himself; he's happy with the life he's living.

'But *if* he's your soulmate,' says Polly, tilting her head as she looks at me.

'What if that's not enough?' I start to feel panicky. 'What if we only fell in love because of that particular path of events? What if we couldn't fall in love again?'

'Firstly,' says Helen, cutting me off, 'we're supposed to be cheering you up and this is heading in the wrong direction. Stay positive, remember? And secondly, it's utter bullshit. Timing is bullshit. You fell in love once before; you'll fall in love again. It's as simple as that.'

'But what if it's not? I mean, us falling in love, it was so fast but full of those little moments, you know, like when we'd played mini-golf as friends and we didn't want the night to end so we kept on playing and playing until we got kicked out. Or when he took me to Paris for a romantic mini-break and told me loved me for the first time. Or all the times in the run-up to our wedding we spent practising our first dance, and each time I had to pinch myself as I thought how lucky I was that I was going to spend the rest of my life with him.

'How could we possibly recreate all those feelings from those moments?'

'I've got it,' says Polly, wriggling forward in her chair and clapping her hands together. 'You do it all again.'

'I do what all again?' I say, confused.

'You do all your memories again,' she says. 'It's absolutely perfect. You were just saying that what if you both only fell in love because of a particular path of events that led you to where you are now? So, by recreating these memories, you could still keep the variables the same.'

'Variables? What is this, a school science experiment?' Helen points down at my bump. 'Besides, I don't think all of the variables are going to be the same.'

'She'll be fine, as long as none of the dates were skydiving,' says Polly.

'I've also got Sasha now. Taking her on a mini-break isn't exactly conducive to romance.'

'Didn't you say that your mother-in-law offered to be there for you if you needed anything?'

'I guess so,' I say, wondering if I should take her up on her offer to help out more with Sasha.

'There you go. I think this sounds like a great idea,' says Polly. 'I'd love to do this with Jason. Perhaps I'll suggest it, although we met at a twenty-four hour dance festival and there's no bloody way that I'd make it even an hour stood in a muddy tent at the moment.'

'It wouldn't work with George either. We got together when he was still living with his ex-wife after they'd separated. And my days of a quickie in the back of his Jag are well and truly over, thank goodness.'

'I feel like we're learning so much about each other,' says Helen, pulling a face. 'But, Ellie, do you think this might work?'

'I don't know. Max is already totally freaked out about the fact that we're together and we live in the suburbs.'

'Oh hun, you don't tell him that's what you're doing,' says Anneka. 'That's not part of the plan. The thing with men is, you've got to take them by surprise but make them think that it was all their idea. That they've fallen in love with you all by themselves.'

'But Max and I aren't like that,' I say, sighing. 'We don't play games.'

'That's when it was an even playing field,' says Anneka, who clearly has too much experience in such matters. 'These are definitely extenuating circumstances. And he is your husband already. It's not like you're trying to seduce a man to leave his wife.'

'We can't wait to hear all about it,' says Polly, moving on swiftly. 'We're going to get you through this.'

'Yes,' says Helen. 'We'll be here, whenever you need us.'

'We'll help you every step of the way,' says Anneka. 'I've never been part of a gang like this before. We'll be like The A-Team.'

'Just without the violence and the bad jewellery,' says Polly.

'Speak for yourself. I could take down a few people, I reckon, and I love a bit of tacky jewellery, me,' says Helen, and we all laugh.

'Thanks, guys,' I say, trying not to cry again. 'I'm so glad that I met you all.'

'Same,' says Polly.

Helen looks at Anneka before nodding in agreement.

I might be experiencing a major life crisis, but, for the first time since Max's memory loss, I feel positive about it. And they're right; I need to start making things happen. Max fell in love with me once; how hard could it be to make him fall in love with me twice?

Chapter 9

Last night's meet-up with the girls was just what I needed. Despite the fact that when I got home at 10 p.m., Sasha was up watching *Peppa Pig* with a flustered Max and Mick, who were like some comedic double act. I needed that time away from Max to remember that he fell for me once and to give me that hope that he could do it again.

I haven't been able to stop thinking about what the girls said. It's such a ridiculous idea, but the more time I spend around him, the more appealing it becomes.

Max is meeting with his psychotherapist at the moment, and I hope that she has found the key to unlock his memories. I did try to go in with him, but I was kindly asked to wait outside and directed to a pile of magazines. It somehow feels fitting that they are years out of date; perhaps it provides a little comfort for his amnesiac clients.

My phone starts to ring in my bag and I fumble around for it, convinced that I'd put it on silent, only to find that my screen is blank. A man at the end of the waiting room deliberately looks up at the big NO PHONES sign pinned on the wall and points at it. But the phone is still ringing, and I realise that it's coming from Max's jacket, which he left on the chair when he went in. I pull out the offending phone, about to decline the call, when I see that it's a London number. I swipe up and answer it.

'Hello,' I say, picking up my bag and Max's jacket and heading out into the corridor away from the disapproving looks of the man.

There's silence on the other end of the phone, but I'm convinced I can hear breathing.

'Hello?' I say again, but then the line goes dead.

I know logically it was probably a sales call, but after the strange few days I've had, I have to check.

I dial the number back and I get an automated answer for the switchboard of Charing Cross Hospital. Without knowing who I want to be connected to, I hang up. Surely that wasn't a sales call? I get my phone and Google the hospital thinking it'll be near Charing Cross station, only to find that it's a large hospital in Hammersmith, just a few minutes' drive from Chiswick where Max lost his memory.

My heart starts to beat faster, but before I can do anything else, Max pokes his head out of the door.

'Ah, there you are. I thought you'd done a runner.'

'No, sorry, your phone rang and I came out here to answer it because I thought it might be important. Sorry.'

'Oh, OK,' he says, taking it back from me and swiping to see for himself. 'Who was it?'

'Someone at the Charing Cross Hospital. They didn't say anything.'

'Probably just a wrong number,' he says, slipping the phone in his back pocket.

'I guess, but it's near to Chiswick, which certainly is

a coincidence. Do you remember being at a hospital? Maybe you went there when you were confused?'

'No, no,' says Max. 'I remember being outside of Chiswick station and not knowing how I got there. That's when I went to Brixton.'

'Right, OK,' I say, thinking that it's a bit of a dead end. I can hardly phone the switchboard asking them to find out who phoned Max. We start to weave our way out of the labyrinth of corridors. 'So, how did the appointment go?'

'It was intense.'

'What did you talk about?'

'Oh, you know,' he says, rubbing his eyes. 'Stuff.'

'Stuff?'

'Uh-huh.'

Glad we cleared that up.

'But it was useful?'

He shrugs and sighs. 'Maybe. To be honest, I'm exhausted; do you mind if we don't talk about it? I guess I usually tell you everything, don't I?'

I'm torn. Max has never been one of those people that pours his feelings out to me, but I desperately want to know what's going on in his head right now. Thoughts of Helen suggesting I use his memory loss to my advantage pop into my mind, even if her ideas were only related to domestic chores.

'Mmmhmm,' I say, not exactly correcting him.

'Hopefully I'll get better at that.'

'Mmm.'

If I don't make anything other than noises, that's not really being manipulative.

I usually feel secure in our relationship, and it's never

bothered me beforehand to need to know every little thought in his head. But what's going on now isn't normal.

We make it back to the car and, as I pull away, I can't help but feel sad. It's not like I truly believed he'd see the psychotherapist and be cured right away in one session, but it's just that each day that ticks by, and he doesn't have that breakthrough moment, it's another day where my Max seems to drift further away from me.

He really does look emotionally wrung-out, though. He leans his head against the window and shuts his eyes. I put the radio on and leave him alone for the rest of the drive.

He stays in the car when I stop and pick up Sasha from nursery and he only really pays attention to his surroundings when we arrive back in Fleet.

'Can we just pop into Mum and Dad's?' he asks.

'Oh, um, I guess,' I say, looking in the back and for once Sasha is wide awake and not snoozing in the car. 'Do you want to give them a ring and see if they're in?'

'But their house is just up there,' he says, pointing. 'We'll just knock and see.'

'Oh, um,' I say, feeling awkward. I'd told Judy that we'd give them notice before Max went round.

I pull up on the drive and park behind Judy's car.

'Aren't you getting out too?' asks Max as he unclips his seatbelt.

'Oh, are we going to be a while?'

'Well, I wanted to talk to them about some of the questions that the psychotherapist asked me. You know, to check that I've got things right.'

'Of course,' I say, wincing slightly.

I take my time unclipping Sasha from her seat before I formulate a plan.

'Do you mind just nipping to the shop for me?' I say. 'I'm having another craving. I would go but my ankles are swelling and—'

'And this craving wasn't there when we drove past the big supermarket?'

'No, just started. It's for… gingerbread.'

'Gingerbread?' he says in disbelief.

'Uh-huh, they do gingerbread men in the bakery section.'

'Right,' he says, as I pull Sasha out of the car. 'Anything else?'

'No, I think that's it,' I say, smiling sweetly.

'Right.' He doesn't move. Instead he kicks his foot into the gravel and I'm wondering if he's going to tell me to get my own gingerbread. 'Before I go, do you, um, know if I've had therapy before?'

'I don't think you have,' I say.

'Right, it's just it didn't feel weird talking about myself, like I imagined it would.'

'Huh, well, you've never told me you have, but I guess you might have seen someone before we met.'

He nods his head slowly, looking down at the hole in the gravel that he's made, before he smooths it over.

'OK, well, I'll see you in a bit. No cherry bakewells to go with your gingerbread?'

'No,' I say, and he turns and walks off down the drive. It isn't until he gets out of sight that I curse, realising that he won't know that my 'no' really meant 'yes'. My Max would have known that and bought the cakes too.

How do I teach him all those little codes again? I try not to let the thought pull me down and I ring the bell.

Mick answers it and he looks alarmed to see me.

'Oh, darling, Ellie's here,' he shouts down the hallway before turning back and looking over my shoulder. 'Is Max with you?'

'Yes, but he's just nipped to the shops.'

'Right, good, sorry, we weren't expecting you. We'll get ourselves sorted. Graham's in the kitchen with Judy.'

'Oh right.'

Judy comes hurrying out of the kitchen and along the corridor.

'Did the psychotherapist help?' she says.

'Not in the way I was hoping for.'

She sighs but I notice Mick looking a little pleased. I think he's torn between wanting Max to get his memory back for his sake and enjoying his time with his son again.

'Max will be back any minute. Did you want me to pretend you weren't in, if Graham's here?'

'No, it should be fine. Judy's got some story concocted,' says Mick.

'We couldn't just not come up with something. Max still thinks he's your best friend so it would look a little weird if he never came over.'

'Come and have a cup of tea,' she says, beckoning me down the hallway. 'You can come too.'

She points at Mick and I get the impression that the two of them are staying as far away from each other as possible whilst Max isn't around.

'I'm going to go and get some tennis racquets from the

shed first. I was going to ask Max if he fancied a game, like old times.'

As Mick heads off, Judy rolls her eyes. 'He's loving this, you know. It's like none of the awful things he did matter any more.'

I rub her arm.

'Max'll remember again soon,' I say, and I release Sasha from my arms and she toddles up to Judy.

'Hey, sweetie.' She bends down and gives her a big squeeze. 'Grandma will see if she's got a biscuit for you.'

Judy stands back upright and turns to me.

'I'm glad that you're here without Max so we can brief you up.'

'Brief me up?' I say, slipping my shoes off and padding down the hallway.

'Oh yes, so we all have the cover story straight.'

'OK...'

'So,' she says, leading me into the kitchen and waving her hand to present Graham who's sitting at the table. I do a double take because he doesn't look like the usual Graham that we all know and love; he's now in Technicolor.

'Hi, Graham. Are you... OK?'

'Yes, I'm fine apart from looking like I've been Tango'd,' he says, glaring at Judy, his arms are folded.

I bite my lip, trying not to laugh at the fact that he's bright orange.

'Dare I ask?'

Graham shakes his head and then pulls me out a chair at the table for me to sit down.

'Graham had to go and get a fake tan for his cover story,' says Judy.

'Ah, this famous cover story, which is what exactly?'

'Well, you know that he's supposed to have been off playing golf with Mick – and we've seen what colour *he* is.'

'I still don't see why we couldn't have just said that I used Factor 50,' says Graham, tutting. 'Do you know how ridiculous I felt? I had to go into a little booth and they gave me paper pants.'

I try with all my mental might not to picture him in paper pants, but I fail miserably and now I don't think I'm going to be able to look at Graham in the same way ever again.

'Well, I wasn't going to ruin my bathroom to do it. Besides, Max would probably see the signs or recognise the smell,' says Judy.

She's giving Max too much credit. Like most men he's naturally unobservant; Graham could dye himself purple and he'd barely notice.

'It's still ridiculous. I had to come over here in a hoodie in case anyone recognised me.'

'Which looked even more ridiculous than the tan. You looked like one of those ASBOs.'

I laugh. I should correct Judy that an ASBO is a police charge and not a generic term for a young person.

'How's it been with Mick?' I ask. Graham scoffs loudly. He'd taken Mick's sudden departure badly too. He'd felt cheated that his best friend hadn't confided in him. Which ultimately pushed him closer to Judy as they comforted each other, and now with the two of them dating it looks even less likely that Mick and Graham will ever be friends as they were before. 'Have you two spoken?'

'Not exactly,' says Graham.

'I've told the two of them that they're going to have to pretend to be civil with each other, even if it's just when Max is around,' she says, putting her hands on her hips.

'We're not all good at acting like you are, Judy. What Mick did,' he says, getting cross, 'it's hard to forgive.'

'Mick won't talk to him either,' says Judy. 'He says that Graham took my side from the beginning and it was all because he wanted me for himself.'

Graham blushes.

'That wasn't true.'

'I know,' says Judy.

'It seems a shame – you two were best friends for years,' I say.

'And he was also married to Judy for years,' says Graham.

Judy plonks my tea down in front of me and it splashes over the sides.

'You know, if it's easier, we could just tell Max the truth,' I say.

'Thank you,' says Graham. 'That's what I've been saying. Save us all pretending.'

'We can't. Ellie, we've been through this: I'm not letting him get hurt unnecessarily. We're just going to have to grin and bear it.'

The back door to the kitchen opens and Graham sits up straighter. Mick strolls in with a tennis racquet in his hand.

'Look, I found one,' he says, swinging the tennis racquet a little too enthusiastically and it nearly knocks over the mug tree.

'Careful, they're Royal Doulton,' shrieks Judy.

'Royal Doulton, my arse. They're Marks and Spencer's and you know it,' says Mick.

Judy folds her arm and the two of them look like squabbling children. I dread to think what it's like when I'm not here.

The front door rings and everyone freezes.

'Everyone act natural,' calls Judy like a film director. 'Ellie, you get it.'

I do as I'm told and when I answer the door Max holds up a brown paper bag of gingerbread before he follows me back into the kitchen.

Mick's leaning up against the worktop, casually resting his tennis racquet around the back of his neck. Judy's grabbed a tea towel and is standing by him. Graham's sat down at the table holding the newspaper in front of him. So much for natural.

'Darling, how are you feeling?' says Judy, gliding across to him and putting her arm around his shoulder.

'Um, I'm OK,' he says, looking round at everyone and their catalogue poses. 'I'm sure Ellie told you that I still can't remember. Hi, Graham, um, nice to see you.'

'Good to see you too,' he says, getting up and shaking hands.

Max studies Graham's hands but doesn't say anything about his colour.

'Did you have a good holiday?'

'Yes, it was excellent. We stayed at the Quinta do Lago resort near Vilamoura and it was fantastic. I would heartily recommend it,' he says in a robotic voice that makes me think he's been forced to rehearse.

'Great,' says Max. 'I've not been to Portugal. I've heard it's nice.'

'Well, your father certainly likes it,' says Judy before she elbows Mick in the ribs.

'Ow. Excellent golf,' he says. 'And the food and the drink.'

'Steady on, Dad, you'll be getting Mum to retire out there next,' says Max, smiling.

'Ha ha ha,' says Judy with canned laughter that would be right at home in any sitcom. 'Did they cover much in your session today?'

She tries to steer the conversation back onto safer territory.

'This and that. Mainly stuff about what I could remember. Questions about you guys and the family.'

'Oh, that's so typical of psychotherapists, isn't it? Blame the parents. It's always our fault,' she says.

'No one said anything about fault. But she was asking me what had happened in the family and I realised that you've been filling me on my life and not anyone else's.'

'Oh,' says Judy. 'Well, you remember your grandpa died, that would have been six years ago. And then, Aunt Susan died a couple of years ago; she's your grandma Lilian's sister, so I doubt you'd remember her anyway. But other than that, all is the same. We're still here in this house.'

'Hmm,' says Mick.

Their house has been a bit of a sticking point in their divorce, but they've just about come to an arrangement and in the New Year the house is finally going on the market. It'll be the end of an era for everyone, but I think it will do them the world of good to move on.

'Right, so nothing significant has happened to you at all?' he says. 'It's just my life that's changed dramatically.'

'Mmmhmm,' says Judy through a forced smile. 'Look, you've had a long day. Why don't I make you a cup of tea? Talking about yourself can be exhausting.'

'You'd know, you've had enough practice,' says Mick.

Graham throws him a look that makes me worried that he's going to launch himself at Mick across the table.

'Tea would be great, thanks, Mum,' says Max, oblivious. 'What's with that tennis racquet, Dad?'

'I dug it out of the shed. Thought we could play tennis like old times.'

'We haven't played tennis since I was about sixteen, or have we started to play again?'

'No, we haven't,' says Mick, 'but we've talked about it. We keep saying we're going to.'

'OK, well, if you think you're up for it.'

'I'm up for it.'

'OK, but you have to be careful, you know, if you're not used to playing. At your age you have to think of your heart,' says Max.

'Don't worry about me, I'm as fit as a fiddle now. I go to three gym sessions a week.'

'And he does Pilates,' says Judy, folding her arms over her chest while she waits for the kettle to boil.

'Pilates, you, Dad?' says Max, screwing up his face. 'I thought you said nothing had changed. Blimey.'

'It's actually very manly,' he says.

''Course it is, darling,' says Judy.

'It is,' he says with a huff. He puts the tennis racquet on the side and lies down on the floor before lifting his torso and his legs up at the same time, then reaching his arms towards his legs.

'Bloody hell,' I say in pure amazement.

Judy's jaw drops and Graham does not look happy.

'That doesn't look too hard,' says Graham and he gets off his chair. The next thing we know he's lying on the floor next to Mick, trying the same moves, only he's wobbling about all over the place.

'Get up, Graham, you'll do your back in,' says Judy, pulling on his shirt.

'Stop manhandling Graham,' says Mick. 'He's OK.'

'I'm fine,' he says, puffing. His cheeks are going bright red, which is an improvement on the colour of the fake tan.

'You don't look fine,' I say to Graham, who seems to be caught up in some macho competition. 'Perhaps it's best if you both stop.'

'I'm. Perfectly. Fine,' he pants, before he exhales loudly and collapses on his back.

Mick laughs. 'Now who says it isn't manly?'

Graham's still panting from the exertion.

Sasha, who's been sitting on the floor, watching, goes over to Graham and sits on his belly, which makes us all laugh. I try and usher her away and she gets up and waddles over to Max.

He picks her up and puts her on his knee.

'Dada,' she says. 'Dada Pig.'

'Oh, hello, Sasha Pig, oink, oink,' Max says. Sasha bursts into fits of giggles and claps her hands.

He looks up at us all staring at him; it's such a contrast from his hands-off behaviour over the last couple of days.

'I was saying that to her last night when we were watching *Peppa Pig*,' he says, his cheeks flushing. 'She seemed to like it.'

He's looking embarrassed as we're all still staring.

'She does, she loves it,' I say, pleased they're having a moment.

'So, Max, when's your next session with the psychotherapist?' asks Judy.

'Same time next week.'

'What, really? You'd think that they'd do it a bit quicker, wouldn't you, what with Ellie and the baby being due soon.'

'I know, tick tock, it's nearly baby o'clock,' I say.

'What are you going to do in the meantime?' asks Graham.

'Dad's giving me a hand with the DIY and tomorrow afternoon I'm going up to meet my boss at work.'

'You are?' I say, surprised. I didn't know he'd spoken to him.

'Yeah, I just wanted to check in about the whole not going back thing. You were right, but he told me to pop in. He said that we could go through some of my projects and he would give me some files that might help fill in some of the blanks.'

'Good for you,' says Judy.

'I could go with you, if you like?' says Mick.

'I'd like to go alone, if you don't mind.'

Judy and Mick look at me and I shrug my shoulders. We've not left him alone since it happened, but I guess we've got to do it sometime.

Polly's words from last night pop into my mind about recreating our memories and it gives me an idea.

'Judy, would you mind babysitting Sasha for us tomorrow night?'

'Of course,' says Judy.

'Max, perhaps I could meet you after you go to your office? I know you want some time on your own, but we don't have to meet until the evening,' I say to him. I've just the perfect place in mind. We could go to the mini-golf where we had our first date.

'I guess that would be OK,' he says, shrugging his shoulders.

'Great,' I say, ignoring his lack of enthusiasm.

'It will be nice for you to go out on a date,' says Judy, and I watch Max's facial expression change and he no longer looks so sure.

'Not a date. I thought we'd just go the pub, keep it nice and casual,' I say hurriedly, and he visibly relaxes. 'Plus, it'd be good to try and jog your memories by going to the places you've been to before.'

'Sasha might as well stay over if you like,' says Judy.

'Are you sure?' I say, thinking that would make the logistics easier.

'Yes, we've still got the travel cot made up from the weekend. I said I was here to help.'

'We're here to help,' says Mick, putting his arm around Judy and she pats him on the chest.

'Great, thank you,' I say.

Max nods before he turns to Graham. 'Are you OK – you're still looking really red in the face?'

I look over and see Graham's nostrils flaring. I'm presuming it's more to do with Mick's arm around Judy than the Pilates.

'Oh, don't mind him; he always goes like a tomato whenever he's exerted himself,' says Judy, and I try not to wince. 'I've seen him when he's out running,' she adds quickly. 'Tea?'

We all accept and this time she actually makes us a cup. Max turns to Mick and Graham and starts talking to them about football and I start planning in my head just how I'm going to recreate our first date. I can't believe that I'm going through with Polly's plan, but with his memory not coming back any time soon, I need to try and do everything I can to help it along.

138

Chapter 10

I'm on the train to meet Max, and I can't remember the last time I was nervous about going on a date with him. I wonder at what point when I was dating him that those nerves disappeared and it just felt normal. If it was under any other circumstances, I'd probably enjoy the tingly feeling of anticipation.

The train pulls into the station and I follow the hordes of people descending the stairs and moving into the tunnels underneath the tracks. I head to the St John's Hill exit and I can't help but smile when I head through the ticket barrier and spot Max waiting outside the coffee shop for me.

'Hey you, come here often?' I say, sidling up to him.

He smiles awkwardly and I wish I hadn't made a joke.

'So, where's this place we're going to?'

I tuck my freshly straightened hair behind my ears.

'Not far from here,' I say, disappointed that he hasn't complimented me on how I look. I squeezed into some skinny maternity jeans and a plunging tunic top that gives me impressive cleavage, but he hasn't noticed that I've made an effort at all.

'How did it go at the office?'

'It was nice to see Simon,' he says with a shrug. 'Which way is it?'

'It's this way,' I say, wishing he'd be a bit more relaxed.

We walk out of the mini shopping centre and on to the busy street outside. It's just after 6 p.m. and people are weaving around us, rushing home from work.

A big double-decker bus swoops towards the bus stop and Max flinches.

'Are you OK?' I ask. He backs away to the far side of the kerb.

'It just took me by surprise,' he says, and we start walking along again.

'So, did you recognise people in your office?' I ask.

'Er, a few people are still there that I know. But there are a lot of fresh faces that I didn't recognise.'

'And what about the projects? Did Simon show you what you'd been working on?'

He takes a deep breath.

'He did,' he says, without elaborating. 'But I don't want to talk about work. Simon's not budging on the month off, so there's nothing to say.'

That's me told then. I don't know why he's suddenly treating me with such contempt. Up until now, he's not exactly been acting like my husband, but at least he's been nice to me, even if he was treating me like his sister's best mate. But this – this is different.

We walk along in silence. This is so far from how I wanted it to be. I'd wanted to tell him about the night I'd bumped into him in the nightclub and how we'd come here on our first date – that wasn't a real date – and how we'd got together, but the vibes he's giving off are hostile.

'Which pub are we going to?'

'It's called Four. It's actually quite cool, it's got a mini-golf course inside.'

He stops walking for a second.

'Mini-golf?'

'Yeah, it's fun. I thought we could play a couple of rounds. We've been before,' I say, tailing off as he looks so unimpressed.

'Will there be somewhere I can get a beer there?' asks Max.

'Uh-huh, it's like a proper bar, just with mini-golf too.'

'Good,' says Max. 'I could do with a few beers.'

Me too, I think to myself, wishing I could actually have one.

We reach the pub and I push open the door and we walk over to the barman to book a slot.

'Hiya, can we do unlimited rounds of the crazy golf, please?' I ask.

The barman wrinkles up his face.

'I'm really sorry, the crazy golf is closed at the moment; it's being refurbished.'

'But we came all this way,' I say in disbelief. 'I was on your website this morning and it didn't say that it was closed.'

'I'm pretty sure it does, on the home page,' says the barman, folding his arms.

I pull my phone out of my bag to prove a point, but when the page loads, I can see it there in black and white. I'd seen that on the website there was no need to pre-book, and I hadn't thought to scroll down any further.

'But we came all the way from Fleet to play.'

'I have no idea where that is; is that Zone 6?' says the guy, squinting.

'No, it's even further than Zone 6.'

The man sucks in his breath in a way reminiscent of Max when he realised that's where he lives.

'I'm really sorry, that sucks.'

'It's OK, Ellie. We could just have a drink elsewhere or go home?'

'No, no, we have to be here,' I say, my voice rising in pitch. 'We're trying to jog your memory, we've got to go to the same place.'

'I'm sure there must be other places that we've been to in Clapham.'

I tap my fingers on top of the bar. He doesn't know why this place is so special to me.

'No, it's got to be here.'

Max looks around the bar.

'If it helps, none of it seems familiar. It probably wouldn't have worked anyway.'

I want to scream that it's not about that, but instead I take a deep calming breath.

'You can play beer pong if you like? We've got some space on the tables in the back room.'

'Beer pong?' I say incredulously.

'Oh, I love beer pong,' says Max. 'I played it when I went to visit my mate Dom at uni in Texas.'

'Cool, so what package do you want: beer, prosecco?' says the barman.

'Orange juice,' I say, pointing to the bump. 'I can't drink.'

'I can give you a pitcher of water for your cups,' says the barman.

'That could work?' Max says.

'Yes, because at seven months pregnant what I want to do

is down a pitcher of water. I already have to pee all the time as it is.'

'Then I can drink the beer for you,' says Max. 'We'll take a table.'

The barman nods and leaves the pitcher to be filled whilst he takes payment.

'This is going to be so much fun. And I'll have you know that I'm awesome at this game,' says Max. 'I am definitely going to be the king of it.'

'Awesome.'

He misses my sarcasm and I'm left wondering how this has gone so horribly wrong from the plan I had in my head.

Max takes the full pitcher and we walk out to the back room that smells like a brewery thanks to floor covered in spilt beer. There are groups playing on most of the tables that are screaming and shouting as they throw the ping pong balls into each other's cups. It looks fun with a group of mates, but definitely not for a first date, especially when one half of the couple isn't drinking.

Max sets up the cups at each end into their triangle shapes and he explains the rules to me, shouting to make himself heard over the cackling group of hens on the table next to us playing prosecco pong.

'Right, yep, got it,' I say, slightly unimpressed. I throw my first ball and it lands in the middle cup.

'Holy shit,' says Max, 'good shot.' He picks up the cup and downs it. 'I underestimated your hand-eye co-ordination. I seem to remember when Rach brought you to the tennis club once and you got hit in the head with a ball. Didn't my mum have to take you to A&E?'

I remember that day so well. I'd chosen my shorts and Aertex T-shirt so carefully as I knew that Max would be there. During the warm-up, when one of the older kids served to me, I'd gone to hit the ball, only to wildly miss and have it hit me square in the head. Let's just say I never went back again.

'Yes, yes, thanks for that. So pleased there's nothing wrong with your long-term memory.'

He laughs and it feels like a small victory that he's no longer scowling. Perhaps I can get this back on track after all.

He takes a shot and hits one of my cups on the back line. 'Score,' he shouts before he walks over to the table and downs my beer. 'This is just what the doctor ordered.' Max walks back to his side of the table.

A woman comes along dressed in tight leather trousers and a vest top, wearing a gun holster filled with shots bottles. She's carrying a tray of shot glasses.

'Who wants shots?' she asks, looking between me and Max.

I point at the bump and she sighs before fluttering her eyelids at Max.

'I'll take one, and perhaps I'll drink Ellie's, too,' he says, digging into his wallet to pay for them.

'Er, Max, are you sure you want to drink shots on top of all the beer you're drinking?'

'I'll be fine. Shots don't affect me,' he says, slamming back the green-coloured drinks in close succession before rapidly shaking his head afterwards. 'They were vile.'

He picks up the cup of beer that he was supposed to down and uses it as a chaser.

'Right, where were we?' he says. 'I bet this is much better than mini-golf, isn't it?'

'Mmmhmm,' I say, trying to block out the chanting of the hen party on the table next to us as they down their shots. Who has a hen do on a Wednesday night?

I throw the ball and it hits a cup. I'm delighted because the quicker the game's over, the quicker we can leave.

The bride-to-be staggers past me on the way back from the toilet and she bumps into me as she passes.

'Ooh, sorry,' she says, noticing my bump and then pulling a look of horror.

'I'm not drinking,' I say quickly. 'My husband's doing that for both of us.'

'Right,' she says, giving me a look and it makes me feel even worse about being here. I turn back to Max to see if he wants to call it a night, but he's talking to a tall blonde woman with a bridesmaid sash draped over her shoulder. The shots woman has come round again and Max and the bridesmaid down a green shot before the bridesmaid hands Max a glass of prosecco to chase it with.

'Woo,' says Max, cheering to much whooping from the hen party.

Max has always liked to party but I haven't seen him drinking like this for a long time, not since we had Sasha, anyway.

I cough loudly and he looks up in surprise.

'It's your go,' I shout.

'Right,' he says, and he gives the woman a small shrug and she sashays off to her table.

He misses and I catch the ball and throw it so forcefully that it splashes beer out when it lands in a cup.

'Easy,' says Max, picking it up. 'You nearly lost all the beer.'

Another big group has started playing on the table to the other side of us, and it's almost impossible to hold a conversation without shouting, so we give up.

'Isn't this great?' he says with a hint of a slur, when he comes over to my side of the table to pick up a cup for a drink.

'Do you think you might have had enough?'

'*Had enough?* Who are you, my mum?' he says with a laugh. 'Come on, this is nothing.'

'You know, you don't really do shots any more,' I say.

He scoffs and rolls his eyes.

'I always do shots,' he says. 'And I can handle my booze, OK?'

There's an edge to his voice that doesn't belong there, and I don't like it.

I watch him walk back around with a slight stagger and I worry about how I'm going to get him home.

Max is steadying his arm, getting ready to throw, when a ball lands in one of my cups.

'Oops,' says the bridesmaid, giggling, and she wanders over to retrieve it. I'm not entirely convinced that her throw was so bad that her ball happened to hit our table, but Max doesn't seem to question it when he walks over and retrieves it for her. 'You might as well drink the cup; Ellie's pregnant and can't drink anyway.'

She doesn't even turn and look at me. She merely downs the beer and swishes her long hair over her shoulder.

'Thanks,' she says, putting the empty cup down and leaning her hand on the table with her back to me. 'You know, I could do with some aiming tips. I seem to be hopeless at this.'

'I'm sure you're not that bad,' says Max. 'I'll help you.'

They both walk round to his side of the table; she holds her arm up and Max corrects her posture.

I can't hear what they're saying but whatever it is must be hilarious from the way she's tipping her head back laughing.

I can feel my heart pounding, watching another woman flirt with my husband. I've never been jealous of Max spending time with anyone else. I know the Cara Worthingtons of this world would think I should be. He, after all, is one of life's naturally beautiful people and whilst it's taken me a long time to accept that I too am pretty in my own way, I'm not the kind of woman that would stop traffic. But for us – as a couple – looks played such a small part in our relationship. Yes, I am physically attracted to Max, of course I bloody am, but it's so much more than that. It just works on so many levels, or at least it did. It's not like I'm naïve enough to say that he's never found another woman attractive since he met me, because of course he probably has, he's only human after all, but he's never let me see it – until now.

The woman throws the ping pong ball and it hits me in the face.

'Ow,' I say, wiping off the stray beer that's streaked across my cheeks.

'Sorry,' shouts the woman, clasping her hand to her mouth, but I can see that there's a smile spread across it.

I rub at it and it surprisingly hurts an awful lot.

This couldn't be any further from our first date. Back then, half an hour in, Max had his hand on the small of my back, guiding me between the holes, and it was me holding onto his hips, leaning into him, trying to coach him with his mini-golf technique. It was somewhere around then that things changed between us and the chemistry started fizzing. Whereas now, the only thing fizzing is the prosecco on the adjacent table.

'Are you OK?' says Max, walking towards me, the bridesmaid following behind. 'I hope you're not going to have concussion from that ball.'

'How could she get a concussion from that?' The bridesmaid folds her arms over her chest. 'It's an air-filled plastic ball.'

'But she's pregnant,' he says, taking a step back from her.

'What? It's not like it hit her in the bump.'

Max turns away from the bridesmaid and she huffs and walks back to her friends – no hip-wiggling this time.

'No trips to A&E needed,' I say to him, wiping away the beer from my cheek.

'Good,' he says, tracing his fingers over my cheek to examine for himself. My body shudders and he looks me straight in the eyes as if he feels it. His hand lingers on my cheek and I can't help but turn my head so that he's cupping the side of my face.

'Shall we go?' I whisper.

'Are you sure you don't want to finish the game first?' says Max, pulling apart, like we weren't just having a moment. 'We've only got a couple more shots to play.'

'Quite sure,' I say with a sigh.

'OK,' he says, turning round and downing the remaining cups on the table.

'Um, Max, I'm not going to be able to carry you home.'

'What? I can't waste them,' he says, downing the last one.

I turn around to leave the beer pong annexe and the shots woman blocks the doorway to the main bar.

'More shots?' she says, picking a bottle out of the holster and pouring it into a glass.

I try to weave around her but Max is already downing another couple of green ones.

'I thought they were really bad?'

He shakes his head involuntarily.

'The more I have the more they grow on me. So what's the plan next?' he says, rubbing his hands together.

'Train home and then bed,' I say, already dreaming of sleeping off this awful date.

'Home and bed? Ellie, it's not even eight o'clock. Let's get food, or even more drinks.'

He makes a beeline for the bar and signals for the barman's attention.

'You don't need any more drinks.'

He orders a shot of sambuca before turning to me.

'And I've told you, you're not my mother,' he says.

The moment we shared only seconds ago now seems to have gone.

We hold each other's gaze and I can feel the anger starting to pulse around my veins. The baby kicks and it grounds me. It's not good for me to get this cross.

'Fine,' I say, taking a step back. 'I'll go home on my own.'

'Ellie,' he calls, but I'm already leaving the bar.

I'm storming off, or at least I'm trying to storm, but it's difficult when you're as pregnant as I am. It's more like a fast waddle.

'Ellie,' calls Max again.

He runs to catch up with me but his breath nearly knocks me out.

'Ellie, come on. Let's finush this.'

'Finush, Max? Listen to yourself, you're slurring all over the place. Let's just get home, go to sleep and we'll pretend this never happened.'

'I thought we were having a great time,' he says, tripping over himself.

'You – you were having a great time. You and that blonde bridesmaid.'

'Oh,' says Max, sighing. 'This is what that was about – you're the jealous type, I get it.'

'No, you don't get it,' I say, stopping short and causing someone behind me to walk into me. 'I'm not the jealous type at all. Just like you're not the flirting type. We're different than that, we're beyond it. We never play games with each other. We got together, we fell in love and it was easy. This,' I say, pointing between him and me, 'this is bloody hard. The Max that I know would never have taken me to play beer pong when I couldn't drink. He'd never have drunk shots with a stunningly beautiful woman. He'd never have called me his mother. I was an idiot for even thinking this was a good idea.'

Max opens his mouth and I think he's going to apologise, but instead he turns around and vomits on the pavement. Fuck. My. Life.

I'm stuck in London with a husband who doesn't know who I am, who's now too drunk to get on a train. What the hell am I going to do?

Chapter 11

'Thanks for coming,' I say, standing up from the bench with immense relief at the sight of Owen.

Without me holding him up, Max slumps over.

'Bloody hell, how much has he had to drink?' says Owen, pulling a face.

'Enough. I'm so sorry to ruin your night. I didn't know who else to call. I didn't think I'd make it back on my own.'

'You did the right thing,' says Owen, standing back and surveying the options. 'Is he still being sick?'

'No. I think he's over the worst of it.'

'OK, let's get him up. I'll take his weight if you can steady him a bit.'

With a heave, Owen slips Max's arm under his shoulders and pulls him up to standing. Max starts to struggle a little.

'Mate,' he says, realising who it is, and he latches on to him squeezing him in an almost hug before he continues looking down to the ground.

'Mate,' Owen mutters back, groaning under the strain of holding him. 'OK, I was going to suggest a taxi, but I'm not sure we'll find one that will take him. We're going to have to get him on the train.'

I look at Max who barely has his eyes open.

'We can go back to mine in Surbiton; it's eleven minutes on the train and a five-minute walk from the station. You guys can crash there tonight. Judy's got Sasha at hers, right?'

'Yeah, but I'm sure if you helped me onto the train to Fleet I could get him off at the other end. I don't want to put you through any more trouble.'

'Don't be silly, it's no trouble, and I don't think you'd manage him on your own. You and Max can have my room and I can sleep on the sofa bed.'

'Oh,' I say, looking Max up and down.

'Or we can put him on a mattress on the floor, if you'd rather,' he says, and I wonder if he's a mind reader.

'Might be the safer option. One that's close to a bathroom.'

Owen smiles. 'Come on, then, let's get going.'

When I was pregnant the first time, I hated the fact that I could never sleep a whole night through; only now do I realise it was probably nature's way of preparing me for the sleep deprivation that was to come. This time around – with Sasha more or less sleeping through the night – I enjoy the quietness of being awake, and the fact that no one is making demands of me. But tonight, lying in an unfamiliar bed, I'm feeling restless. When it eventually becomes unbearable, I get out of bed and creep past Max, who's passed out on an airbed in the hallway. I find my way into the kitchen and I'm surprised to see Owen standing by the sink.

'Shit, sorry, did I wake you?' says Owen, filling up the kettle. 'I thought I was being quiet.'

'You were, I didn't hear you at all. I just couldn't sleep.'

'Want one?' he says, holding up a box of tea bags.

'Hmm, I shouldn't really drink caffeine.'

'What about a hot milk?'

'Perfect.'

I sit down at the table and rub my bump.

'Everything OK with you and the baby?'

'Yes, fine, thanks. I'm just finding it difficult to sleep at the moment. It's hard to get comfortable.'

'I bet,' he says, widening his eyes. 'I take it you haven't figured out what happened?'

'No, still none the wiser. Although Max did receive a call from a hospital in Hammersmith. They didn't say anything, and when I rang back, it went through to the main switchboard. Without knowing who called, I couldn't do anything about it.'

'Was it a bad line?'

'No, I was convinced I could hear someone breathing. Not like heavy breathing – not that kind of call – but I guess I was aware that someone was there.'

'Probably just a wrong number,' he says.

'Yeah, that's what Max says,' I say, looking out the door as the sound of snoring drifts in.

'He's out cold,' says Owen. 'I haven't seen him like this in years.'

'Neither have I. He drank a lot in such a short space of time.'

'It's easy to do at beer pong.'

'I guess.'

He places a pan of milk on the hob and lights the gas.

'You never did tell me why you were up here playing beer pong in the first place. Doesn't strike me as the kind of thing you'd do when you're not drinking.'

I groan.

'What?' says Owen.

'It's going to sound stupid.'

He shrugs. 'I think with what you're dealing with at the moment, things are allowed to sound stupid.'

I smile. I've always liked Owen.

'I thought it might nudge Max's memory if we went to the place where we had our first date – it was where he'd stopped seeing me as his sister's dorky mate and started fancying me.'

'That doesn't sound stupid at all. In fact, it was a nice idea. What went wrong?'

'They were renovating the mini-golf and the barman suggested beer pong instead and Max leapt at the idea and he decided he'd drink all my beer.'

'Ah,' he says, pulling a face. 'That's how he got so drunk?'

'Yep, and the shots with the flirty hens from a hen do.'

'Ah,' says Owen. 'Classic Max.'

'Yeah, exactly,' I say with a sigh. 'Classic pre-me Max.'

We're silent for a while and I try not to let my mind wander to where we've ended up. 'When I first started dating him, Rach was really worried.'

The milk is finally warmed through and he pours it into a cup. 'Really?'

'Uh-huh. She told me that as much as she loved him that he was never going to grow up, that he'd break my heart and that I should get out while I still could.'

He nods as he slides the cup across the table to me, before he goes back over and gets his tea.

'The truth was I was worried about that too at first,' I say, taking the drink and warming my hands. 'He'd always been a player, even when we were at school, and I thought that whatever was going on with us was only going to be a fling. I was prepared for it just to be a few dates, a bit of fun. But he was so different to what I was expecting. The crazy benders that he was known for seemed a thing of the past and whilst we had some mad drunken nights, they weren't out of control. He didn't behave like he did last night. We wouldn't have had a future if he had.

'I just don't get it. What happened between the version of him I saw last night and the version I met a year later? Why did he suddenly change?'

'I expect it was an age thing,' he says, stirring his tea. 'You and Max, you're a great couple, you'll work it out.'

'You and Sarah were too,' I say, before cursing myself. 'I'm sorry, I didn't mean that to come out the way it did.'

'No, you're right. We were. But it was different with us. We were fresh out of university when we met. Neither of us knew who we were, or what we wanted to be. We grew up together but grew apart. Whereas you and Max grew up and then found each other.'

'Only now he's lost his memory of that bit.'

Owen smiles. 'Look, don't worry so much. The doctor said he'd get his memory back any day now.'

'But what if he doesn't?'

'What if he does?' says Owen, blowing on his tea as he walks over to the table and sits opposite me.

'Then everything will be hunky-dory, but I can't keep living in this weird limbo of waiting; I need to plan for the worst-case scenario. I'm going to have a baby in a few weeks and I want him to be in love with me again.'

'And he will be.'

'But how? We can't just carry on pretending we're married when he's never fallen in love with me. He looks at me like I'm still that geeky teenager. And it's not even like I could parade around in a tiny Wonder Woman costume like I did last time.'

Owen laughs a little before coughing.

'Ellie,' he says softly. 'You're beautiful, especially now.'

'I wasn't fishing for compliments,' I say, blushing. 'It's just that I want Max to look at me how he used to. You know – with that twinkle in his eye that made me shiver. I sound so ridiculous.'

'No, you don't.'

'He just had this way of looking at me that made me think like I was everything to him,' I say, wiping a tear away.

'And he will again. You've just got to see it from his point of view. He's gone from being the kind of guy who had a revolving-door policy with girlfriends to suddenly being married with a toddler and a baby on the way. It's going to be terrifying for him to suddenly have to play that role.'

'I know and that's why I didn't want him to play it. I want him to be actually living it.'

Owen looks at me with a look of pity.

'My NCT friends convinced me that I should redo some of our memorable dates. That's why I tried to recreate the magic of our first date.' I sink my head into my hands. 'It was such a crazy thing to do.'

'That's what being in love does to you, though. Are you going to do any more?'

I shrug.

'Rach thinks I should focus on why he lost his memory in

the first place. Try and find out what Max was doing when it happened.'

'I thought you'd hit a brick wall?'

'We did, but maybe I could recheck his messages, see if there's anything he missed.'

'No, don't do that,' he says a little too quickly.

'Why not? Do you think Max is hiding something?'

'No, no,' he says, clearly flustered, 'I just meant that I wouldn't like anyone going through my phone without my permission. And there are things that you might find that are totally innocent – jokes or messages that could be taken the wrong way.'

'I don't know, it might be—'

'Ellie, the phone's been checked. Concentrate on getting to know each other again.'

'You're right,' I say, knowing the messages would have been a long shot.

'Just as long as you're not going to recreate that dinner party we had before you guys were married.'

'Oh God, when Max was still in his flat in Brixton?' I say, cringing at the thought. Owen starts to laugh and I join in.

We thought we were so grown up hosting a dinner party, only Max and I had tried a bit of the Calvados that we were using in a sauce and we'd ended up drinking most of the bottle before our guests arrived. The fact that we ended up ordering Thai take away at 12 a.m. tells you everything you need to know about how bad the food was.

Max walks into the room, squinting and clutching his stomach.

'What's so funny?' he says.

'We were just reminiscing about a dinner party we had,' I say, the laughter falling short. It's the kind of memory where you had to be there to find it funny. 'How are you feeling?'

'Like a bit of a dick.'

Owen stands up, putting his cup in the sink.

'Well, you've had a lot of practice,' he says, patting Max on the back as he walks past him. 'I'm going back to bed.'

'Night,' I say, hugging my cup towards me. 'Thanks again for the drink and the chat.'

'Anytime,' he says, leaving the kitchen.

'I don't think those shots were a very good idea,' says Max with a slur. He staggers over to the table and sits down, rubbing his temples.

'They never are.'

'I'm guessing that wasn't the best night out we've ever had.'

'No, it was probably the worst,' I snap. I didn't mean it to come out so harshly but I'm still angry.

'I'm sorry for all that,' he says. 'I was such an arse.'

'It's OK.'

'No, it's not. Not at all. I mean, I can't remember all of it,' he says, wincing, 'but the bits I can remember were pretty awful. And my head. Did I drink many shots?'

'Four or five.'

'Oh,' he says, groaning.

'Have you been awake long?'

'No. I was lying there, trying to make myself get up for a glass of water, but my head's spinning that much. Then I heard laughter and realised you were up.'

I get up and fill him a glass of water from the tap and pass it to him.

'Thanks,' he says, taking a tiny sip. 'I feel awful.'

'I'm sure you do,' I say, sitting back down.

'You know, a lesser woman would say that I deserved it.'

I bite my lip.

'And they'd be right. I'm sorry for how I acted yesterday. The drinking and insisting that we played beer pong. I know that would have been the last thing you wanted to do whilst sober.'

'It's OK,' I say, batting a hand.

'It's not. I'm sorry. I was in a bad place last night. This whole thing finally got to me. You know I went into the office and people were coming up to me and chatting to me and I had no idea who they were. I didn't recognise the projects that I'd worked on. Everything seemed to be written in a different language with all new abbreviations and jargon. I guess it hit me: what if my memory doesn't come back? What if I'm stuck in this big hole forever?

'Which I guess might be OK if I was on my own, but I'm not. You're on maternity leave and if I lost my job how would we afford the house or the kids?' he says, clutching at his head again. 'And it's not only the financial stuff. I don't know my own daughter; what if I can't bond with her again?'

And I thought my head was spinning. He's been so non-chalant about this whole memory loss that I haven't stopped to truly consider how overwhelming and difficult it is for him.

'You will.' I'm stunned at the sudden outpouring. 'You're already doing a good job with Sasha.'

'It doesn't feel like it. I don't have a clue what I'm doing and you're such a natural.'

'Believe me, I wasn't at the start, but it just takes time to

159

get your confidence and find your feet. I'll help you,' I say, reaching out and taking his hand.

He looks down at it before giving me a small smile.

'Thanks, it means a lot to have someone supporting me through all this. I couldn't imagine doing it alone.'

'It's our wedding vows. For better or worse.'

'I'm guessing that you were cursing them last night.'

I take my hand back because it's getting all clammy where he's sweating out booze.

'Yeah, about the time you vomited on my shoes. Or maybe when you were flirting with the hot bridesmaid.'

He wrinkles his nose up.

'I've got flashbacks of you shouting last night. No wonder you were mad.'

'To be honest, it doesn't take a lot to make me mad at the moment. You've got to imagine that my hormones are going bananas at this stage of the pregnancy, anyway, and throw in your amnesia and that muddle of a house we have – to be honest, I'm amazed that I haven't been losing it more than I have.'

He smiles but it's a sad kind of a smile.

'What happens if I don't get my memory back or if it takes ages to come back and I've fucked it up in the meantime? With Sasha, with work... and with you?'

'Look, Max, your memory is going to come back,' I say, despite the fact that just a few minutes earlier I was worrying the same thing with Owen.

'But what if it doesn't? Haven't you thought about that? What would we do?' he says, scratching his head.

'I've thought about it a little.'

'You know, it's strange telling you how I feel, but it's actually a bit of a relief. Huh. I can see why I tell you everything,' he says.

'Mmmhmm,' I say, feeling guilty for not correcting him the other day, but it is nice to hear what's inside his head.

'You can always talk to me, I'm here for the freak-outs at five a.m.,' I say with a smile.

'How can you be so calm about this? I mean, you're looking after Sasha and me. And we're having a baby in a few weeks. Oh, the birth! I don't even know what I'm supposed to do when you're in labour. Have you got a birth plan? Is it a water birth? Am I going to have to be fishing out your poo with a net?'

His face is turning even greener.

'No, rest assured we're not having a water birth. It's definitely not for me. But to be honest the birth is the last thing we've got to worry about. It's the only thing that we know that is definitely going to happen. We should focus on everything else instead.' I pause.

'Let's just say, worst-case scenario, it takes you a few months to get your memory back, then what do we need to do to prepare for that?' I continue, going into planning mode like I would do at the office.

'I don't know. I'd have to go back to work, I guess.'

'OK,' I nod. 'So, that's a start. You need to work out what those new acronyms are and get up to date with developments.'

'I guess I could try and spend more time with Sasha. You could teach me the routine and what I usually do.'

'Oh yes,' I say, thinking that fits in nicely with Helen's idea to make him the perfect husband/dad.

'And then it would just leave us,' he says.

'Ah,' I say, looking at the foam of milk at the bottom of my empty cup. 'Yeah.'

'I'm guessing that doesn't come with such an easy fix,' he says. 'You haven't even told me how we got together in the first place.'

'No, I haven't. That's one of the reasons I thought it was a good idea for us to go out last night, just the two of us. Give us a bit of time so I could tell you things like that.'

'And then I went and fucked it all up,' he says, sighing loudly. 'What about today? Why don't you tell me about us? We can go home and I can shower and then you can tell me everything.'

'OK,' I say, nodding. 'I can dig out the photo books.'

'Great,' he says. 'And then I'll be up to speed about my new life in no time.'

I smile and wish it was that easy.

Chapter 12

True to his word, Max has spent the last couple days knuckling down and trying to get to grips with the life he's forgotten. He's started jotting down notes and timetables for our family routine, to the extent that he hasn't quite got the go-with-the-flow-on-occasions memo and I'm worried he could give Gina Ford a run for her money.

He's looked at our photo albums and the loose photos I have, as well as the ones on my phone. He learnt how we first re-met at the cheesy club in Clapham on Dodgy Rodge's stag do. Why we moved to Fleet. What holidays we've been on. What my favourite ice cream flavour is.

But while he knows about my favourite ice cream, he doesn't know that whenever we have a bowl of ice cream, I'll save the last spoonful for him, and then I'll kiss him after as he'll taste all lovely and ice creamy. It's a silly habit that started on a holiday in Italy, after Max had asked me for the last bit of my gelato, and we've kept it going ever since. The thought of him not automatically doing it pains me and I can't bring myself to tell him.

'Right, the notes just say *free play*,' says Max, looking up over his notebook and then down again to Sasha.

'Uh-huh, you just let her play with toys or play a game with her. I'm just going to make lunch.'

'But she's not really interested in the stacking cups or the shaking things.'

I pop some eggs in the pan of boiling water and turn to him. He's sitting on the floor of the kitchen with his brow furrowed in a way that he usually reserves for building flatpack furniture.

This is the first time we've properly spent time together as a family of three, as Mick had some things to do today and couldn't come and help with decorating the lounge.

Max's sitting on his knees trying to do peekaboo but Sasha's never been into that. She just bats his hand away like she knows he's there.

'When you say play?' he asks.

'You just play,' I say.

'Um, OK.'

He's floundering so I pick up my phone and search for a pop playlist, and a couple of seconds later, Taylor Swift comes out of the speakers.

Sasha's whole face lights up. She loves music and pulls herself up against the little kid's table that's in the corner and starts to rock from side to side.

'Great,' says Max, getting up and going to walk away but Sasha starts to wail.

'Oh no, you've got to join in. Here, look.' I press the pause button. 'And freeze.' I put my hands up and stand still and Sasha looks up and does the same, although she holds on for balance. I press play again and she starts her rocking/dancing.

'Oh, I see,' says Max. 'OK, I can do this.'

He looks a little bit uncomfortable at first.

'I'm guessing you've seen my bad dancing before,' he says and he starts to do what can only be described as awful dad dancing. I purse my lips together, trying not to laugh.

Sasha immediately wobbles across to him and he bends down almost instinctively and takes her hands and they start to dance together. I press pause and they both stop and I notice that Max pulls a face at Sasha that makes her giggle.

I press play again and watch as Max starts to really get into the music and dance with her, and the more he moves, the more she laughs.

'This is actually working,' he says, looking all pleased with himself.

'Sometimes it's the simplest of things that work; she just wants your attention.'

Max is smiling in a way that reminds me of when he first held Sasha, with a look of awe and wonderment and pride. Tears prickle in my eyes and I turn back to preparing the food.

I keep moving around the kitchen, sorting out the lunch, watching them and pausing every so often. The more I do it, the more they seem to bond over their frozen moment in time.

I try and ignore the green-eyed monster that's growing in my belly. It's not like I'm jealous that they're bonding; I am absolutely over the moon that they are. I'm just jealous that Max and I don't seem to be able to do it that easily.

'Despacito' starts playing from the little speaker and Max wrinkles up his face.

'What the hell is this?' he says. 'Sounds like the kind of song that you only hear on holiday.'

I gasp, forgetting that he won't have heard it before.

'This is one of the biggest songs of the last few years, it was absolutely huge.'

'I'm obviously not some Simon Cowell.'

'No, clearly not,' I say as I pop some bread in the toaster.

Max's hips start to wiggle and he does a salsa move.

'Whoa,' he says, standing still. 'What the hell was that? My hips had a life of their own.'

'Oh, that's right, we learnt to dance to this song when we were taking lessons before the wedding.'

'We took dance lessons before the wedding?' he says. 'Bloody hell.'

'You said that you'd been to too many weddings where the groom just rocked back and forth looking all sweaty and awkward.'

'Don't tell me we did a choreographed dance? Not one of those ones where everyone joined in? I couldn't imagine Owen dancing.'

I try and picture Owen doing one of those mass dances and it makes me laugh.

'Um, no, you did try and talk me into doing the *Pulp Fiction* one, but it was going to be too tricky to do it in my dress. So, in the end, we danced to "I'm Gonna Be (500 Miles)",' I say.

'By The Proclaimers?'

'No, it was a cover; it's really lovely and slow. We'd chosen it because when we were mini-golfing for hours on our first date, The Proclaimers' version kept coming on in a loop.'

'Why did we mini-golf for hours?'

'I like to think it was because we didn't want the night to end, but I think it was more because I kept beating you and there was something about your masculine pride that wouldn't let us leave until you'd at least tried to beat me.'

'Right. I still don't wholly believe this story. Having seen my performance with beer pong on Wednesday, I still think I'd have beaten you at mini-golf.'

'Well, I guess we won't find out now, will we?'

I think about the moment at mini-golf when The Proclaimers had been playing. I'd gone to hit the ball and Max had tried to stop me by pulling me back by my belt buckle and spun me round and we'd ended up kissing.

'You'll have to play me the song,' he says. 'Who knows, maybe the moves will come back to me like it did with the salsa.'

He does an exaggerated hip move and both he and Sasha giggle.

'It's so weird, the psychiatrist said that I might have skills that come back automatically because it's like muscle memory. Have I got any other talents that I've learnt over the last few years?'

'Hmm, I can think of a few,' I say, in a slightly husky voice without thinking. 'Shit, Max, sorry, I didn't mean it to come out that way. Um, let's see. You can play the ukulele now. You learnt just before Sasha was born.'

'Really?'

'Uh-huh, I'll have to dig it out from the spare-room boxes.'

'Ah, good to know, and I, um, look forward to finding out my other new talents too,' he says with a bit of a blush before he turns back to Sasha.

I'm cutting up the toast whilst Sasha's egg cools down and I stop. That's the closest he's come to hinting that something might happen between us.

'Now this, this is a tune,' says Max, tapping his toe to the beat as 'Gangnam Style' starts to play.

'I haven't heard this song in years,' I say, turning to watch Max who's got out his imaginary lasso and starting to do a little pony dance. He's never been the shy type, but he's not usually the person to be found lassoing in the kitchen in the middle of the day.

'I never knew that you knew the moves,' I say, wondering how this has never come up before.

'It was a bit of a party trick a couple of years ago,' he says before he starts to sing along and trot across the floor. I glance at my phone to see the release date: 2012. Blimey, I hadn't realised it was that long ago.

He looks absolutely ridiculous but Sasha is in fits of giggles and I can't help but join in. He's out of time with the music and the moves are a little dodgy, but he's smiling like he's having the time of his life.

He gives us a wink as he does his lasso and trots along to us, and for a minute I think he's going to scoop me up along with him, but instead he picks Sasha up from my feet. He puts her on his hip and stretches out her hand with his and spins her around.

'Come on, Ellie, surely you know the moves. Do you want Mummy to join in?'

'Mama, Mama,' Sasha chants, pointing at me.

'Nuh-uh, you're not getting me doing this dance.'

'Come on, I know you would have learnt it. You and Rach used to spend ages learning Steps dances in her room. I bet you know some of it.'

He does his little sideways shimmy across the kitchen, Sasha clinging on to him and screaming with delight at the same time.

He raises an eyebrow at me. It's so stupid that I feel self-conscious because this is Max. He's seen me dance around different kitchens loads of times before, and he's got no inhibitions, so why should I?

There's the pause between the verse and the chorus where the music goes quiet. Then as the chorus kicks in I start to do the trotting-pony move, and Max gives me a little whoop.

'I can't believe I'm dancing to this song,' I say, secretly enjoying myself. This is the closest I've felt to us being a family of three in the past week, and I really throw myself into it.

By the end of the song, I'm knackered. I'd forgotten how much of a workout the dance was. Max looks like he's worn out too and I take Sasha and pop her in her high chair. She rubs her eyes and I hope that she manages to make it through her food before she falls asleep.

Max and I have some soup whilst Sasha eats, and we've just about finished when she throws the last of her peach slices on the floor and yawns with her whole mouth wide open.

'Ooh, someone's sleepy,' I say to her. 'Is it nap time?'

Max looks down at his list. 'But it's fifteen minutes early.'

'Ah, yes, but you can't mess with sleepiness. If she goes past this, she'll get over-tired. And, believe me, you don't want to meet her when she's cranky.'

'OK, got it,' he says, standing up. He washes her face with the flannel that I had put on the table ready to use and then unclips her. 'I'll put her down. Does she just sleep in this?'

I'm too stunned to reply at first. Before the memory loss Max never volunteered to take her up. I guess I've always done it or he just assumes I'll asks him if I want him to do it. 'Um, yeah, you can just slip off the dungarees but keep on the bodysuit. Also, you need to check the nappy to make sure it's dry.'

'OK, dungarees off, fresh nappy, and then I put her in the sleeping bag?'

'Uh-huh, and flick the monitor on.'

'OK, got it,' he says.

I can't help tiptoeing to the door and listening in on Max and Sasha as they babble and giggle at each other while going up the stairs.

I tidy away the plates from lunch, stacking them in the dishwasher. Before I tidy up the rest of the worktops. I'm clearing away some of our post off the side when I spot a loose photo. It's from the stack I'd been showing Max earlier, only it must have dropped out before I showed it to him, as I haven't seen it for ages. It's of us at Comic Con the year after we got together. I pick it up, but before I get a chance to properly study it, my phone rings with a video call from my mum.

'Hey, Mum,' I answer, relieved this time that it's not all pixelated.

'Oh, darling, it's so wonderful to see you. Although I'd much rather see my gorgeous granddaughter.'

'Max is just putting her down for a nap.'

'Oh, missed her again, but that video you sent me yesterday was adorable. So, how are you?'

'Good, good,' I lie, resisting the urge to cry and tell her everything. 'Where are you now?'

'We're just off Guadeloupe,' she says, playing some imaginary maracas. 'It's stunning, absolutely stunning and the food…'

She smacks her lips together and groans.

'Where's Dad?'

'Oh, he's gone to some talk on astronomy,' she says, pretending to yawn. 'He's in his element with the guest speakers. I barely see him.'

I laugh; that sounds like Dad. More than anything do I wish that they were here now.

'Sasha was out like a light before I changed her— Oh, sorry,' says Max, wincing as he's sees that I'm video chatting. 'I'll go,' he mouths.

'Is that my favourite son-in-law?' she says, looking behind me like she's trying to see round my kitchen.

'Uh-huh, he's also your only son-in-law.'

She bats a hand away. She absolutely adores Max.

Max peeks nervously over my shoulder and holds his hand up in a wave.

'Hello, Mrs Smith,' he says.

I wince. I guess that's who she is to him, as he only knows her from when we were kids.

'Oh, Mr Voss, when did we get all formal?'

Max panics and looks at me and I hastily scribble on a pad in front of me: *Don't say anything about your memory – she doesn't know!!!*

'Ha ha, just trying to be funny,' he says, eventually answering her.

'Always a kidder, I just wish I could pinch your cheeks,' she says, leaning forward, doing the action to the screen.

Max laughs along but looks a little terrified.

'You'll be home soon and then you can,' he says with some canned laughter.

My mum beams back.

'Yes, only another four weeks to go. That's if I can fit on

the plane home; I'm going to be the size of a house with all this food I'm eating.'

My mum turns her head to the side and I know what she's waiting for. I quickly scrawl:

Pay her a compliment!!!

'Oh, um, I like your top,' he says. 'Brings out the colour of your eyes.'

'Max, you're such a darling.'

'I think that's Sasha crying? Max, can you?'

He looks a little confused at first, but then I put my hand out of the screen shot and point towards the door.

'Oh yes, sorry about that... Mrs... um, speak soon.'

He turns and runs out of the kitchen.

'Was he OK?' says Mum. 'He didn't quite seem himself. And it's Friday? What's he doing at home?'

My mum has a sixth sense about these things.

'Oh, he's fine. Just tired; he's been working hard on a project. Thought he'd make a long weekend of it.'

'Right, you'd tell me if there was anything wrong, wouldn't you?'

'Of course. He's fine, really. Listen, I can still hear Sasha. I might have to go and give him a hand – can I call you back later today or perhaps tomorrow.?'

'Yes, no problem. I'll be lying by the pool all day today but then we're ashore for the next two.'

'OK, I'll phone soon. Love you and love to Dad.'

My mum blows a theatrical kiss just as I hang up and it pauses her mid 'mwah' for a second whilst it shuts down.

'The coast is clear,' I say, and Max comes back in from the hallway. 'Sorry about all that.'

'That's OK. Your mum is a little bit…'

'Over the top? Yeah, she's always been one to play to the cameras. You do this whole sucking up thing to my mum and she laps it up. I should have warned you but with her away on holiday…'

'I understand. How come you haven't told her?'

I shrug my shoulders. 'I don't know. I worry that she'd cut her holiday short and come back to help out and there's not a lot she can do.'

'I guess I can understand that. My dad cut *his* short and I feel a bit guilty.'

'Hmm,' I say, picking up the photo.

'What's that,' he says, peering over my shoulder.

'Oh, I think it must have fallen out of that box of photos I showed you yesterday.'

I hand it over to him.

'Is that you in a wig?' he says, squinting at the photo. 'Why are you dressed like a slutty policewoman?'

'I was being Amy Pond from *Doctor Who*.'

He looks at me blankly just like he had when I'd first dressed in the outfit.

'She was a kissagram dressed in that outfit when she met the Doctor. Or at least re-met the Doctor – long story – you'd have to watch the series.'

'Any particular reason for the costume? Or is that a regular thing for us? Dressing up, pretending we're other people. You know there was that thing in Mum's kitchen, and I read those messages about a caterpillar costume.'

My cheeks flush.

'No, we're not into that. The thing in the kitchen, well, that

173

was related to an article that I'd read… and the caterpillar costume was um, from Sasha's birthday, and in that photo we were off to Comic Con.'

'I went to a Comic Con?' he says, frowning. 'Isn't that where everyone dresses up?'

'Uh-huh, it's amazing,' I say.

'I didn't dress up, I take it,' he says, studying himself.

'Well, I told everyone you were dressed as Rory, who was an assistant along with Amy Pond, but only because he always wore a shirt and jeans, which is what you were wearing.'

'I look terrified,' he says with a little laugh.

'Oh, you do, actually. I'd never noticed. I remember you being a tad uncomfortable. I mean, it was a bit out of your comfort zone.'

'Have I got better at going?' he asks.

'We've not been since. You booked a trip to Seville for us the year after so I couldn't go. Then the year after I didn't want to leave Sasha as she was only small, and then this year, well, it's in a few weeks but I hadn't even thought about it.'

'You look so happy,' he says.

'I was. There's something about going to them; it's like I've found my mothership.'

'You haven't changed at all, you're still such a geek,' he says, and he laughs.

I know he didn't mean anything by it, but it stabs at my heart. He still sees me as Rach's nerdy friend.

'Hey, um, do you think we could ask your parents if they could babysit Sasha tomorrow night?' I say, more desperate than ever to get our romantic connection back on track.

'I guess so. They offered, right?'

'Yeah.'

'What did you want to do?'

'I think we should go out, just the two of us.'

'OK,' he says.

'No, I mean we should go *out*, just the two of us on a...' I hesitate before plucking up the courage to say it. 'On a date, you know: a proper one.'

He looks at me and my heart starts to pound. I actually feel like I'm asking him out for the very first time. What if he says no? How awkward would that be?

'That would be nice,' he says.

'Nice,' I say, repeating it. Not quite what I was going for, but at least he's agreed.

'Where are we going to go?'

'I don't know,' I say, going through all the restaurants in Fleet until I think of the perfect one. 'La Flambé? It's the French place out in Church Crookham.'

'Oh yeah, Mum and Dad always rave about that place.'

I don't add that it's where we went on an early date when we both found ourselves visiting our parents in Fleet. It's the perfect way of kicking this re-dating into action.

I remember it as being the date that we first started to talk about our future plans and when we both acknowledged that we were in a relationship. I just need to keep my fingers crossed that it works out better than the beer pong fiasco.

Chapter 13

I kiss Sasha's head and, taking one last look at her sleeping form, I creep away from her room. I know I'm supposed to leave her to settle herself to sleep but I can't help it. It's my favourite time of the day when we're all snuggled up together. Especially as I know that when the new baby comes, I won't have as much time for this.

I creep along the hallway, and back down the stairs. Mick and Judy have come over to babysit Sasha. I think Judy wanted some alone time, but Mick is taking the whole charade very seriously and he's come along to keep her company. I can hear them laughing with Max in the kitchen and, as I get closer to them, it doesn't take me long to pick up on the story that they're telling. It's a famous one in the Voss family. The time that Max and Rachel got stuck in the apple tree in Nasty Nigel's garden. They're so engrossed in it that they don't notice that I've walked in. It seems so strange to see Judy and Mick united in their tears of laughter as they chip in with elements of the story.

'And then when Nigel came out of his house with his rolled-up newspaper, that look of horror on Rach's face before she jumped down,' says Max, his eyes creasing as he laughs.

'That was nothing compared to the look on your mum's face when she heard that blood-curdling scream. Then the two of you appeared through that hedge with scratches and trailing half the garden with you and Rach flashing her bright-pink pants.'

'I could have died,' Judy says, laughing and wiping away a tear, and Mick smiles at her warmly. 'Ah, Ellie, I didn't see you there, love,' she says, standing up and coming over. 'You look nice,' she says, spinning me round slightly, making the skirt of my maternity dress swish. 'That's a lovely dress. Is it new?'

'No, I bought it when I was pregnant with Sasha.' It's understated in the sense that it's a sleeveless, turtleneck dress that brushes my calves, but there's something sexy in the way that the fabric clings to the body and gives me more of a defined shape than the rest of my flowy maternity gear.

'It really suits you. Sasha fast asleep?' she asks.

'Yes, out like a light. Max wore her out this afternoon at the park.'

I'm still in shock that he suggested taking her to the park all by himself so that I could have some time to 'chill out and relax', another thing that Max wouldn't normally think to do off his own back.

'Lovely, hopefully she'll stay that way,' she says.

'Yes, hopefully, we won't come back to find her watching *Peppa Pig* tonight,' I say, looking at Mick who gives me a sheepish grin. 'We should probably get going.'

'I'll go and get my shoes,' says Max, standing up.

He walks past me and I miss that once upon a time he would have trailed his fingers across my waist as he went.

'Things seem to be going well between you two,' says Judy, leaning towards me like she's settling in for a gossip.

'Yeah, since we had our trip to London, things have definitely got better. He's taken more of an interest in our life and trying really hard to learn Sasha's routine,' I say, trying to sound positive.

'And you're going out for a meal tonight?' she says, encouraging me along.

'Yeah, it's a step in the right direction,' I say.

'Where are you headed?' asks Mick.

'La Flambé,' I say, and Judy winces.

'Really, you didn't want to go to El Costellos or The Exchequer?' she says, tilting her head to the side.

'I thought of it, but Max and I had one of our first dates at La Flambé when we were both in Fleet.'

'Oh, I remember that,' says Judy. 'He went out for a mysterious dinner and we didn't find out until a couple of months later that it was with you. But you know, the other restaurants might be a better choice.'

'I like the idea of you going somewhere you've been before,' says Mick, with a twinkle in his eye. 'Stir up a little of that old magic.'

'Steady on, Mick, you're coming across as an old romantic,' says Judy.

'I've always been romantic,' he says, sighing.

She scoffs and the easy-going atmosphere between the two of them ebbs away.

Max reappears. 'Right, I'm ready.'

'You're going to love Le Flambé, one of our favourites, eh Judy?' says Mick.

She doesn't look so sure but she nods along anyway.

'Shall we?' says Max.

'I guess. Are you sure you're going to be OK?'

'We'll be fine,' says Judy, ushering us out the door.

The short drive to the restaurant is filled with Max asking me questions about our first trip here and by the time we arrive I've been properly interrogated about it.

'I think this place has changed hands since we last came, but it's still French,' I say as we pull in, keeping everything crossed that it hasn't changed dramatically like the mini-golf.

'Is it open?' asks Max as I park in the empty car park.

'Yeah, I phoned to book a table this afternoon. Strange, you'd think on a Saturday night it would be heaving.'

We get out the car and walk through the door, relieved to see another couple a bit older than us sat at a table in the corner. I begin to relax.

The interior hasn't changed since we were last here. It's still got the red net curtains hanging in the windows and the wine bottles encrusted with wax used as candle holders on the table.

A waitress who looks like she's in her late teens breezes up to us with an air of confidence that I certainly never had at her age or, perhaps, any age. She's dressed in skinny black jeans, a floaty white blouse and a black waistcoat with her hair plaited to one side and she's wearing bright-red lipstick.

'Can I help?' she says in a heavy French accent, almost shouting over the loud accordion music that's being piped out of the speakers.

'We've got a table booked for two, under the name of Voss.'

'Voss, very good,' she says.

She looks around the almost empty restaurant and puts us at the table next to the other couple.

'Is it possible to sit somewhere else?' I say, gesturing to the empty restaurant.

'But this is the best table,' she says, lowering her voice so that the other couple don't hear.

'OK, then,' says Max, taking the menu and sitting down.

'Chef's recommendations today are the boeuf bourguignon and the fish of the day is cod. Would you like a drink, some wine?' she says, looking at me.

'I'm not drinking, because of the baby,' I say, patting my belly.

She looks down at the bump.

'But you can have one glass, surely?'

'I think I'll just stick to fizzy water, thanks.'

'And I'll just have a large beer, thanks,' says Max.

She nods curtly and walks off.

'Why are French women so intimidating?' says Max, peering over the top of his menu.

'I know, and they're so glamorous too.'

'So are you, in your dress,' he says, not looking up from his menu. 'You know, it's brave to wear a dress with a rollneck like that. Let's not forget the last time I saw you in a top with one.'

'Yeah, yeah,' I say, cringing at the thought. The night he'd pulled the tissue paper out of my bra when we were teenagers, I'd been wearing a rollneck cropped top. I'd felt self-conscious enough with my belly on display and the tissue paper in my bra, but then Max had told me that girls only wore those tops so they could hide love bites. I'd spent the whole night avoiding any boy that came near me, worried I was giving out some kind of secret signal. 'You know, someone once told me that girls only wear them for one reason.'

'Oh yeah,' he says, unable to hide his smile. 'I remember that. I don't think I've given anyone a love bite since I was about that age. Oh God, don't tell me that you're going to correct me?'

I shake my head.

'I've never had one.'

'Really?' he says. 'Not even when you went to Sixth Form?'

'Nope,' I say, not sure if I've really missed out from not having that teenage rite of passage. 'I'm sure you won't be surprised to hear that not many boys kissed me in Sixth Form.'

'Why wouldn't I be surprised?'

'Come on, the whole Spider thing? Max, you keep saying it yourself that you find it hard to see me as anyone other than who I was when I was younger.'

What am I doing? This is supposed to be a date where I try and convince him to see me as something other than that teenage girl and I'm *reminding* him of it?

'Yeah, but that doesn't mean to say that I didn't think you were pretty,' he says.

'Max, you don't have to say things like that. Cara Worthington said the other day that they voted you Most Fuckable 1997; you and I were in different leagues then.'

He laughs out loud. 'God, I'd forgotten that.'

'You knew?'

'Oh yeah. I think they even gave me an award that someone had made in woodwork. I wonder if Mum's still got it in the loft.'

I shake my head.

'You know what I was voted in our school leavers' book? Most Likely to Do Your Tax Return.'

Max laughs again. 'Just because you were good at maths doesn't mean to say that guys didn't find you attractive. You remember your leavers' ball when you and Rach were having your photos taken in our garden? You were wearing that long backless black dress?'

'Oh, that dress. I had to wear stick-on bra pads and I spent the whole night terrified they were going to fall off.'

'Well, you didn't look terrified in the garden. You were posing and laughing with Rach and you looked hot in it. And I remember thinking that you'd finally realised that you were pretty.'

'What?' I say. 'You've never told me this before.'

'Have I not? Huh.'

I can't quite believe it. In all these years I never thought he'd once thought that about me when we were younger.

'You've always been pretty, you were just a massive nerd,' he says with a genuine smile.

'Hey,' I say as if to protest, but I've got no leg to stand on. 'Just because we liked different things.'

'You dressed with a long, knitted scarf round your neck for an entire year after you and Rach watched all those *Dr Who* boxsets.'

'Oh my God,' I say, thinking about how much I loved my younger self for not giving a shit. 'I'd forgotten about that.'

'I bet you still watch the new *Dr Who*?'

'Of course I do. But I've never been able to get you to watch it.'

My neck starts to tingle and I become increasingly aware of how close the couple next to us are. I sense I'm being watched and I glance at their table and they're both staring at me. They turn back to each other quickly, but they still don't talk.

'Didn't they just get a new Doctor? The guy from *The Thick of It*?' says Max, bringing me back to our conversation.

'Oh, Peter Capaldi, yeah. But now they've got a woman playing the first female Doctor and it caused a lot of controversy.'

The man at the table next to us does a huffing sound and I turn and glare at him before he looks back at his companion.

'Why would that cause controversy?'

'I don't know, because some people are big supporters of the patriarchy,' I say loudly.

'So is *Dr Who* still your favourite programme?'

'No, that's reserved for *Dark Energy* – it was probably on TV just before you lost your memory, but you didn't watch it.'

I'm about to launch into the premise of the show but I stop myself. I can't keep reminding him of how little I've changed since I was teenager.

The waitress unceremoniously plonks our drinks down on the table before wiping her wet hands on the apron that's appeared around her waist.

'Have you chosen what you want?' she says, her accent appearing stronger.

'Actually, we haven't really looked at the menu yet,' I say with an apologetic wince.

She tuts and turns on her heel.

'Did she just tut?' I say, looking at Max for clarification.

'Uh-huh. It's not like she's rushed off her feet. You'd think that we'd be doing her a favour giving her something to do.' He pulls a face. 'Right then, I guess I'd better look. What did you say I went for last time? Steak frites?'

'It's always a classic,' I nod. 'I think I had the mussels and they were surprisingly good, but I'm not supposed to have shellfish, so I might go for the bourguignon. It's the closest I can get to wine for the moment.'

'Do you miss it?'

I look at the bottle of red on the table next to us.

'I do and I don't. Sometimes more out of habit than anything, if everyone else has got a glass, but I guess we haven't really been on the booze much since having Sasha.'

Max sips his beer.

'I think after Wednesday's escapades, and how rough I've felt since, that's probably not a bad thing.'

The waitress is back and she's tapping her neat little shoes and arching an eyebrow to the sky.

'I'd like the *chèvre chaud pour l'entree et le steak frites pour* the main, *s'il vous plait*,' says Max in clunky Franglais. The waitress doesn't look impressed at his attempted effort.

'How would you like your steak cooked?'

'Medium-rare,' says Max, closing his menu.

'And I'll just have the beef bourguignon, no starter.'

The waitress snatches the menus back and hurries off.

'Service with a smile, huh?' says Max.

'I know, and after you went to such lengths to practise your French. You usually just stick to "can I have a beer, please."'

'Always the first thing you should master in any language.'

'Obviously,' I say, sipping my fizzy water. A noisy jingle sounds from the door and another couple walks in, doing a double take when they see how empty it is. The waitress walks over, grabbing the same menus that we had, and starts heading in our direction. She points at the table next to us.

'For fuck's sake,' I mutter under my breath. All I wanted

was one romantic evening, just the two of us, not six of us all cosied up.

Max looks up and the woman from the couple smiles as she sits down.

'Cosy, huh,' she says, beaming back.

The waitress hands them their menus and slouches off.

'It's our anniversary,' says the woman.

'Nine years,' says her husband, beaming like his wife.

'How about you?' asks the woman as she puts her napkin on her lap.

'It's our anniversary too,' says Max, and the couple's faces light up.

'How long?'

'One week,' says Max with a smile.

I laugh into my fizzy water that I pretend to sip.

'To this time last week, then,' she says, obviously thinking that Max is joking.

'This time last week I was in A&E,' he says.

'Long story,' I say, turning back to Max. This is not quite what I had in mind for our evening. I think ahead to the next date that I've thought about organising. I can't keep leaving Sasha with Judy and Mick, so next time I'm going to bring her along. 'I spoke to Rach today about the festival she and Gaby are off to next week; we'd been talking about going with them.'

That's not a total lie; whilst Max was leaning towards a no, on the day of his memory loss he'd said that we'd chat to Rach about it.

'We just love festivals,' says the woman, overhearing. 'Don't we, Howard? We went to Glastonbury this year for third time!'

'Wonderful,' I say, turning and pulling my best-good-for-you-but-please-stay-out-of-our-conversation face. I feel terrible as usually I'm quite friendly, but tonight I just want it to be all about Max and me. Luckily, the waitress goes over to their table and they start chatting to her.

'A festival,' says Max. 'What, like in a tent?'

'Uh-huh,' I say. 'And it's family-friendly so we can take Sasha.'

'To a festival? In a tent?'

'Uh-huh.' This was where I started to lose Max originally. 'I was thinking of inviting Owen and Claire.'

'That would be good. Daniel thought it would be good to keep seeing friends, to fill in the gaps of my missing year.'

It takes me a second to remember that Daniel is the psychotherapist.

'Great, that's settled then. So, what's all this about the missing year?'

'Hmm, well, you've done a great job for the last four, but it would be good to find out more about that first year. Did I ever talk about it with you?'

I can't obviously tell him about his parents; it's not my place.

'A little. You had another girlfriend before me – well, quite a bit before me, as in I wasn't a rebound, or anything,' I say, hating myself for feeling the need to clarify it as now it makes it sound like I was.

'Right,' he says. 'Was I with her long?'

'I think you were only together a few months before she moved abroad.'

'Well, maybe I should talk to her; she might be able to help fill in some blanks.'

'I don't know all the details but I got the impression that you didn't keep in touch.'

'So, it ended badly then?' he says, wincing.

'You never really told me about her, so I don't know. Perhaps Owen might know more,' I say with a shrug.

'That's a good idea. I'd like to get a full picture of what happened.'

I try not to laugh. It'll be Owen's turn for an interrogation soon.

'Of course, the more you know, the more you might remember.'

'Exactly. Right, I'll ask him. It would be good to see him and Claire anyway. Even if it is weird seeing him with someone other than Sarah.'

'I know, I thought that too, even though I really like Claire.'

'Yeah, she seemed really nice. But Sarah's become a mate over the years. Do we still see her?'

'I still message her occasionally, but we haven't had her down to the new house yet. I think you feel disloyal to Owen or something.'

'It's always tricky when people break up.'

The chatty couple next to us start howling with laughter with the waitress, and it makes me wonder why she's such fun with them and so cold with us.

'So, you said on the way that last time we ate here we talked a lot about what we wanted in the future,' says Max.

'Yes.' I nod and brace myself for further interrogation. 'We were at that corny stage of dating; you know we'd already found out lots about each other and were talking more about hopes and dreams. Where we thought you'd be in five years' time, you know, that kind of thing.'

I reach forward and take a sip from my glass of water.

'And I'm guessing you didn't see yourself in five years' time being married to someone who couldn't remember you.'

'Ha, no, funnily enough. Even in my wildest of dreams that night I'd never imagined it would work out between us the way it has and that we'd end up married.'

'Really?'

'Yeah, I guess it took me some time to believe it would work out. You know that I had a bit of a crush on you when we were at school.' He looks a little sheepish. 'Don't worry, you've told me before that you knew.'

'It was quite obvious sometimes,' he says, smiling.

'Yeah, yeah,' I say, thinking of the times that I'd suddenly need to 'go to the toilet' just as he was leaving the bathroom after a shower, so that I could see him for a split second in just a towel, or sometimes I'd like to go into the steamed-up room after him and deeply inhale the smell of his Lynx bodywash. I cringe; teenage crushes were brutal.

'But that doesn't explain why you thought it wouldn't work out?'

'I guess I couldn't believe that you would actually choose to go out with me.'

'And I take it that wore off pretty quickly when you realised I was all smoke and mirrors,' he says, laughing.

I laugh along even though sometimes I'm still pinching myself when I think that I'm with Max Voss.

'So where did you say you'd see yourself in five years' time?' he asks.

'I think I said something clichéd like taking a sabbatical and travelling around the world.'

'Did you ever do a gap year?'

'No, I went straight to uni thinking I'd do one afterwards and then I ended up getting onto a graduate scheme and didn't quite have the chance. I wish I had, though, looking back now. It's hard when you're young, isn't it? You think to yourself that you have your whole life stretched out in front of you, but you don't realise how quickly it can start to slip through your fingers the more the years tick by.'

'Yeah, my years are racing by. Five years literally flew by in what felt like a minute.'

I laugh.

'But we're not that old now, are we?' says Max.

'OK, maybe not old, but we have responsibilities. We've both got our jobs, we've got our mortgage, a child, a baby on the way. That ship has well and truly sailed.'

I take another sip of my drink.

'Sorry, this isn't what you want to hear, is it? I'm supposed to be selling you our life.'

'I get it,' he says. 'I probably should have taken a gap year too. I was supposed to. Owen and I were going to go after uni, but then he met Sarah and I didn't fancy going on my own.'

I smile weakly at him.

'You already know this,' he says, shaking his head.

'That's the problem, isn't it, when you know each other so well?' says the woman, leaning across to us. I look at her in horror. 'We're the same. I tell the same jokes and stories over and over, and this one just laps them up.'

Her husband shrugs. 'I do the same.'

I smile back at them and raise my eyebrows.

Although not as cataclysmic as the beer pong date, it's still not going great. What with my constant reminders to Max of my teenage self, and being sandwiched between the polar opposite of couples who are both eavesdropping far too much.

The waitress plonks down a plate in front of Max.

'*Buon appetito*,' she says before hurrying away.

'Isn't that Italian?' Max says to me, but I hardly think that's the thing to be focusing on. I'm too busy staring at his limp leaf of iceberg lettuce with a sliver of tomato and a piece of goat's cheese on a thin slice of toasted baguette.

'Well, this looks, um…' says Max, poking it carefully with a fork.

'At least the goat's cheese looks nice and runny,' I say, marvelling at its gooeyness.

'Bloody hell, it's like lava,' he says, draining his beer. 'It's been microwaved to oblivion.'

He picks around at it and does a better job than I would at trying to eat it.

'Did you want some?' he says, proffering a fork.

I recoil from it and wrinkle my nose.

'I can't have soft cheese because I'm pregnant.'

'Ah, right. I wish I was so lucky,' he says, putting his fork down and admitting defeat. 'I'm slightly worried about the main course now.'

'Hmm, me too. The food was really good last time we came.'

I look out of the corner of my eye and the silent couple actually meet each other's gaze for a split second before she picks a piece of cut baguette out of a bowl and starts to pick at the crust round the outside.

'Perhaps I should have looked on Tripadvisor before we came,' I say, looking round the rest of the restaurant. We're still the only three couples in the restaurant.

'But Dad said it was good, and he should know. I bet him and Mum eat here all the time.'

Luckily our friendly waitress comes back and interrupts us before I have to correct him. She picks up Max's starter before she arrives mere seconds later with two steaming hot plates.

'Very hot,' she says, sliding them perilously across the table and stopping them with her grubby tea towel. 'Enjoy!'

She makes it sound like it's a challenge rather than a pleasantry.

'So, this looks marginally better,' says Max, stabbing at the steak on his plate.

'And mine smells nice,' I say, breathing in the winey smells. 'If it tastes bad, I'll just sit here smelling it instead. It's the closest I've been to wine in months.'

'You know, in that case we could have had a very cheap date. We could have sat at home and I could have let you sniff my wine glass.'

'Now there's an offer,' I say, starting to laugh. 'Of all the things you've offered me over the years, you've never offered for me to sniff your wine.'

'What else have I offered you to sniff?'

The woman to the left of me leans over. 'Oh, is that the bourguignon. That's what I'm going for too. Smells delicious.'

'Sure is,' I say, wishing she'd leave us alone.

I put a little in my mouth so then I won't have to talk.

'Fuck me, that's hot,' I say, spitting it into my hand and throwing it onto my napkin. The woman looks shocked, and I give her a thumbs-up. 'Give it time to cool down first.'

The food-spitting seems to have done the trick to get rid of her and she turns back to her husband and starts talking to him.

'Was it at least good?' asks Max.

I pick up my water and it fizzes on my burnt tongue.

'I'm not sure, I think I burnt off my taste buds.'

Max laughs a little. After my experience he waits to try his steak.

The waitress goes over to the table next to ours and picks up their plates.

'Would you like to see the dessert menus?'

'Why not? That was delicious, thank you.'

I don't know what I'm more shocked about, the fact that the woman could speak or that the waitress didn't have a hint of a French accent this time.

'Did you hear the waitress?' I whisper at Max.

'Yes, she lost her accent.'

We both peer at her, and now we're the ones that are guilty of eavesdropping.

I turn back to my food and it's getting even more unappetising by the minute. It's formed into a congealed heap on the plate. The wine smell has worn off and now I don't even want to sniff it.

'How's your steak?'

'It tastes like a shoe,' he says, chewing and pulling a face. 'What about yours?'

I take a bite and at least the meat is tender.

'I've eaten worse.'

'Glowing recommendation,' says Max with a laugh.

We eat as little as we can politely get away with. Max hides a big piece of fatty steak under a lettuce leaf, and I manage to heap all my uneaten rubbery mushrooms into one corner of the bowl.

The waitress makes a beeline for our plates when she thinks we've finished.

'Dessert?' she asks.

'No,' we both say quickly.

'Just the bill, thanks,' says Max.

'Sure,' she says with the accent that sounds more Spanish this time.

'Not feeling well?' says the chatty woman. 'Is it the baby? I had terrible heartburn at the latter stages.'

'Hmm,' I say, 'something like that.'

The waitress appears with the bill and I don't even look at it before I hand her my card.

'Enjoy the rest of your evening,' says Max to them as he ushers me past the empty tables and out the door.

'Well,' says Max, 'I take it that was not what happened when we went last time.'

'No, it wasn't,' I say, shaking my head. It couldn't have been further from what I planned.

'When they put that second couple next to us—' he says, starting to laugh.

'And that waitress with the fake accent. What was that about—' I join in, and the two of us laugh even harder.

'Oh,' I say with a big sigh. 'It wasn't supposed to be funny.'

A tear trickles down my cheek and I can feel more going to follow.

'Hey, hey,' says Max, putting his arm around me and patting me on the shoulder. 'What's going on? It was a funny evening and some dodgy food.'

'Bloody hormones. It's just, this was supposed to be a proper date,' I say, wiping the rogue tears away.

'Well, it was certainly a memorable one.'

I groan again.

'For all the wrong reasons. Every time we go out and try and recreate one of our dates it goes horribly wrong.'

'What do you mean, recreate our dates?'

Shit. I wasn't meant to say that.

'Ellie?' he says with an almost amused grin on his face and it only makes me feel even more ridiculous. 'Is that why we came here, because you were trying to recreate what happened last time? Is that why you got so mad when the mini-golf was out of action?'

He runs his hand through his hair.

'Ah, Ellie, you're trying to jog my memory. Did you think that if we had a similar evening, that it might fall back into place?'

'Yes,' I say a little too quickly. I'd rather let him think that than what I was really trying to do – to make him fall in love with me again. 'Yes, I was totally trying to jog your memory.'

'Maybe if they'd been that disastrous originally, it might have done it,' he says with a smile. 'Look, it's still early, shall we go for a drink? Is The Five Bells still going?'

'I don't know, I don't think I've ever been there.'

'Not even when you were a teenager? It was the only place that used to serve you – no questions asked.'

I shake my head.

'You and Rach, you two were such goody-goodies.'

'We couldn't all be rebels burning down summer houses with our spliffs,' I say with a wink.

His face creases up. 'Something tells me that I told you the real story behind that, didn't I?'

'I can see why you changed it. Burning a love letter in a bin doesn't do as much for your street cred,' I say giggling. 'You've got to be the only person in the world who'd pretend to their parents that they were doing drugs.'

'I know, I felt like I needed to protect my bad-boy reputation. But I was nothing like that, though, not really. People saw what they wanted to see at school, didn't they? We never really made an effort to get to know the real person under the label.'

'Try being labelled a geek.'

'Yeah, I can imagine it was rough, but it wasn't easy being…'

'Most Fuckable 1997.'

Max laughs. 'OK, you win. But I've learnt over the last week that you're different to how I thought you'd be.'

Does that mean that he's stopped seeing me as Rach's geeky friend?

'Let's give The Five Bells a go,' says Max, and he puts his hand on the small of my back and guides me towards the car.

Whilst the whole recreating dates thing isn't exactly going to plan, Max and I are edging ever closer to one another, even if it feels like it's at the speed that continents move.

Chapter 14

It's not only Max and his lack of memory that have been keeping me busy in my maternity leave, but my new mummy friends too. Especially with their worrying about the impending birth of their watermelons – it turns out that string exercise we did in the first class has been giving Helen and Polly nightmares and, short of me exposing my lady bits to them, it's hard to reassure them that it's going to be OK. Of course, Anneka isn't worried as she's having an elective C-section. Instead she's channelling her worry into whether or not her little one will get into the highly exclusive nursery that they're on the waiting list for.

Even though I'm the only one officially on maternity leave – thanks to Anneka not working, Helen using up her flexi-time and Polly taking an early lunch – we've managed to meet up for a mid-morning Monday coffee in the café in the arts centre.

'I just keep looking at Toby's head and I'm sure it's abnormally big. Maybe it's just that his hairline's receding and it's deceptive, but still,' says Helen, putting her card back in her wallet. 'I'm thinking of taking some selfies just to remember the old girl by, as I can't see how she's ever going to be the same again.'

I pat Helen on the arm and laugh.

'Just spare a thought for what's going to happen to Ellie's after having two,' says Anneka.

'Hmm, thanks for that,' I say, thinking it's the least of my worries. 'Don't forget that our lovely husbands will be at our side with their demands for an extra stitch.'

'That bloody extra stitch. If Toby so much as opens his mouth to make that joke that's where that extra stitch is bloody going.'

Anneka picks up her drink from the end of the counter and turns to us before she goes to get us a table.

'Just think, this is the first of many coffee mornings, ladies,' she says, tutting at another couple of women who were making a beeline for the sofas in the corner. She pushes her bump out and gives them a look and they wisely choose another table.

'Yes, but I'm guessing that the "many more" won't be this relaxing,' says Helen. 'And this will probably be one of the last times we're going to be able to have conversations where we can all follow what's going on.'

'Come on, it's not going to be that bad,' says Polly with a laugh. 'Is it?'

Helen raises an eyebrow. 'I can count on one hand the number of serious conversations I've had with most of my girlfriends since they've had kids. In those first few years they're always so exhausted or distracted. Oh, no offence, Ellie.'

'None taken. You're right, it's a struggle to do anything when Sasha's around and when she's not I'm usually mentally drained from running around after her or working. But that's the bonus of Max being signed off work – I get to swan off and leave Sasha with him when I'm meeting you guys. And the best part about it all is that he's not even complaining, because he thinks that he does it all the time when he's not at work – when usually he'd nip out for a run or a cycle by himself instead. That's why I suggested meeting here because he's taken her to the library for Rhyme Time.'

The arts centre also houses the town library. It's the first time that Max's taken Sasha out on his own, other than to the park, and I wanted to be close by just in case.

'Ah, that's really sweet. I hope that Jason does that with our little one,' says Polly.

'I'm not going to be letting George swan off to Rhyme Time, all those yummy mummies there,' says Anneka with a scowl on her face.

'Spoken from a woman who's obviously never been. It's a savage experience: trying to make it there in time before the room fills up, trying to find a spot where you're not sitting on the floor like a school assembly, then for the duration of the class you not only have to sing but also wrangle your baby so that he or she doesn't try to scramble over all the other babies, scream, cry, poo or vomit.'

'So, I take it that won't be in our weekly routine,' says Helen.

'Oh no, it's actually very good for the kids and it's free. I was just trying to make the point that the other mums probably would be too busy to hit on a rogue dad.'

'You'd be surprised,' says Anneka, pursing her lips.

Polly sighs. 'This whole motherhood thing sounds like a never-ending minefield, and I thought sleep deprivation would be the worst bit.'

'On that matter I have something for you all,' says Anneka,

digging into her bag and handing us all copies of a book. 'I figured that if we all read it and got our babies on the same schedule, it would make our lives so much easier.'

I take a look at the book and my heart sinks. I read this one when Sasha was a baby and I cried as much as her trying to follow its strict rules.

'That's really kind of you, thank you,' I say diplomatically. 'Buying us all a book.'

'My friend owns a bookshop,' she says, shrugging.

'Your friend isn't Jeff Bezos, is he?' says Helen.

'No, but I do have a friend who knows him. This is an actual bookshop and I try and buy books whenever I can.'

'Oh good, you're doing it to be nice and therefore I don't have to feel guilty when I don't read it.' Helen puts it down on the table.

'Is this the one where we have to leave the baby to cry?' says Polly, wincing. 'I'm not sure I would be very good at that. I read a book last month that was a bit... gentler.'

'I'm sure that was a very good book, but you've got to take into consideration the schedule,' says Anneka.

'But that one *was* all about the schedule,' says Polly, holding her ground. 'It's just the baby sets it.'

'I'm not talking about the baby's, I'm talking about your social schedule,' says Anneka. 'You don't want to be stuck on the sofa feeding for the whole year when there are so many things to do? I've scoured a five-mile radius for baby activities that we can do and I'm just making up a draft timetable.'

'A draft timetable?' I say, starting to feel anxious.

'Oh yes, there's baby sensory, baby yoga, baby massage, Rhyme Time, Bach for babies, although that clashes with baby massage so that's going to be an issue, but then again Rhyme Time could be their source of music, so maybe it wouldn't be that bad. I've also found a French class, as it's so important for them to learn as many languages as they can at an early age.'

'Hmm, I'm not sure that it's a rounded enough curriculum,' says Helen, taking the piss. 'Seriously, Anneka, I've spent the last twenty years of my life working. For the next year, I plan to do bugger all.'

Polly gives her a look.

'OK, so not quite bugger all; I do realise that I've got to keep a small human alive. But I've been adding things to my watch list on Netflix in preparation.'

Anneka turns to Helen with a shocked look on her face. 'But those first few months and years are so important to their whole development.'

'And I'll give her a history lesson while watching *The Crown* and she'll pick up Spanish from watching *Narcos*. I'll pop a bit of classical music on for us to nap to and voila.'

Anneka goes to speak when Helen holds her hands up.

'Don't worry, I'll still come out and meet you for coffee. But I'll not be doing any classes where I have to sing my name,' she says, and all of us but Anneka giggle. 'Now, the whole point of today is that we're supposed to be taking our mind off our babies with the giant heads and the impending demise of our vaginas, and we're supposed to be making the most of talking. So, shouldn't we be talking non-baby stuff?'

'Oh, we should,' says Polly, and all eyes fall on me. 'How's it going with Max? How was your date on Saturday? You were very vague in your messages. I take it it went well?'

'Yeah. I mean the restaurant was terrible, but the evening was… pleasant.'

'Where did you go?'

'La Flambé.'

There's a collective gasp from the table and Anneka looks like she's breaking out in a cold sweat.

'Why would you have ever gone there?' she says, wrinkling her nose up.

'We went a few years ago and it was good, and Max's dad was very insistent.'

'Max's dad who lives in Portugal?'

'Yes, I see the error of our ways.'

'It changed hands last year and it's gone massively downhill,' she says, shaking her head as if it should have been obvious. 'You should have asked us. We would have suggested The Exchequer or Mamma Mia in Hartley Witney.'

'That's where we went on Valentine's Day and how we ended up in this position,' says Helen, pointing to her bump.

'Have they still got that waitress at the Flambé who pretends to be French?' asks Polly with a laugh.

'Is she not French?' says Helen.

'No, she's born and bred in Fleet. Apparently, she does it to get better tips,' says Polly.

'I guess she'd need to do whatever she could to get tips there,' I say.

'But you said it was good for you and Max?' says Helen.

'Yes, unlike the beer pong debacle, we made a joke about how awful it was and I guess it was the first time he started to relax. We talked the whole time and it stopped feeling like an interrogation, which is what it's felt like since the incident.

'He even told me things that were really sweet, things from when we were teenagers that he'd never told me before.'

'That sounds like progress.'

'Yeah, it was. He's almost let his guard down in a way that he hasn't before. He thinks I know everything so he isn't holding back like he normally does.'

'Interesting,' says Polly. 'So why aren't you happier about it?'

'Because she didn't have sex,' says Helen, biting the head off a gingerbread man.

'How do you know?' says Polly.

'I can tell these things,' says Helen.

'Still watching *Magic Mike*?' I say to her.

'No, now I'm onto watching *Warrior* with Tom Hardy. He's shirtless a lot in that movie,' she says, practically drooling. 'I don't know what's wrong with Toby. Aren't men always moaning that their wives don't want sex and I'm offering it to him on a platter and he keeps turning me down and muttering about Sigourney Weaver and things poking out of my stomach.'

Anneka cringes and Polly giggles.

'That's not the reason I'm not happy, though,' I say. 'It's just that the whole thing was *nice*.'

'Isn't that a good thing?' asks Anneka, stirring her tea before chinking her spoon loudly on her cup.

'No,' say Polly and Helen simultaneously.

'You don't want a date to be *nice*,' says Polly.

'He told me I looked nice and it was lovely chatting. But there was something missing. I guess it was the flirtation. I mean, I don't know if he even fancies me any more.'

'What?' says Helen. 'He'd be nuts not to.'

'But that's the thing, isn't it? When we met I was all

athletic-looking with glossy hair that was all short and sleek and now it's all long and a bit frizzy at the ends and it's more mousy than glossy. I never seem to find the time to go to the hairdresser's like I did pre-Sasha,' I say, examining the split ends with my fingers.

'Don't be ridiculous,' says Helen. 'We're probably all a little guilty of not being the same women we were when we first met our significant other. Just like they're probably not the same men they were when we met them. I know Toby's not; he's lost most of the hair on that massive head of his and he's carrying a few kilos that he wasn't before. But I don't fancy him any less. I wish that *was* the bloody case as it would make the sex starvation easier to bear.'

Polly hands Helen her gingerbread man, recognising that she's in need.

'But that's the point though, isn't it? We grow with our partners, don't we? And it doesn't matter if you let yourself go a little when you're with them because by that point they should love you regardless. But with his memory loss Max only knows either seventeen-year-old me, which was pretty horrific, or me now, with my ginormous stomach, my cankles and my knickers that are so big that I'm worried they could eclipse the moon. And as much as I love the bump, I can't imagine that he's standing there thinking, Cor, I'd love a bit of that woman who's waddling like a whale.'

'You're hardly big, and it's his baby,' says Polly.

'Yes, but although I've told him that I don't think he really gets it. I mean it's an odd concept to get your head around when you don't remember having had sex with someone.'

'All roads lead to you two getting it on,' says Helen. 'Seems like it's the answer to everything.'

I half smile at her.

'Perhaps you need to nudge some intimacy along. Where are you going on your babymoon?' asks Anneka.

'You don't have a babymoon when you've already got another child at home.'

'Why not?' asks Helen.

'They're like an essential part of the pregnancy, just like your folic acid,' says Anneka.

I'm not going to point out how wrong that sentence was.

'George and I are off to Stratford-upon-Avon next week for ours,' she continues.

'Nice,' says Helen. 'Toby and I are going to London for the night to a spa. We'd originally booked it as a dirty weekend, but I think I've got no chance of that, so I booked prenatal spa appointments instead. If we can't get dirty, we might as well get clean. How about you, Polly?'

'We're going to Bristol for a friend's wedding in a few weeks so we're making a weekend of it.'

'See,' says Anneka. 'You've got to do one, Ellie.'

'What about Sasha?' I ask.

'I'm sure your mother-in-law would have Sasha,' says Helen, waving her hand to dismiss the problem.

'Is there anywhere that you could go that would bring back romantic memories for you?' asks Polly.

'Our best mini-break was when we went to Paris,' I say, my cheeks flushing at the memory. 'I know it's a big fat cliché but Max had gone for a conference and I'd flown over for the weekend last minute and it was so romantic.'

'I love Paris,' says Anneka. 'I've got many a happy memory there.'

'With George?'

'No,' she says, a twinkle in her eye. 'George doesn't really do short haul. He says it's a waste of effort to get to the airport only to arrive an hour or two later.'

I'm desperate to meet George. I'm building up the craziest impression of him from Anneka.

'You should definitely go to Paris,' says Helen. 'Everyone has sexy time in Paris. You can catch the Eurostar,' she says, 'avoid the whole doctor's-note-flying thing.'

'Much better for the environment anyway,' says Polly.

'But I don't know if it's a good idea going abroad so late in my pregnancy.'

'Why not?' says Anneka.

'What if I go into labour? Second ones aren't usually late.'

'They have hospitals there too. Just take your notes with you.'

'I couldn't give birth in a French hospital. All I can ask for in French is directions to the discotheque.'

'You're going to Paris, not deepest, darkest Peru. I'm sure you'd be able to find a doctor that would speak a little English and if not there's always Google Translate. Plus, you'd have a great birth story, wouldn't you?' says Anneka. 'Ooh and you could call them something really cute and French like Margot or Hugo.'

'You know – before we even get ahead of ourselves – the chances of you going into labour in the next couple of weeks are pretty slim,' says Helen. 'Just make sure you stay somewhere central so that you don't have to walk around too far.'

'Paris,' I say, thinking of the lazy afternoon Max and I spent sitting in the gardens of the Palace of Versailles in the spring. I've never been anywhere quite so beautiful or romantic. We were both lying down on the ground, me with my head propped against his chest, when he suddenly blurted out that he loved me for the first time. 'What if it ruins the memories we have of the city?'

'What if it doesn't?' says Polly. 'Think positive, remember?'

'Positive, right.'

'And, plus, before you go, I'll book you in with my hairdresser. She'll sort you out,' says Anneka. 'I'll text her now and see when we can arrange it. Are you free all week?'

'Well, I—'

'Perfect, leave it with me,' says Anneka.

'OK, thanks,' I say, not thinking I have much of a choice.

'I'll also send you a link to a very good lingerie company that specialises in maternity wear. I'll send it to you too, Helen,' she says, tapping away at her phone. 'You never know, it might just be the ticket for Toby.'

Helen picks her phone up straight away when it beeps.

'When's your next date?' asks Polly.

'We're going to a music festival.'

'A festival. What like one with camping?' says Anneka, wrinkling her nose.

'Yep. It's a family-friendly one, so we're taking Sasha and going with Max's sister Rach and his best friend Owen plus their respective girlfriends. Sasha's going to be so excited – Mr Tumble's going to be there.'

'Mr Who?' says Anneka.

'A man you are going to be well acquainted with by the end of next year.'

'Who's headlining for the grown-ups?' asks Helen.

'Pilot Dawn.'

'I'm so jealous,' says Helen. 'Do you think their lead singer, what's his name – Miles – is still hot?'

'He must be really old now,' says Polly. 'Surely he's in his fifties?'

'That's not that old,' Anneka snaps.

'No, not at all,' I say, remembering that Anneka mentioned that George was in his sixties.

Helen does a quick google and nods her head in approval of his picture. 'Still would.'

'You should come!'

'Ha, in a tent, with this bump, are you kidding?'

'Not to mention the toilets,' Anneka grimaces.

'But I'm sure you'll have a lovely time.' Polly is all upbeat. 'And we look forward to the report about you and Max.'

'And how fuckable Miles is,' says Helen.

'Will do,' I say, draining my drink.

'Oh, I've got to run, ladies,' says Polly. 'This was lovely. We'll have to do it again, yeah?'

'Absolutely,' I say.

She gives us each a hug and then hurries out the door.

My phone beeps and I look down – Anneka has sent me another link.

'It's to a boutique hotel I went to once in Paris,' she says wistfully. 'It's dead central and absolutely stunning.'

'I'm not sure we'll have the budget for anything too pricey; buying our house wiped out nearly all of our savings.'

'Oh no, this was pre-George. It's a bit shabby chic but I think it'll suit you down to the ground.'

There's a noise from the library as the doors fling open and a stream of women file out, all carrying babies. I spot Max in the crowd easily – as the only man – and I give him a wave.

'Ah, hi, um,' he says, walking over to us and suddenly going a little pink in the cheeks like he's embarrassed that he doesn't know them. 'Hi, ladies.'

'Hello,' they chant, smiling up at him.

A couple of women walk out of the library and past him. 'Bye Max, see you next week,' they say, waving.

'Oh, I see you're making friends,' I say.

Anneka has a very smug look on her face.

'I actually went to school with them, they were in my year. I couldn't tell you their names, but they remembered me.'

'Everyone remembered you,' I say.

'Oh, you were that boy in school, were you?' says Helen.

'Yep, that was Max.'

'You're making me blush,' he says. He lets Sasha down as she's been wriggling in his arms.

'And this is Sasha, is it?' says Helen, smiling warmly.

Sasha gives her a smile before she comes to me. I give her a cuddle but it's the crumbs on my plate that she really wants, as well as my spoon, which she starts banging against the china cup. Suddenly my relaxing cuppa with the girls has become anything but.

'Did you want to head home?' I ask Max.

'Yeah, or if you wanted to stay, I could take Sasha to the park. There's one behind here still, isn't there?'

'Yeah,' I stutter, 'there is.'

'Great, well, why I don't take her and then you come join me when you're ready to come home.'

'OK,' I say, trying to pretend this is totally normal behaviour.

'Nice to see you, ladies,' he says before he bends down to Sasha. 'Do you wanna come to the park?'

She starts babbling about the park and takes his outstretched hand and off they go.

I watch them go around the revolving door, still in shock.

'You've got him well trained,' says Helen.

'Hmm,' I say, widening my eyes. 'He's morphed into Super Dad.'

'That's not a bad thing, is it?' asks Anneka.

'Surely that's the dream,' says Helen.

'Don't get me wrong it is. It's just – did you see how they were holding hands and talking to each other?'

'Um, yeah,' says Helen.

'Well, that's it. They've managed to get their relationship back on track so quickly, if not better now that they're spending more time together.' I sigh. 'I'm jealous of it, how awful is that? I feel so guilty.'

'Ellie, don't be so hard on yourself. You're dealing with something huge. No one is going to judge your feelings at the moment.'

'But,' says Anneka, and Helen gives her a warning scowl, 'this is just another reason why you need to go to Paris, and to do your dates, because once you rebuild your relationship with him, all those insecurities will disappear.'

'Paris,' I say again.

'All roads lead to Paris,' says Helen. 'And sex.'

I nod my head slowly. I need to move things along; let's hope it's that simple.

Chapter 15

I glance at myself in our hallway mirror as I pass. I'm not sure pregnant rock chick is a fashion trend that'll catch on. I'm wearing my elasticated denim shorts, a floaty white top, a baggy loose-knit wool cardigan. Along with the Hunter wellies that Anneka's lent me. I don't think I'd fit in at Coachella, but I might just be passable at a family-friendly festival in Dorset. I've also packed a pair of jeans and a fleece that are perhaps less rock 'n' roll but maybe a better reflection of the British weather in mid-September.

I walk into the kitchen, tugging at my shorts, which didn't seem quite so short on the very few occasions I braved them in the summer. Max has his head in the fridge and is pulling a couple of cans of Coke out when he catches sight of me.

'Whoa,' he says, almost dropping the cans as he puts them into the icebox. He tilts his head to the side and blatantly stares.

'You've got legs,' he says, before he shakes his head.

'I know, it's incredible. I've heard that you have them too.'

'I just mean, that it's the first time I've seen you without leggings or a long dress on.'

It reminds me of the night we got together in Clapham,

when he couldn't keep his eyes off my boobs in the Wonder Woman costume.

'Those shorts are cute; you should wear them more often,' he says, unable to look away.

'I hardly think they're that practical, coming into autumn.'

'I don't know, maybe turn the heating up and wear them around the house,' he says with a shrug.

I see a flicker of a look pass over his face. I know exactly what that look means and what it usually leads to. It might have only been on his face for a split second, but it was there and that has to be a good sign.

'I'll, um, just pop this in the car,' he says, lifting the cool box and heading out.

I finish packing up the bits in the kitchen and, hearing voices outside, I pick up Sasha to investigate and find Judy talking to Max.

'Ah, I'm so glad I hadn't missed you, Ellie. I've dropped off some bits for you.'

She points to a pile on the ground near our boot.

'What's all this? We're back on Sunday.'

It seems like an excessive amount of stuff to take for two nights away.

'All essentials,' she says. 'I've found you a camping chair.'

'A camping chair?'

'Oh yes, love, you can't be sitting on the ground at your stage.'

I look at the chair in a bright-green casing, not very rock 'n' roll but I hadn't really thought about sitting down; perhaps it'll come in handy.

'Are you going to be warm enough in those? What about mosquitos?' she says, pointing at my bare legs.

'She'll be fine,' says Max, slotting the bits into the boot.

'I hardly think there are going to be any but I've packed some natural spray just in case,' I say. 'And I've got trousers to cover up for the evening if I need them. What's in the box?'

'That's the stove, saucepan, kettle, first aid kit, plates, bowls – you know, all the essentials.'

'You do know we have to carry this all to the campsite, don't you, Mum?' Max says, stuffing everything in wherever he can find space.

'You'll be fine. There's six of you going, aren't there?' she says, leaning forward to tickle Sasha. 'Is she going to be warm enough in that?'

'She'll be fine,' I say, 'Thank you so much for dropping these bits off.'

'I've also popped some sandwiches in the box for you,' says Judy.

'Mum, I might have lost five years of my memory but still I'm far too old for my mum to make me a packed lunch.'

'Speak for yourself. I'm all about the snacks at the moment. Thanks, Judy,' I say, giving her a quick hug.

'Now, are you sure you don't want me to take Sasha? I'm not sure about her going to a festival.'

'Don't worry, Judy; we'll make sure she doesn't get up to any mischief,' I say.

'It's more you lot I'm worried about. Remember you're in charge of a baby as well as yourselves.'

'I don't think I'm going to be going too crazy. I'm pregnant, remember.'

'Yes, yes, I guess so. OK, have a lovely time,' she says, blowing Sasha a kiss before she heads over to her car.

'We'll see you on Sunday,' I call down the drive.

'Do you need to borrow one of my fold-up ponchos?'

She reaches into her handbag but I shake my head.

'I've got my fleece with me and it's not forecast to rain,' I say.

'Are you sure? It folds up really small.'

'Really sure,' I say, thinking that I've barely got any festival chic going on as it is. 'Thanks again.'

This time she turns and makes it all the way back to her car.

'Right, let's get the final bits and hit the road,' I say to Max.

We meet up with Owen and Claire at the last service station before we have to leave the motorway. We do a quick passenger swap, so Claire comes in my car, and Max goes in Owen's. The night we met her we were dealing with the shock of Max's memory loss and it wasn't conducive for finding out more about her. So the car ride is an excellent time to suitably interrogate her, in much the same fashion Max has been doing to me over the last two weeks. She's 27, works in digital marketing, doesn't know who Mr Tumble is either, and is a fan of Pilot Dawn even if she did call them old skool. I'm already warming to her, although it does make me miss Sarah a tiny bit because of how long we knew her.

By the time that we arrive at the festival, I'm already busting for a wee, despite having not drunk anything on the way and having gone like a good girl at the service station. Everyone knows that toilets are the worst part about going to a festival and I've come prepared. I've got my NHS pregnancy card, which apparently will entitle me to use the disabled toilets and therefore have a better experience, and I've brought one of those female urinal contraptions because their website boasted that they're ideal for pregnant women to use when they're caught short. But neither option is available: there are just two solitary portaloos in the car park acting like beacons for my desperate bladder, and the female urinal is buried somewhere in my rucksack. I can't even do my usual drink-so-much-booze-that-I-don't-notice-how-disgusting-the-loos-are, so I just have to grin and bear it. Desperate times call for desperate measures. Although, when I get there it's surprisingly OK and it makes me wonder if it's actually more civilised because it's a family-friendly festival.

By the time I make it back to the car, everyone's unpacked and Owen's standing in front of a wheelbarrow.

'What's that?' I say, laughing at him.

'I didn't want to carry any bags,' he says. 'Bought it on the way down.'

'I'm sure that'll come in handy for your top-floor flat,' I say.

'You guys can keep it after, call it a housewarming present.'

'Cheers, you know there was a time when you would have brought a bottle of tequila.'

Owen raises his eyebrows and smiles.

'Times change.'

'Don't I keep hearing about it,' says Max, picking Sasha up and putting her on his shoulders.

'She's a bit small for that. Hold on, Sasha, sweetie.'

'She's fine – look, all the cool parents are doing it,' he says, pointing to all the other dads doing the same. 'Plus, with Owen's wheelbarrow I've got my hands free as he's taking our tent and blow-up mattresses.'

'Right then, are we all ready?' says Claire.

'Yes,' I say, grabbing a couple of pillows off her to feel like I'm doing my bit.

We start following the other festival-goers. The stream of people filing into the campsite is pure ordered chaos with children running in and out of the throngs, and harassed parents constantly turning to see where they've gone, trying to keep their pack together.

'Are Rach and Gaby saving us a spot?' asks Owen.

'No, they're not here yet,' I say, checking my phone in case of updates. 'They overslept so they left later than planned.'

'Wasn't this their bloody idea?' he says, pushing his wheelbarrow over the bumpy ground.

I wouldn't say I had to twist Owen's arm to come to a festival, but I think he only really said yes to be a good friend. He's rooting for me and Max to find our way to back one another and he thinks this will help.

'Are you OK?' says Max, as we fall behind the others. 'Do you need to stop?'

'We've gone about fifty metres at best. I'm not that bad. Do *you* need to stop?'

He's looking a bit red in the face.

'I'm fine,' he says, gritting his teeth.

For once we're quite evenly matched in terms of being over-burdened. His backpack and Sasha must be weighing him down. It takes us twenty minutes to reach an open space big enough for us to pitch three tents in a row.

Max gently lowers Sasha to the ground before throwing his bag down. He then takes my camping chair out of the wheelbarrow and instructs me to sit down before he turns and tackles the tent.

I slip down into the chair and immediately love Judy that much more for providing it. 'Are you sure you don't want me to help you?'

'No, it's OK. I'm an expert at putting up tents.'

I laugh wildly.

'Shit, I forgot you know my deepest darkest secrets. But this one looks simple enough,' he says, unrolling the flysheet.

I look over at Claire and Owen, who are giggling away, trying to put up their tent. A stab of jealousy comes over me, wishing that Max and I were more like that. They're in the proper throes of early dating, where everything's stomach-flip exciting – despite my best efforts to get our relationship on a similar path, the only stomach-whooshing happening is coming from the heartburn I've been getting in the latter stages of pregnancy.

'Are you sure you don't want some help?' I ask, as he goes to put the fixed awning pole through one of the holes for the tent pole.

'No, no, you sit there, relax,' he says. 'Save your energy for the rest of the festival.'

'OK,' I say, biting my lip to stop myself from laughing. As I turn around, Sasha makes a beeline for my seat and I just catch my balance in time before the seat starts to tip. 'Oh, pickle. Do you want to sit on Mummy's lap and I can read you a story?'

I pull out *Dear Zoo* from my bag, hoping that it'll keep her still for at least five minutes.

Claire and Owen have their tent up in record time and turn to give a red-faced Max a hand, which he declines, and they instead go to scope out the campsite. I stay seated, trying to move as little as possible because it's some sort of miracle that Sasha is sitting still – too in awe of all the activity that's going on around her. With so many people to watch she can't take it all in.

It takes Max a full forty minutes and the help of two enthusiastic kids from a pitch nearby to put up our tent. He finally accepted help because he was worried that Owen and Claire would come back and see that he'd still not finished.

Thanking the kids and their parents profusely, Max comes over and pulls up a chair next to me.

'See, easy as pie,' he says, as Sasha scrambles down from my lap and goes over to his.

'It looked like it,' I say, examining the beads of sweat glistening on his forehead. 'I'm guessing it's beer o'clock?'

'Actually, I'm not drinking this weekend,' he says, trying to get Sasha to stop wriggling.

'You're not? At a festival?' I look at him as if he's mad.

'You can't drink—' he shrugs '—so I figured that I wouldn't either.'

I'm blinking hard because my brain can't process this.

'Solidarity, innit? Plus, I figured I'd made enough of a tit out of myself when I drank at the beer pong. It'll do me some good to give the booze a miss. Especially when we're around Sasha.'

I nod my head slowly. It's not like Max drinks a lot, but he'd never go to a gig without a drink and the fact that he's decided to stay sober with me makes me love him even more. How is it that I'm the one falling more in love with him and not the other way round?

'I'll make us a cup of tea.'

'No, I'll do it,' he says, letting Sasha down onto the ground and pulling a camping stove out of a bag and a small metal kettle.

'Bloody hell, that's a proper nice kettle. What's your mum even doing with all this stuff? I can't imagine her camping,' I say, trying to wrestle a camping mallet out of Sasha's hand. Max throws her the pink unicorn and she lets go of the mallet, which nearly whacks me in the face.

'She said she did a bit of panic buying because of Brexit. Apparently, that's why one of the shelving units in the shed is full of tinned goods. Was it really that bad? I mean, I read the Wikipedia page, but it didn't really explain my mum's stockpiling.'

'I don't know why you're surprised; this is your mother who starts her Christmas food shopping in August in case all the good cranberry sauce sells out.'

Max laughs.

'I can't believe I missed it all.'

'You're lucky,' I say, watching him fill up the kettle with bottled water. 'It's been painful. But let's not talk about it. A lot of other, more positive things have happened in the years that you missed.'

'Like Greggs and the veggie sausage roll,' he says.

'Yes, like that. See, we've been updating you on all the important matters.'

He lights the camping stove and we spend the time it takes for the water to boil trying to distract Sasha away from the flames. I pop her into our empty tent and try and find the air mattress.

I've just unrolled it when Max hands me my cup of tea.

'I'll do that,' he says, locating a foot pump from the box of camping goodies.

'Judy really did think of everything.'

My phone starts to buzz, and I pick up Rach's call.

'Hey, we're almost here,' she says. 'We're in giant sombreros.'

'I'm not going to ask. They're almost here,' I say to Max. 'Can you stand up and wave.'

He hoists Sasha on his shoulders and waves her arms. We all scour the site until we see them and their giant hats.

'Hello, hello,' they call, and we give them a hug.

'What's with the hats?'

'Thought it would be handy to spot each other,' says Rach.

'Good thinking,' I say. 'Cup of tea?'

'Um, thanks, but we started on the wine,' says Gaby, showing us the bag from a box of wine that looks like it's been well enjoyed already.

'It was bloody heavy carrying everything,' says Rach, 'so we started drinking to make it lighter.'

'Clever thinking,' I say.

Rach gives Sasha a big squeeze and she immediately starts pulling at the dangly bits of her sombrero.

'Not sure how we're going to put up the tent, though,' says Gaby. 'It's gone right to my head. Far too early in the day to be drinking.'

'Max will help you,' I say, watching him pump up the air mattress with a foot pump. 'He did such an amazing job with ours.'

I expect him to give me the middle finger and to playfully tell me where I can shove that suggestion.

'Yeah, I'll just finish this and I'll be over,' he says, much to my shock.

'Max, we're OK; I'm pretty sure Ellie was kidding. Besides,

I know you weren't a boy scout and that you're crap with tents,' says Rach. 'Plus, I reckon I'll be done by the time you've finished that.'

Max starts pumping harder with his legs. Their sibling rivalry knows no bounds.

'I'd like to see you try,' he says.

Rach raises an eyebrow and Max's legs go even faster and the pump begins to squeak.

She dumps her bags and whips out a round bag that has the tent in, unzips and then pulls it out.

'Watch and learn,' says Rach with a cackle, throwing the tent forward and up it pops.

'That's cheating,' says Max, going a bit red in the face. 'But you've got to peg it first.'

'It's OK, Max, the air mattress doesn't need to be firm; I only need just enough air so that it cushions the bump.'

'Now you're taking sides, Ellie,' says Rach, running around and hammering in the tent pegs.

Max conveniently chooses not to hear me and keeps going, and I'm worried that I'll be sleeping on the floor if it bursts.

'Finished,' they both shout as Max hurriedly puts the stopper in.

They both go over to inspect each other's work, neither impressed that it was a draw.

'It'll be fun to watch you get that down and back in the bag,' says Max, folding his arms over his chest.

'Yeah, yeah, whatever,' says Rach, throwing in the self-inflatable camping mats into her little tent.

Gaby comes over and sits in the chair next to me. 'At least some things don't change, huh?'

I'm about to reply when I see Owen and Claire heading back, and I introduce Gaby to them.

'What's the festival like?' I say, as Claire pulls out a little camping stool from her tent and sits on it. I marvel at her tiny little frame and how I'd barely get one of my bum cheeks on there at the moment.

'Pretty good,' she says, raising an eyebrow. 'It's just people sitting around casually drinking tins of gin rather than bottles of vod, for a start.'

Sasha waddles up to her and gives her a big chunk of grass, which she takes, slightly bemused.

'What do I do with this?' she asks.

'Anything to make sure Sasha doesn't eat it,' I say, smiling back, and she nods.

'No gin in tins here, we aren't drinking at all,' says Max, picking up his tea after his leg workout.

'Ooh, I'll take one of those if it's going,' says Owen. He looks over at Rach's tent and nods. 'That was quick.'

'Yeah, but wait until she gets it down,' says Max.

Rach rolls her eyes at her brother as he boils the kettle for Owen.

'You guys can't all be drinking tea,' says Claire. 'Obviously, Ellie's got a good excuse; what's with the rest of you?'

'I keep telling you, we're old,' says Owen.

'Look at us, though. Remember the times we would drink as soon as we stepped out of the car until the time that we left?' says Max.

'We were young then, and we had fresh livers,' says Owen.

'Fresh livers,' says Claire, chuckling. 'I'm guessing your liver will actually be fresher now than it was when you were drinking heavily.'

'She's right,' says Gaby, 'your liver repairs itself.'

'And you're a doctor, right, Gaby?' says Claire, and she nods.

'So, are we going to make a plan of who we're going to see?' says Rach, flicking through the festival lanyard. 'Obviously we're only really here to see Pilot Dawn tomorrow night, but there are some pretty good acts playing tonight.'

'Couldn't we just wing it?' says Claire.

Rach does a sharp intake of breath.

'Winging it is good,' says Max, 'that's how you find hidden gems.'

'Oh no,' says Rach, 'if you don't have a plan, you'll miss people on different stages.'

'Ellie, who do you want to see?' asks Gaby.

'I don't know, really. Obviously there are few baby presenters I'd like Sasha to see, and I'll have to be conscious of her nap schedule,' I say, reading the backs of the lanyard. 'Ooh, are Vengaboys playing later on?'

Rach flicks through. 'At two p.m. We could just make that.'

'I love the Vengaboys,' says Claire. 'It reminds me of junior school.'

We all turn and look at her. How old do we feel? It was mine and Rach's soundtrack to our last year at senior school.

'Oh, and after Vengaboys, there's Mister Maker making crafts.'

Rach gets up and claps her hands. 'Great, then that's a plan.'

'I don't think you all have to watch Mister Maker with us.'

'It's so cool, Sasha going to her first festival,' Gaby says. 'Just think, Rach, when we have our baby, we'll be doing this.'

Max and I look up in surprise.

'Oh my God, are you having a baby?' asks Max.

'Oh no, not yet,' says Gaby, 'it's the wine I've been drinking, it came out all wrong. But one day, soon, I hope.'

'That's awesome,' says Max, grinning.

'It really is,' I say, suddenly feeling awful.

This must have been what Rach was going to talk to me about when we were at the coffee van and Judy phoned to tell us about Max. With everything that's been going on with Max I'd completely forgotten.

I'm about to ask more about it, when Rach claps her hands together again.

'Come on, if we're going to see the Vengaboys we need to get going – now,' she says. I get the impression it's not just us that she's trying to move along but the conversation too. She's not sharing our excitement over the baby news. I'll have to try and find some quiet time to talk to her to get the bottom of it.

'Let's go then,' says Max, popping Sasha on his shoulders again, and we follow the crowds of people heading for the stage.

It turns out that having chairs at festivals is a revelation that I wish I'd cottoned on to years ago. There's a slight slope on the festival site, which means that despite us being further back than I'd usually choose when watching a gig, we can still see the stage perfectly. And what with it being a family-friendly festival, there are people sat around on blankets and chairs so that I don't look out of place in the slightest.

Max has had Sasha on his shoulders for the whole time, bopping away to the music, and she's having the time of her life in her bright turquoise ear defenders.

I've stood for a couple of songs and done the best dance moves I can. I'm actually having more fun than I ever thought I would – but sitting in a field dancing, chatting and singing our lungs out for three hours has exhausted me.

'You're yawning, again,' says Max.

'No, I'm not,' I say hurriedly. 'Everyone's having a really good time and I don't want to be the one that flakes out.'

'Come on, let's get you back to the tent. You can have a disco nap. Sasha looks tired too.'

'I always liked the sound of disco naps, although I will be most disappointed if I don't get to fall asleep to the sounds of Earth, Wind and Fire.'

Max shakes his head at me.

'We're going to head back to the tent,' he says to Owen.

'OK, we'll see you there in a bit,' he says.

'Or we could go with them,' says Claire, grabbing his hands and doing some very unsubtle eyebrow wiggling.

'Oh, we could,' says Owen.

'Great,' I say, putting on my best fake smile.

'How about you guys?' I say to Rach and Gaby.

'We're going to go and take a look at the up-and-coming stage,' says Rach, taking Gaby's hand. 'Come find us after.'

'Cool,' I say, 'we'll look for the sombreros.'

They head off towards the other stage and we go back towards the campsite. I wish that Owen and Claire were going with them. They've barely been able to keep their hands off each other since we got here and now they're heading back to the tent, which is right next to ours. It would be cringy overhearing anything in normal circumstances but the fact that we haven't even kissed since Max lost his memory makes it worse.

The two of us and Sasha fall back a little and I almost hope that Owen and Claire's quickie is over before we get there.

'How are you finding it so far without the booze?' I ask.

'It's all right, actually. It's nice not having to go for a wee every few minutes and I reckon I'm saving a fortune.'

'Yes, there is that. It's cheap being sober.'

He's carrying Sasha in his arms and she's asleep by the time we make it back to our camp. There's a lot of giggling coming from Owen and Claire's tent – we definitely hadn't thought that through when we pitched them so close together. Max pops Sasha down on her little air mattress.

'I'm really tired,' I say loudly, doing a big theatrical yawn in the hope that it might make the others realise how easily sound travels. But they're obviously too in the moment to hear because the noises continue and the shadows of their guy ropes, illuminated on the inside of our tent, start to shake.

Max and I look at each other.

'Disco nap,' he says again. 'Shall I put on the music?'

'Yes, yes,' I say. I wriggle onto the airbed that all the forums said to half inflate – they were bloody right; this is the most comfortable I've been in a long, long time. 'Ring my Bell' starts chiming away and it almost makes me think it's the best lullaby of all time.

I wake up and the tent is pitch-black and Max's phone is no longer playing disco tunes. There's enough illumination from the floodlights in the campsite to see that Sasha's still fast asleep. Behind me I can feel Max nestled up against me. From the sound of the little snuffly, half-snore, half-heavy breathing noise he's making, I'm guessing he's fast asleep. It's so nice being close to him, feeling the rise and fall of his chest. I'm even quite enjoying the light snoring as I hadn't realised how much I'd missed it with us sleeping apart. I don't want to move a muscle as I don't want to disturb him.

I'm wondering what time it is when I notice the pain in my bladder. It's the kind of pain that lets me know I have to go right now. I don't even think I can make it to the toilets.

I fumble in my handbag for my plastic urinal and I'm considering opening the tent and having a sneaky pee outside but there's the sound of people chatting and giggling all around.

I'm starting to get a bit of a sweat on in panic and it's taking what very little pelvic floor I have left to hold everything in and, in a moment of desperation, I swipe Judy's travel kettle.

'Sodding hell,' I mutter as I try to roll down the over-the-bump waistband part of my shorts to a stage where I can pull my knickers down enough to get the urinal into position. The website said it was really easy to use, but in hindsight I should have done a test run at home. I just need to find the right position. Which is easier said than done when you're very pregnant and in a goddamn tent.

'Sodding, sodding hell,' I say, as I hope I've got it in the right place, and I start weeing. A wave of utter relief hits me as I hear the tinkle hitting off the metal kettle. That is until I hear Max beginning to stir.

'What is it?' he says with a murmur.

'Ah, nothing,' I say, wishing that my race-horse pee would stop.

'What's that noise, is it rain?'

'Yes, just rain,' I say, beginning to worry that the kettle might not be big enough; this wee is showing no signs of stopping. 'Go back to sleep.'

I finally finish and sigh with relief. I'm just trying to find some loo roll to wipe myself when Max's head torch shines and I freeze. The whole idea of the portable female urinal is that you're supposed to use it without the need to get undressed, but the makers hadn't really taken into consideration over-the-bump shorts, which I'd unrolled and shoved down to somewhere around my knees, which means that my pants are now fully illuminated in Max's torch beam. And whilst I should be pleased that I'm not mooning him, I think that would have been preferable – for us both – to him seeing me in my giant pants. And it's not even like they're functional tummy-hugging Spanx or anything; they are in fact, floral, high-waisted, full briefs bought in a multipack from a supermarket. They are reminiscent of something that you'd have found on my nan's washing line.

'Um, Ellie...' says Max.

'You know, I'm pregnant and if it's not acceptable to wear granny pants now then when the hell is it?' I say, mortified.

'Um, I think the pants are the least of your worries. I think the pee you just did is leaking out of the kettle spout.'

'Oh shit,' I say, scrambling towards the tent door.

Max climbs over too and wrangles with the zip as I hastily pour it out outside our tent.

'Hmm, I probably didn't want to tip that just outside. I'm really sorry,' I say.

'Don't worry about it, I've peed in worse places,' he says, laughing. 'Bloody hell, though, I thought it was a flood.'

I whack him on the arm. He does a deep belly laugh that's reserved for when I've done something particularly silly. I always love the way it takes over his whole body, making him shake.

'And those pants, they are, um… Did Nora Batty lose them?'

'Hey, you usually find them sexy,' I lie. 'And sssh, you'll wake Sasha. It looks like she's out for the count.'

I hear footsteps outside our tent.

'Great, you guys are still up,' says Claire.

'Hang on a second,' I say, taking a moment to pull up my shorts before I unzip the door further.

'You were well out of it earlier. You missed Jess Glynne, she was awesome,' says Claire.

'Is it that late?' I say, patting round for my phone.

'It's eleven thirty,' says Claire.

'Bugger. So much for our disco nap.'

'At least you're pregnant,' says Max. 'I don't know what my excuse is.'

'Oh, great, the kettle's handy. Shall I make us a brew?'

'No,' Max and I shout and he dives to get it, knocking Claire's hand out of the way.

'We're running out of tea bags and poor Ellie here, it's her only comfort.'

'Oh, of course, I've got some Strongbow in the tent. I'll drink that instead.'

'All right,' says Owen, walking up and stepping right into the puddle of wee. 'I don't think I want to know why my foot's wet, do I?'

Max shakes his head and I hang mine in shame as Owen hobbles off to his tent to sort himself out.

'I take it you two probably aren't up for a nightcap at ours,' says Claire. 'Owen just texted Gaby and Rach and they're on their way back to have one.'

'Probably not. I want to make sure I don't fall asleep tomorrow night. I wouldn't want to miss Pilot Dawn or wake up Sasha.'

'I'll leave you to it,' she says, and she follows Owen back to their tent.

Alone again, Max and I both stare at the offending kettle.

'I'll wash it tomorrow morning,' says Max.

'I think that we should hide it in a bag and take it home to wash in the dishwasher. You brought a saucepan, right? We can use that instead.'

'Much better plan. Are you tired?'

'A little, but to tell you the truth I'm just really comfortable on that air mattress; it's like it's hugging my bump.'

'Then lie back down.'

'Will you tell me a bedtime story?'

'Is that something I'd usually do?'

'Absolutely, you usually tell me silly stories about you and Rach as kids,' I say, crossing my fingers behind my back at the lie. Those are usually the stories he tells Sasha.

'OK,' he says, lying down on his airbed facing me and propping himself up on his elbow. 'Once upon a time there were two children. A wonderful, good-looking little boy and a fussy, feisty little girl...'

I close my eyes and try and concentrate on his words, but really I'm just enjoying lying next to my husband – something I'd always taken for granted, but now it means the world to me.

Chapter 16

I'm in a lovely deep sleep when I hear Sasha start to stir and it pulls me out of my dream. There's no way of telling what time it is, thanks to the floodlights, and as I scramble off the air mattress, I check my phone. 5.45 a.m. Bloody hell. I guess that's what happens when you go for a disco nap at 5 p.m. and sleep the whole night. Max is still fast asleep, emitting his little puff-puff snores and I'm worried we'll wake him. I pop Sasha's fleece on over her pyjamas and slip on her shoes, before I do the same, and then I grab her bottle out of the cooler box and some croissants.

It's still pretty dark out but there's a tiny hint of the sun starting to rise and I can see people walking up the hill behind the campsite, presumably to watch it.

'Come on, sweetie, do you fancy a little walk?'

'Walk, yeah,' she says, or at least that's what it sounds like to me.

We're not far from the tents when Rach runs up to us.

'Hey, I thought I heard voices,' she says.

'Sorry, did we wake you?'

'No, I've been awake for a while. Think I drank way too many sugary drinks last night.'

Sasha loops her hand through Rach's and the two of us swing and walk her.

'No prizes for guessing who got you up so early.'

'None at all,' I laugh.

The hill starts to rise quite steeply and we move up it mostly in silence.

'Are you going to be OK?' asks Rach.

'Yeah, fine, you might just have to take Sasha when it's steeper.'

We eventually get to the top and I'm huffing and puffing, but we're rewarded with a beautiful sunrise.

'Oh my,' I gasp.

'Wow, that was worth getting up the hill for,' says Rach.

'Definitely.'

We take a seat on the ground and I pull the bottle out of my fleece. Sasha curls up in my lap and takes her milk.

'Hey, look at that guy,' says Rach, pointing at a man creeping out of a tent at the campsite and then spinning round trying to get his bearings.

'Classic walk of shame. He's only got one shoe on.'

There are a few people doing mad dashes to the toilets – they obviously didn't have a kettle to hand – and a few that seem to be still up from the night before. There are a few bleary-eyed parents up here with their children running around, full of almost Christmas Day levels of excitement.

'I'm so glad you changed your mind to come,' says Rach, taking one of the croissants I've offered her.

'Me too. It's been a lot of fun so far.'

'Despite the fact that you slept through most of it,' she says.

'Yeah, despite that. I think it's actually been good for Max and me to get away. He seems a lot more relaxed and like he's enjoying himself. We've spent so much of the past two weeks with me telling him about his life; it's nice that he's actually getting to live it with us.'

'I hadn't thought of it that way,' she says, in between mouthfuls. 'I still can't get my head around it. It's all Gaby and I talk about. She's explained the medical stuff to me a million times but I still don't get how all his memories are there still and he just can't access them.'

'I know, it's so weird.'

'But you seem better than the last time I saw you. He seems different with you now. I take it that recreating dates got better after the beer pong disaster?'

Even before the attempted mini-golf/beer pong night, Rach had tried to convince me that it wasn't a good idea and that I should focus on finding the cause of his memory loss instead.

'They did.' I shift Sasha into a more comfortable position. 'Although, obviously, he hasn't fallen head over heels in love with me again, but he's at least accepted that he's a dad and we're getting on better.'

'That's good – you couldn't have expected him to fall in love with you overnight.'

'Couldn't I?'

'No, in fact I'd be very worried if he just fell right back into a relationship with you.'

I sigh. She's right, but it doesn't make it any easier to hear.

The sun is properly starting to rise now and the sky is exploding in colour.

'So, it's exciting that you and Gaby are thinking of having a baby,' I say.

Rach's smile disappears.

'She wasn't supposed to tell anyone.'

'Sorry, I shouldn't have said anything… but was that what you were going to talk to me about, that day when we were having coffee in the woods?'

Rach nods slowly.

'Oh Rach, I'm so sorry, I'd forgotten all about it until Gaby let it slip yesterday and I put two and two together.'

'Don't be silly, it's fine; you've got enough on your plate at the moment.'

'I feel awful, though. Do you still want to talk about it?'

'I guess,' she says, but she doesn't say anything.

We sit watching the sky for a while until she's ready to speak.

'Gaby wants to have a baby,' she says eventually.

'Isn't that a good thing?' I say, trying to gauge how she feels about it. 'I thought you wanted that too?'

'I did, I mean I *do*.'

'Is it a timing thing?'

'No, I'm ready,' she says decisively. 'It's just complicated. And I know for a lot of people having a baby is complicated and people have fertility issues, but for us, it's complicated before we even get to that stage.' She paused.

'When you and Max wanted a baby, you just needed to – well, you know what you needed to do. But for me and Gaby there are so many decisions to make. Would we use a sperm bank or would we ask someone we know? Which one of us would carry the baby? Should we get married to give us more equal rights to the child?'

After she rattles off the list she exhales loudly.

'Oh, I guess I never thought of any of that,' I say, stunned, realising how easy we'd had it.

'Gaby sat me down and explained it all to me so matter-of-factly, as she's probably done with countless patients over the years, and I started to panic... This is going to sound stupid.'

'Nothing ever sounds as stupid as you think it does.' I'm reminded of my chat with Owen.

'I'm terrified that we'll make the wrong decision. What if we got an anonymous sperm donor and then the baby grew up to be a total arsehole because the sperm donor was? Or what if we decided to use someone we knew only for them to start demanding custody rights later down the line?

'But Gaby doesn't have any of these worries; she's all calm and unfazed by it all, probably because she knows more about it from her job. When I try to bring up these fears she thinks it's because I don't want a baby.'

'And are you sure you do?'

I watch her watching Sasha as she and another little boy about her age are popping bubbles that his mum is blowing.

'Yeah, I really do. But sometimes the whole process over-whelms me and I get scared. I mean, what if our relationship isn't strong enough to go through all this?'

'Do you want to know what I think?'

'Yes,' she says, wrinkling her face like she's bracing herself.

'I think you should talk to Gaby. Tell her exactly what you just told me. Explain to her that she's going to have to understand that you don't know as much as her and you're going to have to spend more time talking through the options and finding out about them.

'But the main thing is that you've got to reassure Gaby that this is what you want. It's about focusing on the baby at the end of whatever journey you take to get there.'

She exhales deeply.

'I guess I can do that,' she says. 'I actually feel relieved having told you all this.'

'Good, I'm glad. You know, Rach, you can always talk to me, don't you?'

'I know,' she says, nodding. 'That goes for you too. I'm here for you, OK?'

'Thanks,' I say.

'Just as long as it's not about you and Max getting it on – there's no way I want to hear about your role-play shenanigans.'

'We do not do—'

'La-la-la,' says Rach, putting her fingers in her ears. 'I'm not listening.'

I give her a gentle shove and start laughing.

'I'm pleased we went for this walk now,' says Rach.

'Me too, even if it did nearly kill me.'

'At least it'll be easier going downhill.'

'Yes, speaking of which, I'm starving; those croissants didn't fill me up at all. Shall we go and see if anyone's up and get some proper breakfast?'

'Yeah,' I say.

We thank the kind mum with the bubbles and lead Sasha back down the hill. When we get back to the tent, we find Max sitting outside drinking orange juice.

'Ah, there you all are. I was thinking about breakfast.'

'Me too,' says Rach.

'Bacon sandwiches?' I say, realising I'm starving from missing an evening meal last night.

'Toasted, brown sauce,' say Max and Rach together.

I pull a face; it's tomato ketchup all the way for me.

'Is anyone else up?' asks Rach.

'Gaby is. I haven't seen Owen or Claire.'

'Claire's here,' she says, strolling out of the tent in a short pair of PJs. She slips on a fleece and pops on her flip-flops. 'Did someone say breakfast?'

'Yeah, we were just going to get some.'

'I'll come,' she says.

'We can get it for you if you like?'

'Um, no, I heard you mention brown sauce, which is all kinds of wrong,' she says, grabbing her purse out of the tent.

'I'll stay here with Sasha,' I say, and they head off towards the food stalls.

I fumble around the tent looking for a saucepan and I come across a colouring book for Sasha and some crayons that she'll probably try and eat rather than use. I hand them to her and at least she takes them, which increases my odds in being able to drink a hot cup of tea.

I pop Sasha on her blanket whilst she grips onto her crayons for dear life as if I'm about to prise them out of her hands, and I settle into my camping seat while the water boils on the hob.

Owen crawls out of his tent on all fours and collapses on the edge of Sasha's blanket.

'Bloody hell, that was some night,' he says, groaning.

'I hear Jess Glynne was good.'

'So good,' he says, groaning again and shielding his eyes from the sun. 'We were right in the middle of things. I don't think I'm going to be able to properly hear ever again. All Claire's fault.'

'Things seem to be going really well with you two.'

'Yeah, they are,' he says, nodding, but he's not really smiling.

'Is everything OK? That didn't really sound very convincing.'

'Trust you to pick up on that,' he laughs. 'I guess it's just odd being with someone new. I was with Sarah for such a long time and I knew her so well. It's just hard starting from scratch again, getting to know each other's quirks and how they're going to react to something. I'd forgotten how exhausting it is in the early days when you don't really know each other that well and you have to put in so much effort.'

'Um, hello, welcome to my world.'

'But at least with Max he's still the same person. I'm just finding it really hard that Claire doesn't react the same way as Sarah did to things.'

'And that's all it is? You're not still hung up on her, are you?'

'Oh no, definitely not. And it's not like it's a bad thing that Sarah and Claire are different either, and I'm really enjoying finding out more about her. The more I do, the more I feel like this is really right. But I guess I'm looking forward to when we're further down the line and we're fully relaxed with each other.' With a final groan he rolls over and props himself up on his elbow.

'Tell me about it,' I say with a laugh.

'Hopefully he'll get his memory back soon.'

'Hopefully,' I sigh. 'I'm starting to lose hope that he'll ever remember. I've been trying to fill him in, trying to jog his memory with places, but nothing seems to work. Has he spoken to you about the year before I met him?'

'No, why?'

'Because he wants to find out as much as possible about his missing year; I've been interrogated more thoroughly than I would have been if I was a suspect in *Line of Duty*.'

Owen laughs and immediately winces in pain.

'He was asking about the woman he was dating before me – Anne, I think her name was. I told him I didn't know much other than that they'd dated briefly. Just be prepared for your cross examination on the subject,' I say, laughing.

'I don't know why he thinks he needs to know about her again. That's ancient history,' he says, firmly.

'Oh yeah, I know, but he's just trying to get things straight.'

'Then you and his mum should be telling him about his dad leaving. Surely that's a bigger thing to happen to him than dating Anne. He doesn't need to know about her.'

Owen sits up straight and, considering that he's been wincing at any movement he makes, it seems a little strange.

'I think you should just focus on doing more of your date ideas, and not look backwards,' he says, leaning over Sasha and taking a great interest in her artwork, which is largely her tagging each page with a big black crayon mark.

There was something not quite right about the way he reacted when I mentioned Anne. The trouble is, with him not wanting to talk about her and Max not being able to remember her, I've got no hope in working out what that was all about.

'I'm going to nip to the loos before the guys come back with the sandwiches.'

I watch him hurry off and it makes me even more suspicious, but I don't have time to dwell on it as the smell of bacon wafts towards me and Claire and Max walk up, chatting away animatedly.

Max hands me one of the boxes and I open it to find the biggest breakfast bap ever.

'I'm not really eating for two, you know.'

'Yes, but you've got to keep your energy up. It's going to be a big day. Lots to see,' says Rach. 'And dancing to be done. The only person allowed to nap today is Sasha.'

'Righto,' I say, tucking in and looking forward to the rest of the day, trying to put the odd conversation with Owen out of my mind.

When Sasha shows signs of being sleepy, Max and I tell everyone that we're going to walk her round in the sling whilst she sleeps. Although we actually head back to the tent and take a 45-minute tactical nap, without having to face Rach's wrath or to have a repeat of Owen and Claire's soundtrack from the day before.

'Why is the main stage so far away?' I say with a groan. We've only walked about fifty metres from our tent and I'm already pooped. All the walking round the festival site for the last twenty-four hours has caught up with me.

'Because otherwise it would be too noisy to nap,' he says with a smile. 'Are your feet hurting?'

'Everything's hurting,' I say, plonking my chair down and sitting in it.

'Hang on,' says Max, 'I've got an idea.'

He dashes off to Owen's tent, with Sasha giggling on his back in the sling. He shouts 'hello' to make sure they haven't snuck in while we were sleeping. Satisfied that it's empty he dashes in and reappears with Owen's wheelbarrow.

'What are you going to do with that?' I ask.

'You're going to get in it.'

'I'm going to what? No way.'

He leans into our tent and pulls out one of the inflatable cushions that I'd been wedging between my legs to help me sleep and places it in the back of the barrow.

'You're serious about this, aren't you?'

'Uh-huh, come on, hop in.'

I look at it, relieved that it's reinforced plastic and not metal. At least I'm not risking piles.

'You'll go gently, won't you?'

'Of course I will.'

He pulls me up and helps to gently lower me in. Actually, it's not that uncomfortable. He folds up the chair and puts it next to me, before he takes the handles.

'Ready?' he says without waiting for my reply as he starts wheeling, causing me to squeal a little.

We bound along and I cradle my bump, people cheering us as we pass, and I start waving like I'm a carnival princess, secretly lapping up all the attention. Max picks up speed a little and we rattle along, making it to the main stage in a much quicker time. We meet up with Claire and Owen on the pre-arranged spot where we'd watched Vengaboys. Max gently tips the wheelbarrow and Owen pulls me out.

'I hope you didn't mind,' I say.

'Of course not. It's your housewarming present, after all.'

I giggle and settle into my chair as we wait for the band to come on.

I marvel as Owen spins the wheelbarrow round so that it's balancing on the handles rather than the wheel and then he sits on it like a deckchair.

Max pulls Sasha out of the sling and she starts toddling about us.

'Holy shit, look, there's Rach and Gaby,' I say, pointing to the big screen. They're easy to spot with their sombreros on. They're both sat on two random guys' shoulders, at the very front of the crowd.

'Bloody hell,' says Max, suitably impressed by his sister.

'And I thought we did well last night,' says Claire, 'but we didn't get anywhere as close as that.'

The image changes from Rach and Gaby to a shot of the main stage, and a scream goes up as Pilot Dawn step out on to it. The crowd goes wild and we all stand up. They break out into one of their recent hits and I start pretend-strumming my bump like an air guitar.

Sasha goes back onto Max's shoulders, much to her delight.

'Is this song new?' he says, spinning Sasha around gently. 'It's great.'

'Yeah, it was out earlier this year. We played it a lot.'

He nods and it still amazes me that there's not a teeny tiny bit of his brain that doesn't recognise it, but he's clearly hearing it for the first time as, once you've heard the lyrics, there's no way that you can't not sing along to the '*da da da*s' in the middle of the chorus. It sounds epic with the crowd roaring it back at them and my heart starts to race. There's always something so magical about going to a gig when the crowd's chanting in unison and moving to the rhythm as one. It feels soul-affirming. I'm no longer noticing my slightly puffy ankles, or the weight of my stomach; I'm just in the moment.

Max edges closer to me and his hand brushes mine and causes it to tingle. We've often talked about this moment of absolute gig-love and I know he'll be feeling it too, so I reach over and take his hand.

He squeezes it back and tears prickle at my eyes. It finally feels like we're getting somewhere.

Our hands drop when we feel them getting sweaty and we both clap and air-guitar along as they break into old hits, starting to play the classics that even Max knows. Every so often, when a softer song comes along, he grabs my hand and, even though we're only in the pre-school level of intimacy, it's still giving me butterflies.

When the final song comes on, the band breaks out into a melodic beat, with guitar notes being played as fast as lightning that send the crowd crazy. Max looks at me. 'This is one of my all-time favourite songs,' he whispers, close to my ear.

'Me too,' I say, my heart aching for how many times we've danced to this together in the past.

We start to join the rest of the crowd jumping up and down and Sasha is tipping her head back in delight as Max waggles her arms. I do my knee-bobbing to lessen the movement of my bump and the baby starts kicking wildly.

'Feel this,' I say, gesturing at the bump, and Max secures Sasha with one hand while touching my stomach with the other. The baby seems to be kicking harder than a cage fighter.

He looks at me and he doesn't need to say anything; it's written all over his face. The look of sheer amazement and love for our unborn baby. I can see tears in his eyes.

'Looks like both our babies love Pilot Dawn.'

'They have good taste,' I whisper into his ear.

He turns to me and in that moment, the thousands of people screaming around us seem to fade away and it's like we're the only two people there. He takes a hold of both my hands and leans down to kiss me as I reach up to meet him. Our lips begin to brush when I feel a tapping on my head and I step back. I look up and see Sasha. She's giggling and babbling away at me, and Max and I nervously laugh, slightly embarrassed by what just happened. We were so close. But the spell's been broken now.

It feels like our near kiss was a metaphor for our relationship: so close yet still so far.

Chapter 17

For me, the worst part of going to a festival is not the toilets, but the post-festival blues you get when you arrive home and fall back into the daily grind. The euphoric highs that I felt watching one of my favourite bands – those moments with my friends that I know we'll all treasure as memories for ever – they all seem so far away as I rush to drop Sasha off at nursery.

After watching Pilot Dawn, we all went back to the camp-site. I tucked Sasha up in the tent and the rest of us sat around drinking (fizzy water in my case) and listening to the faint sound of the old rock group who were headlining the last night. The next morning, we'd mooched around the kids' field, letting Sasha have her face painted and trying out as many of the activities as she was old enough for. Then we packed up the kit and headed home last night.

It all seems like a million miles away now, the heady mix of disinfectant and sweaty feet at nursery grounding me back to real life.

I give Sasha a big kiss and a cuddle and I try not to get too offended that she runs off to play with the toy kitchen without even giving me so much as a backward glance. I thank the staff and head out, hurrying to make sure I'm on time to meet

Anneka, seeing as Helen will most likely be late and Polly can't make it as she's working.

I arrive at the coffee shop with one minute to spare and spot her in the corner.

'Hey,' I say, leaning towards her and giving her a quick air kiss.

'Hi, hi,' she says. 'So glad you could made it on time. Of course, Helen is nowhere to be seen.'

I slip my handbag off my shoulder and sit down opposite her. I'm quite nervous being here just Anneka and I; she still slightly terrifies me.

'I'm sure she'll be here soon.'

The waitress comes over, and knowing Helen will probably be late, we order some herbal teas. Anneka also orders us some date squares, which sound like a poor substitute for the cakes that I'm eyeing up at the counter.

'How was your weekend?' I ask.

'Good, thanks. We had a dinner party with some friends of George's. There were twenty of us so it was quite lively.'

'Twenty,' I gasp in shock. 'Blimey, I couldn't cook for that many people.'

'Oh, Ellie, you're so funny. I got the caterers in,' she says, laughing like I've said something hysterical. 'Then, yesterday we went for a big Sunday roast with George's children.'

'Oh yes, you mentioned he had kids. How old are they?'

'Liam is sixteen and Lyla is fourteen.'

'Oh, proper teenagers. Do you get on well?'

The waitress pops our drinks and date squares in front of us.

'I was the evil stepmother for a while and they would do nasty things to me. Put cling film over the toilet seat, empty out my expensive moisturiser and replace it with stuff from

245

Poundland, scorching iron marks into my silk blouses. You name it, they did it.'

'Oh, Anneka.'

She shrugs her shoulders.

'To be honest, I can't really blame them. George and I, well, it wasn't long after he and his wife split when we moved in together. It was a shock for them and a shock for me to have his children in my life. I'm not proud of how I handled it either. I kept buying them presents and it took me a while to realise that I couldn't buy my way in.'

'And are they better now?'

'Mostly. It turned out that they just wanted someone to take a bit of an interest in them. Now I go to dance classes, and I watch my stepson shout into a headset whilst he kills zombies on video games.'

'I'm glad it's worked out.'

'Yeah,' she says, tucking into her date square as if it's actually nice. I take a nibble of the corner of mine and I'm surprised at how good it tastes.

'See,' she says, with a smug look on her face. 'You don't need all that refined sugar nonsense.'

'I still think that double chocolate fudge cake looks pretty good,' I say, trying my best not to look at it.

She shakes her head.

'So, how was your weekend? The big festival?'

'Yeah, it was amazing,' I say.

'Amazing?' she says, raising one of her perfectly shaped eyebrows. 'Does that mean Helen's going to be pissed off she arrived late and missed the saucy details?'

'Ooh, sounds like I'm right on time,' says Helen.

'You're only ten minutes late,' says Anneka.

'And hello to you too,' she says, giving us both a quick hug before sitting down next to Anneka. 'Now this sounds like something juicy.'

'I was just talking about the festival.'

'And?' she says, arching her eyebrow in anticipation.

'And we held hands.'

Helen's face falls and she asks the passing waitress for a decaf latte.

'At this rate I'm worried that the first time Max is going to see your fanny is when you're giving birth,' she says.

Anneka drops the tea bag she was dunking in her cup in shock and it spills over onto the saucer.

'What?' says Helen. 'Fanny isn't a swear word.'

'No, but it's not a word for a café in the middle of Fleet on a Monday morning,' she hisses whilst shielding her hand in front of her eyes in case anyone recognises her.

'What if that's true?' I say, starting to freak out. 'I hadn't even thought about it. He's going to have to be in the room when the baby is born, and what if his memory hasn't come back, and we haven't done it?'

Anneka throws Helen another glare before she turns back to me with a more reassuring look.

'You're going to Paris this week. Did you visit that website I sent you the link for? That underwear could be just the answer to all your worries,' she says.

'And probably get me arrested in some countries,' I say with a groan.

'Take lingerie like that to Paris and believe me there'll be more than hand holding going on.'

'I've ordered some for my babymoon this weekend,' says Helen. 'Not that it'll probably make the blind bit of difference with Toby.'

'That underwear never fails,' says Anneka. 'I'd forgotten you were going away too; we'll have so much to catch up on next time we meet up.'

'Don't count on it at my end. Anyway, what else happened at the festival?' asks Helen. 'Apart from the hand holding?'

'The hand holding that was very nice, may I add,' I say.

'Yeah, yeah,' says Helen. 'Come on, tell us the rest.'

A cup of tea and two date squares later, I've filled them in on the festival and mine and Max's progress over the past week, followed by the conversation with Owen that's left me a bit baffled.

'I still don't think that it's much to go on,' says Helen. 'Sounds like he was really hungover.'

'Yeah, but it was the way he said, "he doesn't need to know about Anne," that made me think that he does.'

'Why don't you know about Anne in the first place? Did you and Max not talk about exes when you first got together?' says Anneka.

'A little. I knew that he'd dated her but he gave me the impression that it was nothing serious.'

'And you left it at that?' says Anneka open-mouthed. 'I've always made sure I thoroughly checked out the exes; that way you know if you're in any danger or not.'

'I had no reason to check her out. Max broke up with her long before me; I didn't think she'd been that significant.'

'Every ex is significant. They're the ones that they compare you to when they're getting bored or restless.'

Helen pulls a face. 'Please don't tell me you actually think that.'

'Of course I do. Don't tell me you've never had an argument with Toby and afterwards wondered what one of your exes was up to and then fantasised about what your life might have been like if you'd stayed with them.'

Helen looks guilty.

'In my defence I've only been thinking of Horny Harry because of my lack of action at the moment.'

Anneka smiles smugly.

'I guess it's too late to do the research now, because I can't ask Max as he doesn't remember and Owen certainly won't talk so I'm at a bit of a dead end. I don't know why it's important, but there was something in his tone. He was almost angry to say her name.'

'This is why you should have found this all out before. I'm not saying you need to do thorough background checks on every man you date, but you should at least do the basics.'

Helen whistles under her breath.

'Aren't there any other friends you could ask?' says Anneka.

I think of Max's friend Dodgy Rodge and his sidekick Jez. As lovely as they both are, they're not the type of friends that Max would bare his soul to.

'Not really; he's only really close with Owen.'

'Is he married?'

'No, he's recently divorced.'

Anneka sits up a little straighter. 'Was he married when Max was with Anne?'

'Oh, I see where you're going. I don't know if I could ask Sarah. We're still friends on Facebook, but I've only seen her once since they split up. We kept saying we'd invite her to the house, but we haven't got round to it and now it's a bit awkward.'

'Nonsense. It's the perfect opportunity. She'd probably love to see you. Text her now.'

'Now?'

'Yes,' says Anneka, tapping the table twice like it's a command.

I throw Helen a look and she shrugs her shoulders.

'Not a terrible idea. Why don't you suggest you go to her?'

'I guess I could see if she can meet me for lunch one day; she works in central London.'

'Today, see if she can meet *today*,' says Anneka. 'No time like the present.'

'I'm sure she'd be busy.'

Anneka glares at me and I hastily obey.

My phone beeps almost immediately with a reply.

'She can make it,' I say, surprised. 'She's suggested a hotel at Bankside at one p.m.'

'There you go,' says Anneka with another smug face. 'You'll get to the bottom of it in no time.'

I find the hotel, a little relieved that the restaurant is more casual than I expected. I had to rush straight from meeting the girls to the train station and I didn't have time to change my leggings and tunic combo.

I spot Sarah immediately and she waves me over.

'Wow, look at you. You look absolutely fantastic,' she says, reaching over the table to give me a hug.

'So do you. Your hair looks stunning.'

She runs her hand through her short bob and smiles self-consciously.

'I felt like I needed a change,' she says, as we sit down opposite each other.

An awkwardness hangs in the air between us.

'I'm so sorry that we still haven't got you down to the house,' I say, starting and not knowing how to explain myself.

'It's OK. I knew that, when we broke up, Owen was going to keep certain people and with you being his best friend's wife, you were always going to be one of them,' she says with a theatrical sigh. 'I'm just glad that we still stayed friends on Facebook. It's so nice to see your bump updates, and to see photos of Sasha – she's getting big now.'

'She is indeed.'

'Where is she today?'

'She's at nursery.'

'And it's not long now is it until the new one arrives?'

'About six weeks,' I say, trying to ignore the reality of what's coming.

'That's so exciting.'

'Hmm,' I say. 'Sometimes we struggle with one, but two...'

'You'll be fine. I've got so many friends that have a second one and they just slot right in.'

There's a pause as the waiter comes over and gives us our menus.

'Anything to drink?'

'Sparkling water for me,' I say.

'Me too, please,' says Sarah, 'just bring us a large bottle.'

The waiter walks away and Sarah turns back to me.

'So, this is an unexpected pleasure. Have you got a meeting out this way afterwards?'

'Actually no, I um, came up specially to see you.'

'Really? Oh, it's not about Owen, is it? Because if you think he and I might work it out... We did try really hard at it. I mean, we even went to marriage counselling for six months. I thought he was doing OK?'

'He is, he is,' I say quickly. 'That's not why I'm here.'

'Oh good,' she says with relief. 'His mum came to see me not long after we separated and I thought that you were... sorry. Well, if it's not Owen...?'

'It's Max,' I say. 'He's um, lost his memory.'

She gasps and I launch into the spiel that flows so naturally now that I've told it multiple times. We're interrupted briefly by the waiter, who brings our water over, and we apologise for not having looked at the menus.

'That's incredible,' she says finally. 'And yet you're still standing? How are you not a wreck?'

'I don't know really. It's getting easier. I think it helps having Sasha to focus on. And he's slowly getting to know me again – or should I say, the adult me. That's sort of the reason I wanted to meet with you today.'

'Oh?' she says, leaning forward.

'The thing is, he's lost his memory from the last five years and I've been trying to fill him in on the lost time. And we've only been together for four of those years, so I'm trying to find out about the one before he met me.'

'Right,' says Sarah, nodding. 'So, where do I come in?'

'I was asking Owen about it and he went a bit funny and then ran off to the loo.'

Sarah laughs. 'I'm sorry, I shouldn't laugh; it's just that that's classic Owen. He's not very good with confrontation, or with lying. Which is why he often runs away during conversations. For the first year of our relationship I thought he had some kind of food intolerance because he went to the bathroom so much.'

'I just wondered whether – with you having been close to Max too – if you could remember any details from back then. Owen got a bit funny at the mention of one of his ex-girlfriends, in particular – Anne.'

Sarah looks a little too delighted when the waiter interrupts us to take our order. I still haven't really looked at the menu, so I quickly choose a salad.

'You know something, don't you?' I say with a pleading look when he leaves. 'I know it all happened long before we met, but I don't understand why he acted so strangely if it wasn't important.'

She looks uncomfortable, but then she lets out a deep sigh.

'Look, you and Max are such a happy couple, are you sure you want to know about things that happened way before you were together?'

My heart starts to race and I wipe my clammy hands on my leggings.

'Yes, I think it's only going to drive me crazy if I don't.'

'What if it changes how you think of him?'

'Is it really that bad?' I ask.

She shrugs her shoulders. 'It depends on whose perspective you look at it from.'

Max and I have never really talked about our past relationships in any massive detail; unlike Anneka, we never saw the point. We talked of exes in abstract terms and we were very much 'the past is the past kind' of people.

She takes a deep breath and then starts.

'So, her name was easy to remember because it was Anne Summers.'

I nearly choke on the water I'm drinking. 'Like the sex toys and lingerie?'

'Yep. I think she actually quite liked the attention it brought her and she'd always make a joke out of it. Although she was always quick to point out the "e" at the end of her name, to differentiate herself.

'She worked for Max's company, although in a different department. I think they met at a Christmas do.'

'OK,' I say. So far, so normal.

'He talked about her a lot at first, which was unusual for Max then. We were used to meeting the many different women he was dating but he never seemed particularly smitten like he was with her. Sorry, is this too weird?'

'No, it's fine,' I say, reminding myself this is all in the past.

'We met her once in the beginning and she seemed really nice, but then we found out she was married.'

'She was married?' I'm shocked. This isn't where I was expecting this to go. 'She was having an affair with Max?'

I can't take this all in; I know it wasn't him doing the cheating, but the fact that he knew she had a husband upsets me.

'Yeah,' she says with a gentle nod, 'when we found out, we thought she was horrid. It was bad enough she was cheating on her husband, but she was also leading someone as great as Max on. That really wound us up. It didn't last long, though. The guilt of being the other man affected Max and his conscience got the better of him.'

I'm left speechless.

'Ah, Ellie. Are you OK? I shouldn't have told you. Owen would tell me off for breaking the bro-code.'

'No, it's fine,' I say, trying to pretend that's true. 'What happened to Anne? Max said that she'd moved abroad.'

'That's right. From memory, I think she moved to America with her husband.'

I take a deep breath and try and process it all.

'Don't think badly of Max. He didn't know that she was married at first, and by the time he'd found out, he'd fallen for her. And he did do the decent thing in the end.'

'I wonder why he never told me? I'd have understood.'

'I think he was probably worried about what you'd think of him; no one ever looks favourably on the person someone's having an affair with.'

'I guess not,' I say, trying to weigh it all up. 'Do you think that's why Owen didn't want Max to find out about her?'

'Yes, definitely. Max was really embarrassed and hurt by the whole thing. I can't see any reason why he needs to relive that part of his life.'

I breathe a sigh of relief. Owen was just protecting his friend.

'I guess this explains a lot. When we first got together Max made a whole big deal about us being monogamous and he was adamant that he'd never tolerate cheating in a relationship.'

'Maybe it made him realise what kind of relationship he wanted,' she says. 'That and what happened to his parents.'

'Yes, I know that really affected him.'

I think of the Mick-and-Judy charade and it makes my stomach feel queasy. The longer his memory loss goes on for, the more uncomfortable I get with them lying to him. I know the doctor said not to upset him too much, but that was when we thought his memory was going to come back in a matter of hours. It's been two and a bit weeks now.

'The important thing to realise,' says Sarah, as the waiter comes over and puts our lunch down in front of us, 'is that none of this has any bearing on you and Max. Maybe it even helped you get together. Perhaps that was the relationship that Max needed to make him stop his womanising ways and to get him to settle down.'

'Maybe,' I say, my head still spinning.

'There's never been any question about how much he loves you, and that's all you need to focus on.'

'Yeah, I guess you're right,' I say.

I think about what Anneka said about finding out exes at the beginning, but she would have been wrong in this instance. If I'd found that out in the early stages of dating him, before I got to know Max like I do now, I might have judged him. But I know Max inside and out, and I know that he would never do anything to hurt anyone. It hasn't tainted my views of him, in fact it makes me thankful for whatever happened with Anne because – if what Sarah says is true – it paved the way for Max and I to have the perfect relationship we had up until two and a half weeks ago. And now I can go to Paris and concentrate on getting that man to properly fall back in love with me.

Chapter 18

I don't know how anyone can arrive on the streets of Paris and not go tingly with anticipation. It just oozes romance at every turn. Even on the brief taxi ride from the Gare du Nord, I couldn't help but pretend that I was in a fancy perfume advert as the car whizzed down the streets lined with the iconic Parisian façades. I'm just waiting for the big finale of the advert where the models end up in the bedroom with the two actors ripping off each other's clothes, the curtains billowing in front of the open window, with a perfectly framed Eiffel Tower in the background.

We booked a room in the boutique hotel Anneka recommended and I gasp as we walk into the lobby. It's beautiful. It's full of black marbled surfaces and dark velvet chairs with chintzy chandeliers hanging from the ceiling.

We walk over to the front desk and the man behind smiles up at us.

'We have a reservation in the name of Voss,' I say, forgetting that we're in France and I scratch my head wishing I'd remembered to gen up on some French. *'J'ai une… reservation?'*

'It's OK, we can speak in English, it's no problem,' he says with a faultless English accent.

'OK, great.'

He taps away on the keyboard and I give Max a little smile. We're here in Paris – the city of love – and I can just tell that he must be thinking that too.

'Here we are, Voss. You have a twin room on the third floor,' he says, tapping away some more. 'I'll just need your passports and a credit card.'

I pull out my passport and put it on the desk before it hits me what he said.

'Hang on,' I say, placing a hand over my passport so that he can't take it. 'Did you say twin room?'

'Uh-huh, it's a very nice room. Good view of the Panthéon.'

'That sounds nice,' says Max, sliding it across the desk.

'Hang on,' I repeat, grabbing hold of his too. 'We reserved a double room, we *need* a double room.'

The man looks down at the reservation.

'The site that you booked on doesn't guarantee that. What you actually reserved was a room for two.'

On any other day I would smile sweetly despite being pissed off and just thank him profusely and take the key. But these are not usual circumstances. I'm going to have sex with my husband for the second first time and I don't want to do it in a single bed. Bloody hell, with my sodding bump I can barely fit on a single bed by myself, let alone getting it on in one.

'I'm sorry but we need a double bed,' I say with pleading eyes.

Max turns and looks at me. 'Single beds will be fine, Ellie.'

I take a deep breath.

'No. They. Will. Not. We did not come to Paris to sleep in two single beds,' I say, loudly attracting the attention the other

258

people milling about in the lobby. Now everyone is looking at me like I'm some horny pregnant woman. Which of course I am, but I don't want everyone to know it.

'I'm very sorry, madam, all of our standard doubles have already gone. They are very popular.'

'I can imagine. Well, this will not do.'

'Ellie, let's just—'

I hold up my hand and don't let him finish his sentence.

'When we walked in and I saw how beautiful this place was, the Tripadvisor review was practically writing itself, only now I think it's going to say something quite different,' I say, my lip curling like a ferocious beast.

The man looks up from his computer screen and his eyes startle.

'Oh,' he says, quickly turning back to his screen and tapping away, 'what do you know, we have a suite available.'

'Perfect,' I say, exhaling loudly and trying to stop my hands from trembling. 'That would be most satisfactory.'

'But, um,' he says a little nervously. 'It's one of the more… exotic rooms. Will that be OK?'

'Is there a double bed in it?'

'Yes, yes,' he says quickly.

'Then it'll be fine. Exotic sounds good,' I say, thinking that he means a few shrubs.

I relinquish my grip on our passports and he photocopies them before handing them back along with our credit card and keys.

'Enjoy your stay,' he says with smile and we turn towards the lift.

'You see, you just need to be firm with people,' I say to Max as I stride across feeling about ten feet tall.

'You know you were pretty scary back there. Should I be worried?'

I laugh.

'No, the bitch rage is all baby hormones. I think I'll lose that somewhere in the first year after the baby's born. Or at least I did with Sasha.'

'Shit, that's a long time. I'll have to make sure I'm on my best behaviour.'

'Yeah, you will,' I say all cocky. We squeeze into the lift and head up to our floor.

We quickly find our room, and when I open the door my hand flies up to my mouth.

'Bloody hell,' says Max as we shuffle in. 'It's um, very red, isn't it?'

'Uh-huh.' It's about the only thing I can manage to say. He's right. From the beams latticing the ceiling to the velvet-textured wallpaper to the thick satin bedspread – everything is red. The only thing that isn't red is the painting hanging on the wall of a nude couple. Just in case you couldn't pick up on the not-so-subtle vibes the rest of the room was trying to give out.

I feel like we've walked into a seedy strip club and I'm just waiting for someone to spring out to give us a private dance.

'Well, at least it's got the double bed that you wanted,' says Max.

It's like a neon sign in the middle of the room taunting me; the concierge and everyone else in the lobby knows why I wanted it. But we're not quite at the stage of the perfume ad where they're ripping each other's clothes off just yet.

'Holy shit,' says Max, walking forward, 'look at that view!'

He steps forward and opens the door of the Juliet balcony.

I stand and look over his shoulder at the square in front of us and I catch myself gasping.

Max puts an arm around me and suddenly the red room and the bed don't seem so scary.

'This is beautiful,' I say to him.

'Yes, it is. At least when the red gets a bit much, we can look out here.'

'We certainly can.'

We stand there, admiring the city, before the chilly breeze whips around us and we step back and close the doors.

'Are you tired?' says Max and he looks at the bed that's become the elephant in the room.

'No, shall we go and explore?'

I peer over at the bathroom that is sectioned off by a small wall, which you can look over. Of course you can. The bath is visible from the bed and there's no shower. Which means one way or another Max is going to have to see me naked because there's no way I'll be climbing in and out of a roll-top bath with this bump. I'd be terrified of slipping.

'Yes, let's explore,' he says. 'It's a good job we're not drinking this weekend; this place with a hangover would be really shocking.'

'Yeah, wouldn't it? You'd wake up wondering if you'd passed out in a sleazy club.'

'I know those chairs are made for some kind of lap dance.'

'I'm sure I could give you one,' I say. 'Could you imagine? Instead of poking my boobs in your face you'd have my big belly.'

'That doesn't sound so bad,' he says with a chuckle and looking slightly tempted by the offer. I can't help but feel chuffed that things could be heading in the right direction after all.

'Let's get going with the exploring, shall we?' I spot my guidebook poking out of my handbag and go and retrieve it.

Max takes it from my hand and throws it on the bed.

'Let's just have a day that isn't planned. We've got two full days starting from tomorrow to see the sights.'

It's exactly what normal Max would always say.

'OK, then, lead on,' I say, holding my hand out for him to go first.

I give one last look at the double bed that I fought so hard for and I wonder when it's going to feel like the right time to use it in the way I'd intended.

You don't really have to go far in Paris to fall in love with it. We spend the afternoon mooching about the Latin Quarter, doing our best to dodge the crowds. We wander through cobbled streets, admiring university buildings and old churches, drifting in and out of tiny parks, past fountains and statues. All are marvels in their own right, but you almost become blasé seeing them all together.

The romance is truly infectious and we hold hands, catching each other's eye as we walk along and snuggle on benches. It's nice just being us, experiencing something together in the present, carving out new memories, rather than being so focused on the past.

Max and I stop to have a coffee at one of the many cafés and we can't resist having a bowl of ice cream too to tide us over until dinner.

I automatically slide over my bowl with the last spoonful of chocolate ice cream at the bottom.

'Oh, have you had enough?' says Max, not knowing what to do with it.

'Yes,' I say, thinking that it's time to put the memories of the past behind us. I'm not going to dwell on the fact he doesn't eat it like it's the last Rolo; I'm going to concentrate on making new traditions.

'Are you ready to go?' asks Max, after he pays the waiter.

'Yes, let's do it,' I say.

'You look tired, did you want to go back to the room and have a nap before dinner?'

I could close my eyes and go to sleep here.

'I don't have a very good track record with naps,' I laugh. 'If you get me into bed, you might never get me out of it.'

Max looks at me and raises an eyebrow.

'Would that be such a bad thing? Especially when you went to such great lengths to get us it?'

'Oh, jeez, the porn room, I've been trying to forget about that mortifying experience.'

'It's not that bad,' he says, trying not to laugh. 'It's a nice room.'

'Yeah, if we kept all the lights down low.'

We start giggling and can't stop. I don't know if it's entirely related to the hideous room decor or more about the embarrassment from both knowing what this trip's building up to.

'So, shall we head back?' says Max. 'I might have a bath before we go for dinner.'

'Uh-huh,' I say, thinking of him in the open-plan room bathing naked. I tug at the collar of my wool dress. Is it just me or is it getting hot?

Max takes me by the hand, pulling me up, and doesn't let go as we walk off.

We head along the banks of the Seine towards our hotel. Just when I didn't think Paris could be any more beautiful, the sky explodes into a pink dusk. The streetlights are pinging on and the lights of the city are flickering on all over the place.

'This place is so beautiful,' I say.

'I know, it's funny, I always thought the whole Paris being romantic was so clichéd but I get it now that I'm here. It's not what I expected at all.'

'Just wait until we get to the Eiffel Tower tomorrow.'

'We don't have to do all that, you know. I can take your word for it that we've done it before. I'm just enjoying this. Walking and talking. I think at this point I'd rather get to know you than a city.'

We walk past a couple who are taking PDA to a whole other level.

'Blimey,' I say, shielding the view with my hand. 'Did you see where his hand was?'

'Maybe he was trying to keep her bum warm. I bet she's cold.'

'Well, maybe if she had bigger knickers on,' I say, thinking of the extra-large ones I'm wearing.

Max laughs heartily.

'That was a nil point kiss,' I say.

'What does that mean?' he says.

So much for me not explaining our little traditions.

'We often rate kisses out of ten – you know, when we're watching movies, or when you're trying to initiate some bed-room action – you try and give me a seven-plus kiss.'

'Right,' he nods. 'Huh, I thought it was a good one; there was certainly lots of passion.'

'It was too much of a public display of affection for my liking.'

'You're a harsh judge. You know there are an awful lot of couples about, aren't there?' he says, looking round. 'It's like they've all seemed to come out now it's getting dark.'

'Like vampires,' I say.

'Well, he's certainly doing a good job of trying to suck her blood,' says Max, pointing at a man nibbling his partner's neck. 'How many points does that get?'

'Three maybe,' I say. 'It's semi romantic.'

We walk along a bit more, and it isn't long before we see another kissing couple.

'Now that kiss is very lacklustre. That's got to be a low scorer,' says Max.

'But look, he's cupping her face. It's a bit Ryan Gosling.'

'And that's a good thing?'

'Oh, absolutely. Five points for that.'

'But he looks like he's trying to squeeze the life out of her. It's a nil pointer from me.'

'Brutal.'

'But I guess you have to be, though, don't you? It's not like every kiss could be a ten out of ten,' he says.

'Exactly. So, what do you think would make a ten?'

'Hmm, I don't know.' We walk a bit further, hand in hand, whilst he thinks about it. 'I guess, first of all, it's all about the build-up. You know, the moment where you get the other's attention, it's got to take them a little unaware.'

'Oh, like they have to have them in that exact second.'

'Exactly, it's got to have that urgency about it. And it's got to have that *bam* moment where that spark hits – you know, when it shakes your entire body.'

'Uh-huh,' I nod.

'And then there'd be the hand creep. It definitely doesn't cup the face, maybe it starts off at the back of the neck and slides gently down the spine before it strokes the small of the back and then maybe down to the bum, but not under the clothes like our friend back there, not at this point.'

'And then what happens?' We're walking so slowly that we've practically stopped and I'm edging closer to him.

'And then for it to be a real ten kiss there's got to be that act of passion. You know, the woman jumps her legs round his waist and he holds her close. Or maybe one of them pushes the other against a wall.'

'And that's a ten?' I say weakly. In all our years of playing this game, we've never articulated what a perfect kiss would be and I've got goosebumps.

'No, that's a nine; to make it a ten it has to have the breathy bit.'

'The breathy bit?'

'Uh-huh. The bit where you pull away for a second and you're breathing so close to one another that you don't know whose breath is whose. And that, Ellie Voss, is a perfect te—'

Max doesn't get to finish his sentence as I stop and pull him round to face me before I launch into a kiss.

He's taken aback for a split second – but only a split second – then he kisses me like he's never kissed me before. I feel his hands reach under my open coat and they find their way to my back and I reach mine up to his shoulders and start stroking the nape of his neck before I pull him even closer towards me. I find myself bending back into the balustrade and he presses up against the big bump. I'm vaguely aware that there are other people milling about and I pull out of the kiss and open my eyes to find he's staring hard into mine and we're nose to nose and breathing deeply.

'Now I get the breathy bit,' I say, trying to get my breath back.

'Yeah,' he says doing the same.

'You're right – that kind of kiss is a high scorer. But it wasn't quite a perfect ten for me.'

His eyebrows narrow. 'It wasn't?'

'No, I think that we perhaps had too many clothes on.'

'Oh right?' he says, and he looks at me like he's going to tear my clothes off right here, right now. A small smile spreads over his face. 'And seeing as we know that you get marks deducted for flashing in public, I take it the only way around that would be to get to the hotel as quick as we can.'

'I think that's the wisest course of action,' I say, dragging him by the hand and hurrying down the side street.

It doesn't take us long to reach our hotel and the receptionist behind the front desk chuckles when we practically run through the lobby.

We squeeze into the tiny lift and Max pulls the concertina'd iron door across. All I want to do is kiss him but we can barely fit the two of us in as it is. It eventually pings to announce our floor and Max prises the door open and we hurry along to our boudoir.

The door's barely shut before I'm shrugging off my coat and he's unbuttoning his then he starts kissing me and tugging at my dress at the same time, only separating as he pulls it over my head, and I rip his jumper over his. His T-shirt comes next and I fight with his belt to unbuckle his trousers and they fall to the floor.

'I'm going to need some help with my tights and shoes,' I say, breaking away with an embarrassed laugh. I've got way too much of the pregnancy horn to feel self-conscious that my giant boobs are housed in the nursing bra that's probably the least sexy underwear I own, or the stretch marks spreading over my skin. Max doesn't look like he cares either. He's as hungry for this as I am.

'You are so beautiful,' he says, catching his breath.

I blink back a tear and my heart starts to pound.

He gently guides me down onto the edge of the bed before he bends down and slips my feet out of my boots. He then reaches up and tugs at the waist band of my tights and slides them gently down my legs, before he runs his hands all the way down the inside of my leg causing me to shiver. His hands linger at my giant knickers and then he slips them off too. I have no idea what he's seeing as I haven't seen down there for so long thanks to the giant bump.

He pulls me up to standing and I pull down his boxers and he reaches over and unclasps my bra.

I can't remember the last time that we had sex that wasn't just a quick fumble late at night on a rare occasion when neither of us wasn't knackered from work or looking after Sasha. This is so slow and deliberate that the whole of my body is aroused and I almost feel like it's our first time; it's certainly the first time that we've slowed right down and that I'm taking in every single second of it.

He tucks a loose bit of hair behind my ear and I reach up and hold my hand on his and we're doing the nose-to-nose breathing thing again and the anticipation is driving me insane. Just when I think I can't take it any longer, he surges forward and kisses me.

And this time there's no doubt in my mind it's the perfect ten. The kiss that would put all other kisses to shame.

'Fucking hell,' says Max, lying back against his pillow. 'Is it always like that?'

'No, most of the time we're knackered and don't even bother taking our socks off.'

He exhales loudly again and holds his hands up to his head as he lies flat on his back. I roll towards him and prop myself up.

'You know, you're not finished with your duties just yet,' I say.

'What, you want to do it again…? Ellie, I don't think I can just yet.'

'No, I'm talking about you – I'm talking about me and you know… finishing me off.'

'Finishing you off?' he says, brow furrowing.

'Yeah, you know.' I wiggle my fingers.

He rolls over and props himself to mirror my position; he looks dumbfounded.

'Did you not—'

'No.'

'Huh. I thought you—'

'No,' I say with a smile and a shake of the head. 'Don't get me wrong, it was amazing, but, you know, sometimes you have to do a little work after.'

'Right…' He's looking perplexed. I have a vague memory of a similar conversation with him years ago, only then it was through a fog of tequila. 'You know, I'm usually pretty good at this and I haven't ever really had any complaints. And I would have thought I'd have known if I was doing it wrong.'

'Believe me, you weren't doing anything wrong at all. But you might have a left a few ladies frustrated in your wake.'

'Huh,' he says, and I lean over and kiss him.

'I shouldn't have said anything.'

'No,' he says, pulling back. 'You absolutely should. Do I normally just crack on and do this automatically?'

'Uh-huh, I don't have to ask; I can just lie back and off you go,' I say, lying heavily. I usually have to elbow him in the ribs to remind him.

'Right, then,' he says again. 'I'll have you know that I'm very good at this too.'

'I know, Max Voss, get on with it, please.'

'OK, but I'm going to have position myself down there so I can see what I'm doing – and with the bump you won't be able to see me.'

'Believe me, I don't need to see you.'

'But my face is my best bit,' he says, looking up at me.

'I'd argue right now that your fingers are the best bit.'

'Oh, really? Right, well… I was just going to go for it straight away but if you're going to be like that…' he says, tracing his fingers along my thighs, 'I might just have to take my time.'

He rolls me onto my back and I collapse into giggles and longing. I can't remember when Max and I were last like this. It's made me realise that we don't have to follow the same roadmap to falling in love that we followed last time – it feels like this will lead us to the same place in the end.

Chapter 19

The rest of our trip to Paris passed in a blur of perfect-ten kisses, more sex than is probably advisable for an almost eight-months-pregnant woman, meandering strolls through picture-perfect streets and eating my new body weight in delicious meals. We might not have done any of the big sights but I think we did what really mattered, which is find our way back to each other. I know that sounds cheesy as hell, but after the last month I don't care.

More than ever, I've realised that Max and I have to start living our life again rather than focusing on the past we've forgotten. So, in a bid to getting this new chapter in our life together started, when I collected Sasha from Judy's yesterday, I convinced her and Mick that it was time to tell the truth about their relationship. It's been three weeks now, and Max's memory is showing no sign of coming back and the longer it goes on the more uncomfortable I feel lying to him.

They're on their way over for dinner; officially it's to say thank you for looking after Sasha when we were in Paris, but unofficially it's to break it to him gently about their divorce.

Steam rushes out of the oven as I open it to check on the lasagne, which is bubbling away nicely.

'She went out like a light,' says Max, walking back into the kitchen.

'Ah, good. Thanks for putting her down.'

'No problem. It was my turn; that's how it works, right?'

'Absolutely,' I nod at Max 2.0. I know I should correct him that he's not a Stepford Husband but I can't do it. If I'm honest, he's acting out the fantasy of how I imagined him as a dad, and clearly based on all this, it's how he imagined himself as one too.

'It smells delicious. What should I do?' he says.

'Um, the salad's done and the garlic bread is prepped. Open the wine maybe?' I point to a bottle of red on the side.

'Is that all you want me to do?' He walks behind me and slides his arms around my waist. He plants kisses down my neck and I stop tidying away and I turn round and kiss him properly.

'Max, where are those hands going? Your parents are going to be here any minute.'

His hands keep wandering and he starts to giggle in between kisses, as I slap his hands away.

'We don't have time.'

'I can be quick.'

'Just what every girl wants to hear.'

'Or I can be slow,' he says, planting a long lingering kiss on my neck that makes my toes curl.

There's a gentle knock at the door and we practically leap apart.

'Shit, my parents are here,' he says, running his hand through his hair.

'I did try and tell you they were due over imminently before you started to get me all worked up.'

He looks delighted that he's got me hot under the collar.

'To be continued,' he says, with a wink as he goes to answer the front door.

I take a few deep breaths and try and fan my cheeks with an oven glove and when that doesn't work, I open and close the oven in a bid to make it look like they've pinkened from the steam.

'Ah, Ellie, that smells delicious,' says Judy, walking in. She's closely followed by Mick, and Graham.

'Oh,' I say, not able to hide my surprise at Graham being here. I know he's part of Judy's new future, but I really thought they'd be better off telling Max the truth with just the two of them.

'Oh, Ellie, I forgot to say, I invited Graham,' says Max, wincing. 'It slipped my mind.'

Graham looks flustered.

'Oh, Ellie, you weren't expecting me, I can go,' he says, turning to leave.

'No, stay.' I walk forward and give him a hug hello. 'You're more than welcome. We've got plenty of food.'

I give Mick a quick hug and he clings to me like it's the last hug he's ever going to give me.

'I brought you some nice apple juice,' says Judy, handing it over to me.

'Thanks, Judy. Max, are you OK to sort out the drinks?'

'Sure,' he says. He's still got that horny teenager look on his face and I try to ignore him. My cheeks are still flushed.

'Sasha go down all right?' asks Judy.

'Yes, Max got her down in record time.'

'It was all that sweeping up she did today,' says Mick. 'She kept following us around in the lounge with her little brush.'

'Making a mess, more like,' I say, with a little laugh.

I see the sadness in Mick's eyes. It's not just Max who he's developed a relationship with over the last few weeks, but Sasha too.

'So, do we get to see the lounge, or is there going to be some big grand reopening?' says Judy.

'I'll show you if you like, Mum?' says Max, handing out the glasses of red wine.

'Come on, Graham,' she says, reaching her hand out only to stop halfway, giving him a little tap on the arm as if she suddenly remembers he's not supposed to be her boyfriend. 'You haven't seen it either.'

'How are you feeling?' I ask Mick when the others have gone.

'OK,' he shrugs. 'I know we can't keep putting this off, but...'

'It's hard. You worry you're going to lose him and Sasha all over again.'

'Oh, Ellie,' he says, shaking his head. 'It's the biggest regret of my life that I lost him in the first place, and as for Sasha... It's the main reason I haven't been over from Portugal to meet her before. When I'm away I can pretend that here doesn't really exist and that she's just someone in a photograph, but now I know her personality. The little shuffle she does when music comes on, and the way her eyes almost pop out of her head at the sight of a biscuit.'

He squeezes the bridge of his nose.

'Come on, Mick, you know that I'll always let you see Sasha. Plus, you never know, this time might be different with Max.'

'No,' he says, sighing. 'It won't be. If anything, it'll be worse because I've been pretending. I shouldn't have gone along with it at the beginning, but when he hugged me when I walked in and he treated me like he used to... I couldn't help it.'

'I know,' I say, reaching out and squeezing his arm.

He blinks back some tears. The others come back in and he walks over to peer out through the patio doors in a bid to hide them.

'It looks fantastic,' says Judy, sweeping back into the kitchen. 'So smart. It's made me think that we could do with sprucing ours up before we sell.'

'Sell?' says Max, picking up his wine glass from the sideboard. 'You're selling the house?'

Judy looks at Mick, and I brace myself for the truth to come out. I'd kind of hoped that we'd have got the meal out of the way first, but perhaps this is for the best.

'We're downsizing. No point in us having a big old place like that,' says Mick.

'Oh right,' says Max, mulling it over. 'I guess it's a bit big for the two of you, but the house is where we grew up.'

'Oh, well, don't worry, we're ages away from putting it on the market,' says Judy.

'I don't think we're quite that far away, are we?' says Mick. 'Start of the new year.'

'Start of the new year?' says Max. Since his memory loss, he seems to have taken most things in his stride, but this seems to have hit a nerve.

'Just an idea, but we can postpone it,' says Judy, trying to reassure him. 'But you know, not all change is bad.'

'Yeah, I know. I'm probably being a bit stupid because I knew you'd sell it one day, but my whole childhood was in that house and right now when I'm missing a lot of memories, I guess it's nice to cling on to.'

He takes a deep breath and I reach out and squeeze his hand.

Mick raises his eyebrows at Judy and she looks back at him with panic.

'Where are you going to move to?' asks Max.

'I've got my eye on a little place in Crookham Village.'

'Near Graham,' he says.

Mick laughs before covering it with a cough.

'Still not very far from you two, though, which is the main thing,' says Judy. 'But there's no rush, really.'

With no big reveals in sight, I open the oven and I declare that the lasagne is ready.

'Excellent,' says Mick, 'I'm starving.'

'Sit yourselves down at the table. Max, can you set an extra place for Graham.'

'Are you sure you've got enough?' he says before he sits down.

'Yes, absolutely,' I say, pulling out a dish of lasagne so big that it could feed the whole street and popping it on the table.

Graham sits down next to Judy and Mick sits at the head of the table, leaving Max and I to sit next to each other.

Everyone starts serving up the food, and I reach over to grab the serving spoon at the same time as Max and we brush hands. He can't resist taking hold of mine and I wonder if anyone else can see the crackle of electricity between us.

'So, you haven't told us about Paris yet,' says Judy. 'It was all such a rush when you picked Sasha up.'

'It was absolutely wonderful.' I'm unable to hide the smile that's crept over my face.

'Did you go to the Louvre?' asks Judy. 'We got elbowed left right and centre when we went last year, and the Mona Lisa was so small.'

'No, we didn't really make it there,' I say.

'Oh,' says Judy. 'How about Sacré-Cœur?'

I pull a little face.

'Eiffel Tower? Palace of Versailles?'

'Um, no, we stayed pretty local,' I say. We didn't get more than a few blocks away from our hotel for three days.

'I guess it's hard in your condition to walk around a lot, and you don't want to have crowds elbowing you,' says Judy.

'Mmmhmm, yes, that was it,' I say. Max squeezes my thigh under the table. 'We just sat about in the cafés a lot, watching the world go by.'

Which is true, in between a lot of sex.

'That's one of my favourite things about Paris,' says Graham. 'I loved sitting in Place Dauphine, drinking and people-watching.'

'In that lovely little café where we had that thick hot chocolate,' says Judy.

'Oh, did you all go together?' says Max, breaking off some bread.

Judy looks horrified at her slip-of-the-tongue, but it's given them yet another perfect opportunity to tell him the truth.

'Yes, we did,' says Judy. 'The three of us went.'

'The three of you went to Paris together?' Max looks between all of them carefully.

'Uh-huh,' says Mick.

I close my eyes momentarily; they promised me they were

going to tell the truth. The opportunities keep presenting themselves but they keep telling more lies.

'I guess it's nice that the three of you get on so well.'

'Hmm,' says Judy, clearly changing the subject. 'This is delicious, Ellie.'

'Thanks, Max helped too.'

'Oh yes, it tastes so good because of my excellent chopping skills,' he says, laughing.

'Don't knock a good sous-chef,' says Graham. 'Everyone needs one, huh, Judy?'

'Yes, of course,' she says quickly, 'and Mick is such a good one.'

Graham's face falls, but Max doesn't notice; instead he laughs.

'That's a joke, right? Or has Dad started suddenly helping in the kitchen?'

Judy and Mick awkwardly laugh and I raise an eyebrow.

'A lot's changed with Mick and Judy in the last five years,' I say, growing tired of this.

'Dad, don't tell me you've started cooking?'

Mick opens his mouth but he hesitates as if he can't find the words. His phone starts to ring and he looks relieved at the distraction.

He pulls it out of his shirt pocket and then freezes when he sees the display. He fumbles around trying to turn it off, but it drops onto the table, and it falls in front of Max.

'Who's Ruby?' he says, picking it up and handing it back.

'No one,' he says. 'Just my Pilates instructor.'

'Your Pilates instructor is ringing you on a Sunday evening?'

'Mick's been trying to set her up with Graham,' says Judy, quickly.

Graham drops his fork and it clatters on his plate.

'Oh, that's exciting, huh, Graham. Pilates instructor,' says Max, with an exaggerated wink.

'As I've told your dad,' he says, hardening his jaw, 'young and flexible isn't everything. I prefer a mature woman with intelligence and a good sense of humour.'

'Being young and flexible doesn't define a person's character, you know,' says Mick, and Judy sighs loudly. 'She is very smart and funny.'

'Does anyone want any more?' I say, worried where this is all heading.

Both Mick and Graham take more but the tension's still bubbling away.

'So, Mick, didn't you tell me that you wanted to say something to Max?' I say, putting my knife and fork down on my plate.

He nods his head and takes a deep breath.

'Just that, it's been a real pleasure working on the lounge with you. I've really enjoyed spending so much time with you, and...'

This is it; I brace myself.

'I can't wait to start on getting rid of the mural too.'

'Ah, Dad,' says Max. 'I've enjoyed it too.'

I purse my lips together.

'Did anyone else just hear Sasha?'

'I can't hear anything,' says Max.

'You couldn't just go up and check on her, seeing as you've got the magic touch at the moment?'

279

'Sure,' he says, getting up.

I wait until he's halfway up the stairs when I lean over the table. 'Are you going to tell him?'

'I don't think it's the right time, do you?' says Judy, looking sheepishly over at Mick.

'No, did you see how funny he got about the house?'

I can't deny that he did look shaken, but that's no excuse for telling all these lies.

'It can't go on forever,' says Graham. 'I'm not cut out for this tangled web of deceit.'

Bless Graham, I think Judy's amateur dramatics are rubbing off on him.

'I know,' says Judy. 'It's eating me up.'

'Me too,' says Mick. 'Plus, Ruby's patience is wearing thin. But,' he adds, 'I do think this isn't the best way to tell him. Don't you think it might seem like a bit of an ambush?'

'Yes,' says Judy, 'I agree. Perhaps we should tell him, just the two of us. We could go for a walk around the pond. We used to love walking there with him when he was younger.'

'Good idea,' says Mick.

'But it will be soon, won't it?' I say, sighing.

'Of course, Ellie. We'll get the hallways done and then we'll tell him next week, I promise.'

'Absolutely,' says Judy, whispering as Max's footsteps become louder.

'Still sound asleep,' says Max, sitting back down. He puts his hand on the small of my back. I've missed these little touches.

'Ah, sorry, I must have imagined the noise,' I say, wrinkling my face up. 'Anyone for dessert?'

I leap up so that he can't tell that I was lying. This really is Mick and Judy's last chance, because if they won't tell him next week, I will. Max and I are heading in the right direction and I don't want that being built on a foundation of lies.

Chapter 20

Max and Mick did such a cracking job finishing off the lounge that I've invited my NCT girls over to christen the room with an afternoon tea. Not wanting to disturb us, Max decided to tackle the jungle that is our garden this afternoon.

I set down a tray of tea on the coffee table and look up, sensing their eyes on me. It doesn't help that all three of them are sat on the sofa in a line reminiscent of an interview panel.

'What? Why are you all looking at me?'

'We want to hear about Paris...' prompts Polly.

'So much for acting cool,' says Helen.

'I'm sorry, I couldn't help it. I'm just such a hopeless romantic and right now this story, it's so dreamy. Can I blame the hormones?'

'You can always blame the hormones,' I say, pouring out the tea.

'That photo that you sent of you two snuggled up at that café,' she says with almost a tear in her eye.

'I know, it was pretty soppy, but I'm really loving all the hand holding and little kisses.' I'm beaming.

'OK, enough with the PG stuff,' says Helen, reaching for

one of the cups I've just poured. 'What we really want to know is: was there full-frontal nudity or not?'

I instinctively look up at the door and strain my ears to hear the strimmer still in action in the garden, meaning Max won't overhear.

'Yes, yes, there was. A lot of it,' I say with almost a giggle. Helen's eyes light up.

'Go on,' she says, settling back into the sofa.

'What? That's it. We did it and now everything is fine.'

'Everything is fine?' says Helen, unimpressed. 'We've been waiting for this moment for weeks and that's all we get?'

'I'm afraid so. But hang on, what about your babymoon? Surely you don't need to live vicariously any more,' I say.

'Ooh yes,' says Anneka. 'Did the underwear do the trick?'

Helen sighs loudly. 'He put his fucking back out, didn't he? He spent the whole bloody weekend moaning about how much his back ached. And whilst I'd hoped that we'd spend the whole weekend in bed, him lying there watching continuous sport whilst his back went in and out of spasm is not really what I had in mind. That's why I need details, I need...'

'We all know what you need,' says Anneka, stirring her tea. 'I'll send you a link to another online shop, and Toby being out of action won't be an issue.'

Helen nods in gratitude.

'So how are the rest of you?' I ask. 'I feel like all I do at these meet-ups is talk about myself.'

'Don't be ridiculous,' says Polly. 'The only thing I have to say for myself at the moment is that my ankles have started to swell up and my heartburn's getting worse.'

'And I found a Burberry onesie for the baby today that brings out the colour in my eyes,' says Anneka.

'Always what I look for in a baby outfit, to be honest,' says Helen with grin.

'You see, Ellie, you're not dominating anything, we've not got a lot to say at the moment,' says Polly.

'Exactly,' says Helen. 'That'll change when the little ones are born, but right now, unless you want to have an in-depth conversation about *Stranger Things* or me not having sex – which are my two specialist subjects at the moment – then I think we're absolutely fine to talk about what's going on with you.'

'OK.' I feel reassured and I tell them edited highlights of our trip. When I reach the bit where we have our perfect ten kiss they sigh collectively.

'That was worth the wait,' says Helen, reaching out for another biscuit. 'I am suitably jealous.'

'Sounds wonderful,' says Polly.

'It does,' says Anneka, her hand hovering over the biscuits momentarily before she thinks better of it. 'So, I was wondering: did you ever look into that Anne woman?'

'No,' I say, 'I haven't really given her much thought since I saw Sarah.'

'Oh,' says Anneka. She seems surprised. 'You've not been tempted to look her up on Facebook?'

'No, I've been so busy.'

'Yeah, all that sex you're having,' says Helen wistfully.

'I couldn't do that,' says Anneka. 'If I had the name, I'd have to look them up.'

'What's with you and exes?' says Helen.

'I just like to know, that's all.' She gives me a look with

a raised eyebrow that says she's not going to drop it anytime soon. I pick up my iPad from the coffee table.

'Fine, I'll look her up, although I don't know how I'd know which one she is – I bet there are loads of Anne Summers.'

'Bring it over here,' says Anneka, patting the chair and making Polly and Helen shift along to make room. There's no point trying to argue with her, so I squeeze in on the sofa until we're wedged in like sardines.

I bring up Facebook and type *Anne Summers* in the search bar.

A big list comes up and we all peer at it. The first few are photos of women in skimpy underwear, but then come the women in actual clothing who seem like real people.

'She could be any of them,' I say, scrolling down.

'Mmmhmm,' says Anneka, 'I was hoping that Max would have still been friends with her and then she would have been listed more prominently.'

'Probably a good sign that he's not, though, right?' says Polly, and I nod.

'Didn't you say she worked with Max? Maybe she has her workplace listed?' says Helen.

'Maybe, but look, you have to click on the person and on the "about" section to see their past workplaces, if they even list them at all,' I say, demonstrating on a random Anne Summers who lives in Canada.

'Maybe if we all looked,' says Anneka, pulling her phone out of her bag.

'I don't think you need to—' I'm thinking this has probably gone too far as it is, but no sooner does Anneka start tapping than she gasps. 'My friend is friends with an Anne Summers,' she says, pointing to the top of her list. 'Ah, it's Ninny Collins, she's got thousands of Facebook friends – you only need to make eye contact with her and she's tracked you down and befriended you.'

Anneka clicks on the about her section of the profile of the pretty blonde woman.

'She's listed her previous companies too. Walsh Knightly Associates, Hemmingfield Brothers, PDCA,' says Anneka, rattling them all off.

'Wait, Max works at PDCA.'

My heart starts to pound in my chest as I find the same woman on my list. I click on the profile photo, taking in her surroundings – a glamorous-looking roof-top bar surrounded by high-rise buildings.

'Do you think it's her?' asks Helen.

'Seems a bit coincidental not to be,' I say, staring at her perfect white smile and mane of perfectly blow-dried hair. 'Max's firm only has an office in London. And Sarah said she moved to America, and this one lives in New York.'

'Is her profile unlocked?' asks Polly.

'No, I can only see her profile picture changes. They're of her looking swanky in New York. Look, there she is on a boat in front of the Boathouse in Central Park,' I say. 'And there she is running on the Brooklyn Bridge.'

'Wait,' says Helen, scrolling back up, 'that's not the Boathouse. I went to a wedding there once; it looks familiar, though.'

Polly and Anneka lean over.

'That's the bar at the Serpentine,' says Anneka.

'Yes,' says Helen, 'that's where I recognise it from.'

I click on the photo that's a recent cover photo change.

'Oh shit,' I say.

'What?' says Anneka, leaning in and reading over my shoulder. '*That's right, bitches, I'm moving back to Blighty.*'

'When was it dated?' asks Polly.

I look on the screen.

'Two months ago. A month before Max lost his memory.'

'That doesn't mean anything, though, does it?' says Polly.

'No, but this does,' I say, pointing to the comments underneath.

Gemma Hartley

OMG! Can't wait to see you. Are you back in London?
X x

Anne Summers

Yes! In Chiswick. Let's meet for a drink soon x x x

My blood runs cold.

'Max lost his memory in Chiswick,' I say slowly. 'What if he was meeting her? Maybe that's why there are no messages about his meeting on his phone. Maybe he deleted them as he didn't want me to find out.'

I suddenly feel sick at the thought. In all my imaginings of what he was doing in Chiswick, I'd never thought of him having a clandestine meeting with an ex.

'And maybe it's a coincidence,' says Polly, only she doesn't sound convinced, and neither are Anneka and Helen, judging from the looks on their faces.

Max walks into the room and we all stare up at him.

Anneka quickly turns the iPad on my lap face down.

'Um, hello,' he says, awkwardly. 'Sorry, did I interrupt?'

'No,' says Polly a little too quickly. 'We were just, um...'

'Looking at birth videos,' says Helen. 'You know, preparing ourselves for the mental scarring.'

'Oh right, um... I might just leave you to it then. That sounds very...' He pulls a face and doesn't finish his sentence. 'I'm going to go and get Sasha from nursery.'

He comes over and leans down to give me a quick kiss on the top of the head and I find myself flinching.

'You OK?' he says.

'Yes, sorry. Birth videos. Traumatised,' I mutter.

'Must have been bad,' he says, heading out the door. 'I'll see you in a bit.'

I raise my hand to wave and just about keep a smile on my face, but when he walks out it falls.

'What are you going to do?' asks Polly as the front door slams.

'I don't know. I mean it still doesn't really help us, does it? Even if it was her that he was meeting, it doesn't really explain why he lost his memory. And Max can't help us as he has no memory of her in the first place,' I say, standing up and exhaling loudly.

'You could talk to my friend Ninny. She'll be at my baby shower on Saturday.'

'Oh yes, I can just imagine that. Hello Ninny, do you know if my husband was meeting one of your thousands of Facebook friends,' I say a little too snappily. 'Anneka, I'm sorry, I—'

'Don't apologise, this is all my fault in the first place

for suggesting it. I honestly didn't think...' I've never seen Anneka look sheepish before.

'There's still nothing to think,' says Polly. 'I'm sure that if he was meeting her it would have been for something entirely platonic.'

I do love Polly, but I don't buy it for a second. The more I think about it, the more I think that Anne is connected to Max and his memory loss, and I've got to find out more.

Chapter 21

Max pops his hand on my thigh as I'm driving.

'You OK?' he says. 'You've seemed distracted over the last couple of days.'

'I'm fine,' I lie. I don't feel I can mention Anne to him just yet, not until I find out the truth myself. Mainly because I don't know how I'd explain that I'd found out. *Well, you know, Max, I was casually stalking your ex-girlfriend on Facebook...* It doesn't exactly scream 'trust'.

We're heading down to the New Forest for a family day out. I love going there at this time of year when the leaves have started changing to autumnal colours, but what I'm most excited about is spending some proper time together as a family. It was lovely and romantic with it being just Max and I in Paris, but I really do love it when it's just the three of us, and I get to watch the bond between Max and Sasha become stronger and stronger each day.

But before we could start making our way down there, we needed to stop off at Judy's to pick up the camping chairs that were so handy at the festival and the big cool box.

'You know, we really must buy all this outdoors stuff, now that we've got a house to put it all in,' I say, pulling up onto the drive.

'I guess so. Is that how you know you're a proper grown-up? When you own a plug-in cool box.'

'Probably,' I laugh. It's then that I notice that the curtains are still drawn. That's odd as Judy is normally an early riser. 'Do you think your mum's up?'

'Oh yeah, she's always up at the crack of dawn. She's probably left the curtains closed because Dad is still asleep. I'll just use the keys, rather than knock, so I don't wake him.'

I watch Max go, and I turn and talk to Sasha who's repeating 'Gran-Gran' over and over, as that's what she calls Judy. I'm chatting away to her when Max knocks on the window. It makes me jump and I wind it down.

'You've got to come in,' he says in a panic. 'Bring Sasha.'

'OK,' I say, trying my best to leap out as spritely I can. I unclip Sasha and carry her across to Max, who's hovering at the open front door.

'What's wrong?' I ask.

'It was Graham. He was walking down the stairs when I opened the door.'

'Oh right,' I say, keeping my tone neutral. 'Perhaps he had a late night and stayed over.'

'He was wearing Mum's frilly pink dressing gown.'

'Oh,' I say again.

'And he came out of their bedroom. Oh my God, Ellie,' he says, turning to me. I brace myself. I guess this is the moment that the truth is finally going to come out. 'I think my parents were having a threesome with Graham.'

'*What?*' I say, wondering how he put two and two together and got ten, not to mention giving me mental images that I now can't unimagine.

'It's the only logical explanation. He's here all the time and the three of them hang out together. They went to Paris as a three. Graham's single and oh… do you think they've always been doing it?'

He's contorting his face in all manner of strange ways.

'Don't jump to any conclusions,' I say, knowing the truth. 'There's bound to be a logical explanation.'

'I can't think of one,' he says with a bit of panic. 'They were all teenagers in the sixties; maybe all that hippy stuff still goes on. But the *three* of them, at *their* age—'

'Max, I don't think—' I stop because I can't explain it without telling him the truth.

'How am I supposed to look them in the eye when I see them all?' he says with a panic. 'Do you think we can go? We'll stop and buy chairs and a cooler on the way.'

'Max,' says Judy, poking her head out of the kitchen and peering down the hallway. She's dressed in a nightie with another floral dressing gown. Her hair that's usually framed neatly around her face is sticking up to one side and she's squinting in the hallway light.

Sasha toddles over the threshold and down towards her and I notice Judy wince as she bends down to give her a kiss.

'Are you OK?' I say, walking towards her, not used to seeing her in a dishevelled state. Max hesitates in the doorway, before eventually he joins us as we follow Judy into the kitchen.

'Yes, fine, just um, a little too much port last night,' she says, breathing slowly and deliberately.

'Oh,' I say, relaxing that it's just a hangover.

'Coffee?' she says. 'I'm just making a big pot. And then I thought I might try and eat a fry-up, if you want one?'

Max looks like he's still processing the thought of Graham and his parents.

'We weren't really going to stop; we just popping in for—'

Judy's hand flies up to her mouth.

'Oh, Ellie, I'm so sorry I forgot. I'll head out to the shed and get it sorted.' She walks towards the back door slowly. 'It hurts to move, after last night.'

Max looks at me and I'm worried his eyes are going to pop out of his head.

'She probably means because of the hangover,' I say, trying to calm him down.

Mick walks into the kitchen, clutching his head.

'Bloody hell, Judy, I didn't think you still had that type of night in you,' he says, before he looks up and sees us. 'Max? Ellie? What are you doing here?'

'We just popped in for the camping chairs. You feeling a bit worse for wear too?' I ask.

'Yeah,' he says, groaning. 'Big night.'

'You, Mum and Graham,' says Max.

'Ah, yes, it got a bit wild.'

Poor Max. He's practically going purple.

'Are you two staying for breakfast? Judy's doing us a fry-up.'

'No, we're not staying,' says Max, keeping himself firmly in the doorway.

Graham walks into the kitchen and he barely looks in our direction.

'I, um, I had to stay over as it was late and I, um, couldn't drive home,' he says hastily.

As Judy has forgotten we were popping in, she clearly hasn't prepped him with an explanation.

'No taxis?' says Max, folding his arms.

'Oh, um, taxi, yeah, I guess I could, but then I'd have had to get the car today and, um...'

Judy walks back in carrying the camping chairs and the cooler and Graham rushes to help her.

'You want to watch that with your back, after last night,' he says. 'Are you in any less pain?'

'It still hurts, I shouldn't have bent over like that, it's been a while.'

'We've got to go,' says Max, clearly flustered. 'We'll leave you to whatever you're all doing.'

'Stay, have some eggs and coffee. You'll only get stuck in rush-hour traffic,' says Judy, leading Max over to the table and steering him into a chair.

Graham fills a glass of water from the tap and drinks a sip, for a second I wonder if he's going to be sick, but then he drinks some more.

'It was a bit of a session last night, wasn't it, Graham?' says Mick.

I can see the vein in Max's neck starting to throb.

'Certainly was. I can't take it like I used to. We were so much better at it when we were younger.'

'We certainly were. Remember how we'd be up all night?' says Judy with a cackle, and Mick and Graham conspiratorially join in. Something's changed between the three of them; the ice has melted.

'So, what are your plans today?' I say, steering the conversation on to more neutral territory before Max explodes.

'To be honest, I expect we'll all be recovering from last night,' says Mick with a wink.

Max pushes his chair back, causing it to screech across the laminate flooring, and stands up.

Everyone turns to look at him and he opens his mouth once or twice before closing it, but before he can say anything the doorbell goes. Judy sighs, pressing down on the table to push herself up like it's a huge effort.

'I'll get it, shall I?' I say, relieved to be retreating out of the kitchen.

I open the door and now it's my turn for my jaw to drop. There standing on the doorstep is the last person I am expecting to see. Dressed in athletic gear and a cropped sweatshirt that hangs loosely off one shoulder and clutching a little carry-on case is Ruby.

'Ellie,' she says, looking equally confused to see me. I've only met her once, but occasionally I speak to her when I'm skyping Mick. 'Look at you. Aren't you massive?'

She seems to stand up a little straighter, showing off her bare midriff, making me feel even bigger.

'Hmm, well, I am due at the beginning of November,' I say through gritted teeth. I've always tried my hardest to like Ruby, but she doesn't make it easy.

'Are you sure it's not twins?' She stares hard at my stomach with disbelief.

'Yes, pretty sure,' I say, wishing I could slam the door in her face. Instead I walk out on to the doorstep and pull the door almost all the way shut behind me. 'Does Mick know you're here?'

'No. I've been trying to get hold of him for days and he won't return my bloody calls.'

'Right, OK, well, I'm sure he's told you about Max and

that he doesn't know about you yet. So, I think you turning up here is more than a little awkward.'

'Perhaps Mick should have thought of that before he decided to play happy fucking families then, shouldn't he?'

She goes to push past me and for once my bump comes in handy as I block her path and she doesn't dare push me around.

'Ruby, I understand why you're upset. If I was you, I'd be livid, but Max is the innocent party in all this. Whatever issue you've got with Mick, please can you take that up with him alone?'

'Mick's left me no bloody option.'

'Look, I'll go and get him for you,' I say, and she looks relieved. 'On one condition.'

'OK, what?' she says, crossing her arms over her chest.

'I want you to promise that you will not let Max know who you really are. I want Mick and Judy to tell him gently.'

She sighs loudly.

'Fine, but I'm coming into the house as it's bloody freezing out here. Why is it so cold?'

'Because it's England and it's autumn.'

'I knew there was a reason I'd left this bloody place,' she says, her teeth chattering.

'Stay here,' I say firmly, as she crosses over the threshold into the hallway.

I walk back into the kitchen and I'm wondering how I'm going to get Mick to come out when I find that Max is now sitting back down staring between Mick and Graham. Sasha walks over to me and I scoop her up onto my hip.

'Everything OK?' I ask.

'I think Max might be having a funny turn,' says Judy. 'Who was at the door?'

'Oh yes, Mick, there was a—'

The kitchen door opens and in glides Ruby.

'Ah, hello everyone,' she says, standing with her leg out and her hand on her hip like she's posing at the end of a runway.

Graham, Judy and Mick spin their heads, their mouths agape.

Max looks up at her with curiosity and I can tell he's trying to work out who she is.

'This is Ruby—' says Mick.

'The Pilates instructor,' says Judy, finishing my sentence.

'Oh, *you're* the Pilates instructor,' says Max, staring at her before he turns to Graham.

Mick looks pale, which is no mean feat with his tan that doesn't seem to have faded.

'Ruby,' he says. 'I wasn't expecting you.'

'Clearly,' she says, folding her arms together. 'And you look like crap. Hungover?'

He hangs his head in shame.

'Graham came over for drinks last night.'

'Oh, did he now? And he's still here this morning,' she says with an exaggerated wink. 'Where was my invite?'

'Oh God,' says Max, leaping up again and backing away from the table. 'You're at it too?'

Everyone turns to look at him, taking in his horrified look.

'Has this been going on for years?'

'A few,' says Ruby, flicking her hair back.

Max shakes his head. 'It was bad enough that the three of you were swinging, but this... is there anyone else I should know about? Is it like some sort of club you belong to?'

I squeeze Sasha in closer, relieved that she's too young to

understand what's going on and that's she's more interested in trying to strangle me with my own necklace.

'Swinging,' says Judy in a high-pitched squeak. '*Swinging...?* Swinging.'

She's stuck on a word and she looks like she's going to spontaneously combust out of mortification at the insinuation.

'Swinging,' says Ruby, her nostrils flaring. 'I knew it, Mick! I knew that you two being under the same roof again would come to something like this.'

'Max, there's no swinging going on,' says Graham, by contrast, speaking in a calm voice.

'I don't know what you call it then – a threesome,' he says. Judy wails.

'There's nothing like that going on,' says Graham.

'And the three of you went to Paris together,' says Max, rapidly blinking like he's trying to process everything.

'Paris,' says Ruby, her hands flying up in the air. 'You told me Max and Ellie went to Paris, not you three.'

'But I saw you coming out of their room this morning. Are you trying to tell me that I didn't see that? And you kept talking about aching and bending over,' he says, shuddering and pointing at his Mum.

'Mick was trying to teach us Pilates,' says Judy.

Ruby scoffs, 'That old chestnut.'

Max and Ruby are staring hard at Judy, Mick and Graham, each of them having got the wrong end of the stick.

'Um, guys,' I say. Ruby looks at me furiously for interrupting and I back up a little, taking Sasha with me.

'You did see me coming out of Judy's bedroom, Max,' says Graham, standing up slowly. 'But it's not what you think. Judy,

Mick, I think it's time to tell him the truth. There's just two of us in a relationship.'

Max staggers backwards and looks between them.

'You and… Dad,' he says, 'I guess that would explain the three-week golf trip.'

'What?' says Mick. 'No, no, no. That's not what's going on.' He looks pleadingly at Judy and she sighs.

'Max, I think it's time to sit down,' she says, guiding him into a chair and sitting down beside him. 'It's not your dad who's having a relationship with Graham, it's me.'

'And you know about this?' he says, looking at Mick aghast. 'And what, you turn a blind eye?'

Mick takes a deep breath and shuffles his chair closer to Max's.

'We didn't want to tell you this at first as we didn't want to upset you, but your mum and I… we split up a few years ago. I now live in Portugal with Ruby here. Ruby is my girlfriend,' he says, sighing.

'So she's not your Pilates teacher?'

'She was, that's how we met.' His voice is raw with emotion. 'I met her when I moved to Portugal.'

Max is looking between them all as he takes it all in.

'You're separated, and you're dating *him*?' Max says, turning to Judy before he turns to Mick. 'And you're dating *her*?'

He looks shellshocked and he closes his eyes for a second. I want to go to him, to hold him, but now's not the time; now he needs to hear the truth.

'But why did you move to Portugal? Why didn't you go, Mum?'

Judy takes hold of his hands.

'Your Dad and I—' she says, taking a deep breath. 'It wasn't really working and I don't think I saw that at the time, but your dad went away and he didn't come back.'

'You walked out on Mum?' he says, turning to him, his face in a scowl.

'Max—' starts Mick.

'No, I don't want to hear it,' he says, standing up again. 'Let me get this straight, you've been pretending to be together this whole time?'

'We didn't plan to do it,' says Judy. 'I hadn't wanted to upset you at first by telling you, but I didn't expect your dad to turn up on our doorstep. So I panicked and pretended to still be married to him. But you have to remember at that point we all thought your memory would be coming back any second and we didn't want to upset you any more in case it made it worse.'

'It's been almost four weeks,' says Max. 'Were you ever going to tell me the truth?'

'Ellie's been trying to get us to,' says Judy. 'That's why we came to dinner last week, but you looked so happy after Paris.'

'I don't believe you. I don't believe any of you. You've been lying to me this whole time. What else are you lying to me about?'

He turns and looks straight at me.

'How much of what I think is true actually is?' There's an edge creeping into his voice that makes me shudder.

'Max, I promise you and me, it was all real,' I say.

'Don't bring her into it, Max,' says Mick, standing up, 'she kept wanting us to tell you. It's all my fault; if you want to blame someone, blame me. Judy was trying to protect you from getting unnecessarily hurt, but I didn't tell you because

I was being selfish. I've never regretted anything more in my life than losing you these last few years. But these past four weeks, they've been the best weeks of my life.'

'Thank you very much,' says Ruby, folding her arms across her chest.

Mick sighs.

'It's true. I thought I'd lost you forever and to have you back in my life... I know it was wrong.'

Mick wipes away a tear that's rolling down his cheek and he takes a step closer.

'Don't,' says Max. 'I don't want to hear it.'

He storms out of the kitchen and I pop Sasha into Judy's arms and go after him.

'Max, wait, please,' I say.

'No, Ellie. Do you have any idea what it's like having no memory of your life and relying on the people you're supposed to trust the most to tell you what has happened? I don't know what to think any more. I just need to get out.'

'Do you want me to come?'

'No, I want to be alone,' he says, walking towards the front door then slamming it behind him.

I can hear raised voices coming from the kitchen and I go in to collect Sasha.

No one notices that I've come back in and they are all shouting at each other, spouting blame at every turn.

'Quiet,' I shout, and the four of them are stunned into silence and Sasha bursts into tears. I go and pick her up from Judy and squeeze her tight to reassure her. 'Arguing isn't going to help to sort this mess out. Max is really hurt that we've all lied to him.'

'Do you think he'll forgive us?' says Judy, sitting down on a chair.

'I hope so, but I've never seen him that angry before.'

'I have,' says Mick, pain in his eyes.

'It's my fault,' says Judy. 'It was my stupid idea. I didn't want to see him get hurt and now we've hurt him worse than ever.'

'No, it's mine for being selfish,' Mick says.

'Look, the question here isn't about blame. You made a decision with his best interests at heart but it didn't pan out the way you intended.'

I try and soothe Sasha who's still making squeaky half-sobbing noises.

'Well, now that it's all out in the open there's no need to stick around, is there?' says Ruby. 'He's back to hating you so you can come back to Portugal with me.'

Mick sighs. 'I'm not leaving him a second time. I'm going to check into a hotel, like I should have done initially. He's going to have questions and I want to be here to answer them. Judy, if he comes back, will you let me know?'

'And I'm going to head off too,' says Graham. 'You're going to have to work this all out as a family.'

'But you're part of the family,' says Judy, reaching out and grabbing his hand.

'Give Max some time to get used to the idea,' he says, leaning down and giving her a kiss on the head. He turns to Mick and gives him a pat on the back. 'The one thing we can take from this is that it brought us back to speaking terms, eh?'

'That it did.' Mick nods and stands up. 'I'll go and pack my suitcase.'

Judy looks over at Ruby.

'I guess I'll go and wait outside. It's frostier in here than it is out there,' she says, walking out with a wiggle in her hips.

'Oh, Ellie, what have I done?' says Judy, hanging her head in her hands.

'He'll come around.'

Seeing as though we're no longer heading on our day trip, I go over and flick the kettle on because everyone knows the only thing to do in a crisis is to make tea.

'I hope you're right because I don't know what I'd do if I lost Max.'

And I know how she feels because I feel exactly the same.

Chapter 22

I've always wondered if anyone actually likes baby showers. As a mum-to-be I hate the idea of everyone gathering to give me presents and play socially uncomfortable games. It's the last place I'd want to be on a normal day, let alone when I feel like I should be comforting my husband.

After finding out the truth about his parents yesterday, Max briefly came home to pick up some of his things and then he headed off to stay with Rach. He didn't want to talk and I didn't want to force him. He said that Rach was the only person that would truly understand what he was going through, and he's right.

I'd thought about not coming to Anneka's baby shower and then I remembered that it's Anneka and she's still pretty terrifying, plus there's a chance that her friend Ninny might be able to shed some light on Anne, who I'd almost forgotten about in all of yesterday's drama. Judy insisted that she wanted to look after Sasha, to take her mind off things, and so here I am.

I could have guessed that any baby shower Anneka had would be extra, but, as Polly and I pull up on the drive, we get a taste of just how over-the-top it's going to be.

'Is that a pony?' gasps Polly.

'I think it is,' I say, walking closer towards it to see that it's got a horn attached to its browband to make it look like a unicorn. Only Anneka would have a unicorn at her party.

'If that's what's outside, what the hell is going to be inside?'

We exchange glances and Polly rings the doorbell. It's quickly answered by someone dressed in a pale-pink dress.

'Welcome to Anneka's baby shower,' she says with a smile. She hands us a unicorn headband to wear. 'Please have your photo taken behind the frame and remember to tag it on Instagram!'

I look over at the cardboard photo booth with a big #babyFernleyMatthewLowe hashtag sign underneath.

'Not exactly a catchy hashtag. You wonder why she didn't shorten it to #babyFML… oh,' says Polly, giggling. We stand behind it and the woman takes the photos for us.

We spot Helen over in the corner and she waves us over.

'What are you doing here? You do know you're here on time, right?' I say.

'I was fucking early,' she says, sipping on a pink drink. 'I'd cottoned on the fact that Anneka keeps inviting me places an hour earlier than you're all meeting, so I've started adjusting accordingly. Today she told me it started three hours ago.'

'So, you've been here ages.'

'Ten minutes. But in those ten minutes I've wanted to tear my eyeballs out. She's even given us a headband to wear that's turned us into an actual dickhead.'

'You know it's supposed to be a unicorn? I take it that unicorns aren't really your thing?' I say softly, not wanting to provoke the rage.

'Nope, and neither are pastel fucking colours.'

'Ladies, you're here,' says Anneka, drifting over. She's wearing a floor-length pastel-pink dress with a giant slit up one side, and her hair has been tonged into loose curls pinned to the side with little flowers that remind me of the unicorn cakes you see on Instagram.

'This is wonderful,' I say, leaning into a hug and bashing bumps.

'It's nothing. Just a little something I threw together.'

Helen rolls her eyes.

'Yes, I can see you blowing up a zillion balloons yourself.'

'Ha, I caught my stepchildren raiding my gin collection and I made them blow them all up as punishment.'

'You're so mean,' I say, secretly impressed.

'Just fulfilling my job as wicked stepmother. I think they've probably been raiding it for years but you don't tend to notice an inch or two of gin missing when you're drinking that every night yourself, but seeing as I've been sober for eight months it's easier to keep track of these things.'

'My mum used to mark all the bottles,' says Polly.

'Mine too, but I used to fill up my bottle and then top up hers with water,' says Helen.

'Didn't they cotton on?' I take a pink mocktail from a passing waiter.

'No, they only brought them all out once a year at their New Year's Eve party, and what was funny was watching all these adults thinking they were super pissed when in reality the vodka Cokes they were drinking were in fact ninety per cent water.'

We all laugh.

'Is George here today?' I say, looking round, hoping to catch a glimpse of her elusive husband.

'Oh no, it's Saturday. George will be on the golf course all day today.'

'Wise man,' says Helen. 'Men have it easy with babies, don't they? They don't have to sit around being polite to people, playing shitty games and spending money on a present for both the baby and the mum. Instead they get to go out on a night out with the other dads and get absolutely shit-faced, all in the name of wetting the baby's head. We're the ones that had our bodies stretched and torn and we're the ones that have to stay at home and look after the baby alone whilst they do goodness knows what.'

'And breathe,' I say.

'But I'm right, though, I'm fucking right?'

'You are,' says Polly. 'I'd never really thought about it before. But it should be us going out and wetting that baby's head.'

'Yes, it should,' says Helen. 'But nature doesn't work that way, does it? We'll probably be on-demand breastfeeding, or so sore we can't sit down, or too fucking knackered to want to leave the house in anything other than sweatpants.'

'And so, anyway, lovely baby shower, Anneka. You've done such a wonderful job with the theme,' I say, raising my glass.

'Oh yes, it's just beautiful,' says Polly.

'Yes, yes, beautiful,' says Helen, reaching for a handful of biscuits that a waitress offers to us. 'And at least there are biscuits.'

'They're kale cookies,' says Anneka as soon as Helen's taken her first bite.

Helen wrinkles her face as she continues to chew and Anneka gives her a little wave and glides off.

'How did they taste?' asks Polly.

'Not too bad,' she says when she finally stops chewing, 'although there is a bit of an aftertaste.'

She reaches for her drink and downs it.

'I've been eyeing up that big unicorn cake for a while but now I'm not so keen. It's probably spinach flavoured,' she says with a sigh.

'Is everything OK with you today?' I say gently.

'What, are you saying I'm being even more of a bitch today?' she says.

'No.' Polly and I quickly shake our heads.

Helen raises an eyebrow.

'Let's just say that you're not your usual happy self,' I say, trying to be diplomatic.

'It's Toby, the saga of his back has got worse. He's been signed off work so now he's at home too.'

'Oh lovely,' says Polly. 'You get to have that extra quality time together before the baby comes.'

'It's the worst bloody thing that's happened. I went to lie on the sofa to eat crumpets and binge watch *Queer Eye* and he'd beaten me to it. He was watching some crime-lord drama and eating all the good chocolate I'd been saving for my hospital bag.

'If it wasn't for the fact that I'm not going to be able to handle the sleepless nights by myself, I'd be calling up Anneka's George.'

'Maybe you should do that anyway; at least then we'd find out what he looked like,' I say, and for the first time since we arrived Helen cracks a smile.

'Hopefully it'll be better next week as I've ordered a new

TV for the bedroom. Figure I can lure him up there and then I can at least have the downstairs to myself.'

'Wouldn't the bed be more comfortable for you?' asks Polly.

'Yes, but I'd be cut off from the kitchen and right now snacks are weighing high on my priority list.'

'Mine too,' I say, looking carefully at the canapés being handed round. 'What is it?'

'Pea puree on puff pastry,' says the waiter.

I take one and pop it in my mouth; it's divine.

Helen looks at it with distrust and the waiter moves on.

'Did you get Anneka a gift?' asks Helen.

'Yeah, I got some of the reusable nappies from her list,' I say.

'Same,' says Helen. 'The mere thought of Anneka and her perfectly manicured nails scraping them and putting them in the washing machine was like giving a gift to myself.'

'You know that she's joined that service where you put them out on the doorstep and they return magically cleaned,' says Polly.

'There's a service that does that?' I say in disbelief.

'Yes, if you're willing to pay for it. But I'm pretty sure you have to scrape still,' says Helen with a twinkle in her eye.

'You're so mean,' says Polly.

'I bet you bought them too.'

'I did, but mainly because everything else was designer and way out of my price range.'

'There was that.' I nod in agreement.

The waiter comes by with more pea puree bites and I take two. One for me, one for the baby.

Anneka walks past with her arm looped through another woman's. She slows down as she passes us.

'Oh, Ninny,' she says, loudly, 'that's hilarious.'

We all stare at the woman with flame-red hair that somehow knows Max's ex. I managed to convince Anneka that I'd talk to her myself if she pointed her out, but now that she's in the same room as me, I don't know how I'm going to bring it up.

'What are you going to do?' asks Polly.

'I don't know. I've been wracking my brains what to say without sounding like a complete stalker. How do I shoehorn that we have a mutual friend in common?'

'Ooh, I know, why don't you get her to add you as a friend on Facebook then be like, *look, we have a friend in common*,' says Polly.

'I thought of that too, but when she looks she'll see she won't have one in common because Ellie's not actually friends with Anne on Facebook,' says Helen.

The woman that answered the door to us when we arrived comes over with some peach clipboards.

'Anneka has made individual ice-breaker games. They're questions about various points in her life that she wants you to ask people you don't know.'

I'm expecting for Helen to tell her where she can shove the clipboards, but she holds her hand out.

'Thank you, that sounds like a wonderful idea,' she says. Polly and I look at her, stunned.

We all take the clipboards and the woman walks over to the next group of women.

'Here's how we do it,' says Helen. 'I'll go over to Ninny and ask her my Anneka questions.'

'Which Sweet Valley High twin did Anneka most identify with?' asks Polly, reading over her shoulder. 'How's that going to help?'

'They're all different, right? Let's just imagine that Anneka's favourite shop happens to be Ann Summers. Wish me luck.'

Helen strides off before we can object to the plan and Polly and I shuffle closer to earwig.

'Hi, I'm Helen,' she says to Ninny. I've never seen her smile so much.

'Hello, now, I'm guessing you must be one of Anneka's yummy mummy friends.'

I watch Helen almost snap the pen in her hand; she hates the name on our WhatsApp group.

'Yes, well guessed,' she says, with a smile. 'And how do you know Anneka?'

'We go way back; we used to work together, back in the day.'

'Oh right,' Helen nods. 'Have you got your ice-breaker questions? I love ice-breakers. So much fun, don't you think?'

'Yes! And these are so great. I'll start – which Spice Girl do you think Anneka would most have wanted to be?'

'Got to be Posh, right?'

'Ha ha, correct!' says Ninny.

'OK, and so for me, what naughty shop did Anneka buy a particular... mechanical rabbit from?'

I nearly spill my drink in surprise.

'Oh, like the toy that walks along and flips?' she says, wrinkling her face in confusion.

'Not quite,' says Helen. 'I was thinking more of an adult toy?'

'Oh right,' she says, still confused at what Helen's getting at. To be fair it's only because I know where she's going with this that I'm able to follow the conversation, otherwise I would be lost too.

'I'll try another one. Which lingerie brand did Anneka borrow the name from once on a night out?'

'Agent Provocateur, that is *so* Anneka.'

It really is *so* Anneka. Poor Helen, she's going red in the face.

'Good guess, but I think it's more high-street.'

'Figleaves? Floosy? Victoria's Secret?'

'Ann Summers,' screams Polly before clasping her hand over her mouth. 'Sorry, I couldn't help it, is that what you were after?'

'Oh, did she really?' says Ninny, laughing. 'You know, it's funny. I actually know someone called Anne Summers.'

'*Really?* What a coincidence,' says Helen with relief.

'Yeah, she's really good friends with a friend of mine. Oh, poor Anne,' she says, shaking her head. 'Anyway, that was really fun. I guess we should circulate and do more ice-breakers. Hey, what's your name and I'll look you up on Facebook?'

Helen doesn't get a chance to reply as I step in.

'Excuse me, sorry, I didn't mean to overhear, but I don't suppose you were talking about Anne Summers that used to work at PDCA? My husband used to work with her.'

'Oh yes, that rings a bell. I think she worked there before she went to New York.'

'Did I hear on the grapevine that she's back in the UK?'

'Yes, although I bet she wishes she'd stayed Stateside.'

'Why, what happened?' I say.

'She got hit by a bus, about a month ago.'

My blood runs cold.

'She what? Is she dead?' I stutter.

My head starts to spin; a month ago is when Max lost his memory.

'No, she was so lucky. Apparently, she broke her leg really badly and had some bad bruising.'

'Oh my God,' says Polly. 'That's awful.'

'But that's not even the worst bit, apparently; my friend was telling me she'd been with her boyfriend and he didn't even wait for the ambulance, he just took off.'

I hadn't realised that Helen was holding on to my arm but it's a good job she is as without her my legs would have given way.

'Where did it happen?' I ask.

'Somewhere up in London, Chiswick rings a bell.'

I close my eyes and my whole world is slowly starting to fall apart. The phone call from the hospital in Hammersmith. It all fits.

'Did your friend say boyfriend? I thought she was married?' I say, my voice shaky.

'No, apparently she and her husband split up. He stayed in New York and she came back alone.'

I only vaguely hear the rest of the conversation... traction... hospital... home.

'Would your friend have an address for her? I'm sure my husband would want to send her flowers,' I say, trying to sound casual and not like she's planted a seed in my brain that my husband might have been having an affair.

'I can get it for you. What's your name? I'll add you as a friend on Facebook.'

She digs out her phone and sends me a friend request, before she goes off to do more mingling.

'You know, it still could all be just a coincidence,' says Polly.

'But it happened in Chiswick, where Max lost his memory around the same time that she got hit by a bus. Ninny said that the boyfriend didn't stop at the scene. What if the bus accident is the traumatic event that caused him to blank the past five years out? What if Max was the boyfriend?'

My mind is racing nineteen to the dozen and I can't think straight.

'What, Ellie? Where did you get that from?' says Polly, shocked. 'You can't be suggesting he was having an affair?'

'Can't I? This is what I do for a living. I connect the dots, and the dots here all fit together with the same outcome – that Max is the boyfriend in question.'

The two of them fall silent and my mind continues to whir.

'He was working late a lot and was constantly distracted. He said it was because he was trying to get things done before the baby was born, but what if it was because he was meeting her?'

'Ellie, don't jump to conclusions,' says Helen, softly.

'I don't think I'm jumping to anything, but there are only two people who can tell me if I'm right about this; one of them has lost his memory and the other's resting at home with a broken leg.'

'You're not seriously going to see her, are you?' says Polly.

'Come on, you two would want to know if it was Jason or Toby having an affair, wouldn't you?'

'If Toby was having an affair I'd at least be relieved, as that might explain why we're not having sex,' she says before she looks horrified. 'I'm sorry, terrible time to make a joke. Yes, of course I'd want to know.'

'Who wants to do a nappy race?' asks Anneka. 'It's going to be super fun. We're all going to be blindfolded and we have to change the nappy super quick.'

'That doesn't really sound like a game, more like what we're going to spend the next year doing,' says Helen.

'Actually, Anneka, I think I'm going to go home. I'm not feeling that well,' I say.

'But you can't leave now. Unless – is the baby OK?'

'The baby's fine, but I really think it's best I go.'

'OK,' says Anneka. 'You do look a bit pale. It's such a shame you're going to miss voting for which is the cutest baby photo of me.'

'Such a shame,' says Helen with a wink.

'I'll give you a lift,' says Polly.

'No, you stay. I'll call a cab.'

'It's no problem.'

'Stay,' I say, giving her hand a squeeze.

'Yes, you can't all bail,' says Anneka. 'Hang on, Ellie, I'll get you a goody bag.'

'OK, great,' I say. The last thing I want right now is a goody bag, but I stand there and wait anyway.

Anneka comes back over. I was expecting a small little favour bag but she hands me a unicorn tote bag that's jam-packed with stuff.

'Text me later and let me know you're OK,' she says. 'I won't get too close in case it's catching.'

'I will do, thanks so much,' I say, turning to leave.

'And us too,' says Helen, pulling me into a hug goodbye. 'I'll drop anything, anytime if you need me.'

'Thank you,' I say, choking up.

After a month of uncertainty and wanting to know the truth, now that I'm on the cusp of getting it I'm suddenly not so sure I'll like what I'm going to find.

Chapter 23

'Max,' I shout a little too loudly in the train carriage. I've already been given scornful looks by the people around me for my phone ringing, despite the fact that I'm not even sat in a quiet carriage. But my signal is terrible; it keeps dropping in and out. 'I'll give you a call when I've arrived at the station.'

'No, don't worry. I'll be...' the signal disappears '...at home... this afternoon.'

'OK,' I say, sighing with relief. He's spent the whole weekend with Rach and Gaby but I'm pleased – from what I've cobbled together from the conversation – that he's finally going to talk to his parents about everything and try to sort things out. 'Good luck.'

We've spoken on the phone a couple of times over the weekend, and whilst I get the impression that he doesn't blame me for not telling him, there's been a slight shift in his trust. I can empathise with that, because I now know what it's like finding out something that turns your world entirely on its head.

After Anneka's baby shower, I spent the weekend trying to think whether there had been any tell-tale signs of Max having an affair. Ninny sent through her address almost immediately

316

after Anneka's party, and I've been trying to work out whether I should confront Anne ever since. Would she talk to me? What if I've got it all wrong and Max wasn't meeting her? Would she think I was a right weirdo for turning up? Or if he was with her, would I be able to handle what I heard? I honestly didn't know if I was brave enough to do it until I dropped Sasha off at nursery this morning but I felt like I was on autopilot; I drove to the train station and now I'm en route to her house.

The train slows as it pulls into Chiswick station, and I slip my phone in my bag and head off very slowly to Anne's flat. The closer I get, the more nervous I become and the slower I walk. I've been so focused on getting here that I haven't planned what I'm going to say or how I'm going to introduce myself.

I reach the outside of the big Victorian house, find the entrance to 11b, which turns out to be a basement flat. I go to knock on the door, but before my knuckle makes contact, it swings open. A middle-aged woman wearing a blue nurse's tunic is standing there with a big smile on her face.

'Ah, you made it before I left, fantastic! Anne was worried she'd have to try and get up. I've left two cups out in the kitchen with tea bags in and along with a packet of cookies. Anne's in the lounge. Have a lovely time,' she says. She slips her bag over her shoulder and heads past me, but holds the door open for me to go in.

'Actually...' I start, before changing my mind. It feels a bit wrong sneaking in when she clearly thinks I'm someone else, but at least this solves the problem of Anne potentially refusing to see me. 'Thank you.'

The nurse smiles and heads up the stairs to the street and I step over the threshold into the flat.

I head straight into the lounge and Anne's sat with her leg elevated in bright-pink plaster, her long blonde hair tied up in a messy topknot. She might have a few scars on her cheeks, but she still looks as pretty as she did in her Facebook pictures.

She looks up and becomes agitated when she sees me.

'Who are you?' she says, trying to push herself up.

'Sorry, I know I shouldn't just barge in like this but your nurse – never mind. I'm Ellie, Ellie Voss,' I add quickly to stop her freaking out.

Anne stops trying to get up. She may no longer look scared at the possibility of a stranger in her flat, but she doesn't look any happier to see me.

'Is Max with you?' she says, looking over my shoulder.

'No, he doesn't know I'm here.'

'Right,' she says. 'Did you want to sit down? You might be more comfortable.'

I perch gratefully in an armchair.

'I'm sorry about what happened to you,' I say, trying to keep my voice steady. 'Will your leg heal OK?'

'The doctors think the prognosis is good. I was incredibly lucky,' she says, 'but I'm guessing that's not why you came all the way here.'

'No,' I say, looking at the get well soon cards lining the mantelpiece and the big bouquets of expensive-looking flowers on the hearth. 'I came to talk to about you and Max.'

'Me and Max?' she says with an almost bitter laugh. 'Look, Ellie, I don't know what Max has told you but, as far as I'm concerned, he can go fuck himself.'

'Right,' I say, trying to keep calm. I'm the one that should be angry, not her. 'It's just that I was hoping that you might help me understand the day of your accident, what you and Max were...' I can't bring myself to finish the sentence.

'You want to understand the day of the accident? You mean, when I got hit by a bus and he left me there alone? I woke up in an ambulance to a paramedic telling me that Max had turned and walked away, instead of helping me when I was injured. Did he tell you that?' she says.

'Actually, he can't tell me that. He doesn't remember.'

'He what?' she says, still angry.

'He's lost his memory. The doctors think something traumatic happened to him and it caused him to go into a fugue that causes temporary amnesia of the last few years.'

I go on to explain how we didn't know what it was that had caused him to shut down and how I now think it was seeing her get hit by the bus.

'His brain shut down? That's why he left me there alone?'

'I guess so,' I say.

Her whole demeanour changes and the venomous tone has been replaced by one of confusion and disbelief.

'So, he wasn't an utter shit for not checking on me?'

'I know Max and there's no way he'd have left under normal circumstances.'

She reaches for a glass of water and winces in pain as she gets it. She takes a small sip before repeating the process and putting it back on the side.

'I can't believe it,' she says. 'It's all so...'

'Far-fetched? It's been a shock to us all.'

'And he doesn't remember meeting you? Or me?'

'No, luckily we've spent a lot of time together and...'

She nods as if she understands.

'I'm glad. Max said you were really happy.'

'Well, I thought we were; that's sort of why I'm here. I'm trying to piece everything together and I found out about you, and he can't tell me about it. I need to know what he was doing meeting you, and if you two were having an affair?' I almost choke on the words.

'An affair?' says Anne, then pauses. Her eyes flit down to my bump before she looks back to my face and sighs. 'No, we definitely weren't having one of those.'

I breathe out and can feel myself going light-headed with relief.

'Before he went up on that Saturday, he lied and told me that he had a work thing, and then when I recently found out he was meeting you,' I say with relief, 'I guess I put two and two together.'

Anne pauses again before she nods.

'Well, it *was* a work thing,' says Anne. 'Not a total lie. I'd asked him to meet me because I had been thinking about applying for a job back at PDCA.'

'Oh, is that what you're going to do?'

'No, actually, I got an offer from another company. I had an interview a couple of days before the accident.'

'Then why were you thinking of applying to PDCA?'

She tucks a loose bit of hair that's escaped her messy top-knot behind her ears. 'I didn't think the interview had gone very well and I panicked.'

'And that was it?'

'Uh-huh, we chatted a little and then I turned to leave and that's when I got hit.'

'And that's when Max lost his memory.'

It was all so innocent.

'Looks like it. Are you going to tell him about my accident?'

'I don't know,' I say honestly.

It didn't exactly go down well that I didn't tell him the truth about his parents, and I'm guessing that telling him that I've been digging into his ex-girlfriend's life for the last two weeks won't exactly go down well either. Not to mention the fact that up until a few minutes ago I'd been convinced he'd been having an affair. I'd hate for him to find out that I even considered he could do something like that. 'I should get going.'

I stand up and walk towards the door.

'Ellie,' she says, stopping me in my tracks. 'Max loves you in a way he never loved me. You'll get through this.'

I smile weakly back to her and head out the front door.

I arrive back in Fleet to find Max at home.

'Hey,' I say, surprised; I thought he'd spend longer at his parents' house. 'How did it go?'

'Better than I thought it would,' he says. He's sat at the kitchen table and I walk over and sit down next to him, taking his hand. 'It's been hard to reconcile what my dad did with how he's been over the last month. I still can't imagine he'd ever do anything like that; it's such a massive shock. And I'm not saying that I agree with how Dad went about it, but seeing them open up about their lives now and how happy they are, I guess I can see that they're better off apart.'

He sighs deeply.

'I don't think my relationship with Dad is going to be quite like it has been over the past few weeks, but I think we're going to *have* one, which I hear is better than before.'

'Much better,' I say, squeezing his hand.

'The whole pretending was a bit fucked-up, though – but Rach and Gaby have been reminding me that this isn't exactly a normal situation that we've all found ourselves in.'

'Tell me about it,' I say, and he squeezes my hand back.

'It's made me realise what a remarkable woman you are, and how amazing it is that you're my wife. The way you've handled this whole thing.'

'I did what any wife would have done, in sickness and in health, right?'

'Right,' says Max, smiling.

It makes me feel terrible keeping the secret about Anne.

'So, I went to visit someone today in London,' I say. 'A woman named Anne Summers.'

'Is that code for you've been shopping for something special,' he says, raising an eyebrow.

'No,' I say, wishing it was. 'She was hit by a bus and has broken one of her legs really badly.'

'Oh, that's terrible,' says Max. 'Is she OK?'

I scan his face for any recognition.

'She will be, she was lucky.'

'Sounds it,' he says, leaning forward and kissing me before I can finish what I was about to say. 'You know, ever since you mentioned Ann Summers, I can't get the image of you in some racy undies out of my head. So, I was just wondering, exactly how long is it until Sasha needs picking up from nursery?'

He kisses me again and I know that I should gently push him away and tell him the truth. He needs to know how he fits into the story. This information could possibly be *the* trigger to bring his memory back. Only I can't do it. His hands start to slide under my jumper, creeping up and up and I don't stop him. Because there's a small part of me that doesn't want our old life back. I want this relationship – the one where we make time for each other, the one where we've found ourselves again.

I know I'll have to tell him, it's only fair, but I can't quite bring myself to do so just yet.

Chapter 24

I'd booked tickets to see Left Foot Forward when I had just found I was pregnant at seven weeks. I remembered being bored by the latter stage of pregnancy when I was expecting Sasha, and I thought it would be good to have something to look forward to. Little did I know that I would barely have enough time to think about it.

'Do you think we should try and find a tout and see if we can get tickets?' says Claire. 'They're not really my cup of tea but it would be fun.'

'But Ellie and Max have got seated tickets so it's not like we'd get to sit next to them,' says Owen.

To make the most of our trip to London, we've had a pre-concert meal with Owen and Claire. I wish they were coming with us to see the band; I've really enjoyed the time we've spent hanging out with them recently. They're really settling into being a couple with their playful banter, and the more I get to know Claire the more I like her, and it's so lovely to see Owen so happy.

'We should get going,' says Max, draining his drink.

Owen picks up the bill, with our two cards sitting on top of it, and looks around at the restaurant that's become really busy since we arrived.

'Perhaps I'll take it up and pay at the bar,' he says.

'I'll come with you,' I say, following him and we join the queue.

'Is Max OK?' Owen asks. 'He seems a bit quiet.'

'It was quite an emotional weekend for him with all the stuff with his parents. I think it's probably catching up with him.'

'Yeah, I guess it would do.'

'I had an interesting time too. I went to see Max's ex, Anne, yesterday.'

'What?' says Owen, his mouth agape. 'Sarah told me you met her and asked about her, but tracking down Anne? Ellie!'

He shakes his head at me.

'I know,' I say, wincing, 'but you sounded so suspicious when we were talking about their relationship at the festival. I was really worried what I'd find out, but now I know the truth and it's not that big a deal.'

'It isn't?' He looks surprised.

'No, I know you were just trying to protect Max, but that's in the past now. You should have told me.'

'Right, sorry,' he says, as the frazzled-looking bar worker appears and takes our payment. 'I didn't think you'd be OK with it, but, um, I guess that's good.'

'Why didn't you think I'd be OK—' I start, but Claire comes up to us and slides her arms around Owen's waist and he pulls her in close, just as Max comes over and takes my hand.

'Have a fabulous time,' says Claire, not realising she was interrupting something.

'We should get going, Ellie,' says Max. He turns to hug Claire goodbye before giving Owen a handshake. And as I lean over and hug Owen, I whisper in his ear, 'Can I call you tomorrow?'

He pulls out of the hug and gives me the same look he did when he didn't want me to look into Anne in the first place, but then shrugs and nods. 'Enjoy tonight,' he says, almost like an order.

Max puts his hand on the small of my back and I feel the familiar crackle of electricity. I try and push Owen's look out of my mind, telling myself that he's just being overprotective of Max, nothing else; Anne's already told me what happened.

When I'd booked our tickets, I hadn't taken into consideration how steep the O2 gets at the sides and I grip the row of seats behind us carefully as I look for where we're sitting.

'Are you going to be OK up this high?' asks Max as I sit down. 'I mean, in your condition.'

'In my condition,' I say with a laugh, clinging onto the base of my seat to the extent that my knuckles whiten. 'In any condition I'd have trouble here. I'm not great with heights.'

'Relax, you'll be fine. I'm here,' he says and he squeezes my thigh.

'Good, you'll have to distract me.'

Max leans over and gives me a kiss.

'Hey, I meant, talk to me!'

'Oh, OK. Hmm,' he says, looking around. 'OK, what's your favourite Left Foot Forward song?'

'"Whispers", definitely. It was one of the first singles I ever bought,' I say, thinking back. 'I was in my last year of junior school and I had such a crush on a boy called Peter Dawson.'

'His name sounds familiar. Would I have known him?'

'Maybe, he was really good at football.'

'Oh yeah, didn't he go on to play for some club?'

'I think he went to play for the Southampton youth team,' I say, pretending like I wasn't certain and hadn't followed his career.

'Did anything happen with you two?'

'I wish,' I say, laughing.

'I can't believe you fancied someone else. I'm truly hurt; I thought you only had eyes for me at school?'

'Oh no, I fancied loads of boys; Matthew Hooper, Tim Knight, Russell Frost.'

'Russell Frost? The one with the mohawk?'

'Yeah, didn't David Beckham have one?' I say, laughing.

'He did, but I think Russell's was more a result of falling asleep at his mate's house and his mate shaving it off for a laugh.'

'Ha,' I giggle. 'It suited him though. I bet you were jealous because you didn't have the balls to shave off your curtains.'

'Ouch, I'll have you know the ladies loved my curtains.' He laughs.

It was true we did. Even if he did keep them too long after the nineties.

I look back down and gasp at the drop again.

'OK, keep talking,' he says. 'Best concert you've ever been to?'

'Foo Fighters in Hyde Park. I think it was in 2006? Some guy put me on his shoulders and it was amazing.'

'I don't think I'll be recreating that tonight, no offence.'

'Believe me, being up here I'm not offended. How about you? Best gig?'

'Got to be the Chilis,' he says with almost a glint in his eye. It's almost like he knows that it'll push my buttons. It's a sore point in our relationship as I've had a long-term love affair with the Red Hot Chili Peppers and have never managed to see them live. But he doesn't know that.

'So that was better than when you went to see 5ive in concert?'

'Don't tell me I told you that?'

'Oh, Max, I know all your secrets.'

His smile momentarily slides off his face.

'Just kidding,' I say, wondering if Owen was on to something – he doesn't seem quite himself tonight. 'Don't forget I was friends with Rach at the time, and I was jealous as hell.'

He smiles again.

'They were actually pretty good, and you know it wasn't a bad place for a teenage boy. All those girls.'

I laugh. Typical Max.

A couple squeeze past us and we have to get up to let them through. Max takes hold of my arm under my elbow.

'Thank you,' I say, feeling more secure with him hanging on to me.

'Anytime,' he says as we sit again, just in time as the lights dim and the support group walk on stage.

Left Foot Forward give a quick thank you to the crowd and walk off to rapturous applause. The arena begins to shake as people start to stamp their feet and cheer for an encore.

I'm willing them to come back, feeling short-changed that they haven't yet played 'Whispers', when an iconic guitar riff starts to play and the crowd roars even louder.

When we arrived a couple of hours ago, I thought that there'd be no way I'd feel comfortable standing up during the concert, but whilst I'd been sitting down for the whole gig feeling like the ultimate party pooper, I have to stand for this.

Max puts his arm protectively around me and kisses the top of my head. If only my teenage self could have known that all those times I played this one song on loop, fantasising about Max, one day I'd be stood beside him watching them live – she never in a gazillion years would have believed it.

The song draws to a close and this time when the band leaves the stage the house lights go up. We hang back and let people leave before us. We're checked into a hotel around the corner. I'd booked that back when I'd booked the gig tickets – it was supposed to be our last little treat to ourselves before the baby came. If I wasn't heavily pregnant than we probably would have gone for a couple of drinks afterwards, but we make do instead with picking up gelatos on our way out.

Most of the crowd heads towards the Tube station and we walk around the back of the Dome, along the path running beside the river. We take our time eating our little pots of heaven and enjoy the fresh air after being cooped up inside for hours.

'I can't believe how good that was,' say Max. 'Or how well you did. You must be knackered.'

'I'm glad we're staying nearby, that's for sure. There's no way I would have made it back by Tube and train.'

'I never thought they'd be as good as that – and especially when we were seated. All those years I've snubbed those seats in favour of standing and actually it was all right.'

'I know, it's so nice going for a pee and knowing that you're going to come back to the exact same spot and not have to spend ages looking for who you're with.'

I'm getting near the end of my tub of gelato and I stop and watch a party boat going down the river. It's decorated with fairy lights around the outside, and the sound of excited chattering and 'Dancing Queen' drifts in the air.

'I'm guessing there's going to be a lot of sore heads on that boat,' says Max, pointing with his little wooden spoon.

'I know, looks like fun, though.'

I'm just about to scoop up the last of the gelato.

'Hey,' says Max, making me freeze. 'I hope you're not going to eat the last bit.'

He leans across to my pot and scoops it up with his spoon, before he leans over and kisses me. Our old tradition. The perfect ending to a perfect night.

We start walking again before I stop when it suddenly hits me.

A tradition that I haven't told him about.

I'm frozen to the spot. My mind's racing – did I tell him and I've forgotten about it? Would Rach have told him about it last weekend? Did I ever tell her?

Max has taken a few steps before he realises I'm not next to him.

He looks back and laughs. 'What are you doing?'

'You remember?' I say slowly, still trying to make sense of it.

His face says it all. He closes his eyes like he realises his mistake.

So many thoughts are whizzing through my mind. How long has he had his memory back for? Why hasn't he told me? Does he remember everything? Has he been pretending this whole time?

Only I can't seem to articulate any of that.

'When?' I stutter.

'Last night.'

'And has it all come back?'

I've thought about this moment ever since the doctor gave us his diagnosis. I'd imagined that he'd sweep me up in his arms and tell me how much he loved me, kissing me and telling me how relieved he was to remember again. I don't understand why he wouldn't tell me.

He takes a step closer towards me but there's still no big moment.

'It was just like the doctor said: it came flooding back. One minute I was putting Sasha down, the next I had this weird feeling – a bit like déjà vu – and then I suddenly spotted things in the room that I knew all about. The shop we'd bought that little print of the bluebird before she was born, the stuffed toy Gruffalo and the Hungry Caterpillar on the shelf to remind us of her first birthday party. Then I looked down at Sasha and I could remember her. Her being born. Her first step. All of it.'

A solitary tear rolls down my face.

'And you,' he says.

He bends down and kisses me and my knees are so weak and jittery that I'm starting to shake. I'm expecting one of the legendary perfect ten kisses, but instead it's a kiss tinged with sadness.

'You remember absolutely everything about our routine?' I wince at the times I didn't correct him from his perfect dad impression.

'Yes, I know that I didn't used to do every other bedtime duty, or take her to the park to give you time alone.'

'Ah, yeah, sorry for all those little... tweaks.'

'Don't be. That's how I should have been.'

We're skirting around the subject and I eventually pluck up the courage to ask him.

'Why didn't you tell me you could remember?'

He stares straight into my eyes and it causes me to shiver.

'It all came back so suddenly. When you told me about Anne's accident, I didn't remember who she was but I knew by the way you were looking at me that there was more to it than you made out. I couldn't stop thinking about getting hit by a bus, and the more I thought about it, the more familiar it seemed. And that's how it happened. And I knew you'd seen Anne – and I...' He sighs deeply. 'You know, don't you?'

I nod my head.

He runs his hands through his hair and closes his eyes. I've never seen Max cry before, but he's got tears rolling down his cheeks.

'I should have told you about it. When it happened. I'm so sorry,' he says.

Any kind of elation that his memory has come back is starting to ebb away because something is not adding up. His reaction is not what it should be. I think back to my exchange with Owen earlier when we spoke about Anne, and Max is acting very guilty. I'm slowly getting the impression that I'm missing something from the story.

'Why didn't you?' I say, wanting to know.

'Because I thought about how I'd feel if you told me you'd kissed someone else.'

My ears hear his words but it takes a minute or so for my heart to catch up. But when it does, it feels like it shatters into a million pieces.

I look at the man in front of me. I feel like I don't know him at all, all over again, because the Max I thought I knew would never cheat on me.

'Did Anne tell you that it was just a drunken kiss? Not that that makes it any better. I don't know what she's told you and I'm worried that she made it sound like it was more than what it was.'

'You should give her more credit,' I say, surprised at how steady my voice is. 'She actually made it sound a lot less than what it was. She said that you'd met up the day of the accident because she wanted to apply for a job back at PDCA. Oh God, that wasn't the only time you saw her, was it?'

My voice sounds so calm and controlled but inside my mind is screaming at him and my heart is pounding. His silence speaks volumes.

'I think there's been enough secrets between us, Max. Tell me.'

He wipes away the tears on his face and takes a deep breath.

'She came back from New York a couple of months ago and she came to the work summer party with another one of our colleagues.'

I think back to that hot night in July. I was supposed to have gone too, but Sasha had been poorly and she was really clingy so I didn't feel like I could leave her with my mum who was supposed to babysit her.

'I was really drunk, we all were, you know what those things are like. And...'

He runs his hands through his hair again.

'Tell me,' I say with force, despite the tears that have started to roll down my cheeks.

'I bumped into her in the corridor on way back from the toilets. She told me that she'd split up with her husband and that she missed me and that she wanted us to try again. Then she kissed me.'

I close my eyes. I don't want to hear any more.

'I was so drunk, Ellie, that I kissed her back – and it took me a moment to realise what was happening but when I did, I pushed her off. I told her about Sasha and the baby, and how I was happy with you.'

'But you kissed her,' I say, thinking: he's making it worse. 'What kind of a kiss was it? A five? A six? A perfect fucking ten?'

I realise that I'm shouting now and the few people walking towards the hotel are trying to listen in in that not-so-subtle British way where they're not looking at us but they're not talking to each other either.

'Ellie, it wasn't like that. I don't think it was even that long before I pushed her off.'

'Then why didn't you tell me? If it meant that little?'

I grip the railings even tighter, feeling sick to the stomach.

'Because I didn't want to hurt you.'

I laugh, because if he'd told me at the time, we could have brushed it off and it might not be as big a deal as it is now.

'Are you sure it wasn't more? Is she the one that got away and I'm just the rebound?'

'Ellie, no, you know that's not true.'

'Do I? How do I know if anything's true any more?'

'It was just a kiss,' he says.

'Just a kiss? It's just a kiss when you're single, a bit of meaningless fun,' I say, thinking of the times that I kissed random men in clubs when I was younger, 'but when you're married a kiss is so much more than that. That's ours and ours alone. What did you really talk about the day she got hit by the bus? I take it it wasn't about work.'

Max sighs, and I laugh out loud at how gullible I've been. It hurts to think that this whole thing was going on in the background. Not only had he kissed another woman, but he was having secret meetings with her. It was forgivable when I thought it had been about work – but this was something more and now I don't know if I can trust anything he says.

'She wanted to meet up and I went along because I wanted her to understand that that part of my life was all in the past, only she kept pushing for us to be together. That's when we started arguing and she turned and stepped off that kerb.' He inhales a sharp intake of breath like he's reliving the moment.

I try and take it all in. He might not have been having an affair, but I still feel betrayed.

'For weeks I've been acting like a fool trying to get you to fall in love with me again to save our perfect marriage. But how could we have had a perfect marriage if there were these secrets between us? And Owen knew, didn't he?'

Max closes his eyes and sighs.

'I had to tell someone and he told me to tell you, but I couldn't.'

'That's why you weren't talking?'

He nods.

'I can't do this any more,' I say.

I can't stand to look at him any longer and I start walking towards the hotel.

'Ellie, wait.'

'No, Max. I'm too tired for this. I'm going to go to the hotel. You go back to your mum's or wherever. I can't do this now.'

'But Ellie, please, let me come with you. I need to explain.'

'No. I'm doing this for the baby and I'm doing it for me.'

I walk away and I don't look back. He doesn't follow me and I'm glad because I meant what I said.

I ignore the looks of the other people in the lobby as I walk through, my cheeks wet with tears, waddling like only an eight-months-pregnant woman who's been at a rock concert can.

I reach the sanctuary of our room and I crawl on top of the bed and pull a cushion into me and curl up.

Now I understand what Max must have felt like when suddenly your whole world falls out from underneath your feet and you have no clue who or what you really believe any more.

Chapter 25

The last thirty-six hours have passed by in a bit of a blur. When I got home, Max was gone. He'd written me a note telling me that he knew I needed time and that he was going to stay at Judy's house, and she arrived a little later to drop off Sasha. He's on his way over now to take Sasha out for the day and my hands are starting to tremble.

I'm thankful that Sasha's been oblivious to everything, and I've thrown myself into playing with her to take my mind off things. We've been making dens, having tea parties, and generally trying to ignore that my marriage is in a shambles. But even still, unwelcome thoughts have a way of sneaking into my mind, whirling around, confusing me even more about what's going on and making me scrutinise all aspects of our marriage.

I'd be the first to be up in arms about anyone's husband cheating, but since I found out about Max, I've realised that it's not that black and white. I'm turning into Rach, asking myself question after question. Does it make a difference that it was a drunken kiss? How much cheating is considered enough to break up a marriage? Is it worse because it's with an ex and there's the possibility of residual feelings there? Does it mean that if he's done it once, he's more likely to do it again? Can I trust him?

I also wonder if things would have been more clear-cut if I'd found out about this before his memory loss. We've changed so much in that time and it's made me realise how guilty I was of neglecting our relationship. I think it was inevitable that after having Sasha I put her first – most mothers do that – but I never really let Max in to our little gang. That's not an excuse for what he did, but it's made me realise that our marriage wasn't as perfect as it appeared to the outside world. I'd been too fixated on the image of it, rather than what was going on inside it.

I double-check the contents of Sasha's backpack, making sure I've put in extra clothes and her favourite soft toys, even though I know that Max is capable of taking care of everything. He knows her routine better than I do now, having followed it to the letter.

There's a soft knock at the door and it stabs at my heart that he's knocking rather than using his keys. This is really happening.

Sasha is all excited and as soon as the door opens, she toddles straight into his arms and he scoops her up and onto his hip, giving her a squeeze like he hasn't seen her in years.

'I've missed you, little pup,' he says, kissing her on the top of her head.

She rests her head against his chest. Another stab at my heart.

'Hey,' says Max, turning his attention to me.

'Hey.'

There's an awkward silence as neither of us knows what to do or say.

'You look nice,' he says.

He's lying. I'm sure some women would dress up for an occasion like this, in order to show him what he's missing, only I've gone the other way, too emotionally drained to care. Greasy hair. No make-up. Unflattering outfit choice complete with stains from Sasha's breakfast.

'Did you want to come in?' I say, not budging from my spot blocking the door.

'No, no, we'll just, um, get off. Unless you want to talk?' he says, a little hopefully.

I shake my head.

'I'll get her backpack,' I say.

This feels so wrong. Is this what'll be like if we can't work things out? Conversations on the doorstep whilst we hand over the kids?

'Great, thanks,' says Max, taking the bag from me. 'I spoke to my dad again last night, and he's going to fly over tomorrow so we can talk properly.'

'Oh,' I say, surprised. 'I'm glad that you're still speaking to him now that you've got your memory back.'

'Yeah. Seeing how he was with me when I lost my memory… I think it's time that we sorted things out properly. I don't think we're going to be best buddies, but I'd like him to know Sasha and the new baby.'

I nod my head again and there's another pause.

'Also, I spoke to my boss, and I'm going back to work next week, part-time initially. But if that goes well, I might talk about doing part-time permanently or taking every other Friday off or something. It would be nice to spend more time with the kids. If that's OK?'

I'm stunned and all I can do is nod.

'Right, well, we'll get going.'

'Have a lovely time, sweetie,' I say, leaning over and kissing Sasha's head. I'm finding it too difficult.

Max says a quick goodbye and turns and walks down the path. That's my family – I should be going with them, but then I think of Anne and how pretty she looked even when she was recovering from being hit by a bus, and the sickness returns to my stomach. I shut the door quickly, trying not to cry.

I'm not sure what I'm going to do with myself. Judy and I are going to a garden centre later this afternoon. She wants to help me choose some plants for our garden. I should cancel but she's been so good to us lately that I don't want to let her down. But we're not going for another two hours and I don't know what I'm going to do until then to take my mind off things. I usually crave alone time, but now that I've got it I don't want it.

I head into the kitchen and I set about tidying it up, when there's a knock at the door.

I walk along the hallway, wondering what Max has forgotten, only to be surprised that Rach is standing on the doorstep.

'Hey,' I say, surprised to see her. I don't think she's ever turned up at my door unannounced before. 'What are you doing here, shouldn't you be at work?'

'I took a day off,' she says. I know instantly by the tone in her voice and her body language that she knows.

'Max told you,' I say.

'I thought you might need a bit of company,' she says.

I nod my head and I can't help but cry.

'Come here,' she says, pulling me into a hug, and I rest my head on her shoulder and start to properly sob.

She leads me into the lounge and sits me down at the sofa. 'Why didn't you tell me?'

I wipe away my tears with my sleeve.

'I didn't want anyone to know. I thought that if Max and I work things out then people will always think of him as a cheater. I don't want them to look at him like he or our marriage are tainted.'

'Oh, Ellie, you can't go through something like this on your own. You can always call me, you know that. I already look at Max and think he's an idiot, so it really wouldn't change anything.'

I laugh; only she can make me do that through my tears.

'Seriously, though, Ellie, forget he's my brother. I was your friend first long before you two got together.'

Once upon a time I would have told Rach everything and it was so easy – but after Max it felt too strange.

'You did try and warn me that Max would hurt me and that I should get out when I could.'

'I've always felt terrible about that. I never expected it to work out between you; none of us thought Max would ever settle down.'

'If anyone was surprised, it was me. I never believed that he would be with someone like me.'

'OK, hold it there,' says Rach. 'This has got to stop. He's the one who should be lucky to be with someone like you.'

'Ha, I—'

'No,' says Rach, cutting me off. 'You are one of the most amazing women I know. You're clever and kind and witty. You don't realise it but you have this kind of... I don't know what you'd call it – radiance – but you sort of light up rooms. And yes, maybe Max dated women that looked like they walked off a Victoria Secret's catwalk, but they have nothing on you. You've got to take Max off his pedestal and you've got to realise that you deserve to be on it instead.'

'Rach,' I say, the tears having started up again.

'I mean it. He's the lucky one.'

'I guess I always wondered if I somehow trapped him in all of it; we got together so quickly and then we got married.'

'What?'

'It's always been a little niggle.' I shrug. 'And now with the whole Anne thing, I know it was just a kiss, but it's made those niggles worse. Because now I wonder if he only rejected her because of Sasha and the baby.'

'I think it was almost easier when we didn't talk about this,' says Rach, with a smile on her face, 'because that is absolutely not true. You only need to see you and Max together to know that it is the real deal. He even fell in love with you all over again when he lost his memory – surely that tells you something?'

'But he forgot her too, so he didn't know he was missing out on her.'

'Ellie! Get a grip,' says Rach in her no-nonsense style. 'I've known Max all my life and I have never seen him care about someone as much as he does you. And yes, he loves Sasha like any father should, but he loves you, he really does.

'Do you know he phoned me to tell me what was going on because he wanted me to come over to you when he took Sasha out? He knew that I was going to be cross and that I'd shout at him – which I did, by the way – but he still phoned me and told me the truth because he didn't want you to be on your own.

'I know that he cheated on you when he kissed Anne and I don't know whether you'll be able to forgive him, but don't make it a bigger thing by bringing in any other worry you can think of; worries that I know aren't true and, if you actually talked to Max, he'd make you understand that they shouldn't be worries at all.'

She reaches out and gives my hand a squeeze.

'I'm sorry if that was tough to hear,' she says.

I nod. 'It was, but I've missed you talking to me like this,' I say. 'No one cuts through my problems like you do.'

'Well, someone needs to talk some sense into you.'

She's right, they do.

'So, how are you feeling, about the kiss?' she says in a gentler tone.

'I honestly don't know. I feel like I've gone back to being a teenager – getting upset over just a kiss – but it's feels like such a betrayal.'

'Of course it is. I know I'd hate it if Gaby kissed someone else. But, from speaking to him, I honestly don't think that it was like one of those big passionate end-of-a-movie kisses. It sounds like it was just a drunken mistake.'

'But the trouble is, he made it more of a thing by keeping it a secret and for sneaking off to meet her.'

'Yeah, like I said, my brother is an idiot,' she says with a sigh. 'Do you know what you're going to do?'

'Not yet. Irrational niggles aside, this whole memory-loss episode has really made me look at my marriage. I naïvely thought that it was all so perfect and so happy, but it wasn't. It's not all to do with the Max-and-Anne situation; I'm to blame as well. I think you're right; maybe I have put Max on a pedestal.' I sigh. 'I think part of me was caught up in this fantasy of getting my dream man. Then when he lost his memory it made us get to really know each other. He finally saw more of the real me, and I saw the real him, or at least I thought I had. I think that's why this has hit me so hard because we'd grown that much closer.

'I just don't know if I can trust him. I'm scared that I'll always be worried that when he says he's going into the office on a Saturday that that's not where he's going.'

'Trust is such an odd thing, isn't it?' says Rach after a pause. 'Don't you think it's crazy that when you start dating someone new you give them a level of trust and the benefit of the doubt, but they've done nothing necessarily to earn that?'

'I guess so; I've never really thought about it like that.'

'We trust our partners with everything. Our hearts, our hopes, our dreams.'

There's a sadness that's crept into her voice and it gives me the impression that we're not talking about mine and Max's marriage any more.

'Have you managed to speak to Gaby about the baby?'

'A little, but now's not the time.'

'Now is *exactly* the time. I've done nothing but speak about myself for the last month and it's about time that I listened to people with real problems.'

'Everyone's problems are real, they're just different.'

'Are you avoiding talking about it?' I say, arching my eyebrows.

'Yes,' she says, laughing.

'Come on, I want to hear.'

She sighs and lets out a deep breath.

'We talked a bit more and I explained my fears to her and she understood them. We discussed the different options and we decided that if we were going to have more than one child we could take turns to have a baby.'

'Well, that sounds fair.'

'Yeah, it does, and I thought once we'd made a decision that I'd stop worrying. But now I'm worrying about new things, like, what if we have a baby and then we don't want another one? Or what if we can't have a second one? Will the one of us that didn't have the baby resent the other one because she did?'

'Oh, Rach. Of course those are genuine worries too, but you can't think like that – you're thinking of the worst-case scenarios. And you know, someone wise once told me not to make a thing bigger by adding unnecessary worries.' I pause.

'You want to have a baby with Gaby, and that's the important bit. No matter how you do it or who does it, you'll both be that baby's parents.'

'And that's bloody scary. What if I'm no good?'

'Then you join the club with the rest of us, as most parents think that from time to time. Or to be honest, all the time. But for what it's worth, you're going to make a great mum, and your baby will be lucky to have you as a mum. And Gaby too.'

Rach, who is certainly not a crier, looks like she's welling up.

'Bloody hell, do you remember when we used to sit in my bedroom obsessing over the latest *X-Files* episode.'

'I know, life was so much simpler when the only things we were scared of were extra-terrestrials and chain-smoking men in suits.'

Rach laughs.

'I'm sorry that we stopped talking like this,' she says. 'It's lovely having a partner that's like your best friend, but it doesn't mean that I don't have room for my oldest best friend as well.'

'Ditto. I'm sorry I ruined it by marrying Max.'

'You didn't ruin anything. Promise that we'll talk more about things in the future?'

'Yes, I'd like that,' I say. 'It sounds silly to say I missed you seeing as we see each other loads at family functions, but I've missed seeing *you*.'

'I know. Me too. Although today you might not just be seeing me on your own,' she says, screwing up her face.

'Your mum,' I say. 'I'd forgotten I'm supposed to pick her up later on to go to the garden centre.'

'Yeah, about that. There is no trip to the garden centre.'

'There's not?' I say, wondering what's going on.

'No, now, I'm not going to spoil the surprise, but you might need a little advance warning. You are obviously still beautiful with tear-stained cheeks and jeans that look like they're covered in food, but you might just want to get changed into something a little flashier and maybe you might want to have a shower and do your hair.'

'Why?' I say. 'Is it Max – has he planned something?'

'No,' she says, shaking her head. 'It's your new friend, Anneka.'

'Oh god, I'm not having a b—'

'No, no, no, don't finish that sentence. I'll be in trouble and I want to reveal as little as possible. But go make yourself presentable.'

'OK,' I say, slowly pulling myself up. 'Am I at least going to like it?'

'I think you're going to love it. Now hurry up, you're due at Mum's in an hour and I'm mega scared of this Anneka. We've only been WhatsApp contacts for three days and I'm already cowering when I hear the notification beep.'

'Thanks, Rach, for this advance warning, and for coming over, and for listening.'

'Anytime. Now go. I imagine Anneka's fury is worse in person than it is on WhatsApp.'

I get out of the car, tucking my freshly blow-dried hair behind my ear. I can hear sshing and giggling as I walk towards the door and then Judy opens it theatrically. As much as I hated the idea of a baby shower, being with my close friends and family today might just be what I need.

'Darling, it's so wonderful to see you,' she says, opening her arms wide to welcome me in.

'Aren't we supposed to be going out?' I say, playing along.

'What?'

'You know, to the garden centre,' I say, raising an eyebrow.

'Oh yes, about that... I have something I thought you might like to see in the lounge.'

'Oh right,' I say, wishing that I shared her ability for ropey acting, although her stint pretending with Mick has really honed her skills.

I open the door and there are balloons everywhere and I almost can't see my friends who are hidden between them.

'Oh my goodness,' I say with canned laughter and a smile that I've been practising all the way over.

'We simply couldn't let you not have a baby shower, especially when you missed out on most of mine,' says

347

Anneka, pushing balloons out of the way to come to the front.

'Oh my God, what are you wearing?' I say, my eyes opening wide.

'Isn't it fabulous?'

It's a long T-shirt with a Wonder Woman costume printed on. It goes down to her thighs so it even has the little shorts printed on it too. I look around the room and notice that everyone is wearing them, complete with little headbands in their hair and little capes.

'Excellent theme choice,' I say as Helen comes up and gives me a hug. 'But what's with all the balloons?'

'Anneka forgot that not everyone else's house is as big as hers when she ordered them.'

I turn round to greet Polly and Rach, before Judy thrusts her iPad in my face. It's mounted on a tripod and I'm wondering what she's doing, until I see my mum on the screen waving at me.

'Hello, Ellie, love,' she says, grinning in the slightly pixelated picture.

'Mum, you made it,' I say, tearing up a little.

'I wouldn't miss it for the world,' she says. 'All you've got to do is make sure you move me round with you and I won't miss out on anything.'

'Now, we would have invited more of your friends,' says Judy, 'but being a Thursday afternoon, not a lot of people could make it.'

'Gaby sends her apologies,' says Rach.

'Oh, bless her,' I say. 'This is so lovely, thank you. You know, I would have hated anything big.'

'That's what I said, didn't I?' says Anneka, looking round the room for confirmation. 'Now, it's time for you to get your outfit on, Ellie.'

'My outfit? Do I get a T-shirt too?'

'Oh no, we've got something much better for you,' she says, pulling out an actual Wonder Woman costume from behind her back.

'Um, Anneka, the bump, it'll never fit.'

'Yes, it will. I had my seamstress fit it with elasticated material – here,' she says, pointing it out. 'The bits that are meant to be rigid are soft. It'll be lovely and cosy for your bump.'

'Put it on, put it on,' chants Helen followed by the rest of the girls. I get hideous flashbacks to the last time I was wearing a Wonder Woman costume and the guys that were chanting at me, although they were chanting for me to take my clothes off, not put them on.

I take the hanger and everyone cheers.

'And that's just the start,' says Anneka, clapping her hands.

My mum gives me a thumbs-up as I walk away to change into my outfit. It's all such a lovely gesture that it suddenly becomes all too much for me and I begin to cry.

'Bloody hormones, huh?' says Polly, giving me a little squeeze.

'Yes, bloody hormones,' I say, for the first time glad that I have them because at least it's given me a cover story for why I'm an absolute bawling wreck.

Chapter 26

It turns out having a baby shower isn't a completely hideous experience, especially at the time of having a secret life crisis. I didn't realise how much I needed to be fussed over and it gave me the courage to tell my new mum friends what had happened. They've rallied around me over the last couple of days, meeting Sasha and me at the park, inviting us over for dinner at their houses, and keeping me laughing with ridiculous chat in our WhatsApp group. I honestly don't know what I would have done without them, and without Rach, who's been sending multiple texts daily, to see if I'm all right.

I still haven't spoken to Max. He's been busy with Mick, who came over from Portugal for the weekend, and it's worked out to be the perfect excuse to not see him as I'm allowing him the space to rebuild his relationship with his dad, while in reality I'm stalling for time, unsure what I'm going to do. I dropped Sasha off at Judy's yesterday afternoon as I knew that Mick would want to see her, and she's missed Max terribly too. She stayed overnight and today they're going out for the day. And they're not the only ones, as the girls surprised me by booking tickets for us to all go to Comic Con.

'What do you think?' I say, tugging at my Wonder Woman

costume. It wasn't that bad wearing it round Judy's for the baby shower, but I'm a little embarrassed to wear it out in public.

'Of what you're wearing or the message you received?' says Helen, looking up from my phone.

'Both,' I guess.

Last night I received an unexpected Facebook message from Anne. She told me that Max had phoned her to apologise for leaving her when she'd had the accident and he'd explained what had happened with us, and that he wished her well but that he never wanted to hear from her again.

'You look smoking hot in that outfit, and I thought it was a nice message,' she says with an apologetic shrug. 'She sounded genuine in her apology. Plus, I kind of get it. She'd just split up with her husband, she'd moved cities and she saw Max, who was all familiar, and she got it wrong.'

'Yeah, that's what I thought. I respect her for messaging me; she didn't have to do that.'

'No, and if there really was something between them then she wouldn't have messaged you, encouraging you to take him back.'

'I know,' I sigh. 'Hey, hang on a second. Why aren't you wearing your Wonder Woman T-shirt from the baby shower – wasn't that the plan?'

'Oh yeah,' she says, unbuttoning her oversized cardigan. 'I had to sneak out wearing this over the top of it. You know, Toby has been like a horny teenager ever since I wore it home last week. I've had to keep hiding from him.'

'But I thought that's what you wanted?'

'I know! It was! And it was all very flattering, but I'd forgotten how exhausting and how much effort sex was, especially when you feel like you're the size of a whale.'

'Well, you never know, it might help move things along; isn't that the old wives' tale?'

'I think I'd rather take my chances with the raspberry tea and a curry,' she says, tucking into the jar of raisins on the counter. 'What's with the healthy snacks? Going all Anneka on me?'

'I do it for Sasha. The good stuff is in the cupboard.'

'Now you tell me,' she says, still shovelling the handful into her mouth. 'Speaking of snacks, do we need anything for the ride?'

'Got it covered,' I say, holding up a bag. There's a beep from outside. 'Speaking of our ride.'

Helen does a little clap of her hands and we head out to the street to see a smart-looking Rolls Royce parked outside.

Anneka pops her head out of the passenger window.

'Hop in, ladies.'

Helen and I slide in next to Polly.

'This certainly beats getting the train,' says Helen.

'I thought at least this way we'll get to have a good chat whilst we're going up,' says Anneka. 'All ready?'

'Yes,' we all chant and I can't help but feel touched that they've done this to cheer me up.

'OK, ladies, next stop Comic Con,' she says, and the driver pulls away.

'You know,' says Helen, looking around when we step inside the exhibition centre, 'I didn't expect to be underdressed wearing this.'

Everywhere we look there is someone in a costume. From *Doctor Who* to *Star Wars* to *The Avengers*, there's truly something for everyone and at such a high standard too.

'Who are all these people dressed as?' says Anneka, wrinkling her nose up. 'I had no idea this was going to be some kind of freak show.'

'You ain't seen nothing yet,' I say, clapping my hands together. 'Now, what do you want to do first? Check out the stalls? Try and get tickets for a signing or see one of the talks?'

Anneka's nose is still wrinkled. 'You know, I thought Comic Con was going to be funnier, like, as in comedian. You know, comics.'

'Um, no, like comics the graphic magazines rather than funny ha ha,' I say, as she pulls even more of a face.

'Why do you think we're all dressed up as Wonder Woman?' asks Helen.

'I thought it was to cheer up Ellie and to get some wear out of them. If I'd known that it was sci-fi then I would have worn my Princess Leia gold bikini costume. I don't get enough opportunities to wear that outside of the bedroom. And I definitely would wear it better than her,' she says, pointing across the room.

'Don't you think your bump might have got a bit chilly?' I say, trying to purge the mental images I have now.

'Oh right, I didn't think of that. Well, I'm sure that I could have found something better.'

She winces and scrunches her face up in pain before she starts walking round in a circle, taking deep breaths.

'Um, are you OK?' asks Polly.

'I'm fine. I've just been getting Braxton Hicks all morning. Nothing to worry about,' she says.

'Right,' says Helen, looking a little alarmed. 'OK, so we've got some time before we've got that pre-booked *Dark Energy* panel.'

I clap my hands together. I'm so excited.

'I can't wait to see Candy Tyler and Evan Wilson.'

The three of them stare at me blankly.

'They played Persephone and Commander Quartz.'

They still look none the wiser.

'You're going to love it,' I say, laughing. 'Come on, let's check out some of the stalls to get us in the mood.'

'And we should head to the toilets too, if we're going to be sitting down for a while,' says Polly.

'Yes, Mum,' says Helen.

We start walking through the crowds that are swarming around the rows upon rows of tables.

'It's nice to see you smile,' says Polly, linking her arm through mine.

'Thank you, it's nice to be smiling,' I say, steering her out of the path of Captain America and Loki who are play fighting.

'Hopefully today will be just what you need.'

'Let's hope so,' I say, trying to banish thoughts of Max and concentrating on enjoying the moment.

The *Dark Energy* panel is everything that I'd hoped it would be. Even the girls seem to be enjoying the atmosphere. There's a magic that comes from being at Comic Con that's hard to explain to anyone who's never been. There's always an infectious ripple of excitement no matter who the speakers are; the super fans are so enthusiastic and responsive that it kicks the audience up into hyper-reactive mode. I'm almost gutted that we're nearly at the end of the hour and there's only time for a few more questions.

'Is there any hope that there'll be another series?' asks a fan near the front of the room. The audience laughs and a few people clap and applaud. It's what we all secretly hope for but we've given up asking.

'Well,' says Candy, turning and looking at the director at the end of the panel, 'whilst I think it's safe to say there'll never be another series—' groans ring out from the room '—there just might be – I don't know if I dare say it – a feature-length movie on a streaming platform.'

She almost whispers the last bit before she claps her hands over her mouth.

The director winks at her and the whole room erupts and suddenly hands go up everywhere for the next question.

'I wish we had time for all your questions,' says Hans the director, 'but I know that a lot of you felt cheated that Persephone and Commander Quartz had missed out on their happy ever after. So all I will say is, when we continue the story, the path to true love might not run smoothly, especially in the gamma quadrant.'

Most of the people in the room, bar my friends, snigger, as the true fans get the galactic reference. I turn to look at Anneka who's fidgeting in her seat. She's been experiencing more and more twinges and every so often she looks like she is in pain, and I'm wondering if we should call it a day after this.

'Do you want to sneak out? I think it's more or less finished,' I whisper.

'No,' says Anneka, almost in horror. 'We must stay to the very end.'

'OK,' I say, shocked but also pleased that she's enjoying it as much as I am.

'Right, last question,' says the host, to more groans.

A steward takes a microphone over to a man dressed in a Batman costume, from the 1960s classic TV programme.

'Hi, um, this is just following on from what you said about fans not getting to see the happy ever after,' says a shaky voice, a voice that sounds just like Max. But it can't be. Max wouldn't dress up or come to Comic Con. 'One of your fans, one of your biggest fans, had the chance of a happy ending and I messed it all up. I did something really silly, just like Commander Quartz did,' he says, nodding at Evan Wilson. That is definitely Max talking. My heart starts to hammer in my chest and I stand up to try and get a better view only for the people behind me to whisper at me to sit down. 'But unlike him, I knew instantly that I'd been a total idiot and—'

'I'm sorry,' says the host, cutting him off. 'We've got a lot of fans here and they all wanted to ask questions. I'm afraid we've got to keep it show specific, so unless you—'

'Hey, man,' says Evan Wilson, holding his hand in front of the host's face. 'I think I wanna hear what this guy's got to say. Quartz might not have got his chance yet, but this guy could. What do all y'all think?' he says to the audience in his thick Southern drawl.

There's a faint ripple of applause and a few people shout out 'Yeah!', and the host reluctantly backs down and a steward helps Max onto the stage.

It's a good job that the people behind me told me to sit down because I'm going weak at the knees seeing Max sheepishly walking across the stage in his costume. He hates dressing up and I can only imagine he's feeling absolutely ridiculous.

I turn and look at the girls and none of them look surprised to see Max. Polly even gives me a thumbs-up, and I get the impression that this has something to do with our sudden daytrip to Comic Con.

'Come on, man,' says Evan, slapping him on the back when he gets to the front of the stage. He stands next to him and gives Max a reassuring nod.

'Hello, everyone. Um, first up I should say to my wife that our daughter is with my mum, before she panics, as I'm supposed to be looking after her,' he says, his voice getting shakier. He's usually a good public speaker, but he's so far out of his comfort zone and it shows. 'I was just going to put my hand up and tell my wife that I was sorry and that I loved her. I hadn't really planned a whole big speech.'

'Tell it from the heart, man,' says Evan, tapping his chest, causing his microphone to boom loudly round the room. 'Tell us the story. We're all rooting for you.'

'OK,' he says, letting out a deep breath and then giving one of his smiles that causes me to melt. 'A few years ago, I was lucky enough to re-meet the most incredible woman and after we dated for a few months, I then felt like the luckiest man alive when she agreed to marry me. I didn't exactly have a good track record with women beforehand and I kept thinking that I would somehow mess it up. But I didn't and after we got married and had a baby, I almost patted myself on the back thinking I'd done so well. But then one night it went so horribly wrong. And I almost couldn't live with knowing that if she found out, I'd have really hurt her, or worse I'd have disappointed her. But before she could find out, I experienced the ultimate plot twist life has ever dealt me – I lost my memory and I couldn't remember us getting together or even our daughter.'

I rub my sweaty hands on my cape and look around the

room. Everyone is transfixed by Max's story, almost as much as they were when the cast of *Dark Energy* were talking.

'And my wife, being the kind woman she is, very patiently taught me about my life and who I was, and who we were as a couple, and slowly, we fell back in love. Only when my memory came back, she found out the truth of my mistake and I lost her all over again.

'I loved her before the memory loss, but what I feel for her now is so much more. It was like I'd underestimated how amazing she was.'

I gulp. I want to shout and tell him that I had, too – I had underestimated him as a partner and as a dad. But I don't. Instead I'm rooted to my chair.

'I came to Comic Con to show her that I love her. I even wrote her a list of all the favourite memories I have of her, which I would have told her about if the tables had been turned and she was the one who had lost her memory. It all sounds so cheesy now,' he says and the crowd laugh.

'I don't even know what I'm doing up on this stage, but I guess I've got nothing left to lose. I want to shout it from the rooftops that I love her, and, well, I guess this is the best equivalent I'm going to get as she's always loved these conventions. And there isn't a better place to do so than right here. So Ellie, I know you're out there somewhere…'

Helen cheers loudly and everyone turns to look round at me.

The people behind me suddenly start pushing for me to stand up and I shakily get to my feet.

Max spots me and he visibly relaxes; he holds my gaze and stares straight at me.

'I love you, Ellie, more than you could possibly know.'

The audience snap their head back to me, waiting in anticipation for my reply. But before I can even open my mouth, an almighty scream sounds through the air and I turn around to see Anneka double over in pain and gripping the back of the seat in front of her.

'I'm. So. Sorry,' she says.

'Shit, Anneka, are you OK?' I say, sitting back down next to her.

'I don't think they're Braxton Hicks,' says Helen, looking alarmed.

One of the stewards rushes over and starts speaking into their walkie-talkie and we manage to get Anneka out of our row. I scan for Max, but the host has seized the opportunity to regain control and is now thanking the guests, with the audience giving them a very noisy standing ovation.

The steward starts to usher us through a fire exit and along a corridor and I desperately search for Max. It's then I spot him running towards us, with Robin, Batgirl and Catwoman in his wake. I do a double take before I recognise them as Owen, Rach and Gaby.

Max looks at me, like he's about to swoop me up into his arms. 'No time for that now. Anneka's in labour,' I shout, and his face changes.

'Shit, is that even safe?' he says.

'She's just hit the thirty-seven week mark, so hopefully it'll be OK,' I say, beckoning for them to follow us into the corridor. Gaby surges forward to take Polly's place supporting Anneka.

'I'm Ellie's friend, I'm a GP. How long have you been having contractions?'

'I guess since last night.'

'*Anneka*,' Helen shouts.

'But my waters haven't broken or anything. This isn't real labour.'

'Waters don't always break at the start,' says Gaby. She sits her down and takes her pulse, whilst there's still more furious walkie-talkie action from the steward. 'You're in labour.'

'No, I'm not. I'm not due to have my C-section for another two weeks.'

'You realise that the baby doesn't know that, right?' says Gaby. 'Let's time this and see when your next one is.'

'Whoa, that baby's not coming right here, right now, is it?' says Evan Wilson, walking over to us.

I'm in actual shock. Evan Wilson is here. Max hangs up the phone call he's on, and he walks over and greets Evan like a long-lost pal.

'I got hold of Anneka's George,' says Max. 'He's playing golf in Richmond, so he's going to meet us at the hospital as he said we'll get there first; apparently we're not far away'

'No, we're not,' says Anneka, 'that's the only reason that he let me come up here.'

'Have you got the driver's number? He can come and get us,' says Polly.

'He's not due back for hours,' says Anneka. 'Goodness knows where he'll be.'

'You need a ride?' says Evan. 'I was just heading out. I've got a car outside. I can drop you at a hospital. Come on,' he beckons.

Before we get a chance, Anneka has another contraction, and poor Owen, who just happened to be closest, takes the brunt of it as she grabs hold of him.

'Yeah, we definitely need to leave now,' says Gaby, as Anneka recovers.

Evan signals for a suited man to follow him and we're off.

Rach grabs hold of my arm, pointing at Evan. 'Ohmigod-ohmigodohmigod,' she babbles incomprehensibly.

'I know,' I say, as we all race after him.

We're halfway out of the building when Anneka stops walking. 'I can't go to hospital,' she says in a panic. 'What if they make me give birth naturally?'

'You mean, like women having been doing since the dawn of time?' says Helen.

'Don't think about that,' says Gaby. 'The doctors will help you decide what's best for you and your baby. The most important thing right now is focusing on keeping you both safe, and giving birth in a conference centre surrounded by people dressed up as comic-book heroes isn't really ideal.'

'But you might get free tickets for Comic Con for life,' says Rach, a goofy grin on her face.

'Trust you to say that,' says Gaby, rolling her eyes and laughing.

'Let's go,' says Evan and there's something about his strong confident voice that makes Anneka start walking again.

Max and Owen help support Anneka and we head out of an exit, finding ourselves at the back of the building.

'Hang on. We won't all be to fit in the car,' I say, realising that, with the arrival of the Batman cast, there are now eight of us.

'Sure we can,' says Evan. 'Y'all didn't think I'd have one of your little British cars, did you?'

A Hummer limo appears as if on cue and stops in front of us.

'Plenty of room for everyone,' he says. The driver opens the door and our motley crew pile in.

It's been such a rush with everything so far that Max and I haven't even had a chance to speak yet, and any hope of talking to him discreetly in the limo is dashed when I find myself wedged between Polly and Rach.

'Oh, here we go again,' says Anneka. She squeezes one of Polly's hands whilst she leans on Gaby, her body rippling with her contraction. After a minute she takes a deep breath and smiles sweetly.

'See, I told you, nothing to worry about,' she says.

'Whoa, you're one tough cookie,' says Evan. 'Do you know if it's a boy or girl?'

'We wanted it to be a surprise,' she says.

'Well, you know if you're stuck for names, Evan is a nice solid one, or I guess Eva if it's a girl, that works too.'

'Or you could call her Persephone,' says Rach. 'That's pretty cool, seeing as you nearly gave birth in the *Dark Energy* panel.'

We all keep chipping away with Comic Con-inspired names until the next contraction.

'Right,' says Gaby, looking at her phone. 'The contractions are getting closer.' She engages with the driver, enquiring how far we are from the hospital.

'About a mile. Should take us about ten minutes in this traffic in this beast,' the driver says through the intercom.

'Shit, we could walk there quicker than that,' says Max. 'We could carry you, couldn't we, Owen?'

'You know you're not actually Batman and Robin, don't you?' says Rach, laughing.

'Besides, she's probably got a few hours left yet,' says Gaby.

'Ten minutes is fine. I just wanted to get her there as quickly as possible so she could be comfortable.'

When we finally pull up outside the hospital, I don't know who's more relieved that she's not given birth in the limo – Anneka or Evan's driver.

'Wait,' I say, staring at the hospital that seems oddly familiar. 'Is this where the Royals have their babies?'

'If it's good enough for a princess,' she says with a wink before she leans over and gives Evan a big hug and thanks him for the lift.

'Don't forget to @ me on Twitter so that I can see the little one,' he says.

We all thank him profusely as we slide out of the car onto the pavement.

'Good luck, you two,' he says, giving Max and me a fist bump as we pass.

'Did that just happen?' I say, stunned. 'Evan Wilson just fist bumped me.'

'And now this day will be remembered for that forever, my grand gesture speech forgotten about.'

'Oh, about that—' I say, but Owen bounds up to us.

'Right, Batman,' he says, hands on his hips. 'Let's get this woman to a doctor.'

'To the maternity ward,' says Max, giving me a look of longing before he turns and helps Anneka up the hospital stairs where they buzz the intercom.

When the doors open, Max and Owen help her down the corridor, with Gaby following close behind, and as they pass through, there just so happens to be a blast of heat that blows through their capes, lifting the back of them up, as if they were real superheroes, making us laugh.

The rest of us hang back, wanting to give them some space. I find myself next to Rach.

'So, what did you think of Max's speech?' she says, her eyebrow raised.

'Did you know he was going to do it?' I ask her.

'I don't think he knew he was going to do it,' she laughs. 'He told me that he'd roped the girls into bringing you, and Gaby and I thought it would be fun to tag along.'

'I'm glad you did. You and Gaby seem more relaxed today – does that mean that you've sorted things out?'

Rach breaks out into a big smile.

'Yeah, I took your advice and talked to Gaby, again. She told me that she was scared of everything too, even if she had all the answers. She said it's completely normal to feel overwhelmed.'

'And you're not alone in that.'

'I know. We've decided that from now on we're going to do the whole thing together, like a team. So,' she says, making an excited face, 'Gaby is going to use her eggs for the IVF treatment and then I'm going to have them implanted. We'll be both involved in the pregnancy then.'

'That's great news,' I say, rubbing her arm.

'Yeah, except,' she says, not looking quite so sure, 'seeing what Anneka's going through, maybe I'll see if Gaby will want to swap roles.'

And we both laugh.

Helen turns around to ask what we're laughing about when a man rushes past us dressed in chinos and a polo shirt, and we can't help but follow him with our eyes, our jaws dropping.

He looks like he could be Hugh Jackman's older brother. He's quite possibly one of the most handsome men I've seen in real life.

'Annie, Annie,' he shouts a little breathlessly and Anneka beams up at him, holding her arms out to him.

'It's time, darling, I'm so pleased you made it.'

Helen, Polly and I all stare at him open mouthed.

'That's George?' I say.

'Bloody hell. I thought she was dating some kind of coffin dodger by the way she talked about him,' says Helen.

'I know, and look at the way he's squeezing her hand and she's stroking his cheek. It's so cute,' says Polly, beaming.

We watch them whisper to each other before an orderly comes over and sits her in a wheelchair.

Anneka points over to us and George nods and makes a quick phone call before he walks over smiling.

'It's so lovely to meet you all, finally, and I wish I could get to know you better, but it looks like I'm going to be a bit busy,' he says with a huge grin. 'Listen, I've called the car you had this morning and he's coming to collect you. Plus, the driver I had is waiting outside, so use both cars, go back to the convention centre or wherever you want to go. Quite frankly, they're both paid for until this evening, so fill your boots. I'm going to have a baby!' he says, his face lighting up.

'Congratulations,' we all chant.

'Now go and be with your wife,' I say.

'I shall,' he says before he stops briefly to thank Gaby as she walks back towards us.

'Is that the husband?' asks Owen as him and Max walk up to us.

'Uh-huh, he's a divorce lawyer.'

'I wonder if he breaks up the marriages beforehand,' says Helen, fanning her cheeks.

Max gives me an uneasy look at the mention of the word 'divorce'.

'Do you mind if we have a quick word?' he asks, pulling me to one side. 'Perhaps we could go outside?'

I nod and we walk out onto the steps. I'm pretty sure we're lowering the tone somewhat dressed as Wonder Woman and Batman.

'Your costume,' I say, looking him up and down in wonder.

'It's very fetching, don't you think? Especially with my pecs,' says Max, looking down at it.

'You do know that I know they're padded, right?'

'I still feel a bit proud of them,' he says and we laugh.

'I can't believe you dressed up. You hate dressing up.'

'But you don't. One of the many things I learnt through the memory loss is that I haven't done enough of what you wanted to do over the years.'

He's looking at me with such intensity that my heart starts to race.

'What was on your list of memories?'

'Do you really want to hear them? Wasn't that speech enough?' he says, screwing his face up.

'It might have been, but humour me with the list too.'

He smiles and pulls out a folded list from his utility belt.

'Number one,' he says, clearing his throat. 'The weekend we spent watching *Game of Thrones* in bed.'

'I don't think we watched a whole episode through.'

'I know,' says Max, 'but we had a very memorable time.

'Number two – the mini-break we had in Seville, finding that food market where we spent the whole day eating different tapas and drinking that great beer.

'Number three – the time we went paddle boarding on the coast.'

'It took me forever to get good at it,' I say, folding my arms.

'I know, but for once I enjoyed being able to help you with something,' he says with a smile.

'Number four – the moment the midwife handed me Sasha and then I handed her to you. What you went through, it was incredible; you were incredible.'

He coughs a little loudly and I'm sure I can see a little tear in his eye.

'Number five – the day we originally went to Comic Con.'

'Seriously? Comic Con? You looked scared out of your mind. You didn't dress up. You were uncomfortable for the entire day.'

He shrugs.

'I felt uncomfortable because I knew when I got there I should have made the effort and dressed up, but that day when you were completely in your element, that was the moment that I knew that I'd fallen in love with you and that you were the woman I was going to marry.'

'You did?'

He nods.

'You know,' I say, 'one of the things I've learnt from this whole situation of you losing your memory is that we spend too much time not only taking our memories for granted, but also lazily living on our memories so that we don't have to put the effort in.

'Did you notice that most of the memories we'd chosen were from the early days when we were falling in love? I worry that once you get married, you forget to make an effort in everyday life. I know I've certainly been guilty of that since Sasha's been born.'

'I think we both have,' says Max, nodding. 'Although, from the last few weeks, I've got some new contenders for my favourite memories. Like the time in the tent at the festival.'

'What, me peeing in the kettle?'

'Yes, but not for that reason; for the fact that it brought us closer. There's also the time I told you those stories – the ones I tell Sasha,' he says, raising an eyebrow. 'Plus, there was Paris.'

'How could we ever forget Paris,' I say, 'and all that it taught us.'

'Some more than others, hey?' he says, causing me to laugh. 'I promise I won't need nudging so much in that department either. But that's not what I meant. It's special to me because I couldn't sleep that first night, and you were half lying on me and the baby was doing all sorts of karate moves and I was thinking how on earth is she sleeping through this,' he says, with a laugh, 'but you carried on snoring through it all.'

'Hey, I don't snore,' I say, gently pushing him.

'Not like big snores, cute little snuffily ones, but the point is, I looked at you and I was happy – like happier than I've ever been – and that's when it hit me how lucky I was that that night wasn't a one-off and that it was forever. It was my life: you, Sasha, and the baby.'

A tear rolls down my cheek. I can't believe it; even without our backstory he still felt that way.

'And then you rolled on my arm and, man, did that hurt,' he says.

'Hey,' I stutter, a little choked-up. I go to gently shove him again, but instead he reaches out and takes my trembling hand.

'I love you more than anything in the world, Ellie.'

'Even more than Brighton and Hove Albion?'

'Even more so,' he says. 'Getting to remember them being promoted paled in significance to getting my memory back and me remembering how I fell in love with you in the first place.

'I was lucky enough to fall in love with you not once, but twice. I would do anything for us to stay together. Counselling, therapy, whatever it takes. I want to prove to you that I've changed and I'm different and that it will never happen again.'

I look so deep into Max's eyes that I can just about see through his Batman mask. I can't believe that he didn't take it off in the limo.

'Do you think you can give us another go?' he asks.

Love is a massive leap of faith. But what this month has taught me is that if you have a love like mine and Max's then it's worth fighting for.

'Yes, let's make some new memories,' I say. 'Lots of them.'

'But not just the big ones,' he says, taking a step closer. 'Let's enjoy the little ones too.'

'Like the kisses.'

'Like all the kisses,' he says, and he steps forward and runs his hand through my hair and it rests on the back of my neck and he pulls me forward and gives me a slow, gentle kiss.

'Perfect ten?' he asks as he pulls away.

'Nah, more like an eight,' I say, biting my lip and giggling.

'What?'

'Well, they can't all be tens now, can they? Plus, the whole mask thing isn't really doing it for me.'

'Huh, and there was me thinking that you'd be really into the whole dressing-up thing.'

'I know. Me too. You know that isn't the sexiest version of Batman?' I say, tugging at the utility belt. 'I was always partial to the Val Kilmer one in the nineties.'

'Noted for next time.'

I'm suddenly delighted that there's going to be a next time.

'I wonder if we'll have more luck getting you out of the Wonder Woman costume than we did that first night in Clapham?'

'Yes, and I hope you don't end up with a black eye,' I say, thinking back to that night. At least this time we're more even with him in his Batman costume, and I begin to blush at the thoughts I'm having about peeling it off him.

'Do you think your mum will mind having Sasha overnight?' I say, feeling like an awful mother. I'm sure in the long run this is in her best interest – her parents working on their marriage and all that.

'I've already asked her. Good job too; it'll be a busy night as now I've got to make it epic enough to make the Evan Wilson fist bump pale in comparison.'

I laugh and Max leans down and kisses me again.

'Get a room, you two.' Owen slaps Max on the back as he walks out on to the steps, and we pull apart. 'I'm glad you've worked everything out.'

'And you two have, as well,' I say, smiling.

'Yeah, well, if Max had listened to me from the start this whole thing wouldn't have happened.'

'But then we wouldn't be standing here in these very fetching costumes, now would we?' says Max, wincing because he knows he messed up.

'Speaking of costumes,' I say, 'have I told you how much I like yours, Owen?'

He gives me a hard stare.

'The things I do for friendship.'

The door opens and Polly, Helen, Gaby and Rach stream out onto the steps.

'Cars should be here any minute,' says Helen, who breaks out into a big grin when she sees Max and me holding hands.

'So, are we heading back to Comic Con?' asks Owen.

'Yes,' claps Rach, 'we're in, right?'

Gaby nods.

'Great, Claire's meeting us there in bit; she's coming as Catwoman as well.'

Polly looks over at me. 'Are you wanting to go back there too? Or...'

'Actually, I could do with going home,' I say, squeezing Max's hand.

'Me too to be honest,' says Helen. 'I'm knackered.'

'OK, so we'll all go in one car and you guys will take the other,' says Owen.

It takes us a while to hug each other goodbye, chattering about our eventful morning, before we split into the two groups and head off in our respective cars.

'So, am I going to carry you over the threshold this time?' says Max, waving to the driver as he heads off down our street.

'Er no,' I say, looking down at my bump. 'And I can't be carrying you either.'

'Hmm, but it just feels like we need to mark this occasion. Our fresh start.'

A woman walks by pushing a pram in front of our house.

'Excuse me,' I say, walking up. 'Would you mind taking a photo of us? We're just moving into our new house.'

'Of course, congratulations,' she says, taking the phone and then staring hard at our outfits.

'We were at Comic Con,' says Max.

'Wasn't going to say anything,' she says, smiling. 'Say, *Cheese*.'

The woman takes the photo and hands back the phone and we thank her, taking a look at it.

I laugh at the ridiculousness of it, but I love how wide our smiles are.

'That's one for the memory wall up the stairs,' I say.

'The memory wall? You're really going to put hundreds of photo frames up those stairs and ruin walls that we're going to get lovingly plastered and painted,' he says with a groan.

'Uh-huh,' I say, turning the key.

'Can't you imagine how nice it would look with nothing on them, just beautiful Farrow & Ball paint.'

'You know, we're standing here arguing about the walls when Sasha isn't here and this little one's staying put. Who knows when we'll get the house to ourselves like this again?'

'You're right,' he says, moving towards me. 'I should be concentrating on something else that would look even more beautiful with nothing on.'

'God, you're cheesy, Max Voss.'

'I know, but that's one of the reasons you love me, right?'

'One of the many reasons,' I say, and this time I don't wait to be kissed; I grab him and pull him towards me. And this time there's absolutely no doubt in my mind that it's a perfect ten.

Acknowledgements

Thank you so much for reading *The Man I Didn't Marry* – I really hope you enjoyed it and please do pop a review up if you have time! I absolutely love interacting with my readers so do follow me on Twitter, Facebook and Instagram. It's so nice to get all your lovely messages as it spurs me on during those tough first drafts and multiple edits. Thank you to all the lovely bookstagrammers and book reviewers who take the time to review my books too and for generally spreading all the book love.

I have used a lot of dramatic licence for this book – so any errors I made in relation to the medical knowledge, local Fleet geography (the imaginary coffee van at Fleet Pond that I wish existed) etc., are all mine.

A huge thank you goes to my long-suffering literary agent Hannah Ferguson, for reading very early drafts and being patient through my yo-yoing between giving up on this book and new ideas to make the plot click – we got there in the end! Thanks also to the rest of the team at Hardman and Swainson for all that they do.

Another huge thank you to my editor Emily Kitchin and assistant editor Melanie Hayes for their enthusiasm for this book, and for their brilliant editorial comments that, as always, the book is so much better for. Special thanks to the rest of the team at HQ – especially Katrina Smedley, Lucy Richardson, Lucy Davey, Fliss Porter, Harriet Williams, Sammy Luton, Angie Dobbs, Halema Begum and Tom Keane. Also, to copy-editor Jon Appleton.

Writing and editing in lockdown has been a particular challenge – but it has reminded me of how much I rely on my friends and family to keep me sane during the writing process. So, thank you to Mum and John, Jane, Laura, Kaf, Hannah, Jo, Sam, Sarah, Sonia, Ali, Christie, Janine and Ken, and Jon and Debs. Special mention to Isabelle Broom, Lucy Vine, Vicky Zimmerman and Katie Marsh for the much-needed daily word races and the Zooms. Also, to writer pals Lorraine Wilson, Victoria Walters and the Mirepoix Writers' Group for all the support.

Lastly, as always, the biggest thank you has to go to my husband Steve and my children Evan and Jessica, for putting up with 'Mummy always daydreaming about her book'. And to the dogs, Rex and Pru, for letting me also daydream on their dog walks.

Turn the page for a sneak peek at the heart-warming and laugh-out-loud romcom from Anna Bell, *We Just Clicked*.

Available now!

Prologue

If I'd known that the last time I'd see Ben was that unusually hot day in April, I would have made more of an effort to tell him something profound. I would have told him I loved him. Told him I was sorry for all the times I'd fought petty arguments with him. Told him how he was more a part of me than I ever imagined was possible. I certainly wouldn't have told him that he had crappy taste in engagement rings and that his hairline was starting to recede. But I guess in some ways that was better than all the soppy stuff because if I'd known it was the last time, I'd never have let him leave that afternoon at all.

He'd taken me to a high-end jewellery shop whose windows I'd only ever drooled over from the outside. I'd never dared enter it, let alone imagined that I, Izzy Brown, would be allowed to touch one of their exquisite rings.

'Holy shit,' I said, my hand flying up to my mouth in embarrassment of my potty mouth. Luckily the man behind the counter was polite enough to act like he hadn't heard. 'Are you sure the rock's big enough?'

I held the diamond up to the light and it practically blinded me. There was no denying it was a beautiful ring, but it was far too showy.

'It's not that big,' said Ben. Beads of sweat had started to form on his forehead as the magnitude of what was happening hit him. Or maybe he'd caught sight of the price tag. 'I just want it to be special.'

'I think it's too much,' I said, shaking my head and slipping it off. 'I think she'd prefer something more understated.'

'Something like that?' asked Ben, pointing to another equally ostentatious ring.

I shuddered, not because the ring was horrid but because it was exactly the type of ring that I imagined that Cameron would propose with. Not that he'd come here. He'd have flown to Antwerp and bought the perfect diamond first before flying back to have it set. That's what the very few engaged or married traders that he knew had done and Cameron hated to deviate from the pack.

'I think she'd prefer something like…' I walked along to the opposite end of the display cabinet and my eyes fell upon the perfect ring, 'like that.'

I stared at the platinum band with a bright blue sapphire flanked on either side by tiny diamonds. It was elegant and understated, but special none the less. It was exactly what he was looking for.

Ben followed my finger and examined the ring before he looked up at me and a small smile spread across his face.

'Bloody hell, that's the one.'

The man behind the counter pulled it out and rested it on the top and glided it over my finger. It was a little tighter than the first one, but it fit well enough. Ben shook a little as he checked the price tag but relief flooded his face when he saw he could afford it.

'It's an excellent choice,' said the man. He started spieling about the cut and clarity of the diamonds and the pedigree of the sapphire, but I could tell Ben wasn't listening. He'd found the ring and he was happy. As was I – my hand had never looked more beautiful. I fanned my fingers out and stared at it twinkling in the lights. It was entrancing.

The man behind the counter coughed and I looked up a little embarrassed.

'I need to pop it back in the box,' he said.

'Of course, of course,' I said tugging it off. 'It's so beautiful.'

Ben smiled as he handed over his credit card, and just like that, my brother had taken his first step to getting married. Or perhaps it was technically his second step as he'd actually got engaged a few years ago when he'd proposed with a ring from a Christmas cracker. He'd told his fiancée that he'd get her a better ring one day, and after a recent work promotion he'd finally been able to make good on the promise.

'I can't believe you're going to do this,' I said, looping my arm through his as we left the store.

'We've been engaged for three years, it's hardly a shocker.'

'I know, but this is really it, though, isn't it? You've got the proper ring and you're going to set a proper date. This is huge. We should celebrate.'

'I was going to head straight back to the station. I don't really want to be walking round London with it.'

He hugged his backpack tighter to his chest. He looked like such a tourist wearing it over his front.

I pulled out my phone and read a message.

'Cameron's going to the Founder's Arms, it's just over the river from here. Why don't we go and have a quick drink with him before I walk you back to Waterloo?'

Ben looked at his watch and I could tell he was uneasy, but I hadn't seen him in ages. The afternoon had whizzed by and there was still so much to catch up on.

3

'OK, but the drinks are on you as I don't think I can ever afford to drink again after buying that.'

'Ben, I hope you're not getting into debt for the ring. It's not like the wedding will be cheap and—'

'Izzy, I'm kidding.'

'Good,' I said with relief. 'Of course I'll buy you a celebratory drink anyway. Plus, I can't wait for you to meet Cameron.'

'Oh yes, the famous Cameron. I'm intrigued to meet him too.'

It felt strange that they'd not met before, but my life in London seemed so far removed from my family and friends back home in Basingstoke. The two might only be an hour apart by train but you'd think I was from Timbuktu judging by the reaction I'd get from Cameron when I suggested we visit. I think he expected that he'd turn to dust if he left the Greater London area, like a vampire entering a church.

I stifled a yawn as we weaved through the empty streets. During the week the same ones would be full of City workers bustling about, but at the weekend they were deserted.

'Late night?' asked Ben.

'Kind of, but it's been one of those weeks where every night's been a late one.'

'I don't know how you do it; I can barely manage going out at the weekend now.'

'That's what happens when you're old and settled. You get a mortgage, you get married and next you'll be losing your hair like Dad.'

He rubbed at his hair. 'Oi, I'm only two years older than you and I'm not receding quite yet. Plus I'm not married yet either.'

Ben's been with his fiancée Becca for fifteen years; they met at school, and I think of them as an old married couple. It's been a cruel wait for my mum to splash out on an over-the-top mother-of-the-groom hat and for me who wants to be their bridesmaid.

'So does this mean you're going to have to propose all over again?'

'Oh God, I don't know. Does it? That was the whole point of proposing with the cracker ring. It was supposed to be whimsical.'

'I think that would have been fine if you'd then produced the real ring soon afterwards, but three years... I think you'll have to do it again, and with a ring like that it deserves to be properly romantic.'

He groaned.

'Don't worry, I'll help you think of something.'

By the time we crossed over the river to the pub, we'd come up with a sneaky proposal plan that was both romantic and personal. I'd shed a few happy tears and Ben was once again grateful I'd helped him out.

We arrived at the pub before Cameron and his friends, so we ordered drinks and took them out onto the terrace. We managed to find a recently vacated table on the edge, still covered with empty glasses.

'Will you take my photo?' I said, looking over at the view over the Thames towards St Paul's on the other side.

I didn't bother to wait for a reply; I simply held out my phone to Ben and struck a pose.

'Is this for your Instagram? I see you're doing really well. Over 500 followers?' he said.

'I know. Can you believe it?'

'I told you I had a good feeling about it,' he said, snapping a couple of shots. He checked his work before handing it over with a nod. 'Not bad.'

I had a look myself and was suitably impressed.

'Perfect, I can post that later with all the appropriate hashtags.'

'Move over Zoella,' he said sipping his drink.

'I don't think I'd ever be that big, it's just nice doing something creative again. And you never know, I could perhaps try and make the move into marketing or PR by showing agencies that I understand how to build a brand.'

'Still having no luck on the job front?'

I shook my head. I took a job as a copywriter for an advertising agency that specialised in medical products straight out of university. I thought I was going to have a glittering advertising career and that it would all be cocktails and swanky parties à la *Mad Men*, only the reality was far from glamorous. I didn't mind when I was younger, when it was all about the pay cheque and where the next party was, but as I'd got older I wanted to start focusing on my career. Only five years writing copy about haemorrhoid creams had left me pigeonholed in the medical sector and longing to do work that people didn't read in desperation because they had piles.

'Well, I think you're onto something with the Instagram thing. From what I've seen on your feed, you're a natural. I'm sure you'll be making a living out of it in no time.'

I laughed hard. 'Do you have any idea how hard it would be to get to that stage?'

Ben shrugged. 'I know you could do it. You know, I'm proud of you for giving it a go.' He chinked his glass against mine.

'And I'm proud of you, finally getting married. Can I see the ring again?' I said, clapping my hands together.

He looked around to see if anyone was watching and he leant down into his bag, which he had looped around his leg. He pulled the little ring box out and flipped it open, holding it out to me.

'Oh, it's even more beautiful than I remember it being,' I said, looking at it longingly. 'Can I try it on?'

'I guess so, it's probably safer on your finger than it is in my bag,' he said as I picked it up and slipped it on.

I held my hand out and it felt complete again. The table next to us burst into applause. I looked around to see what they were clapping at and it took me a good few seconds to realise they were all staring at me and Ben.

'Congratulations,' one of them shouted whilst raising their glass.

'What the… Oh no, it's not what it looks like. He's my brother,' I said in slight horror as I tried to slip the ring back off my finger but it didn't want to budge.

The clapping petered out and they all looked a bit embarrassed.

'I was just trying it on,' I said, feeling ridiculous and yanking it even harder, but it wasn't moving in the slightest.

'Well, I hope the actual proposal goes better than that,' said Ben, taking a large sip of his drink.

'Um, that's if I can give you the ring back,' I said, holding up my hand. My finger looked like a plump sausage and it was at least double its normal size.

'You're joking, right?' he said, laughing a little awkwardly before he realised I wasn't laughing back. 'Izzy!'

'I'm sorry,' I said, wincing. 'It won't come off.'

I tried to pull it as hard as I could.

'Don't do that,' he said, screwing up his face. 'You might break it.'

He took an audible deep breath before he stood up.

'Ice, you need to put it in ice. Your hand will shrink,' he said.

'I can put it in my cider,' I said, about to plunge it in.

'Don't you dare, it'll get sticky. Hold tight, I'll get some from the bar.'

Hold tight, I muttered to myself as I sat there looking at my ever-increasing sausage finger.

'Izzy,' shouted a voice and I looked up to see Cameron and a few of his work colleague friends heading across the pub terrace, glasses in hand. 'I didn't realise you'd already be here; I would have got you a drink,' he said as he sat down next to me and gave me a quick kiss on the lips. 'So how did the engagement ring shopping go?'

'Really well,' I said holding my hand up. 'I decided I'd save us the trouble and get the ball rolling.'

I'd been about to laugh, thinking he would too, when his whole face started to crumple.

'Er, Izzy, I don't know what you were thinking but I really don't think we're there, are we? I mean, we only live together because you were living in Balham and I don't go further out than Zone 2. I mean, you know how much I care about you and all—'

'Prosecco on the house,' said a woman, cutting Cameron off mid-flow. 'For the happy couple, I hear you just got engaged!'

Cameron looked up at the barmaid in absolute horror, his face turning pale. I risked a glance at his work colleagues who were all trying to look anywhere but in our direction. All except Tiffany, who was giving me her usual pursed-lipped, narrowed-eye look. I'd long suspected she fancied Cameron, even though he denied it.

'Actually, we didn't,' I said, mortified. 'It was all just a misunderstanding. I was trying on a ring for my brother and it got stuck.'

'Oh well,' said the woman, looking unbothered. 'You might as well have it now anyway, it's been written off by our boss.'

She placed the tray with the bottle and glasses on the table and I muttered a thank you.

'Here's the ice,' said Ben, rushing over and putting it down in front of me.

He grabbed my hand and plunged it into the water.

'Bloody hell, that's cold,' I said, wincing in pain as my hand started to go numb. 'How long have I got to keep it in there?'

'I don't know,' he said, still panicked. 'Until it comes off?'

He turned and noticed Cameron, who was sitting there mute.

'Cameron, this is my brother Ben, Ben this is my boyfriend Cameron, or at least I think he's still my boyfriend, but he's definitely nowhere near being my fiancé,' I said.

They muttered a hello and shook hands, both distracted: Ben by the ring stuck on my finger, Cameron by the conversation we'd just had.

I pulled my hand out of the glass and, much to my and Ben's relief, the ring came off my finger.

Ben cradled it like a newborn baby, wrapping it up in his T-shirt and drying it carefully before depositing it back in the box and in the safety of his backpack.

'So it's *your* ring?' Tiffany said to Ben, with obvious relief.

'Yes, and I think I'd better take it home before anything else happens to it,' he said, downing the rest of his cider. 'Do you mind, Izzy?'

'Of course not,' I said lying.

I got up and gave him a quick hug and he said a quick goodbye to the others before leaving, clutching his bag.

It was the last time I ever saw him.

Two weeks after the pub incident I was on my way to work when my phone rang. My mum's number flashed up and at first I thought she'd phoned me by mistake because it was so early. When I picked up there was a rustling sound on the line, and I was about to hang up when I realised it was Mum sobbing. Eventually my dad took the phone from her, and when he spoke

I barely recognised his voice. It was so quiet and soft, nothing like his usual boom.

'Izzy, are you sitting down? Something awful's happened to Ben.'

I'd immediately started to witter on about an accident and asking if he was in hospital when Dad went quiet. He didn't need to tell me the next bit; I knew from his tone that Ben had died.

The world started to spin and my body and mind seemed to drift away from each other. I could hear Dad telling me details and words jumped out at me – cardiac arrest... arrhythmia... in his sleep – but I couldn't absorb any of it. I was too numb to take it all in, too numb to be able to say anything other than I was coming home.

I was near Paddington, and so I jumped on a train to Reading in the hope of changing from there to Basingstoke. It's not a route I'd usually take going home but I couldn't face travelling across London in rush hour. I went into some sort of a survival mode, putting one foot in front of the other and was amazed to find myself on the right train.

I managed to hold it together until I got to Reading and then it hit me – like slapped me in the face as if a freight train had hit me – and I found myself stranded at the station not knowing how I was going to find my connecting train. All I could think was that Ben was gone and that I'd never see him again.

My legs started to wobble and my phone slid out of my hands, and I couldn't stop myself from falling.

'Whoa, there,' said a man, catching me under my arms and keeping me upright. 'Are you all right?'

My head was throbbing and my legs had gone to jelly.

'Are you all right?' he said again, but it felt like it was coming from somewhere distant.

He continued to hold onto me and I took a moment to look at him. He was dressed in a smart blue shirt that matched his eyes.

'Do you speak English?' he said, elongating every word and speaking very loudly.

'I, um, yes,' I said, confused.

'Sorry, you weren't answering me and I thought… Look, are you OK? Is there someone I could call?'

I shook my head. There really wasn't. Cameron was on a business trip to New York, I'd planned to call him when I got to my parents' house. There was no rush; it was the middle of the night there and it wasn't like he'd be able to do anything from there. I thought back to the one and only time that Cameron had met my brother and my heart started to ache about it – my last afternoon with Ben. 'I'm on my way to my mum and dad's and I… I don't know where the platform is for Basingstoke.'

A breeze whistled through the station and my curls blew into my face. I'd left the house with them wet, I'd planned on putting my hair up at some point on my journey, but I'd forgotten and they'd dried out of control.

'Your mum and dad,' said the man kindly, 'in Basingstoke. OK, OK, we can do that.'

He looked up and scanned the departures board. I couldn't believe that I'd been standing so close and I hadn't noticed it. My mind felt full of fog.

'OK, so Platform 4 at 9.52, you've got ten minutes. I'll take you there,' he said.

I closed my eyes and I was flooded with relief.

'Thank you, I…' I took another deep breath. 'Just thank you.'

'It's no problem, really. Um, OK, can you stand on your own, do you think? You look a bit unsteady.'

'I think so,' I said, focusing on breathing in and out.

He pulled his arms away from me slowly and I successfully proved that I could stand on two feet, much to both our amazement. My hair blew in my face again, and I scraped it out of the way the best I could, but curls kept getting stuck on my tear-stained cheeks.

'Now,' he said, pulling the hair band off my wrist. 'This looks like it's bothering you.'

He scooped my curls up into the messiest topknot ever, but in that split second I was just so grateful that he'd got them away from my face. I stared down at the red ring the band had left on my wrist, wondering why I didn't remember I had it there in the first place.

He bent down and retrieved my phone and wrinkled his face.

'It's a little cracked,' he said, handing it to me. I slipped it into my handbag without looking.

'Least of my worries,' I said, and he nodded.

'Let's get you on that train.'

He steered me by the elbow towards a platform, taking care not to rush me, as I tried desperately to hold the floodgates of emotions shut.

The man walked me halfway along a platform and he continued to hold my elbow until the train arrived, like he was propping me up. It was only when he escorted me onto it that I noticed he wasn't leaving.

'Your train,' I said in protest. 'You don't have to take me to Basingstoke.'

He guided me to a seat, and sat down on the one next to me.

'It's fine, I can catch a later one. I just want to make sure you get there safely. That's all.'

'But really, I'll be fine,' I said, trying to hold back the tears.

'You're not fine, and you don't have to be either,' he said. 'I'll

make sure you get to your mum and dad's. Do they live near the station, or do you need a taxi?'

'Taxi,' I just about managed. His kindness was starting to make me choke up.

'OK, then I'll make sure you get in one.'

I stopped protesting and nodded and then the tears started to fall. I cried all over his blue shirt and he sat there patiently passing me napkins that he'd nabbed from the buffet trolley.

I didn't even realise we'd reached our final destination until he gently guided me out of the seat and led me out of the doors. I walked down the stairs into the tunnel to the main entrance, not caring what an absolute state I must have looked like.

I found my ticket and put it into the machine on autopilot and he followed me through the barrier using the ticket he'd purchased on the train. Then he led me to the black cabs waiting outside the station.

'Are you OK from here?' he asked, helping me inside the cab.

I nodded back, 'I am.'

He leant into the front of the cab and handed the driver a £20 note, asking him to take me to where I needed to go.

'She hasn't been drinking, has she? I don't want to clear up any sick,' said the driver.

'No,' he said, shaking his head. 'She's just had a really awful start to the day.'

He turned to me and smiled with his head tilted.

'I'm so sorry for whatever's happened to you,' he practically whispered.

'Thank you. Thank you for everything,' I stuttered. It didn't seem adequate for what he'd done.

He shrugged his shoulders. 'It's what anyone would have done.'

'I don't even know your name.'

'Aidan,' he said softly.

13

'Thank you, Aidan,' I said.

'You take care,' he said, stepping out of the car and gently closing the door.

'Where to, love?' asked the taxi driver.

I gave him my parents' address and he pulled out into the road. I turned back and looked at Aidan standing there on the pavement. He waved and I waved back. But then I remembered that Ben had gone and the rest of the journey became a blur.